Shadows of Empire

Novels:

Change and Decay in all around I see

The Last Peacock

The Death of Men

One Night in Winter

Augustus

A Question of Loyalties

Tiberius

The Hanging Tree

The Sins of the Fathers

Caesar

These Enchanted Woods

The Ragged Lion

King David

ALLAN MASSIE

Shadows of Empire

SINCLAIR-STEVENSON

First published 1997
1 3 5 7 9 10 8 6 4 2
Copyright © Allan Massie 1997

Allan Massie has asserted his right
under the Copyright, Designs and Patents Act 1988
to be identified as the author of this work

First published in the United Kingdom in 1997 by
Sinclair-Stevenson
Random House, 20 Vauxhall Bridge Road, London SW1V 2SA

Random House Australia (Pty) Limited
20 Alfred Street, Milsons Point, Sydney,
New South Wales 2061, Australia

Random House New Zealand Limited
18 Poland Road, Glenfield,
Auckland 10, New Zealand

Random House South Africa (Pty) Limited
Endulini, 5A Jubilee Road, Parktown 2193, South Africa

Random House UK Limited Reg. No. 954009

A CIP catalogue record for this book is available from the British Library

Papers used by Random House UK Limited are natural,
recyclable products made from wood grown in sustainable forests.
The manufacturing processes conform to the environmental
regulations of the country of origin.

ISBN 1 85619 688 7

Typeset by Deltatype Limited, Birkenhead, Merseyside
Printed and bound in Great Britain
by Mackays of Chatham PLC

first: for Alison
then: for Alex, Louis and Claudia

I

Father died fifty years ago today, and a fortnight ago I received his royalties: £3,816.73. Down on last year and the one before. The surge in interest caused by the television adaptation of *Corners of Foreign Fields* is on the ebb. Well, it is no mean thing for a man who regarded writing as merely another string to his bow to have provided for us so comfortably so long after he was in the grave.

The television success of *Corners* surprised many. I can't think why. It was just the sort of thing, half-true, half-trashy, bitter-sweet, nostalgic, sentimental, to be a popular success even in its third manifestation – book, film, serial on the telly. This last time round it fed a mood which was already established – regret for the days when Britannia ruled the waves, and the flag flew over a world-wide empire – a mood which Mrs Thatcher may be said to incarnate.

My old friend Tony Powell has often remarked that self-pity is an almost invariable element in any bestseller, and of course Father wallowed in that emotion. Despite his oft-proclaimed stoicism – how he loved to echo Sir Walter's *agere et pati Romanum est*: 'of all schools commend me to the Stoick' – he would loudly bewail his misfortunes. But he was full of pity for others' suffering too, and of indignation. Though he delighted in the company of youth, he came to think poorly of my generation. We couldn't compare to his friends who marched to war in 1914 and died in Flanders mud. He thought us greatly inferior. Maybe we were, but we had perplexities they never knew, and indeed their fate was one of them, sapping our willpower and self-confidence. All they had to do, it sometimes seems to me, was to know how to die. No one can say they didn't do that well: a hundred-thousand casualties before lunch on the morning of 1 July 1916. We stood aghast at the enormity of the sacrifice, and told ourselves no nation could do that again. Scott Fitzgerald, in the best scene in *Tender Is The Night*, called it an Empire marching to its death, one step at a time. He wasn't far wrong. Oh yes, I can understand why Father felt as he did, though his bitterness never extended to Haig, whom he knew, served, and revered.

One thing they got wrong in the TV version of *Corners* – one of several things of course – was Father himself. He is there in the character of Sandy Dalrymple, the man denied service at the Front, denied the comradeship of the trenches, because he was deemed 'indispensable'. There's a scene in which he goes to comfort the fiancée of one of the closest of his dead friends, just after the telegram announcing the death has been received. The girl, you will remember, insists, almost hysterically, that he take her dancing. In the book the end of the evening is veiled; in the TV version you see them in bed. But it isn't that – even that coarsening – I meant to talk about.

No, Father's voice, that was it. They got his voice all wrong. The actor played him with a pinched Edinburgh accent, with narrow vowels. Perhaps they thought it went with his admiration for Mussolini. Well, he got over that, in 1940, just before he died. The stab in the back of the fallen France cured him of that imbecility. He died talking of Napoleon and Stalin. He died, as it happens, drunk. He keeled over the table, spilling the glass of Armagnac I had just poured for him. He had never been accustomed to drink heavily. I had scarcely ever seen him the worse for liquor. Indeed he prided himself on being abstemious and was given to repeating the Greek tag 'water is best' – in the Greek, of course, for he had kept up his classics. But in the last months of his life, after the news came about Alastair, he turned to

2

whisky, as his grandfather, the Glasgow shipbuilder, had done. That evening he asked for Armagnac, perhaps on account of the talk about Napoleon and the number of Gascons among his marshals. Alastair was his favourite, the apple of his eye as the Bible has it. I couldn't regret his death, for it spared him further heartache; I could have wished he had gone earlier.

But his voice – it wasn't Edinburgh at all. He had lived only briefly in what Toby Macrae used to call 'Scotland's sad city', and, though, on account of its beauty and history, and his love of Scott and Stevenson, he sometimes spoke of it fondly, in other more frequent moods he would call it 'a place in mourning which has lost its function and lacks the energy to forge a new one'. No, his voice was conventional public school English, though he hadn't in fact gone to an English public school, but had acquired that manner of speech at Balliol; except when in moments of emotion he would revert to the soft tongue of the Scottish Borders where he had spent the happiest days of his childhood.

They say, critically, that he worshipped success. I was never sure of that. He was easily dazzled by the successful, and by the flashy, such as Beaverbrook and Birkenhead, but there was a kernel in him, a stern residual Calvinism that despised the material trappings of success. He liked, to my mother's irritation, to quote that line of Stevenson's – 'where about the graves of the martyrs the whaups are crying'. He was – as perhaps we have all been – a divided man, and, if he strove for worldly glory, he was half in love with failure too. I have often thought it was the naive side of his character that responded to the glamour of success, but he was more truly himself fishing a hill stream than in the Ritz Hotel, where, however, he loved taking us as children and ordering an elaborate meal of which he nevertheless ate little. He often spoke, with some relish, of being 'in the wilderness'. A lot of his life was acting, and he liked alternating his roles.

Success – the power to shape things, real achievement

3

rather than celebrity – in any case eluded him. He had little interest in making money. Thanks to the Glasgow ship-builder, he lacked nothing, though even in his lifetime the capital dwindled. He aimed high in politics, and missed the mark. The true professionals thought him a dilettante, and were irritated by his eagerness to see both sides of any question. Many of his closest political friends were on the other side of the House. He early abandoned the bar where, it was said, a glittering career awaited him. In literature he knew himself to be third-rate, beginning as a disciple of Stevenson, and ending as an inferior Hugh Walpole. He didn't even see that Stevenson, or at least his reading of him, represented a dead end.

Who am I to sneer? I was to be a poet, was indeed – bad sign – showered with praise by Edith Sitwell while I was still at Cambridge, and spent near twenty years as foreign editor of a middle-market newspaper, my importance declining as the British public withdrew its interest from foreign affairs.

Now, solitary, I watch the rain drops slide down the window-pane, start on the gin bottle too early in the morning, and am addicted to the turning over of old photographs.

Self-pity?

I take my stick, call to Dandie the terrier, and set my face to the brae. The wind has dropped and the rain eased. Away to the West the hills are folded under a pale sky. This country has been sucked of its people. It is a land of abandoned cottages and crumbling sheep-folds, where gloomy regiments of spruce are drawn up like an elaborate old-fashioned battle-plan. It suits me. I sit on a broken dyke while Dandie hunts a rabbit.

II

Scots have ever loved to dwell, often ironically, on matters of heredity. The great national put-down has long been 'I kent his feyther'; ergo, the son can't be what he would have you think he is. Now I often catch myself in gestures which uncannily recall Father. But whatever geneticists may say, it's not all in the genes. The author of Ecclesiastes was wiser: 'Time and chance happeneth to them all.' So, for instance, when I last saw Hector, in his retreat in the hills behind Carpentras, it was as if I had come on my father's father, and yet my grandfather's life was one from which self-reproach was absent, and which the world judged a success.

The son of the Glasgow shipbuilder, he became a minister of the Church of Scotland at a time when ministers were still figures of great consequence. Since he also enjoyed a handsome private income, he lived in some style, in a large manse in Roxburghshire, with half a dozen indoor and outdoor servants; when horses gave way to motors, his chauffeur drove him in a Daimler. He married a Miss Scott, who was a distant – very distant – connection at some remove of cousinship, of the Scotts of Harden, and therefore of Sir Walter himself. He was certainly, to my mother's amusement – but she did not care for him – more willing to dilate on his wife's relationships than on his own.

That was not in those days surprising, though now I fancy anyone in his position would be more likely to dwell on his own father's humble origins – not of course that he would use the word 'humble', but rather, proudly, say 'working class'. But it was otherwise then, and my grandfather, in his way a man of great kindliness and even generosity, preferred to leave his paternal origins in decent obscurity. It was years before I knew – and the knowledge then pleased me – that the shipbuilder's father had come from Protestant Ulster as a navvy in the years after Waterloo, and that his wife, Mary Benzie, was the daughter of a farm labourer from Buchan. She had, it seems, gone into domestic service in the manse of her home parish, and when the minister removed to a charge in Glasgow, young Mary accompanied the family. She met the young Ulsterman, perhaps at the kirk, and married him, both, I think, being well on in their thirties. The shipbuilder, who ended life as Sir William Allan, was their only child or, at least, the only one to survive.

He was born in 1830, and therefore came of age in 1851, the year in which, with the Hungry Forties and Chartist agitation behind them, the Great Exhibition set the Victorian Age under sail. The years of glorious expansion were ahead. Now, of course, there are many to cast doubt on its achievements. There is a fashion for pushing the British loss of competitiveness further and further back in time. One recent study even identified what are said to be the congenital failings of the British economy – waste, contempt for the workforce, low investment, neglect of scientific research – as far back as the 1830s. Perhaps if I live long enough, some clever young don will discover that we were in decline even before we rose to take the lead in making the Industrial Revolution.

Be that as it may, it was not how it seemed in the middle of the nineteenth century. Then everything was galloping ahead. The great dividing line, as the historian G. M. Young put it, was not between rich and poor but between those who were respectable and those who were not. And young Willie Allan was certainly brought up by his God-fearing mother to be respectable; to learn the shorter Catechism with its challenging first question 'What is the chief end of Man?', and what Stevenson called 'the noble, if obscure, reply': 'To

6

glorify God and enjoy him for ever'. Young Willie may, I fancy, have questioned that in his heart, but the long intelligent head revealed in the Sargent portrait of him in old age would then have known better than to utter any doubt.

So he was a dutiful and obedient son. The erstwhile navvy had set up his own joinery business, and prospered sufficiently to send young Willie to the High School of Glasgow and then to the university, which still stood in Old College Yard before its removal to Gilmorehill. There he studied under Kelvin, and emerged as an engineer, and, because it was then in the air of Glasgow, as what we would now call an entrepreneur – having to use the French term because the concept has become so unfamiliar.

A man of genius in his way, which is not a way that has flourished in the family since, except perhaps in my brother George, he built up a great business with a flourishing yard, and, before long, a shipping line of his own. By the 1880s he was a notable figure in Glasgow, friend of Sir Charles Tennant and one of the princes of the city Establishment. Then, because his only son had turned away from manufacture and trade, and gone into the Kirk – the Established Kirk, not the Free Kirk to which Willie's mother, following her former employer, had adhered at the time of the Disruption – he withdrew from the active management of yard and line, and retired to the mansion he had built himself on Loch Lomondside, to indulge, among other pleasures, his taste for collecting works of art.

That he had, from his background, and despite his immersion in business, found time to acquire and develop such a taste says much for the intellectual and aesthetic energy of Glasgow. He didn't, I have been told, rely, as other rich men did, on a dealer to guide him. He was quick to latch on to the merits of 'the Glasgow Boys' and later was ahead of the times in buying a Cézanne. It is said that he attended the famous Post-Impressionist exhibition of 1911, organised by Roger Fry, and came away muttering: 'I dinna

7

ken, but there's siller in the air.' Though for years he had ordinarily spoken standard English, he was apt to revert to his mother's Aberdeenshire Doric for his gnomic utterances.

Perhaps he employed it in memory of his wife, Catherine Johnstone, who was the niece of that minister in whose service Mary Benzie had come to Glasgow. In the old Scottish fashion Mary had always kept up with her former employers, regarding herself, and indeed being regarded, as a member of the family rather than as a mere domestic servant, and so the young Willie was introduced to Miss Johnstone while she was on a visit to her aunt and uncle. I possess a daguerrotype of her, which suggests a girl of uncommon sweetness and rural simplicity; her smile is shy but extends to the eyes, and she captivated the ambitious young man who had just embarked on his first independent business adventure. He was twenty-one, she was eighteen; they were married the next year, and eighteen months later she died, giving birth to my grandfather.

No doubt the young widower was wretched. He threw himself with still more energy into business, and handed the child over to his wife's mother to be reared in Aberdeen-shire, while he set himself single-mindedly to making his fortune. Unlike most widowers then – and perhaps now – he never married again. He carried a locket with his Catherine's portrait in his waistcoat pocket to the end of his days. In middle-age, his fortune assured, he took up with an actress. She lived with him as what the young of this county would now call a bidey-in for the better part of twenty years. She was the daughter of a Frenchman, a journalist who claimed to be a refugee from the new Bonapartist tyranny, and perhaps because, like many of his contemporaries, Sir William (as it seems convenient to call him, though he was not knighted till King Edward came to the throne) thought the French a frivolous and untrustworthy lot, he never married her. When she died and was buried in the little churchyard at Luss by the edge of the loch ('Dearly-loved friend of William Allan, Shipbuilder' is the brave inscription on the tombstone – and I wonder how he got the local minister to agree to that?) the old man's taste turned to housemaids and the like. They were often very young. No doubt there were whispers of disapproval, but he was by now rich enough and, I should guess, sufficiently indifferent, to pay them no heed. There are still old gentlemen in the neighbourhood of Loch Lomond whose physiognomy recalls that Sargent portrait.

He lived to be ninety-four.

I have only two memories of him myself. The first dates from that summer when the world he had helped to build came to an end. I was four and have no idea why I was taken to visit him at Ardlochish House. It was the year my youngest brother, Alastair, was born, so he cannot have been there. I believed, indeed, for many years that I was the only child present, but some time ago Kirstie assured me she was there, and also, she thought, Hector. George, she said, certainly wasn't; he had measles. Perhaps Father had brought us north to escape infection.

All I remember is that the old man had a parrot, and that he took me by the hand and led me to the stables to admire his carriage horses. 'You'll not ride behind horses, laddie,' he said, 'but I'm too old for motors, and the cuddies'll see me out.' Then, back in the house, he showed me a painting of his horses with a lady in the carriage; it may have been the French actress and I have a notion it was a Crawhall, but I have no means of checking, for his collection was dispersed long ago. The next day we went to Helensburgh where he kept his yacht, and sailed down the loch and into the open sea rounding Islay and Jura, though of course I didn't then have the slightest idea where we were. Finally he gave me five golden sovereigns and told me to put them in my kilt sporran and not tell anyone I had them.

It was high summer and we may have been there the day the Archduke was killed in Sarajevo, but if so the news did

9

not impinge on me. My memory is of a remote benevolence. I sat on Father's lap and admired his gold watch, and, yes, he pulled out that locket and showed me the portrait of my great-grandmother. I suppose it was a ritual he went through with all his descendants, of whom, however, there were, in the legitimate line, no great number – only eleven then, and fewer when we made our second visit, in 1923, the year before his death.

It was in autumn turning to wet winter. In October the little-known Prime Minister, Stanley Baldwin, had announced that Protection was the only remedy for the post-war Depression, and that he intended to seek a mandate to reverse the policy of Free Trade, which had been the Ark of the Covenant since the days of Cobden and Gladstone. The election was held in November, and my father stood as the Liberal candidate for Inverclyde. The need to defend the sacred cause of Free Trade had brought Asquith and Lloyd George together again for the first time since 1916, L.G. even appearing on the same platform as Asquith in Paisley.

I should myself have been in my first term at Glenalmond, but I had been ill during the summer holidays and the doctors recommended that I should not start there till the New Year. I found this irksome, the rest of the family being away at school, even Kirstie (despite Mother's belief that school was unsuitable or unnecessary for a girl); all the more so because by October I felt thoroughly well again and full of energy. Since I had, in the last eighteen months, developed a sudden and passionate interest in party politics, which, provoked doubtless by the excitement occasioned by the break-up of the Coalition, vied with county cricket for the chief place in my list of enthusiasms, I prevailed on my father to let me accompany him during his campaign. As a result I actually attended that historic meeting at Paisley, and so can claim to be one of the very few now about, and not a native of Paisley, to have seen Asquith and Lloyd George on the same platform, and heard them speak. I don't, naturally, recall anything they said, but I remember Asquith's manner. He seemed impossibly remote, indifferent almost, and very old. Of course politicians went on longer in those days than most of them – thank Heaven – do now, and Asquith, I suppose, must have been about seventy. No great age really, but he gave the impression of one so bruised by the misfortunes he had endured in the last seven years as to be very much older. Brandy no doubt contributed to it. Lloyd George, by contrast, made me laugh, and so won my allegiance, which held for another six or seven years.

The day after the poll, when Father had been safely returned, we went to visit my great-grandfather.

'I don't know how much sense he'll make, Alec,' Father said. 'They tell me he's getting very frail, and sometimes wanders. But you'll be a gentleman and pretend to follow what he is saying even if it makes little sense, won't you?'

We found him ensconced in a high-backed chair in a drawing-room that I recognised, even then, as a period piece, with its Turkey carpet, Benares brass, tapestried chairs and heavy gilt-framed paintings – not the good ones; they were in his gallery. He had a tartan plaid wrapped round him and his beard had lost the neat shape I remembered. The green and yellow Amazon parrot was still there in the cage behind his right shoulder, and he was sipping a glass of hot milk laced with whisky, and smoking a cigar. Fifty years of Havana smoke hung heavy in the velvet curtains.

'So, Walter,' he said, 'you're in, I see. Laura not with you.'

'She doesn't care for politics.'

'Sensible woman, man's business. And what will Asquith do?'

'He'll put Labour in,' Father said, 'and quite right too. The fact that they don't have an overall majority and will depend on us if they are to survive will teach them to be a responsible government.'

'Taxes will go up. Well, I'm too old to worry.'

'Besides, Baldwin's set on Protection,' Father said. 'We can't have that, we're a trading nation.'

'What about you, young man?'

He turned to look at me and the cigar slid from his fingers. I picked it up and restored it to him. He waited and his gaze was still keen and lively, appraising.

'Well,' I said, 'I'm glad Father's won of course, but I don't see what's so wrong about Protection. I mean, we came north by train and we passed through all those towns in Lancashire with factory chimneys and no smoke coming out of them, and then in Inverclyde, well, you see men standing about at every street corner with their caps pulled down over their eyes as if they want to hide from the world, because they have no jobs. So if Protection will bring back jobs for them, then maybe I'm for it.'

'No, Alec . . .' Father began, 'that's very well reasoned and does you credit, but, you see . . .'

'I've been a Free Trader all my life,' the old man said. 'Glasgow was built on Free Trade. So was the Empire. When Joe Chamberlain came to Glasgow and spoke up for Protection twenty years ago, I gave him dinner at the Club and told him why it was wrong, wrong in principle and wrong in practice. We depend, I said, for our prosperity on the Free Market in goods, with no restrictions and no tariffs. It enriches everyone, I said. Joe adjusted his eye-glass – you know he always wore an eye-glass – and touched the orchid in his buttonhole, and said: "Sir William, with all due respect, it ain't one of the Ten Commandments. It's not an iron law. There ain't no such thing as an iron law in political economy." I didn't believe him then, but now I don't know. I'm old and I know less, with less certainty, than ever. So, you may be right, laddie . . . help me up, will you.'

I got my arm under his and let him steady himself against me as he found his balance. Then he directed me to guide him, his steps shuffling and him leaning on me, to a recess in the L-shaped room. He told me to light a candle and hold it up to the painting on the wall. It showed a steam ship making its way down the Clyde, with mountains in the distance.

'First ship of the line,' he said, 'beautiful. The first of the Allan Line. Painted on her maiden voyage. Can't remember the fellow's name. You can read it, I suppose. Took to drink and died young, but he could paint. Could paint a bit, don't you think? What are you going to do with your life, laddie . . . can't remember your name.'

'Alec, sir.'

'Alec, then . . . what you going to do? Doesn't matter to you now, you'll be thinking, and I'll be gone long before you have to decide. So listen to an old man. Make things. Doesn't matter what, but make things. That's what the country needs, people to make things. People like you, laddie. Not like your grandfather, a poor thing, preaching sermons. Sermons. There are better sermons in iron and steel than ever came from a pulpit. But now, they don't want to make things and so there's this talk of Protection. Well, they may be right. If you're weak you need Protection. We were strong when I made that ship, the *Catherine Johnstone* – that was my wife's name and that was the ship's. We were strong then, and there was no talk of Protection. Take me back to my chair, laddie, I'm weary.'

Well, I let him down. I never made anything, not what he would have recognised as a thing being made. I couldn't even make the poems I thought I had in my head. Sometimes I think I made nothing except mistakes.

Later in the evening he said: 'Death duties. They'll go up if Asquith puts these Socialist rascals in. Well, Walter, it all goes to you, now that you're the only one of your generation. You'd better set up a trust for your wife and bairns, and the nephews and nieces. I never liked trusts myself. I can do more with my money than a set of canny Scotch lawyers, I said when they ettled at me to establish one. But I'm a businessman and you're not, Walter. So set up a trust, it's too late for me to do it now and I'm over-weary. I made a settlement on your father when he went into the Kirk. That'll keep you for life, I said, and it's a deal more than a minister needs. Christ preached to the poor . . . blessed are the poor in heart . . . and those with a low bank balance, I said. Your father didn't like that, Walter, but then he never did like much that I said or did. And then he married that thin-flanked woman and she brought money to him too. I asked him what he thought about the rich man and the needle's eye. But he wouldn't answer me. I think I had the better of him there. So it all goes to you. May temper your enthusiasm for putting the rascals in.'

'I've no great enthusiasm, but I think it has to be done,' Father said. 'In any case, most of the Scots Labour MPs, who are the ones I know, are decent chaps, practical men some, Romantics others, but decent fellows. You'd like them well enough yourself.'

The old man grunted. He shifted in his chair. His head dropped. I wondered if I might slip off and view the paintings in the gallery. Then he stirred.

'It was a sore disappointment to me when your father went into the Kirk. I've never forgiven him, you know, I don't have a forgiving nature. There's kirk on both sides of the family, kirk or preaching, and a sour cauld morality, and I wouldn't give a docken for any of it. There's no God waiting to call and judge me. I made up my mind on that a long while back, when your father was a boy. I took a voyage on one of my ships as far as Italy. I went to Rome and saw all the priests and friars and monks and cardinals and him they call the Holy Father – a beastly sight. And then I travelled down to Sorrento on the Bay of Naples and sat on the rocks looking out to sea, and I said to myself, but out loud, "You're a pagan, that's what you are, Willie, a pagan." And I've never regretted it, never changed my mind. Your father's but a poor thing, and he's got an ulcer. I may outlive him yet. I'd like fine to do that.'

Again he sank into abstraction. My father took a book from the table and glanced at it. I watched Sir William, fascinated by the craggy features, and trying to see behind them to the young man who had gazed towards Capri and rejected the Christian God. The veins stood out in ridges on the hand that rested on the arm of the chair. The parrot cackled and the old man's head jerked up.

'The damned doctor tells me to drink my whisky with milk, but I want a proper dram before bed. Pour me one, Walter.'

My father obeyed and took one for himself.

'Give the boy one.'

'He's too young, far too young.'

'Give him one. He can drink my health.' The old man laughed like the parrot. 'Come away, Walter, a wee dram'll no' harm him, and it'll aye be something for him to be able to say that he's taken a drink with a man who was born when George IV was king. He died just six weeks after I was born. They hated him in London, you know, laddie, but he came up here to Scotland – it was Sir Walter who brought him – and he stood on the battlements of Edinburgh Castle in the rain and cheered the people who were cheering him. He liked a dram too, though his tipple was cherry-brandy. Well, laddie, drink my health and tell me how you like it.'

I sipped, my first taste of whisky.

'It's grand,' I said, and the parrot laughed again.

'Twenty years old, that malt, and tasting of Islay peat that was formed before there were men in Scotland. What d'you think of that? I bought the distillery last year. It was going to close. Would you call that Protection – of a sort, eh, Walter? Laddie, pull that bell-rope and Jock'll come to see me to my bield. Always remember, it's bad whisky that rots the liver. I've aye held to the good stuff myself. But I'll no' live to drink what they've been making in my distillery since I bought it . . .'

III

'My father was killed ten years ago today.'

Colin lay on his back on the shelf of rock, in navy-blue rugby shirt, bathing-trunks and sandshoes. I looked up from frying the burn trout he had caught. He was staring through the lattice-work of the birch trees at the deep blue of the summer sky. A fat Turkish cigarette (bought by me in Rattray's tobacco shop in Perth on my last visit to the dentist) was held between his lips, and his profile was sharp. A little pebble prinked his thigh. Feeling my gaze, he sat up and pushed the soft tawny hair out of his eyes.

'Fish is nearly done.'

'My mother wanted to take me out,' he said, 'but I couldn't stand it, not again.'

'What do you mean?'

'In memoriam the dead hero.'

'Oh,' I said, 'won't there be the devil of a row?'

''Spect so. That hurt look. How could you, Colin, don't you care? I don't like rows, but what can you do? Anyway, it's all rotten now she's married again.'

'What does your stepfather think about it?'

'Oh, the Major's like me, not good at thinking.' Colin rubbed his nose. 'Tell you something, though. If we weren't both in the XI there'd be a row about us being off here together, different houses and you a scholar and me not good at thinking.'

'Oh, rot.'

Cricket brought us together. Colin was my friend of three

summers then. The friendship was nipped annually by the first cold winds of autumn, then hibernated, no more than a pleasant memory, till it revived with the green grass and the sound of bat and ball. I felt guilty towards him in the dark days. He looked pinched and miserable as he sidled along the cloisters through which the winds whistled. But in summer he glowed and blossomed. Every summer he became the most important person in the school and my life. It was only in summer that he was possessed of the freedom of youth; in winter his vitality sagged, oppressed by the ageing weight of memory.

I passed him the fish on a tin plate and a bottle of ginger-pop from the cool of the burn.

'Did you say, just, I don't want to come, or did you make some excuse?'

'I told the truth. I said I wanted to spend the day with you.'

'Crikey. There will be a row.'

'I don't often tell her the truth, but I thought it was time I started.'

'I'm afraid you may have started something else.'

'Anyway, if she had wanted me to, she shouldn't have married Bunny.'

'But that was years ago.'

'So?'

'I know it's difficult for you. I'd only uncles killed. Three of them, two on one side and my mama's favourite brother, Uncle Ned. That's hard enough to live up to. But a dead father with the DSO and you an only child. Much worse, I can see that. Well, it can never happen again, not like that. Don't know why you're going into the army, Col.'

'Only thing I can do. We've no land, I've no brains. I say, this fish is jolly good, isn't it?'

'Jolly good. Bit like school again, the army in peacetime. You'll even have to ask your colonel's permission to get married.'

'Daresay I won't want to.'

We slept in the heat of the June afternoon, then, vigour of boyhood replacing its delicious languor, bathed in the deep cold pool under our rock, wrestled like young puppies, and at last, orderly like good, well-schooled children, tidied everything up, smoked a last defiant cigarette, and made our way down the burnside towards evening chapel, in a pale blue and yellow evening that was still warm and scented with dog-roses, honeysuckle, and beyond the river the sharp odour of pine needles.

We parted under the archway to go to our separate houses.

'Be good. Don't do anything I wouldn't do.'

'Couldn't.'

Our friendship would, indeed, have been viewed with suspicion, regarded even as 'unhealthy', if we had not been in the XI. Even so, my housemaster frowned on it (as did Colin's mother) while my chum Toby Macrae amused himself by pretending mystification.

'I can see he's got a pretty face,' he said, 'and you tell me – I bow to your superior knowledge of such matters – that his cover-drive is a joy for ever, but tell me, does he ever say anything remotely interesting?'

'I get interesting conversation from you.'

'I see. So it really is *formosum Alexim* and all that.'

'Absolutely. *Ardeo* like Hell. Fool.'

'Fool yourself, I should say.'

I was certainly in love with Colin, that summer as other summers, but, despite my jesting with Toby, I didn't think of it that way. Love was something that would happen later, with girls. This was only friendship. Such analysis is of course retrospective, for it did not then occur to me to define my feelings in this manner, even when, for example, I experienced intense jealousy – equal to any felt since – if Colin occasionally preferred someone else's company or even seemed to smile too eagerly across chapel at another. I couldn't think of it either as a crush, because that was something you might have on a younger boy, not on an equal, and was, we most of us thought, rather reprehensible, if carried even a small step beyond facetious conversation.

Colin came to stay with us in the summer holidays while he and I attended every day of that famous Oval Test of 1926 when Hobbs and Sutcliffe had one of their greatest opening stands, and then the young Larwood and the venerable Rhodes brought about an astonishing Australian collapse, as a result of which the Ashes were regained for the first time since the war. We got merry in a South London pub, and only just managed to catch the last train to Oxford, arriving at Blankets as the moonlight lay athwart the lawn.

Father had bought Blankets soon after the war. He said that the mood of London now grated on him. At Blankets, on the fringe of Otmoor, he took possession of England. He developed an enthusiasm for the history of the locality, and delighted in the conversation of the older villagers. There were men who had never travelled even to Oxford, less than an hour's bus-ride away. He found a quality absent even from his beloved Borderers; they were rooted in the soil and had what he called 'a settled habitation'.

In my youth I found this fanciful. His absorption in life there seemed a retreat from life. He had invented a safe place for himself where the hum of the world was inaudible.

Colin, that summer, pushed his hair out of his eyes and said: 'The war might never have happened. You can't believe in it here.'

Yet there were thirty-one names on the parish memorial,

almost all from the local Yeomanry regiment, the Queen's Own Oxfordshire Hussars.

Father liked us to bring our friends to stay. Youth refreshed him. He still had hopes that we would measure up to his own dead friends. He circulated the claret jug and encouraged us to air our views. Colin was shy and silent while my brothers' friends from Oxford or Eton put themselves on display. Father said: 'He has the natural Calvinist reticence of the well-bred Scot.' It was the sort of phrase he relished. 'Besides,' he added, 'he is a fisherman, and that is proof of virtue.' For him, that word had a Roman ring.

I introduced Colin to the dry-fly, which he had never used on fast-running northern streams. After a couple of days his skill surpassed mine.

Lord Birkenhead came for the weekend. His way of flattering the young was to dazzle us with the daring of his wit and the extravagance of his opinions. Father had broken with him over Ireland; yet found the audacity of his conversation irresistible. He spoke to us of glittering prizes as the candles guttered.

Colin said: 'I couldn't understand the half of what he said, but he's a bit of a cad, isn't he?'

Birkenhead took me aside, and said: 'And so you're a poet, young man. We need poets. Where there is no poetry the people perish. It is our great national art.' He quoted Matthew Arnold. 'A sublime pessimism,' he said. 'I have sat on the Woolsack and thought the world dross. But it is through poetry that men learn to reach for the stars.'

It was the middle of the afternoon, and he reeked of brandy.

'What would I give to be sixteen again, with the world spread out before me to feed my dreams? Ah youth, youth. *Carpe diem*, young man. There is poetry too in the romance of politics, the march of events, the great decisions, the drama.'

Four years later he was dead, at fifty-eight.

Historians call him a failure, remark something coarse and rotten in him, suggest his extravagance was pathological. Yet he inspired me that afternoon, as his speech rolled like blank verse over the lawns.

Father saw Blankets as a refuge, but for us it was a private Eden. The apple was still on the tree.

My determination to go to school in Scotland had distanced me from George and Hector, who had gone to Eton. Alastair, still at his private school, was father's delight whenever he was at home. So I was closest to Kirstie who shared my passion for Scotland, devoured the Waverley novels, and thought Oxfordshire 'tame'. With Colin, Kirstie and I spent brisk mornings riding, afternoons on the croquet lawn, and evenings on the trout stream to catch the rise before sunset. Colin sighed, 'If life could always be like this.' The only book he had read with pleasure was *The Wind in the Willows*.

Hector brought undergraduate friends, mostly Etonians in whose bright confident voices one could discern preparation for Government. I disliked their assurance that the world was theirs for enjoyment and exploitation; but their knowledge of that world dismayed and diminished me. When I argued with them in defence of that summer's General Strike, they brushed me off with disdain born of privilege and ignorance.

'I say, are you a Bolshie?' one said.

He was a tall fair handsome boy, with loose lips, very blue eyes, and wandering hair. He looked more generous than his sentiments seemed. His name was Guy Holland, and his father, a Member of Parliament, had been killed at second Ypres.

'I don't know,' I said, 'but they're at least trying to make a better world in Russia.'

'You're an idealist,' said Edwin Pringle, heir to the ground rents of a square mile of some Midland city. 'But I fancy idealism's a luxury we can't afford.'

'I was an idealist once,' said Robin Maltravers in his creamy voice. 'In my Shelley period, I recall.'

'And when was that, Robin?'

'When I was twelve.'

The port circulated, the candlelight danced; in the garden a nightingale must have sung.

Father said: 'I've been looking into local history. Did you know this house and land were held by a connection of yours, Guy? It had been monastic property, and was acquired when the monastries were dissolved. The Holland who held it at the time of the Civil War, Gervase, fought for the Parliament, but he opposed Oliver's Protectorate and was knighted at the Restoration. His son turned Catholic – interesting? The family became Tories and Jacobites. During the '45, the then Holland, Sir Benjamin, was visited by one Alastair Maclean, an officer in the French service who was sounding out English Jacobites. He promised he would join the Prince if the Jacobite army won a victory in England or reached London, but – he pointed out – his was a peaceful country, he couldn't bring any fighting-men, for the use of weapons had been long forgotten in this quiet land, and his obligations to family and tenants were such that he couldn't undertake to lend support to a still doubtful cause. And so, of course, he sent Captain Maclean away, with the same answer that so many English Jacobites gave: our hearts are yours but we dare not commit ourselves. I think there's a lesson for our own times there.'

Father's lessons were ever oblique. He saw lessons where other men didn't. I doubt if anyone at the table understood him. They listened politely, because they had been taught good manners.

But there were, I thought, two lessons; and they contradicted each other. Either you devoted yourself, body and soul, to a cause, for better or worse; or you recognised that

23

you had other personal loyalties that deserved priority. And I had no idea which lesson Father approved.

'My dear,' said Robin Maltravers, 'it's very naughty of Hector to have kept you hidden for so long, but now that I've found you, I'm not going to let you go, not even when you retreat to your northern refuge. Though I hate the North, all wet knees and tweeds.'

Robin alarmed me, and I wasn't sure that I liked him.

'I wish I could take you to the Riviera with me. I wish I didn't have to go. But duty, in the shape of my mother, calls me, and I'm a slave. But oh the fatigue of the casino life, too enervating for words.'

His eyes danced.

'But then,' he said, 'it's on to Italy and marvellous Baroque art. Don't tell Sachie though, but I'm almost certain I'm rather a Rococo boy at heart.'

It was typical of him to assume that I knew who Sachie was – and might indeed be in a position to tell him anything. But Robin was an aesthete and modernist, on lunching terms with the Sitwells and Nancy Cunard. My tastes, depending on mood, still ran to Kipling and Housman. Robin mocked the first and deplored the second.

'All that English self-pity, Shropshire,' he said, 'like living in a salad, my dear. And Kipling, boom, boom, boom, you might as well like Newbolt and his ghastly hush in the Close tonight. This is the Chapel: here, my son, your father learned the ways of whatever it was. I ask you. We have changed all that, we who live in the wasteland of Western civilisation.'

Yet, if he frightened me, he also appealed. I was ready to rebel against Father's values – 'All that dismal Liberalism and high moral tone, my dear' – and he offered me one rebellious path. When he began to write to me the next term, from Oxford, I was exhilarated. I showed his letters to Toby Macrae.

'Well,' he said, 'you are going it. "Love or what you will".

I say. Would this be the love that used not to dare to speak its name? If so, it's learned to proclaim itself pretty clearly.'

But Toby was impressed all the same. Like me, he was ready to kick against the decent middle-class standards of the College and the muscular Christianity of the headmaster. Toby came from a solid professional Edinburgh background. His father was a Writer to the Signet, partner in a long-established firm, an elder of St Giles, the essence of Edinburgh respectability. Their house in Moray Place spoke eloquently of the virtue of things that were taken for granted. Donald Macrae was a kind man, but he drove Toby to distraction by his unquestioning acceptance of the way things were ordered. Sitting at their mahogany dining table, I was aware of Toby's leg twitching as Mr Macrae pronounced on eternal verities. 'Dr Pangloss, I presume,' Toby would say as soon as we were free of the parental presence.

'One thing for sure,' he said, 'wild horses will not drag me into the legal profession.'

We would slip from the house into the cavernous Edinburgh winter night, to Rutherford's in Drummond Street, frequented by medical students, or the low howffs at the top of Leith Street. Our revolt at that stage rarely carried us beyond drinking a couple of pints of beer – all, I daresay, that we could afford – and such wild talk as youth has always indulged in. But Toby fancied himself in love with a barmaid, Morag, who flirted her dark curls at him, and treated him with a rough but kindly condescension.

'Only compare,' he said, 'Morag with the girls we meet at dances. Vapid creatures. All the vitality of Scotland is now to be found in what my father would call the lower classes. Do you suppose, Alec, that there is any city in the world, any single city, half as class conscious as Edinburgh?'

'It seems unlikely,' I said.

'But Dr Pangloss will tell you that Scotland is distinguished by the respect in which all classes hold each other. "We are not egalitarian, but we recognise that we are all Jock

Tamson's bairns." I tell you, it makes me want to scream and scream and scream.'

He emitted an illustrative yelp, which, though it fell far short of a scream, caused Morag to tell him to behave himself.

'We want none of that in here, I'm warning you.'

'What strength of character,' Toby said, 'and then in the next breath Dr Pangloss will deplore the rough manners of those people "who simply don't know how to behave".'

To my surprise Toby found nothing Panglossian in my father. Perhaps it is only against one's own parents that one needs to rebel. Perhaps not; many of us then, and in the next few years, were to feel it was a war between the generations. Toby however responded to my father's own enthusiasm for youth. It impressed him that Father encouraged us all to hold forth, whereas Mr Macrae was merely irritated by his son's opinions.

'You have no right,' he would say, 'to an opinion which you have not earned by experience.'

Casting his resentment aside at Blankets, Toby was acute in his judgements. He pointed out to me that George was really rather intelligent; I had been accustomed to think of him as a fool because he was the only one among us who had no taste for books. George was not illiterate; he wasn't even what is now identified as dyslexic. He could read perfectly well, had no trouble with schoolwork; he wasn't interested. That was all. It wasn't that he was a hearty; he despised games players. At school, where necessary, he had done enough to pass muster on the games field and waited till he was sufficiently senior before declaring it was all a sad waste of time. He had no use either for the field sports in which Father delighted. If he wanted to eat fish, there were perfectly good fishmongers. Talk of politics bored him equally; people, he once said, invented problems in order to discuss them.

His indifference to almost everything gave him, now that I

was ready to believe he wasn't a fool, an air of authority. There was nothing he wanted to do, and yet, though impatient, he was not discontented.

'George might be a great man,' Toby said.

In the middle of his second year George left Oxford. Father was bewildered. He couldn't conceive that anyone should do such a thing. He went to the length even of having George see an alienist in Wimpole Street. George – surprisingly? – consented. I put the question mark there because I had supposed that in his terse economic manner he was acting in accordance with some settled idea. But it wasn't, it seemed, like that at all. He knew that Oxford was not for him. He viewed the enthusiasms of undergraduates with frigid contempt. But he didn't know why. It wasn't even as if, then, he was driven away on account of the near-absence of women. He was still an unambitious virgin.

He attended the alienist over a period of six months. One day I found him drinking tea in the drawing room at Hyde Park Gardens when I had supposed he would still be in Wimpole Street.

'I gave him a bloody nose,' he said, 'and told him he was a fraud.'

'Why?'

'Because he is.'

That was all. Nobody got any more of an explanation from him. The alienist called the police. There was some question of a prosecution. Then the complaint was withdrawn. George appeared unmoved though the whole family, and especially Father and Mother, had been in a state of anxiety.

He turned his blue gaze on them as if to say: so what?

Then, a little later, in the spring of 1928, George left home. He gave no warning. One day after breakfast he ordered one of the housemaids to pack a suitcase and call a taxi.

No word came for weeks. Father wanted to call in the

27

police; Mother prevented him. He went to the police morgue, instead, to gaze at unidentified bodies. Then a cable came from Spain. George was following the bulls. 'Extra-ordinary,' Father said. 'I've always loathed the idea of bull fighting.'

'Spaniards,' said my grandmother, his mother-in-law, 'have no feeling for animals. I can't think why. They all have English nannies, you know.'

Sunlight lingered pale-gold on her lined late-Victorian face; her tea-gown gave off the merest whiff of moth-balls.

Father had not expected his children to be troublesome. George bewildered him. He himself had been a good son, alert to duty; had followed the *cursus honoris*. Won respect. He wasn't a wholly worldly man; and yet he valued his worldly success. And now here was George.

'He is probably smitten by some gypsy,' I suggested. 'Like Carmen.'

'Opera!' Father said. 'Shrieking sopranos! I could under-stand it if George was of a different temperament, if he revolted against "this strange disease of modern life,/ With its sick hurry, its divided aims,/ Its heads o'ertax'd, its palsied hearts . . ." Yes, I could understand that. But that's not George. There's no poetry in him. And yet he's not a waster. Something's gone wrong somewhere, and I wish I under-stood.'

He looked to me for enlightenment, and I had none to offer.

Father knocked out his pipe, sighed deep and theatrical as a Tennysonian lover, and shuffled off to his library.

Toby shook his head.

'There are three sorts of people in this country,' he said. 'There is the generation that grew up before the war, formed its opinions and tastes then, was too old to fight, and now looks back on the lost gardens of the Edwardian afternoon. There are those who were broken in the trenches and who

28

can never believe anything again. And there is our generation, which is searching for a faith and, not finding one, delights in dissipation.'

'That's all very well,' Hector said in his light high tenor, 'but old George is just jolly selfish. He doesn't care how his actions affect the rest of us.'

Alastair looked up from *Point Counter Point.*

'I should say that old George is just acting as his instinct tells him, cutting loose like this. And he's jolly well right. That's what we've got to learn to do, isn't it? And if he has got a gypsy girl, jolly good luck to him.'

'You're too young to understand,' Hector said.

'Hector,' I said, 'that's the sort of remark They make.'

'And who are They?'

'The forces of unalterable law.'

IV
Berlin 1931

Looking at the young man who set off for Berlin as he stands below the blue-grey hissing steam of Victoria Station, I feel a certain irritation and impatience. He is for one thing so very evidently a member of the British ruling class – and yet he is determined that he isn't. He sees himself as a rebel, but no foreigner or member of the working class could ever be deceived into regarding him as such. His coat is good Scotch tweed, as is the dark, herring-bone suit. He wears a cloth cap, also tweed. He is even obeying one of his father's dicta: 'Always keep a cloth cap for travelling by train.'

And his eagerness of expression is of a naivety no Continental of his age would have been capable of.

What's more, he is running away, even though ostensibly he is in search of experience. But he has no right to hope for anything very intense of that sort. He is only going to stay with his brother Hector who has just received his first, very junior, posting at our Berlin embassy.

But in fact Hector, when he greets him at the station in Berlin, looks different. He no longer seems to be ever ready to take offence. The bad smell of which his nose has always betrayed consciousness would appear to have evaporated. Something of Eton and Oxford has vanished too. Perhaps someone has told him life isn't a matter of winning marks.

Outside it is raining as it was in London's January. But – for Alec – it's again a different sort of rain, indefinably foreign, though he would be lost if you asked him to account for what is different. English rain, he thinks, is just rain, but this German rain is aimed directly at him.

They come out into a wide square and the rain leaps from the puddles which the streetlights make gold and purple. But he has got the rain wrong. He realises this almost at once. It isn't aimed at him, it isn't aimed at anyone. It belongs to the vast uncaring indifference of Berlin. It is then liberating rain, the rain of a city where he isn't going to have to pretend to be what others think he should be, these others being, of course, his elders.

It is also bitterly cold, with a raw frigidity that cuts through his expensive tweed coat and into his bones. And this too is as it should be – no half-measures. There is something splendidly mocking in the air. Even the buildings, which are huge, heavily-ornate, demanding of admiration, have an unreal look. It is as if they shouldn't be standing here, in a city that is like a dream out of control. All round Berlin – he knows this even then and can sniff it in the air – is emptiness. The city stops abruptly, and beyond is the desolate landscape of the Teutonic Knights.

Hector calls up a taxi and they drive, not as Alec expects to his apartment, but to a bar on a wide boulevard which in the grim light of January has a brutal contemptuous look. The bar itself is bright with electroliers, and full of gilt and velvet and mirrors. It is crowded and steam rises from damp coats and sausages.

Hector has directed the taxi-driver to take Alec's luggage to his apartment, and for the rest of the evening Alec will wonder whether it is wise to have trusted a foreign cabbie with his things. (But it was, of course, quite safe, and the luggage was waiting for him when eventually he got there.)

Alec has come to Berlin because, six months after coming down from Cambridge, he has no job – this is the autumn of 1931 and the Slump. Lack of a job doesn't trouble him – he is a poet after all – but he has persuaded his father that it might be a good idea to learn German.

Really, he says to friends, I want to be able to read Nietzsche in the original. If you don't understand Nietzsche, he adds, then you are lost in the world of today. Most of those he speaks to haven't, as he well knows, read Nietzsche even in translation; and he himself hasn't been able to get through *Thus Spake Zarathrustra*, but has only dipped into it, and extracted a few apposite aphorisms. But this doesn't matter. He feels sure he has got the 'essence of Nietzsche', and, in certain moods, he persuades himself that he will really get to grips with him when he knows enough German. But of course, though in time he does learn the language well enough, he never really tackles Nietzsche. In any case he discovers that very few of his German friends have read him either.

Then there is Kafka. But at this stage Alec isn't quite confident enough to lay forth on that subject.

Hector says: 'We're meeting Guy here. He's always late.'

'Guy?'

'Guy Holland of course.'

Alec is not immediately sure that he is pleased to learn that Guy is in Berlin. There is something disquieting about Guy. What is he doing there?

'Oh,' Hector says, 'Guy doesn't need to "do" anything. He's one of the lucky ones. But there is some film he's interested in, I believe.'

Then Hector turns the conversation to their parents and the 'impossibility' of Father. This is new. Hector has never found Father impossible till now. On the contrary, he has been the dutiful, unquestioning son; his being here in Berlin, accredited to His Britannic Majesty's Embassy, proves that. But now Hector says: 'Sometimes, I understand why old George made his getaway. Father doesn't realise the whole ship is sinking.'

'Because of the Slump, you mean?'

'My dear boy, the Slump is a symptom, not a cause, of the shipwreck we are about to experience.'

Even then, Alec wonders where Hector picked up this phrase. It doesn't sound his own wording. And, indeed, Alec soon meets lots of people who tell him that the Slump (or the Depression) is a symptom, not a cause of . . . oh, the terminal exhaustion of the capitalist system. That kind of thing.

But Guy Holland, when he is seen crossing the crowded floor towards them, moving as if the throng should part like the Red Sea before the Children of Israel, which in fact it does, looks like an advertisement for the continuing vitality of the system that is about to suffer shipwreck. He is beautifully dressed. He has left his overcoat with the porter (for this is the sort of bar where there is a cloakroom and a porter), and he is wearing a wonderfully negligent, loosely-cut, dove-grey suit, a cream silk shirt and a burgundy red tie. There is an orchid in his buttonhole, and his wandering blond hair gives him the incongruous look of a Georgian poet.

He smiles at Alec as if it is too much trouble to speak a greeting.

'I can't think why we come here,' he says, and, as explanation, directs their gaze, following his, across the gangway to a table where two large grizzled men, looking like superannuated officers – and one, indeed, has lost an arm – are struggling for possession of a bottle of champagne (wrapped in a napkin, but probably German) which the one-armed one has taken from the waiter. They are competing for the right to pour the wine for their companion, a lady whose warpaint fails to disguise the galloping years, and who wears a creamy fox fur round her shoulders, even though the room is so hot that Alec is regretting his tweed suit.

Alec soon settles in a pension, or boarding house off the Nöllendorffplatz, in a thin street where the dirty plaster frontages, with their scuffed scrollwork and heraldic devices, can't conceal that the district is teetering on the verge of social decline. He is pleased to be on his own. Hector, in Berlin, may be livelier than Hector at home, but he is still

33

Hector. All the same he is somewhat offended when Hector doesn't press him to stay on in his apartment, where there is certainly room for both. Indeed, he doesn't even make the excuse that he likes to keep his guest room free, so that he can accommodate visiting English friends, but simply agrees that Alec's German will make much faster progress if he moves to a boarding house where he will be forced to speak the language.

It is some time before Alec realises why Hector was so immediately acquiescent. It had never occurred to him that he was cramping Hector's style; but then it hadn't occurred either that Hector had a style to be cramped.

In the mornings, though he often has a hangover, Alec works conscientiously at his German. He tackles the language methodically, using a grammar book and a good dictionary. He learns lists of irregular verbs. The German he hears in the streets, cafés, shops, and bars, is not the language of Nietzsche, whom anyway he soon discards. For some weeks he can make nothing of the harsh Berlin accent. Then, all at once he clicks, and the subversive mocking humour, characteristic of the city, delights him.

Guy Holland cultivates him and demands his company. He is not sure if he likes this. There is something about Guy that disturbs him. It is not his homosexuality. Alec now admits to himself, though he wouldn't say it to others, that his feeling for Colin had been what the world would call homosexual. (Nowadays, more accurately, I judge it to have been homo-erotic.) But he has put that behind him, he is sure of that. He is on the lookout for a girl. So he is ready to be amused and complacent when Guy takes him on a tour of the Boy Bars.

Guy is frank, even boastful.

'For me,' he says, 'Berlin means boys.'

He explains that he had not known true sexual release till he came here. In England, though he recognised his own nature early, he never experienced that. It is a matter, he says, of class. If he is in bed with a friend, from his own background, he can't take it seriously, he even starts giggling. But a working-class German boy . . .

It is the first time Alec has seen him animated.

'They enjoy it,' Guy says, 'even when they really prefer girls.'

While he is speaking in this way, Alec realises why Hector too is relaxed since he came to Berlin. He has been a fool not to see it before, an utter fool. But he didn't. He now understands why Hector preferred that he should move out of his apartment. It wasn't, he hopes, that Hector thought Alec would split to the parents. It was just what Guy has been describing. With Alec there, Hector would have felt himself British, constrained by the respectable bonds of England and class.

After this conversation Alec is much easier with Guy, and is able to enjoy his company. He had been afraid that Guy fancied him and might embarrass him by making a pass. Now he sees how silly his fear was, and finds Guy charming in his absolute lack of concern that allows him to go to the lowest quarter in his Ritz Hotel suits.

He is happy to accompany Guy on his jaunts. One night they go to a *Lokal* in a working-class district. There are about twenty boys sitting around, gossiping and playing cards or dice. The room is heated by a big iron stove, and because it is so hot the boys have mostly taken off their jackets or jerseys, and unbuttoned their shirts to the navel. Most of them, perhaps all, as Alec realises, are waiting for customers. But they don't appear impatient. The bar is a sort of club.

Alec and Guy sit down and order beer. Two boys throw down their cards and saunter over to join them. They greet Guy by name and one gives him a quick kiss. It is little more than a peck on the cheek, and speaks of affection rather than flirtation. They probably know that later in the evening, whatever happens, whether they go off with Guy or not, he will give them some money. He is English after all and the English are rich.

The one called Otto puts his arm round Guy's neck, letting it rest lightly, companionably, on his shoulder, and begins to tell him a story. Alec doesn't listen. He is more interested in taking in the whole scene. Some middle-aged men, very fat, like prosperous butchers, have arrived and are dancing with boys; the music is an old waltz tune, played on a gramophone. The record has a crack in it, and spits on every revolution. But they don't seem to mind.

Then the other boy, Heinzi, shifts over to settle on the bench beside Alec. He snuggles up to him. He says he is just out of the Reformatory, and hasn't been reformed at all, but it is nice to be out.

'You wouldn't believe the vice in places like that. The things they get up to,' he says.

He is quite pretty with a rather squashed face, and he is wearing leather shorts to display his thighs, which look very bronzed for a boy who has been in the Reformatory.

'Put your hand in his pocket,' Guy says.

'What?'

'Put your hand in his pocket.'

Guy smiles as he gives the order. So Alec obeys and discovers that the pocket has been cut away so that his hand goes straight through to Heinzi's cock, which immediately stiffens in response. This excites Alec and he kisses the boy on the mouth and finds Heinzi's tongue searching out his.

Guy is pleased by the success of his experiment. Much later in the evening he tells Alec that he had had him worried.

'Which puzzled me when I remembered that beauty you brought to Blankets.'

Alec doesn't think it worth explaining that he and Colin have never even kissed. He shrugs it off, hoping to suggest that he is a man of mystery, a deep one. But he realises that he is quite gratified.

He forms the habit of dropping in to this *Lokal* once or twice a week. Usually he has a couple of glasses of beer and spends a few hours chatting to Heinzi and some of the other boys. He is fascinated by what seems to be their easy acceptance of things as they are. None of them has any ambition, though they would like to be rich, if it just happened. But the notion of making it happen doesn't occur to them. They would think the idea ridiculous. They live in an eternal present, and it is – he thinks, sentimentally – very agreeable. A couple of times he takes Heinzi home with him, and that is quite jolly, but it is not serious.

What he is doing then, and in the *Lokal*, is acting out a sort of fantasy. It is like public school life if all restrictions and inhibitions were removed. It is as if he is doing what they would all have liked to do four or five years ago, but dared not.

Of course this is fantasy, he recognises that, like making up stories about being shipwrecked on an island. But this *Lokal* is a sort of island, and that is why it appeals to him.

The second reason it is not serious is that he has fallen in love with a girl.

Trude is the daughter of Father's only German friend. Alec has been in Berlin for more than two months before he carries out his father's instructions and calls on Professor Liebknecht. The professor has written a study of Sir Walter Scott; he sent it to Father with an inscription thanking him for awakening his interest in Scott when they first knew each other at Oxford.

He tells Alec, almost straight away: 'Sir Walter was a Tory, but I am a good Social Democrat.'

This is true. It is not long before Alec learns that the professor's cousin, Karl Liebknecht, was a Deputy in the Reichstag who opposed the war, was imprisoned, and murdered by right-wing extremists in 1919.

'So, you see,' the professor says, 'I have to be careful.'

Alec is not quite sure whether this is a joke. At first he

thinks it is, then he thinks it is a sour joke with an edge to it. He is expected to regard it as a joke, and yet the professor means it.

Professor Liebknecht lives in a large gloomy apartment with Turkey carpets (like old Sir William's – perhaps from the same Kidderminster factory) and too much stained mahogany furniture with elaborate carvings and awkward sharp corners. The walls are lined with bookshelves right up to the ceiling, and between them are dark representations of mythological or legendary scenes. Alec thinks *The Ring* might have been composed in such an apartment, though in fact he knows little about Wagner. It also occurs to him, for the first time, that what we call 'Victorianism' was not a purely British phenomenon.

He would like to talk to Professor Liebknecht about Nietzsche, but is too shy to do so. He is afraid to expose his ignorance. Instead he listens, carefully, while the professor dilates on the beauty of the Trossachs. It is not very exhilarating till Trude joins them.

She has come in from the street where it is still very cold and her thin face is flushed. She has dancing eyes, her hair is cut fashionably short, and her arrival takes twenty years off the atmosphere of the apartment. Indeed there is something absurd about such a place being her home, she is so light and airy. The professor looks at her, Alec thinks, even that first day, when he is still ignorant, with a mixture of love and anxiety. She talks very rapidly for two or three minutes about where she has been, whom she has seen, and what she has been doing. You can see that she does so to please the old man.

Alec can't take his eyes off her, and this embarrasses him. When she speaks and he tries to reply, his German deteriorates. He feels an awful fool.

If Trude notices this, she forgives him. Soon they are going about together, to cinemas, exhibitions and theatres; and of course cafés. Trude has lots of friends – she is a student at the university – and they meet in cafés and talk, talk, talk. They gossip and chatter of course, but most of their talk is serious. Trude has the air of a butterfly but she is a serious girl.

She is permitted an unusual degree of freedom, partly because her mother is dead, and partly because to grant her this freedom is in accordance with her father's political principles.

'He is modern,' Trude says. 'Why do you smile, Alec?'

'I don't know, really.'

'It is because of our apartment, I think. That, I agree, is not modern. My father is not modern in his tastes, but in his ideas. He believes in the equality of the sexes. This is something, I think, you don't have yet in England, but it is what we believe in, in progressive circles, in Germany. Women are not made just for the kitchen and child-bearing, my father thinks. Why do you smile?'

Alec is fascinated by Trude. She is different from anyone he has ever met. She has precisely what they lack at home. Sincerity. Trude says exactly what she thinks, when she thinks it. It is not always intelligent; she can be irritatingly and abruptly dismissive: 'That I do not care for!' Poof! it is gone, swept aside. But it is still magnificent.

And she can be absolutely earnest even when eating cream cakes, of which she is inordinately fond. 'I do not get fat,' she says simply, and Alec believes her. It is, clearly, simply a question of will. And Trude's is very strong.

He is careful not to let her meet Guy. They wouldn't get on at all. Trude has no time for persiflage. Her own variety of make-believe is different; she trusts in the supremacy of reason, or says she does. Actually, even in his infatuation, Alec can't but observe that she never stops to think. She reacts.

Some of Trude's friends are Communists and they are much more serious than the Communists Alec has known at

Cambridge. They argue its theory passionately. That is one difference, but the other is more important. The Communists have a real chance of coming to power in Germany. The revolution may happen tomorrow. The dawn is pink turning to red. That is how they see it, and no wonder then, that their excitement is tremendous. It might even be catching, except that Trude herself remains staunchly loyal to Social Democracy.

'We must build,' she says. 'Social Democracy is constructive.'

'We must destroy before we can build,' her Communist friends reply; and the matter is argued for hours.

Of one thing they are certain however: capitalism is finished. Four and a half million unemployed prove that. You can't walk the streets of the capital without being aware of the reality of its failure. It rises to your nostrils like the smell of roasted chestnuts from the braziers on street corners.

And they are certain, also, that Hitler and the Nazis cannot come to power. They are so certain, that they are not even afraid.

'The German soul will reject them,' they say. 'It will spew out that poisonous nonsense.'

Alec is not so certain. This is impertinent of him, so he keeps quiet. But he wonders if these idealistic students from solid bourgeois homes where intellectual achievement is a sort of household god, are incapable of hearing the murmurous rancour that whispers to him as he walks the shabby streets full of boarded-up shops.

Moreover, Guy has introduced him to some young men who are proud to proclaim themselves Nazis. In comparison with Trude's friends, they are stupid. But their confidence is alarming, and he can't but think it may be justified. Of course these are socially respectable Nazis, but they are the ones Alec has met. The reality of the movement is still only, for him, a distant drumming deep in the forest of unknown Germany.

★

Hector also tells him that it is the opinion in the Embassy that the Nazi movement will not come to anything. He himself has talked with the Conservative leader von Papen. Papen, he says to Alec, knows the game he is playing with Hitler. Hitler is his tool, that's all. He is using him to destroy the constitutional republic, and when that is done von Papen will head an old-style authoritarian regime, he may even restore the Kaiser, or his son, and 'Master Hitler will be discarded'. Hector says that the Nazis are like the seed which the sower sowed on stony ground and which sprang up quickly and then withered because it had no roots. Hector is giving him the benefit of educated opinion; but the use of the parable reminds Alec of their father. He is always quoting the Bible to make points.

Trude says: 'Von Papen is a bag of wind. He is so stupid, you can't believe. He is so stupid people think he must be cunning. But he is just stupid.'

Hector also believes that von Papen's authoritarian regime, when it is established, will not last, because 'it will be built on a contradiction and a lie. There is no future for that sort of Germany, it belongs to the past, and will be swept away.' By whom? By the forces of history and its ineluctable logic.

Hector is not, he quite often tells Alec, a Communist. He couldn't be a Communist because it would be incompatible with his position. Nevertheless, he is a Marxist. He knows how and where history is going.

All these political arguments swarm like bees round Alec and through his head. He is entranced by them. They are so marvellously real, not like politics back home, where it is all a question of whether dear Reggie will get a ministry and whether they can contrive to keep 'wild men' like Winston and – his old hero – Lloyd George in a position where they can do no harm. And yet, in another way, part of the excitement he feels is because he knows very well that at any moment he can take the train and be in London in thirty-six hours. It is theatre, that's all.

Only Trude is not theatre. He is beginning to know that. They haven't even kissed, because for all her devotion to what is modern and to Social Democratic liberty, Trude remains a nicely brought-up girl from a good family, one which, in its notions of morality is, indeed, considerably more straitlaced than his own. (He thinks of his great-grandfather and village girls.)

Moreover, though he very much wants to kiss Trude, and more, he is not at all sure that she wants to be kissed, even if her principles permitted it. This uncertainty torments him, and he takes refuge from it in those other activities of which she would be certain to disapprove vehemently, and which are therefore better kept hidden.

The months pass. Alec is now at home in Berlin. Summer comes, and talk of holidays. Hector is going home, but Alec fears to break the spell that Berlin has laid on him.

He gets a letter from Colin, now with his regiment, and due leave. Can they meet somewhere? For a moment he likes the idea. Then he thinks of how they must both have changed, and also of how what he has learned in Berlin will make it impossible for him to be natural with Colin. He is fond of him, of course, but as a memory. So he does not reply till he is sure it is too late and Colin will have made other plans. This is shabby.

Alec has discovered what he wants to do with himself. He will become a newspaperman. Berlin is the perfect point of departure. This is where the future shape of things is unfolding, and he has a seat in the front stalls. The idea intoxicates him, he can hardly wait to start. He writes to Father informing him. Father replies that he has connections with the *Morning Post* and will see what can be done. The *Morning Post* is not, however, the paper that Alec has in mind. He couldn't write what he wants to write for something so stuffy and Conservative. Instead he struggles over an analysis of the political scene, and at last dispatches 2,000 words to the *New Statesman*.

And then comes the great Crash. One day he goes into the street and finds that the banks have closed their doors. Hundreds of depositors are to be seen outside the Darmstadt and National Bank. One old man with a Hindenburg moustache is in tears. He keeps on saying: 'This is the third time I am ruined, and I am too old, too old.' Someone else, not identifiably a Nazi, cries out that it is all the fault of the blood-sucking Jews, but a stout, middle-aged man in a linen suit says: 'What do you mean, blood-sucking Jews. I'm a Jew myself and my blood is being sucked as fast as yours, let me tell you.'

When Alec returns later, the street is empty, and an unnatural silence seems to hang over the city, as if the plague has struck.

Two weeks later he does go on holiday. There suddenly seems no reason not to join Professor Liebknecht and Trude in the Harz Mountains where the professor has a summer chalet. Alec has had no reply from the *New Statesman*. His journalistic career can wait till the autumn.

Trude seems delighted to see him, though Alec doesn't think she has been bored. Every day the three walk in the mountains, the old professor with his alpenstock setting the pace. He says: 'There is a Chinese proverb, "The virtuous delight in mountains, the wise in rivers and lakes." I am not afraid to be classed among the virtuous. Perhaps in Germany today we have more need of virtue even than wisdom.'

Because they have no servant with them – the chalet has only three bedrooms, and in any case the professor insists that holidays demand the simple life and their good servants require a holiday also – they eat every night in the *Gasthaus*. The innkeeper is pleased to have the professor – 'Such a distinguished man, an honour to our district,' he tells Alec – as a guest. They eat brook trout and ox-tongue with brown

43

onion sauce, and venison and *Kaiserfleisch*, and huge quantities of roast potatoes; and cucumber salad sprinkled with paprika, and beetroot with cummin seed; and then of course pancakes or *Apfelstrudel* or the little wild strawberries which are still in season in the mountains; and they drink quantities of a greenish wine, slightly acidulous but wonderfully refreshing.

The professor talks about the decay of German culture, destroyed by militarism and vanity.

'This is what I admire so much about the English,' he says. 'You have a sense of proportion, which we Germans have always lacked, and so you do not feel tempted to throw yourself into the abyss. No *Götterdämmerung* for the English gods. We Germans have done things of which the English would never be capable. It is impossible to imagine an English Hegel or an English Wagner. But we always go too far, even Hegel and Wagner are, how shall I say? Excessive? There is something gross about their appetite.'

The professor rubs his belly, stuffed with *geröstete Kartoffeln*, and calls for another bottle of wine.

'Too far,' he says. 'We feel the perverse attraction of disaster. But you English smile politely and say –' he breaks into English and a parody of the Oxford voice – ' "That's a bit much, old chap." I admire that. Here in Germany we must prepare to suffer, for there is a madness abroad, and I fear it will soon have us by the throat. Well, then, like Sir Walter, I shall say: "*agere et pati Romanum est.*" '

Later Alec and Trude walk in the moonlight. He takes her arm.

'No, please,' she says, 'don't be sentimental, Alec. I find I do not care for the sentimental.'

He tries to tell her that he loves her, but she shakes her head. It is not what she wants to hear. Then, since he doesn't know what else to say, they walk in silence, up into the pinewoods above the village. There is a light breeze and the scent of the pines reminds him of Scotland. The pale moonlight of summer flickers between the branches and dances on the floor of the forest which is thickly covered in pine needles. They have now climbed high enough to be clear of the sounds from the village. A deer breaks from the trees ahead of them and then, in one bound, is out of sight crashing through the wood. They look up and they can see beyond the trees to the bare line of the hilltop. Now it is very still and a night for summer dreams. It would be pleasant to lie under the trees and sleep with his girl in his arms.

Only she is not his girl, and she is not in his arms.

She says: 'I am afraid.'

He knows she doesn't mean afraid of the dark or even the half-light.

She says: 'Father is fearless and believes in speaking the truth.'

'I know, I've noticed it.'

'And so I am afraid.'

He can't argue or reassure; her fear seems reasonable. But he feels ashamed, and the shame corrupts his tenderness. He is ashamed because what is happening in Germany is exciting for him; it doesn't touch him, but he knows it may break the professor. And Trude? Yes. Trude also.

V
Berlin 1931–3

Despite the air of menace there was something idyllic about those first months in Germany. That is why I have written of myself in the third person and of what happened in the present tense. An idyll has always belonged to another person, different from the one you subsequently become; and yet the idyll is never entirely lost, it remains ever-present. But after that holiday in the mountains my feelings changed: I stopped believing that things there didn't concern me. Instead it seemed that their working-out would determine the next years of my life.

My article had been returned by the *New Statesman*. They had in any case kept it so long that it was now out of date. There were other letters waiting for me, among them one from Father and another from Toby Macrae. I stuffed them in my pocket, and, having given my landlady the bottle of Kirsch which I had brought from the village, I went out.

The air was sultry and the city had a rhythm like a beating of distant drums.

I sat in a café and ordered beer, and read my letters, Father's, dutifully, first.

Dear Alec,

You will have seen from the newspapers (if you have seen English newspapers, but in the mountains you may well not have done so) that I have been persuaded to join the National Government. It was a difficult decision. As you know, I have no political ambition – that vanished a while back. But I have an affection for Ramsay, who is an honourable man. In consenting to lead the National Government against the wishes of the majority of his own party, he has sacrificed much. It is a hard thing to cut yourself off from your friends and to expose yourself to taunts and insults. He has, however, in putting the national interest before the interest of his party, acted as I should wish any statesman to do; as you know, I have never been greatly enamoured of party. In this moment of crisis, lesser loyalties must give way to greater, and so I accepted his invitation, reluctantly and yet in the end unquestioningly. I stipulated only that my health would not permit me to undertake heavy departmental duties, and I am glad to say he accepted this condition. My post is therefore one where I may trust to exert some influence, but will have no real power. I was greatly gratified, and – it goes without saying – honoured to receive a note from His Majesty, in his own hand, welcoming me to office. 'The Empire,' he wrote, 'must hold together in this time of trouble.'

I have given much thought to your own immediate future. I understand why the *Morning Post* does not appeal to you. You have often heard me say that the man who is not a Socialist at twenty is a scoundrel. Accordingly, I have spoken with Edward Harbottle, the editor of the *Globe*. He understands your position and quite sees that you do not wish to do an apprenticeship on a local paper – the usual way into journalism, as you know. He has talked with their correspondent in Berlin, Ian Forbes – an Aberdeen man – and Forbes will be happy to see you, and believes you may, for the time being in an unofficial capacity, make yourself useful. I trust this will appeal to you, and that you will make something worthwhile of the opportunity vouchsafed you in this manner. I am certain that it is unnecessary to remark that it is a rare and exceptional favour that has been offered you.

Hector has talked much of the situation in Germany. While I respect his power of analysis, I cannot find myself concurring with his conclusion. Germany requires, above all, stability and the restoration of the value of the currency. Without that, recovery is impossible. I daresay we would be wise to abandon the claim for reparations. I never thought them desirable, and nor, I believe, did L.G., but the French insisted. As ever, the French influence on international politics has been pernicious. I love France, revere the French contribution to civilisation, but politically they have been trouble-makers since the days of Cardinal Richelieu!

There is clearly much that is wild, brutal, and unsavoury about the National Socialists, but Hayes-Hayward of the FO, with whom I had a word in the Club yesterday, is of the opinion that Herr Hitler is fundamentally sensible and patriotic. H-H thinks he will discard and subdue the wild men if he is admitted to the Government. Certainly it seems to me that Germany needs a strong man, who will do for the nation what Signor Mussolini has achieved in Italy. Herr Hitler seems the only candidate – so thin is the field.

Your mother sends you her love. She has been in better health, but pines to see you. It's a sair day for a mither when her bairns gang a-wandering. But ye maun dree your ain weird – she kens that fine.

I remain as ever your loving and affectionate father,
    W.A.

P.S. I grow forgetful and remiss in my old age. Do, pray, convey my affectionate respects to Professor Liebknecht, and my gratitude for the interest he has taken in you. If only there were more such Germans! He reminds me of what Carlyle had to say of Burns: 'Here was a piece of the right Saxon stuff: strong as the Harz rock, rooted in the depths of the world; rock, yet with wells of living softness

in it!' A true man, as I recall, such as is rare to find today.
W.A.

Poor Father, I thought, poor, dear, unseeing Father, to be so reassured by some pin-striped ninny in his club.

Two nights before, in the village *Gasthaus*, the professor had been talking of the two strains in German culture, of how 'we both long for reason and fear it, we recognise its limits and shrink from it. And this shrinking, my dear Alec, manifests itself in two fashions. On the one hand, you have someone like Thomas Mann – I say, someone like, but in reality he is beyond compare in his acuity and sensitivity. Now Mann is pre-eminently an artist, and as such he knows with a wonderful apprehension how intuition and the unwilled call the operations of reason into question; and yet even while aware of this, Mann remains rational, wedded always to the light. And he contrives to balance in this delicate manner because he does not feel himself diminished or threatened, but rather enriched, by what goes beyond reason and for ever bubbles below it. But on the other hand, there are Germans who feel themselves inferior, who are made to feel inferior by what they recognise as the sceptical spirit which inheres in the true man of reason. Scepticism is abhorrent to them for it calls into question the very basis of their own insecure character. And so they fling themselves into unreason, denouncing reason, as Luther did, as a whore. They think themselves strong because, rejecting reason, they reject scepticism and throw it onto the rubbish heap. Instead they abandon themselves to dark dreams of a primitive blood-force when what they deem natural man stalked the German forests in primeval and unchallenged freedom. They call themselves strong, when in reality they fear to stand in the lucid light of day. They flee the complicated, infinitely intricate, world of qualification and scepticism, which man in his march towards the light over the centuries constructed and explored with such difficulty and courage. Yes – and courage – for scepticism is the mark of courage; it requires a man to look reality in the face. Now this creature, this Hitler, is a child of the dark, a coward who dare not do that, one for whom scepticism is impossible, because it would reveal even to him his essential inadequacy. And his appeal rests precisely in that inadequacy. Inadequate himself, he preaches a message which calls on men to deny reality – and then, being a liar as well as coward and clown, he pretends that what he offers is reality, the reality of the eternal struggle, the reality which calls weak strong and declares that this feeble strength has the right to govern the way we think, what we believe, how we act. For the call to action which he shouts forth, has ultimately but one purpose: to annihilate thought, to reduce man to a condition only of feeling. Scepticism being an essential property of thought, he inevitably, in his shrill terror of reality, abominates . . .'

And at this moment, from the table behind me, I heard a chair pushed back. A young man in a brown shirt loomed over the table.

'Scum,' he said, and spat in the professor's face, 'Jewish scum. When we come to power . . .' and as if intoxicated by the word power, he swung a blow at the professor. I threw up my arm and knocked it aside, and leaped to my feet and grappled with him. A fist thudded into my kidneys and I gasped with pain. At this moment the innkeeper, Herr Schwarz, struck the Nazi on the shoulder with a thick stick which he kept behind the bar. The Nazi yelled and let go. Herr Schwarz, a sturdy thick-set fellow with the strong arms of a man accustomed to heaving barrels, ordered the Nazi and his friends out. Seeing three or four villagers ready to come to the landlord's aid, and conscious that they were strangers in the place, the group obeyed, with threats and mutterings, beating a retreat as sour as it was lacking in dignity.

'Thank you, Johan,' said the professor, 'we are grateful to you, but I am not sure if you were wise.'

'I don't allow people of that sort to behave like that in my house,' the landlord said.

Trude was trembling.

'Even here,' she said, 'even here.'

'My dear,' the professor said, 'we have many friends. Thank you, Alec, even scepticism would not have protected my old bones from the blow that lout could have delivered.'

But Herr Schwarz arranged that a handful of villagers should escort us back to the chalet.

'I don't know what the world's coming to,' he said. Then he scratched his head. 'Herr Professor, it's not for a simple fellow like me to give advice to a learned gentleman like yourself, but an innkeeper sees a bit of the world and gets a sense of how it's going, so if you will forgive my presumption, I would just advise you to be more careful of how you speak in public. These are nasty times we are living in, and I wouldn't like to think of a learned gentleman like you getting hurt. I know you like spinning words, and, Lord help us, words never did anyone any harm, but that's not as everyone thinks, and this young gentleman, the Englishman, might not be so quick next time, nor might I be here with my club.'

Poor, dear Father, I thought again, and took my beer to the bar.

'Franz,' I said to the bar boy, 'let me ask you a question.'

He pushed back his thick blond hair and leaned over the bar. He had a habit of pouting his lips and moving his face close to yours as if about to kiss you. He did this to everyone. Some customers, I had observed, found it exciting, others disconcerting, even repulsive. I don't suppose he was even aware of it. What may have begun provocatively had become simply habit, so that Franz appeared to flirt even when he was in reality uninterested in the customer.

'Is it intimate?'

'Very.'

'Well, then.'

'Well, then, Franz, what do you really think of the Nazis?' His lips pouted.

'Oh,' he said, 'that's not my sort of question. I have friends who fancy them no end.'

He darted off to serve a party that had just entered. There were two provincial businessmen in tired suits and two girls, not their wives, whom they had recruited for a night out on the town. The girls were not quite professionals; they inhabited, I would guess, that middle kingdom disputed by tarts and chorus-girls. They looked bored, as if their escorts felt they had acquitted themselves sufficiently by the mere act of picking the girls up, and that no more could be demanded of them. When the men got home they would be able to hint to their colleagues of their wild times in Berlin. They had ordered a bottle of champagne, and, pouring it, Franz seemed to be entering into a conspiracy with the girls.

I pulled out Toby's letter. It was written in a style that he had copied from Stevenson's Thomson and Johnstone letters to Charles Baxter, a style sadly affected even when Stevenson employed it.

Weel, weel, my auld and trusted that's aye gallivanting wi furrin hoors. Hae ye nae mind tae yer chiels condemned to bide in Auld Reekie? The lassies in the howffs are eident tae see ye. 'Wull he no come back again,' they speir, gin ye were Chairlie himsel. 'Wae's me, wae's me!'

And what's the clash o' the toon? This puir prentice sawbanes got unco fou last Setterday nicht, and sae finds himsel in black disgrace wi Dr Pangloss, the whilk is o' the opeenion that 'nae guid will come o' sic cairryings-on'. And wha's tae say the auld fule is wrang? No me, laddie, no me.

The ither nicht I accompanied a marrow o' mine, a fellow student o' the mysteries that the guid Dr Knox enlisted Burke and Hare tae help him reveal, tae a meeting

52

o' the National Pairty o' Scotland. Alas, puir countree! Stands Scotland whaur she did? Niver hae I see sic a thrang o' knobblie knees that suld hae been concealed in the decent obscurity o' trews laid open to the licht aneath the cutty kilt.

Oor nationalists are no like thon they breed in Gairmany, for siccar.

Gin, in unregenerate hours, your hert still pines for the bonnie laddie o' the cover drive, I hae sair news for you. He's taen up wi wumman or sae they tell me. Sae there's nae yeese setting your hert on thon sodger laddie.

Seriously, Alec, I miss you. Auld Reekie is a dour soor vratch o' a toun wi'oot a glisk o' your bonnie sonsie face. Haste ye back, an we'll owre the hills wi' Chairlie.

Toby or Thomson.

I felt what everyone in a foreign city must sometimes feel, that home-tugging wrench, and saw the wind shift the haar as it raced up Leith Walk, and heard it rattle in the lum-tops of that city where I had never lived and yet recognised as home. I began on the blank sheet Toby had left to pick out some lines of verse.

The bar of the Eden Hotel was usually beyond my means. Nor was the atmosphere of anxious luxury appealing. It was Barbara Jakobsen who took me there. She was an American journalist, already celebrated in her late twenties. She was a Communist, though with her short-styled hair, short straight nose, full red lips, and the metallic chic of her dress, she looked the very picture of the daughter of an American millionaire, which indeed she was also.

She said: 'The Eden is a microcosm, Alec. I could write my column without ever moving from this bar.'

She had a sharp way with waiters: 'Only a sentimentalist, only an Englishman, would suppose that just because I'm a Communist, there's any reason for me to tolerate poor service. I believe in people doing their jobs properly. Communism is about efficiency. I guess Stalin gives sloppy waiters short shrift.'

She liked to proclaim her Communism in strong, clear tones in the Eden, where it was a toss-up whether she would be overheard by Jewish bankers or fashionable Nazis.

She drank Gibsons, and said it had taken her a full week to train the barmen to make them properly.

'They try to put too much vermouth in. That way they make on the deal.'

Barbara was usually accompanied at the Eden by a German girl called Sophie. Sophie was as blonde and vague as Barbara was dark and decided. Sophie would have looked at home on the top of a Christmas tree. Barbara always found occasion early in conversation with a new acquaintance to make it clear that she and Sophie were a ménage. 'The slut's so weak and amiable she would otherwise go off with the first man that asked her.' She had a habit of talking about Sophie in her presence as if she wasn't there. Sophie didn't seem to mind.

'But tell me, Barbara,' I said, 'don't some men regard that as a challenge?'

'And you think I can't beat off any challenge? Be your age, Buster.'

Barbara had an ambition to interview Hitler. She knew many of the leading Nazis, and, by her account, they found her fascinating and infuriating because she contradicted their ideas of what women should be. She liked that a lot.

'All the same,' she said, 'they can't resist me.'

But she hadn't succeeded in nailing Hitler.

'You know of course that he's impotent. Fact. Yes,' she raised her voice, and exaggerated her accent, which was normally mid-Atlantic at most, so that it sounded as if she came from the Deep South, 'that poor little man just cain't get it up.'

She paid no apparent heed to the looks such remarks attracted. Likewise she was happy to let it be thought, on

54

account of her name, that she was Jewish. She even encouraged the belief, and I had known her for several months before she confided that her grandfather, a Lutheran minister, had emigrated to the States from Denmark in the 1880s.

'Why didn't you tell me before?'

'Why should I? 'Sides, I liked watching your "ever so embarrassed and good form" attempts to avoid saying anything which might be construed as upper-class English anti-Semitism.'

'Thanks. Anyway, I'm Scots, not English.'

'Scots, English, it's all the same. You're part of the same imperialist racket.'

'You don't look Danish, but then you don't look Jewish either.'

'No, my nose is too short. But I'll thank you to keep my secret.'

'You mean you're happy to be taken for a Jew?'

'Sure, it disturbs them no end when they find me attractive.'

I had been nervous going to see Ian Forbes. He could easily resent having me foisted on him. I could imagine that foreign correspondents had no great love for suggestions emanating from their editors. One of the attractions of the job is its independence. So it was a few days after I had got Father's letter that I presented myself at Forbes's office.

I found a slight man with sandy-reddish hair and watery blue eyes who cut my apologies short.

'I don't know your father,' he said, 'and my politics aren't exactly his, but there's scarce a Scotsman for whom I have greater respect. He has the root of the matter in him and is wise like Ulysses. And so, I'm blithe to extend a helping hand to his bairn, and I'm sure, laddie, from the look of you that you'll deserve it. And, for it'll be ill talking with a new acquaintance – and I hope I can soon say friend – when the pair are drouthy, we'll just away round the corner, and as my own old father – God rest his soul – would hae said, wet oor thrapples.'

Forbes described himself as 'an auld-farrant Radical'. Born a Liberal (like Father), he had long since despaired of the party, and now found none to satisfy him. He had a hatred of war and violence, and deplored imperialism.

'I'll no deny that the Empire has been a grand thing for mony a Scot,' he said. 'We have plunged deep there, and profited. And yet I can't like it, I canna like it, Alec, or think it right that we should hold dominion over palm and pine, far less the folk that bide there. I believe in the Brotherhood o' Man, and there's an end on't.' His father had been a horseman on a Donside farm – 'forty year on the same placie, he was that good' – and young Ian himself was the classic Scots Lad o' Pairts, proceeding from the village school to the local academy and then to the university in Aberdeen.

'I was to be a professor, but then the war came, and four years in the trenches with the Gordons knocked all the scholarship out of me and the taste for war. So here I am.'

He didn't mention that he had been commissioned from the ranks, and won the DSO. Instead, 'I've sometimes thought that if I had directed my machine-gunners better at Ypres, we might have finished off Master Hitler there and then.'

Ian Forbes loathed the Nazis, whom he called always 'the Nasties'. Yet unlike Barbara Jakobsen, or indeed Professor Liebknecht, he sometimes, late at night over a bottle of whisky after Ilse, his German wife, had gone to bed and we were left in the sitting room of his comfortable apartment, spoke of them in a different way.

'When I look at a man like Roehm – or wee Adolf himself – or the rank and file of the movement – the old soldiers – I sometimes find myself saying, 'There, Ian Forbes,' (which he pronounced in the old-fashioned and, I believe, correct way, as two syllables) 'There, Ian Forbes, but for the Grace of

God, go you. You see, laddie, their resentment touches me. I can understand their sense that they've been betrayed, that a world is coming into being that would deny them. All their ranting against the Jews is an abomination, but when a man finds everything he has believed in stripped away from him, it's a rare comfort to find an enemy to blame. And what's worse, they do not appeal only to the baser side of man; with their call for national renewal they appeal also to noble instincts.'

In October 1931 I accompanied Ian to Brunswick. Hitler had had his first interview with the aged President Hindenburg the week before, and it had gone badly. Ian said that Hindenburg had muttered afterwards to the Defence Minister, General Schleicher, that the queer little fellow would never make a Chancellor, but might do as Minister in charge of the Postal Department.

'One of Schleicher's aides passed that on to me. You can imagine that wee Adolf would be fair scunnered to hear sic a judgement. They say he spoke at the old man for half an hour without a stop, and him deaf as a post.'

Then Hitler had attended an assembly at which all the right-wing nationalist parties were represented, and hadn't cared for that either.

'Too many frock coats and brass hats,' Ian said.

The Brunswick rally was supposed to demonstrate the vitality and strength of the Nazi movement, and, while Ian was going to write a straight news report, he had suggested that I should do 'a colour piece'.

'After all, laddie, you're the poet.'

This then was my first appearance in print, outside school and university magazines.

All day the lorries had rolled in, five thousand of them, and debouched their platoons of Hitler's Brownshirts. Thirty-eight special trains from all over Germany had brought others to this gentle peaceful northern city.

In the pale autumn light the Nazis formed themselves, with much jostling and a disorder that the Brigade of Guards would have despised, into marching columns. But when the columns were formed discipline reigned, and the sight was formidable, even awful.

Contrary to received opinion, and their own propaganda, even the young Nazis, even the most admired and feared stormtroopers of the SA, do not all resemble blond Nordic gods. They come, like the rest of common humanity, in all shapes and sizes. Roehm, the commander of the SA, is short, bullet-headed and pot-bellied. He looks like a butcher and his reputation is that of a butcher of men. While waiting for Hitler to arrive, he stood, legs wide apart, laughing and joking with his intimates, and you were certain always that the joke was at someone's expense.

Then all was ready and Hitler arrived in an open Mercedes to an exultant yell. He stood on the saluting base and the columns filed before him. They moved with a swing and swagger that was truly frightening. Hitler talks of the will to power, and here was that will made flesh and steel.

Our military parades are formal and dignified things. There is even a reverence to them, and that is the only emotion permitted. But here, there was no reverence; adulation there was, and the keen expression of a will so naked and brutal that it expressed what can only be called lust. It took six hours for the procession to march past him.

Then it was dark and the torches were lit, thousands of torches bright in the encircling night.

And then Hitler spoke. He spoke for more than an hour, and the tens of thousands did not move except when his words compelled a cheer that came, it seemed, from their innermost soul, a cheer that they could not have repressed by any mental effort.

He speaks in a south German accent, and, people say, he speaks coarsely and often ungrammatically. But of the power of his words there can be no doubt. We have no such speakers in England and never have had, nor will. The English language does not lend itself to this sort of rhetoric.

He spoke, and Milton's lines came to mind:

'and to confirm his words, out-flew
Millions of flaming swords, drawn from the thighs
Of mighty cherubim; the sudden blaze
Far round illumined Hell: highly they raged
Against the Highest, and fierce with grasped arms
Clashed on their sounding shields the din of war,
Hurling defiance toward the vault of Heaven.'

At present it is the din of civil war that sounds through Germany, but the march of tramping feet and the cry 'Heil Hitler' are sending a sinister message throughout Europe.

It is a message against which many may choose to stop their ears.

They will, I fear, do so in vain.

As a matter of fact, Milton's words had not come to mind. I had to look them up when I was back in Berlin.

Ian Forbes said: 'The sentiments are fine, but the style . . . never mind, we'll send it and I'll see they print it. For the sake of the sentiments . . .'

Barbara was scathing: 'Operatic nonsense,' she said. 'The Nazis are a product of economic circumstances. That's all. They represent the last knee-jerk reaction of a doomed *petit-bourgeoisie*, supported by Big Money.'

'It doesn't feel like that.'

'Oh, you are hopeless.'

Trude was rather kinder.

'Yes,' she said, 'it makes me see. That is good. But I don't like the implication that the Nazis are the soul of Germany on the march. I think you were more impressed than you should have been. But I insist, that is not the real Germany.'

'It seemed real enough,' I said, 'when those Nazis attacked your father in the *Gasthaus*.'

'No, but I see, it is always your English way to remark the particulars rather than what lies under appearances.'

Barbara and Sophie lived in a long street of apartment blocks that were melancholy and mysterious by night, drab in the winter rain of the afternoon. Barbara liked to say that Sophie kept house, or perhaps it was Sophie who first claimed that. But I couldn't believe it. Sophie was a girl whose body was so touchingly right that it always looked as if she had nothing on under her dress. Her beauty was all freshness, skin, complexion, youth, but there was a fat little old lady waiting to take over. Once, when I offered to kiss her cheek, she drew back, and said: 'I am so sorry, Alec, it is not you, but I have a horror of men touching me, it is so sad. It is because of my half-brother.'

Her half-brother, Barbara said, had been an army officer. Since the family had lost their estates in what was now Poland, he had become a banker. Also, she said, a Nazi.

'Sophie has a horror of him, don't ask her why, it's too painful. Well, you can guess why, I guess.'

Barbara and Sophie were having a Christmas party. Bring a girl, or a boy, they said, and Sophie giggled. So I invited Trude. I did so with some hesitation, but she had expressed a desire to meet Barbara when I had spoken of her, and, since I didn't think they would agree, this party seemed a safer way of gratifying that wish than a meeting in a café.

'Are your friends Bohemian?' she said, considering what she would wear.

'They are lesbians.'

'That I know. It does not help me to decide.'

60

'You'll look beautiful whatever you wear' – and she did in a black fringed dress with a wide white collar.

'If you don't like the party or the people, you will say, won't you, and we'll leave.'

'Why are you nervous, Alec, do you think I am some poor little girl that knows nothing?'

I was deliberately late, so that the party was in full swing when we arrived. A drunk American novelist, of some celebrity, was marching up and down the hall, singing, to the tune of 'I didn't raise my boy to be a soldier', words – he broke off to tell me – of his own composition.

'Listen, bo' . . . "I didn't raise my boy to be a bourgeois,/ I raised him to be, The Third International's pride and joy,/ But the son of a bitch, has gone and gotten rich,/ my boy, my boy, my boy" – pretty swell, eh? The girls are through there. They don't like my singing.'

He took a swig from a pint flask and resumed his chant. We moved through double doors to the main salon. A gramophone was playing ragtime, and a black girl was dancing. She clicked her fingers and kicked up her heels. She was a performer in a cabaret Barbara had taken me to.

There were about twenty people in the long room. I was surprised to see Hector among them.

'I didn't know you knew Barbara.'

'Everyone who is anyone knows Barbara.'

'I didn't know she was that famous.'

'Over there,' he said, pointing to a small man in a shabby grey suit, 'is Karl Meyer, who is the coming man in the Communist Party. I hope to have a word with him later in the evening. It was the promise of Meyer which lured me here. I prefer to meet him in surroundings like this.'

Meyer was talking to an elderly gentleman, who, as I watched, removed a glossy chestnut wig to reveal a head bald as an egg. For a moment he rested the wig on a bust of Lenin. Then he replaced it on his head.

'Who's that?'

'That is Gerald Hamilton. He may be the wickedest person here. Some say he is the wickedest man in England.'

'Why is he so wicked, please?' said Trude.

'I don't think I know you well enough, Fraulein Liebknecht, to tell you that.'

Hector giggled, and I realised that he was nervous.

'Don't worry,' I said to Trude, 'I've never heard of this wicked man either.'

'Then he cannot be so very wicked, I think.'

We moved away.

'Your brother seems different,' she said. 'When I have met him previously, he has been so stiff, so correct, so English.'

'I expect he is just letting his hair down. Call it the humanising influence of Berlin.'

To my surprise Barbara and Trude took to each other. There was a rapid moment of assessment, and then Barbara seized Trude by the arm and led her off. Half an hour later they were still deep in conversation, and Sophie's lower lip was trembling.

'It is so unfair,' she said, 'I cannot bear it when she does this to me. It is cruel, I think.'

My attempt at reassurance, and suggestion that we might dance, were brushed aside. And yet, as the tears welled up in her eyes, it seemed to me that Sophie might in reality be the dominant partner. Barbara, thoughtless and immediately interested in a new acquaintance, would suffer for it, like a husband who has forgotten time and obligations in the intimacy of a bar, but must return to a cold and nagging wife by a dying fire. Every couple manages things in their own way, and yet, ultimately, there is a limited variety of pattern which the married relationship can take; and Barbara, I saw then, was caught whether she knew it or not, in the coils of marriage.

I watched Hector in conversation with Meyer. There was something disconcerting, obsequious, in his manner. I thought: Hector shouldn't be paying court. And then I thought: why not? The idea that, by reason of his birth and upbringing, Hector was naturally superior to this little man in a crumpled suit, who looked like an office clerk or minor trade union official (both of which he had been in his time), was a relic of my expensive education. It was part of that relentless need to label and place in categories, characteristic of English society; something which, in other contexts, I had identified and determined to be rid of. A man like Meyer – though of course I knew nothing of him personally – represented the future, certainly the only desirable future Germany might be offered, but, more important than that, the future as it must inevitably unfold in the upward and onward march of history. So Barbara had told me, and I was some way to conceding that she was right.

'But I think Hitler cannot come to power.'

The speaker was a young man with pop eyes behind very thick lenses.

He said: 'You must not be deceived by the enthusiasm of his followers. It is light as thistledown. I know.'

'That must be very comforting.'

'Yes, it is. You see, I am a banker. That is how I know. There is not one Nazi leader to whom my bank would grant a loan. They are not worthy of credit. And so you must take my word.'

'You look very young, if you'll allow me to say so, to be in a responsible position in a bank.'

'That is correct. I am very young, quite ridiculously young, to be in a responsible position in a bank. But it is my father's bank. That is why I must be worthy of him. So, you see, it is not true what Hitler says, that all banks are controlled by the Jews. It is not true. Only some of them are. Excuse, please, I think I am going to be sick.'

He brushed past me, heading with a swaying but rapid step towards the bathroom.

Meyer now had his arm round Hector's neck, and was

63

drawing him down so that he could speak, as I supposed, more confidentially. Hector dropped to his knee to let Meyer, who had been stretching up while Hector leaned towards him, settle himself more comfortably in his chair. Hector's mouth hung a little open as he listened to him.

Sophie was dancing with a tall woman in a dinner jacket. When she saw me watching her, she led her partner over.

'Please, Alec,' she said, 'I would wish to present you to the Countess Arnazy. The Countess has asked me to visit her estates in Hungary. It is not possible, but perhaps all the same I shall go.'

'Please to tell me,' the Countess said, 'how Vita is?'

'Vita?'

'The Honourable Vita Sackville-West. I am a great admirer and so I wish to know how she is.'

'Very well, I believe.'

'That is good. Come, Sophie, even if you will not come to Hungary, let us dance.'

They began to waltz. The Countess, older than I had first supposed, played the man, propelling Sophie in a stiff military manner round the little square that had been formed for the dancing in the middle of the room; Sophie let her chin rest on her partner's shoulder, and closed her eyes. They didn't speak. The Countess's determination was impressive. I sat down resting my back against the wall and drank brandy. The black dancer was now being embraced by a German journalist I had met at the Eden with Barbara. He was called Helmut and was a Communist without hope. He had told me that there was no question, no question at all, but that Hitler would come to power, if not this year, then next. He would toy with the Conservative Right, the way a child might pull the wings off flies, Helmut said. He himself had acquired a Norwegian passport. There would be no place for him in the 'new Germany'. His fatalism had impressed me deeply. 'We are entering a new Dark Ages,' he insisted; but it was nice to see that he himself was welcoming the New Year agreeably.

A body slumped to the floor beside me. It was the American novelist. He waved his pint of scotch aloft.

'Not a drop spilled till it's ten years old,' he said. 'I didn't raise my boy to be a bourgeois. 'S a matter of fact, son, I dunno where he is. His mother took him with her, you see. Part of the divorce settlement. I got the cat, she got the boy, but what the hell, my boy, my boy, my boy. See that fella with the toupée, son? That's the wickedest man in Germany.'

'I was told he was the wickedest man in England.'

'That so, son? He might be that and all. But what the hell. I didn't raise my boy to be a bourgeois, and do you know why?'

'Because his mother took him?'

'Hell, no, son, because there's no future in the bourgeoisie, that's why. I write novels for them. For them and about them. So I should know. If they buy my novels – and they do – and praise them – and they do – and make me rich – and they do, son, they do, helluva rich – why hell, there's no future for them. Because I insult them, that's why. I insult them in every line I write, and they lap it up the way the cat – that's the one I got as part of the divorce settlement – laps up cream, when it gets it, poor beast. So, I say, Wall Street's in ruins, Herbert Hoover's finished. You heard of this guy Hitler? Well, let me tell you something. He's no good. He wouldn't play in Peoria. I wouldn't advise him to venture into the Bronx. Let me tell you, son, where you will find the real America. On the wrong side of the tracks, that's where.'

He took a swig from his whisky, and put his free arm round me.

'You're a Britisher, son. Hell, I can always tell, I'm a novelist. My last novel sold . . . hell, I don't recall just what it sold. But do I care? Do I?' For a moment he seemed doubtful. I couldn't believe he didn't care. 'You know

Barbara? She's a great girl. But let me tell you something, son. She wasn't born on the wrong side of the tracks. She was born rich. And she can't forget it, poor little rich girl. She's never known the great beating heart of the real America. My gums bleed for her.'

Hours later, with the fog yellow on the window panes of the morning, Barbara cooked bacon and eggs for Trude and me. Sophie had retired to bed in tears, and the other guests had, mostly, departed, though a few, including the American novelist and the pop-eyed banker, still slept on the floor or stretched or huddled in chairs.

'Never,' Trude said, 'have I known such a party.'

'Par for the course, honey. Alec, you oughta keep a hold of this girl. She might make a man of you yet.'

'Didn't think you thought that desirable, Babs.'

'If there have to be men, let them be men. Hey, what about your stuck-up brother, eh?'

'What indeed?'

'The long arm of the Comintern reaches even within the august portals of Her Majesty's Foreign Office. What a story!'

'But you can't use it!'

'And for why not?'

'The Party.'

'No,' she said, 'I guess not. Pity.'

Berlin was playing on my nerves. It was because I no longer felt a tourist. I attended party meetings with Helmut. His father had been killed at Verdun, and during the twenties his family had known hunger.

'Imagine,' he would say, 'my mother, a professor's daughter, the widow of a lawyer, took a job in a department store. Her mother was horrified, but it was good for her, though she will never admit it. My elder sister became a tart. Not the kind you see on the street corners, but a tart all the same. Now she is married to a Jewish film producer. She is his fifth wife and he is already looking to exchange her for a newer model. That's how it goes, Alec.'

I asked him how he could be a Communist without hope. Wasn't it a contradiction in terms? Communism promised certainty. It knew the direction of history. And so on. I expounded the theory, as I understood it, at length.

'All you say is true,' he replied. 'Intellectually, you are right. Nevertheless . . . so a Communist without hope is absurd? Very well, I am absurd.'

'Perhaps you lack the ruthlessness to be a true Communist?'

'Communism is pity,' he said. 'You don't understand. Communism is pity. That is why I am a Communist and why I do not believe in the historic inevitability of its victory. How can pity win? Answer me that.'

With Helmut I walked for many hours through the city streets, arguing, listening, often laughing, but always disturbed. He had an eye for the incongruous, and a sharp ironic humour, often directed at himself. And yet he took himself and Germanity with the utmost seriousness, brooding for hours on the nature and destiny of his race.

'We are the greatest people in Europe,' he would say, 'and the least. We soar to the heights and wallow in the mire. That is why the English, who are average, are our superiors, and despise us. We lack moderation. We have no common sense. That is why people are mad for Hitler.'

'What will you do if he comes to power?'

'I have a Norwegian passport. I told you so.'

'Yes, I forgot.'

So much of life was bound up in this question: will Hitler come to power? And in its sequel: what will you do if—? and then?

Trude still refused to grant it as a possibility. To do so would, for her, have been to deny the truth of the Germany she knew. Loving her father, she was able to believe in the strength of goodness. She had been much impressed by Barbara, and talked admiringly of her, but she still resisted the Party.

'How can I deny that I am a bourgeois?' she said. 'It would be spitting in Papa's face.'

But that of course was what so many of my generation were determined to do. It was for them a necessary mechanism of release.

To my dismay she still declined to let me make love to her. I even thought of proposing marriage. But I wasn't ready for that, and nor, I knew, was she. Yet whenever we had arranged to meet, I waited for her with apprehension, in case she was prevented, and her entry to the bar or café was like a field of poppies dancing in the breeze.

Her father was causing anxiety. There had been a scene at the university. Some Nazi students had disrupted the lectures of a Jewish professor of anatomy. Perhaps they had protested at the use of Aryan corpses for demonstration, I don't know. That is my memory. It seems absurd. So I am probably right. That is how things were then. In any case, Professor Liebknecht, who wasn't, as it happened, personally acquainted with the professor of anatomy, had taken up his cause. He wrote to the newspapers. His colleagues were furious. It was insupportable, they said, that he should dishonour the university in this way. He replied that the university was dishonouring itself by its inertia. He was officially censured.

Ian Forbes wrote an account for the *Globe*. Two days after a couple of paragraphs, severely mauled by the subs, appeared, he was visited by a policeman who told him that while he himself was in substantial agreement with Ian and believed that such things should be known, there were those higher up who took a different view. Accordingly he was obliged to warn Ian that reporting of this sort was viewed with disfavour, 'even though the Nazis are not yet in power,' the policeman finished with a sigh.

'What will it be like when they are?' I asked Trude, but she looked away, lips drawn together, and shook her head. I urged her to persuade her father to leave the country.

'He is too rash to stay,' I said.

'Never. He is too proud to go. Oh, Alec, you are lucky to be English.'

In July there were elections for the Reichstag. The Nazis won 230 of the 608 seats, with thirty-seven per cent of the vote. They had more than thirteen million votes. The Social Democrats got under eight million, the Communists five and a quarter, and the centre parties four and a half. The other right-wing parties – the Nationalists and People's Party – had only 44 seats in the Reichstag – and yet it was to them that the aged President looked to form a government.

About this time I began to keep an occasional diary.

August 10: Helmut came to my apartment early with news of the murder of a Communist miner, called Pietrzuch, kicked to death by six Nazi thugs, in front of his mother, in the Silesian village of Potempa.

Helmut: 'That clown von Papen has announced the death penalty for "clashes which lead to people being killed". It's a joke. The Nazis have protested at this "inhuman" decree.'

Helmut always makes me feel adolescent. Nothing surprises him.

Ian thinks that in view of von Papen's decree, we can use the story. All the same, it's asking for trouble. We both know that.

August 14: To the Eden. Barbara and Sophie there. Barbara says Hitler may have overplayed his hand. When he demanded the Chancellorship and control of police from Hindenburg last week, he lost his temper and talked of massacring the Marxists. 'Give the SA control of the

69

streets for three days and we shall have a new Germany,'
he screamed. Hindenburg's response? That communiqué
calling on Adolf to conduct the opposition 'in a chivalrous
manner'. Chivalrous! My God!

August 16: The Eden again. The pop-eyed banker (whose
name I can never recall) was there again saying, 'You see,
they are not men to whom any reputable banker would
extend credit.' When he left, Barbara said: 'All the same,
you watch. When Adolf does come to power, he'll offer
him full banking facilities and any loan he asks for. They'll
need it. They've got a cash crisis, you know.'

While we talked politics, Sophie ate cream cakes and
smiled. Barbara went to the powder room and Sophie told
me the Countess was still eager she should go to Hungary
with her. 'But it is not possible,' Sophie said. All the same
she's tempted. The idea delights her.

August 22: The Nazis responsible for Pietrzuch's murder
have been sentenced to death. All members of the SA.

Letter from Father: George is coming home, without
plans. Alastair wants to visit me next month. Father asks: is
it wise? Is it safe? He says the National Government has
stabilised things. 'S.B.'s deep humanity is reassuring to all,'
he writes of Baldwin. So that's all right.

Went for old times sake, to the Rosebud Lokal. Quiet,
nervy, like all Berlin today. Heinzi told me the other boys
had gone to the beaches.

'I've a new lover,' he giggled, 'an American who can't
swim.'

But Heinzi is frightened.

'Sure,' he says, 'lots of queers in the SA, Roehm's boys.
But that won't last. I don't want to be kicked to death, so I
ask my friend to take me to America, but, shit, he's
fascinated by the Nazis and won't move.'

How longingly he dwelled on the word 'America'.

These boys all love the idea of the place. I once told Barbara their enthusiasm was enough to make me doubt Communism. She wasn't amused.

Heinzi said: 'I'll come home with you tonight.'

'Won't your friend be angry?'

'Shit, I'm not his possession. I'm a free German boy.'

But for how much longer?

August 23: When I got to the office Ian handed me a copy of Hitler's telegram to the boys who kicked Pietrzuch to death. It expressed total support.

Later in the day the Nazi Press Office released the text of a 'manifesto' Hitler has issued.

'Herr von Papen: I understand your "bloody" objectivity now. I wish that victory may come to nationalist Germany and destruction upon its Marxist enemies, but I am certainly not fitted to be the executioner of nationalist fighters for the liberty of the German people.'

Ian poured himself a glass of whisky, gave me one too.

'The liberty of the German people! Saved by kicking a poor bloody miner into the grave.'

I suggest this outburst shows that Hitler is running scared of losing the support of the SA, without whom he would be only an ordinary loud-mouthed politician.

Ian shook his head.

Later we went out and had beer and sausages.

Ian said: 'My wife says she couldn't be happy in any other country.'

He talked about the decadence of the German upper classes, of how they will lick Hitler's boots if he comes to power.

'When,' I said.

'When . . . there's still a remnant of decency in ours,' he said. 'They'll accept a social revolution, surrender political power, to keep their country houses. That's what they really care about.'

I spoke of Father's admiration for Baldwin.

Ian drank deeply of his beer.

'As an old-fashioned Presbyterian radical, I find it hard to say a good word of any Tory. But there's a decency about that man. His mother's a MacDonald, mind you.'

'I've heard him say his ambition is to prevent the class war from becoming a reality in Britain.'

He glanced round the beer cellar.

'There's maybe something to be said for that intention,' he said.

Ian puts everything on a basis of personal relations. I like him for it, but it does mean that he is blind to the economic determinants of History.

What a phrase!

Hard to read that young man's reflections without embarrassment; harder still to realise how saddened he would be to meet the weary thing he has become. That's one sort of knowledge the young are spared.

VI

Berlin 1932

I waited, beyond the barrier, for Alastair. I thought: this is how Joseph's brethren felt. But Alastair, when the throng parted to let him through, was dressed not in a coat of many colours, but in irreproachable West of England flannel, morning-grey with a chalk stripe. He was bare-headed in that dull-hatted crowd, and his hair was just a little longer than Father would have thought proper. He wore his Old Etonian tie like a heraldic device and looked ridiculously English, soaring with Olympian assurance over the realities of our age.

He greeted me as if he had just slipped down on the 3.30 from Paddington to my country place for the weekend. 'What fun,' he cried, and looked round for a porter. It hadn't occurred to me to get one. I had grown out of the way of porters. Yet the distaste I felt for the thought that one man should carry another's bags was without economic justification in a world in which men were required to do just that to feed themselves and their families. No doubt in an ideal world – the world for which I was ready to work – we would dispense with servants. But since the real world had its servant class, servants must be employed or starve.

In any case Alastair whistled one up with imperial command, as if, indeed, he was the elder brother who knew his way about.

'Old George is home, I suppose you'd heard. We must face it,' he said, 'old George is mad. Do you know, he mooched about for three weeks speaking nothing to anybody, and then announced that he had got a job as a rubber planter in Malaya. He's going to manage an estate. Crazy. Can you credit it?'

'How did he fix that?'

I knew, from my reading of the financial pages, that the rubber industry had been hit hard by the Slump and that many estate managers had been laid off.

'How would I know? But he's crazy, old George in the gorgeous East, I say . . .'

Alastair had come, not from London, but from the Côte d'Azur. He had been staying with the Mosleys, or at least near them, and was full of talk of 'Tom'.

'Tom really is the future, you know. He's so utterly alive, not like those old men with one foot in the grave and the other trembling on the verge. I mean, to think of an Empire like ours being governed by the likes of Ramsay MacDonald and Baldwin, well, it doesn't bear thinking of. It's the most feeble and wrong-headed government since Lord North's. Of course dear old Father can't see how absurd it is, but then he's the same generation, isn't he? They're all finished and don't know it. You must see the absurdity of it, Alec.'

'I see the absurdity of trying to prop up the capitalist system.'

'Oh, Tom agrees with you there. He says capitalism as we know it has had its day.'

I waited for him to add that it was all a Jewish conspiracy.

'I can see Hitler's no gent,' he said, 'but then consider the mess the old gentlemen have landed us in.'

Father had said he didn't wish Alastair to spend much time in Berlin. 'I fear for him there,' he wrote. 'He's an impressionable youth with something wild in his imaginings, and that city of *rastaqouères* is not for him. He's not a robust moralist like you, Alec.'

Though uncertain what I had done to earn this tribute –

for, coming from Father it was a tribute, even if I would have resented such an assessment from any other quarter – I took Alastair into the country, 'the real Germany,' I said disingenuously.

'But Germany is the home of idealism, not reality, isn't it?' Alastair laughed.

So, knowing that it was the sort of thing of which Father would approve, indeed the kind of mind-and-spirit-cleansing holiday he awards the heroes of his novels, we set off on a walking-tour in the Harz Mountains. If Alastair had been looking forward to urban dissipation in the European capital of Decadence and Depravity, he, nevertheless, acquiesced in this proposal with that sunny ease and zest that made him so lovable.

It rained in the early morning and the evening, but the middle of each day was soft and blue, with the scent of pine resin, and the sound of cow bells jangling from every hillside. We walked modestly – by Father's standards – no more than twenty miles a day; and rested in the warm afternoon eating a lunch of bread and cheese and sausage. We drank with this water from clear unpolluted mountain streams, and smoked our pipes and talked of the things that young men talk of; future, family, girls, philosophy.

'You must realise,' Alastair said, 'that we have got beyond thought. What do we know now? That thought and words are evasions. It is in action that man realises himself.'

Alastair's assertion was, like Sartre's similar boast, the cry of weakness – a refusal to look facts in the face, to admit that we have got beyond the stage when man can act spontaneously, uncorrupted by thought. There was an absurdity in it: Alastair was always conscious of the mirror.

'Are you really a poet, Alec?' he said to me.

'No,' I said, 'it's beyond me.'

It was beyond me because I was incapable of joy. I had

75

read enough Nietzsche, grasped enough of the importance of light-heartedness, to feel this, even to admit it.

But it remained necessary for me to play the part in public for a few more years, even to publish verses, and to delight in the false praise they received.

When we returned to Berlin, Alastair seduced Trude. 'Seduced' is my word.

It was after he had gone away, back to London, that she told me.

We were in a park. It was early evening and just beginning to be chill. Sunlight still lay red on the little lake. I had placed my arm round her neck, soliciting a kiss. I felt very close to her.

'I must tell you,' she said, 'I went to bed with your brother. I am sorry, but I am not ashamed.'

What could I say? Small boys were sailing model boats on the lake. A tramcar jangled past beyond the railings of the park. Somewhere, distant, a violin was playing a dancing folk tune.

'No,' Trude said, 'I am not ashamed, but I am miserable.'

My arm lay heavy on her, as if it was not part of me.

'It is my misfortune,' she said. 'I fall in love with men who are not my type.'

She turned to look me in the face. Her eyes were candid. I could see it all, still found nothing to say. I heard a voice calling out to the small boys to collect their model boats, saying it was time to go home to Mummy.

'He has great charm, your brother, and the fact that he is not my type made it impossible for me to say "no". Is that crazy? And now he has returned to London and I do not suppose it will ever happen again. I'm not asking you to forgive me, because . . .'

'Because I have no right, I'm not in a position where I have a right, to offer forgiveness? Is that it?'

'Because it's not a question of forgiveness,' she said. 'These things can't be a question of forgiveness.'

'I don't understand you.'

'I don't understand myself. It's something in the air of Germany now, I think, that we do things we can't account for.'

I thought of them waking together. It made a beautiful picture, and left a hungry emptiness within me.

VII

London and Scotland 1934

'So the devil has that unfortunate nation by the throat.'

'I would still like to go back there.'

Billy Hughes pushed a packet of Goldflake towards me.

'Mr Forbes was pleased with what you did. So were we all. But there's a feeling, just a feeling, that some of your reports were without that impartiality we like to cultivate, which we think necessary. If we are to maintain our reputation, that is.'

'I don't think impartiality is what's required.'

I thought: he's fifty, if a day, and a Methodist lay preacher, he can't begin to understand.

'You talked of the devil, yourself, that doesn't sound so impartial.'

'Our editor is of the opinion that the regime will mellow, now that they've got rid of what he calls the wild men. He thinks Herr Hitler is open to reason. And he admires the way he is putting Germany back to work.'

'Got rid of the wild men' was good, I thought, a nice gentle-English way of describing the Night of the Long Knives.

Hughes smiled.

'In his opinion,' he said, 'and Mr Harbottle's a man of vast experience as he'll tell you himself, things will settle down now that the gangster element has been eliminated.'

'And we'll have a nice Liberal regime?'

'I don't think our editor would go as far as that. But he's confident that the policy towards the Jews will be modified.'

Hughes himself had lost his left arm at Gallipoli. I liked the note of scepticism I heard in his Welsh lilt. Yet, as so often since I had come home, I despaired of making the reality of what was happening in Germany comprehensible.

'I'm sure Ian Forbes doesn't agree with that analysis.'

'There's a feeling that Mr Forbes is too much affected by certain relationships he has formed, loyalties – as you might say – to be the most reliable of judges.'

I had spent six months in the London office. There was an agreeable decency to the place, and I was enjoying the rhythm of newspaper life. I liked becoming part of Fleet Street. I liked my colleagues. I had come to feel an affection and a respect for Hughes, the paper's foreign editor, even though I wondered at a foreign editor who took his holidays at Llandudno. It was even possible sometimes to feel that English life was reality, and Germany a bad dream. It was comforting to hear people talk of Bradman and Ponsford's batting feats – they had just put on 451 together at The Oval. I derived pleasure from the decency and good-mannered order of the London streets, from the quiet conversation of pubs, from the men who pored over the racing page and made notes with pencil stubs, from the sweet forgetfulness that seemed to reign everywhere.

'After all,' Hughes said, 'the editor thinks we've our own house to put in order. He has asked me to suggest that you take a break from the foreign desk. And, well, he'll tell you himself what he'd like you to do. Meanwhile, you're due a holiday.'

At Blankets I encountered the same complacency, at once seductive and exasperating. Weekends of talk arrived nowhere. Cabinet colleagues of Father's burbled platitudes. India, and Winston's hostility to the proposed bill, were of more concern than what was happening in Europe. Father said, repeatedly: 'We are not a European power. That was our mistake in 1914. We need to return to the old Blue Water policy and cement our imperial links. The white Dominions are our truest friends. And the United States. I foresee a Confederation of the Anglo-Saxon race.'

Meanwhile we played tennis and lazed in the sun.

Early in September my grandfather died. His ulcer had not prevented him from outliving old Sir William by ten years. We took the night train from St Pancras to St Boswells for the funeral. Father spoke of filial piety. The church was thronged. Whatever the deficiencies the old shipbuilder had discerned in his son, it appeared that he had been respected in his own country. A fellow minister spoke of 'a soul that had journeyed untroubled by doubt or fear to meet his Maker'. At the manse afterwards, tea and scones were served, with home-made gooseberry jam. Old ladies talked in lowered voices of Grandfather's qualities, then, more animatedly, of local scandal. Kirstie and I wandered into the garden, and sat on the stone dyke that divided it from the fields beyond. We looked over to the Eildon Hills.

'I used to love coming here when we were children,' she said. 'It seems so long ago.'

'I never liked him,' I said.

'It worries me, Alec, you seem to dislike so many people now. Grandfather was a good man, I think, in his way.'

'In his way.'

'What other way can there be, for anyone?'

'I don't know. He was a self-satisfied beast, though.'

'Oh, Alec,' she said, 'you sound bitter, you're not judging him as he really was. I don't like to see you unhappy. There's so much we don't need to say to each other, and I know there are things you don't want to talk about with anyone. But remember I'm here. Don't shut me out.'

The proud curve of Kirstie's nose stood out in profile

against the sun setting behind the Eildons. Grey crept across the land, and black cattle stood in the shallows of the Tweed.

'I wish I lived here,' she said. 'It feels like home. How strange that a country which has seen so much war should be so peaceful.'

In the morning we visited Dryburgh Abbey, a ruin since Hertford's army burned it four hundred years ago.

'Those cedars of Lebanon,' Father said, 'were brought back from the Crusades.'

Scott is buried at Dryburgh, Haig also; both heroes of Father's, who had served under the Field-Marshal, and revered him. To my generation Haig was a callous and incompetent brute who sent waves of men to their deaths through sheer stupidity. Father would have none of that.

'In the long drawn-out ordeal of battle,' he said, 'the glittering cavalry officer was transformed into a man who had made a Covenant with the Lord.'

Father could make that sort of remark without embarrassment. I left him, to watch the waters pass. Now, I do not know. I have seen war myself and reported war, and I know it has its own unforgiving momentum. Napoleon on St Helena thought Borodino his finest battle – 'because it was so far from home' and so horrible perhaps. German subalterns at the Somme were colonels and generals at Stalingrad. I turned and saw that Father had been joined by Peter, Grandfather's handyman, who was chauffeuring us in the Daimler to Edinburgh. Peter had served in the Royal Scots throughout the war, and limped on account of the shrapnel still lodged in his right knee. Now he pulled off his cap as he stood before the Field-Marshal's grave. There was a wreath of red Flanders poppies there, and a simple wooden cross with the Field-Marshal's name printed, like a private soldier's, on a strip of aluminium.

In Edinburgh we lodged at the North British and dined at

81

the Café Royal under stained-glass depictions of Edwardian athletes. Toby Macrae joined us, and we ate lobster and drank Montrachet. Father questioned Toby about the progress of the National Party, founded the previous year. Toby scoffed; he was a junior partner in a practice in Gorgie, a poor quarter of the city, and had – to Dr Pangloss's dismay and social horror – joined the Labour Party. I suggested that the Nationalists were probably Fascist. 'They haven't,' he said, 'the spunk even to be that.'

But Father was sympathetic.

'Every Scot,' he said, 'is, as dear old Rosebery put it, a Jacobite at heart, and a revived Scotland, within the Empire, would be a fine thing. I see Scotland as a self-governing Dominion within an Imperial Federation. Why shouldn't the Duke of York become Prince of Scotland and live at Holyroodhouse? He has, after all, a fine Scottish wife. I know that my old friend, Monty Mackenzie, who is one of the founders of the National Party, would leap at the idea. As for Fascism, Alec, you take too sour a view of the movement which is essentially one of national renewal. Signor Mussolini has given Italy a sense of its own worth it hasn't possessed since the Renaissance. In any case, I fancy a Scottish Fascism would be a different beast from any of the Continental varieties.'

He dilated on this theme till we reached the pudding. How hard it is not to make Father sound absurd. And yet he wasn't that then. There were others who shared his dream of an Imperial Federation, and if the thing had come about, I suppose a semi-independent Scotland would have fitted into it comfortably. After all, it is not so different from the relationship the Scottish Nationalists now propose for Scotland within the European Community.

VIII
England 1935–6

It was unusual for me to be invited to lunch by Hector at his club. His face was a relief map of bewildered unhappiness, as if life couldn't be doing to him whatever it was doing; and his club embarrassed him too. He pointed out a couple of Permanent Under-Secretaries, and I was puzzled because I had thought this was what he had always wanted, and now he had it, it was strange that it tasted sour. The Party, I remarked, would surely approve of his membership.

'I don't want to talk of that here,' he said. 'It's something much worse. Anyway I don't belong to the Party. I can't. You know that.'

We ate cold veal and ham pie, followed by rhubarb tart. Hector talked, vaguely, about the French – their terrible unreliability.

'You sound like Father.'

'Do I?'

'Yes, he thinks the French are the chief obstacle to a peaceful settlement in Europe.'

Hector ate little, picked at his food. After a very small cup of very bad coffee, he suggested we walk across the park.

'I couldn't talk to you there. I thought I could.'

It was still the lunch-hour. Clerks and office boys, and typists in pretty dresses lay on the grass. People were feeding the ducks and cormorants.

'I feel trapped,' he said. 'I wish I could speak to Meyer.'

'Not much chance of that. He's in a camp, I've heard. Or dead.'

Hector shuddered. He was made to be a sententious Victorian parson, like our grandfather, and he found himself in the wrong part, in the wrong drama.

'I wish I could leave the Office.'

'Why don't you then?'

'It's impossible . . .'

'Well,' I said, 'take the afternoon off. You don't give yourself much fun.'

He shook his head and sat down on a bench, clutching his umbrella between both hands and leaning on it. I waited.

'I keep thinking of Meyer,' he said. 'I have nightmares. About being tortured. I couldn't stand it.'

'We none of us have the right to suppose we would. But there's no immediate likelihood of being put to the test.'

'People don't understand.'

Poor Hector, I thought. Of course they don't, they're English, even after the first German war they know they are different, they know nothing awful can happen to them, because dear old London Town and the Crazy Gang and Buckingham Palace and the Derby and potted shrimps at Brighton and lunchtime in the park, all add up to a life that is as life should be. They can even forget the dole queues because they're away up north and it's there that you have the factory chimneys that are no longer smoking. Down here we have the tranquil suburbs and what we can think of as the warm cosiness of the East End or the still life south of the river.

That's what I thought. I was wrong of course, with the arrogance of youth. England was more complicated than I allowed myself to admit, but it was still a family, and a place where manners and decency prevailed, at least in people's minds; and perhaps that is what really counts – what you believe your society to be.

Hector's melancholy disturbed me. It occupied my mind

84

as I retraced my steps across the parks, up Piccadilly, through the narrow and lively streets of Soho, over Oxford Street, and into the grimy purlieus of Fitzrovia where I had an assignment with Annie, a young actress with whom I was then involved. Hector, I thought, had a faith which should have kept him buoyant. But that was a stupid reflection. It is one thing to be confident that history is on the side of the cause you have embraced; another, and a natural thought, to fear what you yourself may have to undergo before victory is achieved, to dread the trials that may be imposed upon you and, perhaps, the likelihood that you will fail them. The success of the collective does not offer any guarantee that the individual himself will come through. Hector was afraid that he was both a physical and moral coward, though brave enough to acknowledge that fear to himself. His admiration for Meyer was corrupted by envy for the fortitude he was certain Meyer possessed.

Well, it is rare for admiration to be free of a tinge of envy, certainly when it is directed to qualities one fears oneself to lack.

But Hector's single-mindedness and his determination, despite appearances, to be himself even to rashness were, though he never guessed it, at least in part what drew Max to him. Max was an American dancer, with a zest for life that gave him a fresh, spontaneous charm; he had close-cut, chestnut-coloured, curly hair and a wide mouth which opened in a movie grin. It was easy to see why Hector found him irresistible – even while the boy's uncritical eagerness for experience irritated him. He was forever urging Max to be serious, impressing on him the importance of educating himself, and berating him for that frivolity which was, after the first smile Max had bestowed on him, the very quality that had turned desire into love. But because Hector could not forgive himself his homosexuality, which, precisely, as it seemed to me, for that reason he was sometimes rashly ready to make manifest, it was natural for him to reproach Max for what most drew him to the boy. So also, for instance, when they went on holiday to the South of France, he resented the time Max spent on the beach because the tan he got made him still more beautiful and desirable to Hector. He resented also the fact that it was the South of France they had gone to; yet he chose the Riviera because his awareness of Max's pleasure in being there was a mortification for him. And it pleased him, self-willed as he was in the ordinary business of life, to submit his will to Max's, or at least to allow Max to believe that that was what he had done. It is a common ploy in the battle of wills inescapable from any love affair. To seem to yield is to claim a moral advantage. In the same way, and for the same reason, Hector would indulge in brooding jealousy.

'And yet,' Max said, 'I don't understand it. He would accuse me of trying to get off with every queen in Cannes, but he bought me the most fetching outfit and paraded me as if he was renting me out. Do you get it?'

Max sat, with his knees drawn up and his hands clasped around them, on the window-seat of Annie's sitting room. Clouds had gathered, and the light of the late afternoon was yellow and murky. It looked as if a storm was on the way.

'And did he?' Annie asked.

'Did he what?'

'Offer to rent you out?'

'Like hell he did.'

'I don't understand your brother,' Annie said.

'He doesn't understand himself.'

'Who does?' Max said. 'Now that we've all read Freud, we're further from understanding ourselves than we ever were.'

'Let's go out,' Annie said. 'I've been in all day. Let's go out.'

I had come hoping to make love. Now it seemed that was off the menu. It wasn't Max's unexpected presence that made it so. Max and Annie were good friends. They had known

86

each other at least a year, since they had been in the same show. It was as a result of their friendship that Hector had met Max. I had brought Hector along to a party Annie was giving. But if Annie had wanted to make love with me that afternoon she would have been happy to do so with Max in the other room. So, when she said: 'Let's go out', it meant she wasn't willing.

'Where shall we go?'

'Gaston's?'

'Must we? Oh very well, then.'

'Gaston's' was a restaurant – it had some other name, but I have forgotten it because we never used it – in Charlotte Street. The restaurant would not be open at that time in the afternoon, but there was a club in the upper room where drinks and sandwiches were served when the restaurant was closed. Gaston himself was seldom seem. He was a melancholy man of, nevertheless, great good humour and charm, who suffered from ulcers. The club was the domain of his wife, Zita, a Neapolitan, once a beauty.

'You would not think it now to look at me,' she used to say, 'but I have been kept by three dukes. That was before I met Gaston and came down in the world. It is true they were only Sicilian dukes, but nevertheless, it is something to boast of.'

The rain was starting as we turned into Charlotte Street, falling in big drops heralding thunder. The sky was shot with purple. At the corner of the narrow stair that led to the club room Annie turned and kissed me, hard on the mouth.

'I'm sorry,' she said. 'I know what you wanted, but I'm not in the mood.'

'That's all right.'

'Later.'

There were only two people in the club, Alfred Moss and a young girl with long red-gold hair and a *Country Life*, twinset-and-pearls face. Alfred was a fashionable portrait painter, who flattered his sitters and mocked them in conversation. He introduced the girl as Vanessa Stuart-Styles.

'We saw it was going to rain,' she said. 'So we took shelter.'

She spoke as if she had said something witty.

Zita fetched a bottle of Chianti and some ham sandwiches.

'I'm going to do a mural for Zita,' Alfred said. 'To pay my bill. The Commedia dell'Arte. You could be Harlequin, Max.'

'So I could.'

Conversation languished. Alfred began to make a card-house from the pack that lay on the table. They were Neapolitan cards. After a little his house collapsed.

'The story of my race,' he said. 'And my career. I read your pieces on the Distressed Areas, Alec.'

Vanessa took some lipstick from her bag and applied it.

'I do think it's terrible that people are allowed to live like that. So demoralising.'

'What do you suggest?'

'I'm sure they could find work if they really wanted it. After all, there's plenty of work to be done. Of course, what can you expect from this government?'

Max, quicker than I, let his wrist fall limply. 'I think your Mr Baldwin's sweet, I guess I do.'

'And Herr Hitler's doing wonderful work,' I said.

'Oh, but he is, surely. If we had a man like that . . .'

'Oh, Christ, must we talk bloody politics?' Annie said.

'Honey,' Max leaned, confidingly, towards Vanessa and opened his eyes very wide, 'I guess you could be a great success with Adolf. But, as for me, like the man says, include me out.'

I poured more wine and ate a sandwich. The ham was good and salty. I felt Annie's leg press against mine, in apology or for reassurance. I lit a cigarette and passed it to her, putting it between her lips, then another for myself. Time passed.

Alfred said: 'Actually we're waiting for your brother.'

'Oh, are you Alastair's brother? You can't be.'

'But I am.'

'But it's too amusing!'

'Yes, isn't it?'

We called for some more Chianti.

'Why's he always so bloody late?' Vanessa said.

Hours later, at a studio party, there was dancing. Annie clasped her hands behind my neck.

'I'm sorry I was beastly this afternoon.'

'Yes, you were.'

'I am sometimes, I don't know why, but I'm sorry.'

'That's all right.'

'Not as beastly as that awful girl. Say I wasn't.'

'You weren't.'

'Not half as beastly.'

'Not even a quarter.'

'I couldn't be. Could I?'

'You couldn't.'

'She really was beastly, wasn't she?'

'Absolutely.'

'I wish I loved you, Alec. I really do.'

Later, her skin warm and damp, she lay in my arms and wept.

'I don't know why I'm crying. I just don't know. I'm happy, but I'm crying.'

I kissed her, first on the brow through straggles of curls, then on the lips. Our tongues played. We made love again.

'That was lovely, but I still want to cry. Happiness doesn't last, does it?'

'Oh, I don't know. It might.'

'It doesn't. It can't.'

She fell asleep. In a little her leg moved, to lie over mine. My hand rested in the sticky softness between her thighs. I thought: after all, there is nothing better than this, to lie, having made love, with a sleeping girl who for the moment at least seems to be fond of you. And we never have more than the moment.

A taxi stopped in the street below, its engine throbbing. Then after its fare had at last found the coins required, it moved off. For a little there was silence in the city, a silence so deep that you could, paradoxically, hear it. I was conscious of the swell of Annie's breast as she fell into heavy sleep. Like the sea, I thought, like the sea. Her cat leaped onto the bed, and nestled on my pillow, purring and pushing its face into my hair.

Footsteps sounded in the street. Then a voice was raised in song:

'How you gonna keep 'em down on the farm,
After they've seen Paree?
How you gonna keep 'em away from Broadway
Jazzin' around . . . that's the mysteree!'

There was a letter in the pocket of my jacket which was draped over the chair by the bed. It was from Trude.

Dear Alec,
    I wrote a letter to you the other day in a little Wilhelmshöhe café. But I did not send it. I found its English so bad, so naif and clumsy that I was ashamed. And then it was full of self-pity. Shocking, yes?
    So now I write at home with the dictionary at my side. But it is not the words I lack – the vocables, as I remember you saying one of your students called them. It is something else.
    Alec, dearest Alec, you used to say that I was brave but blind. Perhaps you said that I was brave because I was blind, I cannot remember. But now my eyes are open, I see very clearly, and I am not brave but very much afraid.
    A catastrophe and a wickedness are being prepared here.

There is a madness to which my people have willingly consented. That is horrible.

Father sees that it is mad and wicked, and he is not afraid. He speaks out.

You remember that scene in the *Gasthaus* in the mountains when you saved him from that lout of a Nazi?

Well, he continues to speak out with the same rashness. He calls the Nazis scum, and he made a speech in which he said that whatever was fine in German civilisation owed much to the genius of the Jews. You cannot imagine the fury this has aroused, which is all the greater because so many have respected him. I wish that he will leave Germany and become a refugee, but he refuses.

So I have had an idea. It is that you should ask your father, for whom he has such admiration, to arrange perhaps that he should be invited to lecture at Oxford. I believe he would accept, it would please him so greatly to get such an invitation, and then when he is in England, perhaps we can persuade him to remain.

What do you think? Is it possible? I wish so much that it may be.

You understand my desperation and the urgency. I do so wish to save my father from the consequences of his own nobility.

But, dearest Alec, there is another course which I have been considering, and which I may have to adopt if this first one that I have outlined does not succeed. It is one of which you will disapprove.

It is that I should join the Party. Yes, become a Nazi. Not of course that I should do so sincerely, you know my opinion. But if it is the only way to protect my father, then I shall take it. You must understand, his safety is my first concern. He would himself be horrified at such an act, and it would be difficult to explain why I had taken the step. Nevertheless, I foresee that it may be necessary. Do you think I am mad?

Or do you understand?

You may not, because I have heard you speak of your own father without reverence or even respect, with a touch of mockery, of which I must say I could not approve. But my father is all in all to me, and his security is my prime concern.

Try to understand, dearest Alec, if I do as I say I may. Think of me kindly.

You write beautiful and loving letters. Alastair does not write at all. And yet . . . oh, I am so sorry, it is such a mess, it makes me weep.

Barbara was in Berlin last week, and looking beautiful. The Nazis are very nervous of her, and would like, I think, to declare her persona non grata in Germany. But Goebbels is fascinated by her, he can never resist a pretty girl, they say. She asked after you, and asked me to send her love. Sophie, alas, has deserted her, fled to the terrible Hungarian. Barbara just says: 'Guess it was too hot in the kitchen for Baby.' She is rather wonderful, isn't she?

Do you know, when I am with her, I even feel just a little bit lesbian. But no, I say, that would complicate matters too much, and they are already altogether too complicated.

I do not think our post is examined. Nevertheless, I think it is safer to give this letter to a friend who is going to Switzerland and have it posted there. Isn't that awful?

Oh dear, I shan't ask you to give my love to Alastair if you see him because that sort of love is not what I feel for him. You know what I feel, and I am sorry that it pains you. But believe me, I am ashamed.

Do please, please, dearest Alec, do what you can about my request. I really do not wish to feel obliged to become a Nazi.

Your unhappy friend,
    Trude.

I so often think of those days in the mountains when we were happy.

Trude was wrong to suppose that her letters were not examined. Recently they had come to me resealed and with the official stamp: *Zur Devisenüberwachung zollamtlich geöffnet* (Opened by the customs office for foreign exchange inspection). Of course I could not know just how carefully they were scrutinised.

Thinking of her letter, I found myself wakeful, and slowly, with as great a gentleness as I was capable of, I drew myself from the bed, without disturbing Annie. I made a pot of tea in the little kitchen. The brick wall across the alley gleamed damp in the reflected light.

I read Trude's letter again. Once before she had written that we could not be lovers − she had always known it − because such a relationship would render ordinary and impermanent what we already had, which was something higher and more valuable. 'Truly, my dear, bodies are not so important, I think.'

Annie would not agree. Or Hector and Max? It was hard to say. Hector saw in homosexuality a certain defiance. It was the statement of his emancipation from the system he served and detested. And yet that system was more tolerant of such deviation than the other which he also served with a greater purity. Were Annie and Max, who seemed to act spontaneously, more admirable than Hector and myself?

I thought of George. Had he taken a Chinese or Malay mistress? Or did he, like a Maugham character, seduce the wives of fellow planters? Of us all, George, since his return from Spain, was the one who had most certainly committed himself to the 'real' world − the world, that is to say, of the ordinary everyday business of getting a living, which I can call 'real' because it is after all the world inhabited by the majority of mankind. In doing so, George had rejected abstraction, the vice of the age which insisted on seeing everything in terms of movements and concepts. For George, it seemed to me, phrases like 'the revolt of the masses' or 'the crisis of capitalism' had no meaning. The question was how much rubber could be extracted from so many trees. A practical straightforward business like ploughing a field. And yet it was the crisis of capitalism that would determine the market for his rubber.

Of course my speculations about George's state of mind could be only that – speculative. He was a poor communicator. His occasional letters home – addressed only to Father – were concerned with the minutiae of daily life. On the one hand, you could say old George knew a thing or two; on the other that he was an ostrich, a willing accomplice to the crime of the century: the reduction of everything to a question of pounds, shillings and pence – or, indeed, Malayan dollars.

Haskins, the gardener and keeper, was burning leaves when I arrived at Blankets. It was cold and grey and very still, merely the faintest breath of wind from the east. Veils of mist hovered over and around the stream. Haskins stood, pipe in mouth, hands dug in the pockets of corduroy breeches, watching the smoke rise from his bonfire. Then it hung above him, unwilling to disperse. He grunted, without removing his pipe, when I greeted him. A pheasant rose with a clatter and cry from the copse.

'We'll have an early winter,' Haskins said. Except for two years in training camp and trenches, he had never been twenty miles from Blankets. He hadn't, he once said, been in Oxford, ten miles away, since the war. Every morning he rose early and checked his rabbit snares. As a boy I had often accompanied him on his round. His son, Frank, my age, was employed in the Morris Works in Cowley. Frank was married to Agnes who had come to us from the village as a parlourmaid. They had two small children and had, last year, put down the deposit on a three-room bungalow. Frank was

94

doing well at the works. I had found myself thinking of him as a symbol of the times, like the Mars factory in Slough. That was not foolish, yet to reduce Frank to an abstraction seemed wrong. We had played cricket together for the village; he bowled off-spinners, and voted Labour. Old Haskins was a Gladstonian Liberal, with no time for Socialism and other foreign ideas. Father used to quote him as an oracle. He liked to tell visitors that Haskins's name, like many others in the village, could be found in the medieval abbey rolls. 'Haskins grips the past like a vice,' he would say, proudly.

Father was full of such sententious observations. They came to him as naturally as the wild duck fly. There was neither pose nor insincerity in them, however they might sound to others.

'I have been reading Isaiah,' he said to me. 'How trivial and insignificant he makes the business of man seem against the rolling desert of eternity.'

Yet he had just embarked, that weekend, on what was to be his last election campaign, and later in the evening he was full of speculation as to how the outcome might alter things, the desert of eternity apparently forgotten, or put on hold. His seat was a safe one, not much required of him.

'I am sorry, Alec, that you think so ill of us Parliamentarians,' he said as we climbed, the following afternoon, up to the sheep pastures, 'for we cling to what is old and familiar. In the war and the years after it, I had a recurrent nightmare, that the stable universe was dissolving around us, that everything we have come to understand as civilisation was in danger of perishing. Well, here we have kept the faith, and I believe we can claim – I will not say "boast" – that we have come through. And if we have, then it is Ramsay and S.B. above all others whom we have to thank. Yes, there is hardship and poverty, and unemployment is a curse. I admired the generosity of your articles about the Distressed Areas, but what I admired most was the spirit of fortitude that shone through. Believe me, I know the misery of these poor people, but yet their response proves to me that as a nation we have not lost coherence. If we can avoid war, and I believe we can, then their fortitude will be rewarded.'

I thought: is he simply complacent, or does he see something that I don't?

When I raised the question of inviting Professor Liebknecht to lecture in Oxford, he was first enthusiastic, immediately naming dons whom he might enlist to support the proposal; then hesitant.

'He has spoken too forcibly against the regime, and that could create difficulties. We do not want to give the impression that an invitation, which would be interpreted, however mistakenly, as having official sanction, betokens British hostility to the National Socialist experiment. I know that you share Liebknecht's views concerning that, Alec, but my own opinion is less certain. Herr Hitler's language is wild and regrettably harsh, his anti-Semitism repellent. And yet he has restored the pride of a great nation, and confidence to a large section of a class – a respectable and industrious class – that seemed ready to give way to despair. No, Alec, the jury is still out.'

'Does this mean that you are not prepared to get Professor Liebknecht an invitation. . . ?'

'No, no, dear boy, it means only that we must move with circumspection.'

The light was fading as we returned through the dripping chestnuts to the house. Dogs barked from the keeper's kennels.

'Partridge shoot next week. Come down for it, will you?'

A long, grey Lagonda sports coupé swooshed to a stop, scattering gravel, before the front door. Alastair leaped out, then, languorously, Vanessa emerged. Father affected surprise, displayed unaffected delight.

'Surely Mother told you? This is Vanessa.'

'Vanessa?'

96

'Stuart-Styles.'

'Ah, I was at Balliol with your father. Ronnie's girl, how nice.'

'Can you afford it?' I said.

'The car or the girl?'

'I meant the car.'

'Have to, in the film business. They get in a funk if you don't seem rich.'

'Tea,' said Father. 'Tea and muffins.'

At the word 'muffins' the spaniels dashed into the house. We followed more sedately. Vanessa's hips swayed as she inclined the upper part of her body towards Father.

Alastair came to my room as I was dressing for dinner. He threw himself on the bed, careless of the white tuxedo which I recognised as a prop of his new film image. He ran both hands through his hair, in a gesture that seemed self-consciously careless.

'You're not still angry about Trude, are you?'

'Angry . . . no.'

'I behaved badly there, I realise that.'

'Just who is Vanessa?'

'At the moment of asking, old boy, she's Alfred Moss's mistress.'

'But you plan to change that.'

'Say I'm in with a chance.'

'So this is a seduction weekend.'

'Don't think seduction's quite the *mot juste*. Don't think much seducing will be necessary.'

'Ripe fruit?'

'And juicy.'

I concentrated on knotting my tie. In the mirror, Alastair's face was blank of expression. Was that how he looked when alone, deprived of an audience?

'This film business?'

'It's the coming thing. Film's the language of the century.'

'Well, yes, but what do you do exactly?'

'Hard to say, hard to say. Call me a producer.'

'What have you produced or are you producing?'

'Company's just set up, we're not really at the production stage yet. So far the Yanks have had it all their own way. We aim to change all that. Leopard Films, that's the name to look out for.'

'Does this mean you're through with politics?'

'For the time being. Thing is, Alec, Tom says I should establish myself in this first. Then I'll have the independence that he advises. By the way, he really liked those pieces you did on the Distressed Areas, really liked them. He wants to have a chat with you.'

'Oh, does he?'

'Yes, he's like us, against the old men, you know.'

During dinner Alastair held forth on the subject of the film industry. Father asked searching technical questions. One of his thrillers – 'shockers' was his name for them, and he could dash one off in six weeks of the summer at Blankets – had recently been bought by an American company. 'They can do what they like with it,' he said.

'And will,' I said. They would have to inject a love interest, something of which Father's books were devoid.

Alastair's replies were full, verbose, unconvincing to me. He was a small boy showing off, the pet of the Upper Sixth. One of the guests, a junior minister whose name I could never remember, took out a little book and made notes.

Alastair said: 'We live in a collective age. Film is the art of the collective. And yet it celebrates individualism. That's why it creates such a marvellous tension.'

The junior minister nodded his head, then drank the glass of claret which Stubbs, the handyman who doubled as butler when we had guests, had just filled.

'It's the first authentic mass medium which is also an art form,' Vanessa pronounced, and looked to Alastair for approval. I thought: that's something he said to her in the car on the way down.

A vixen barked way down the valley. Mother collected Vanessa and the other ladies, and left us to our port. The junior minister drew up his chair beside Alastair and began to question him. He was, I remembered, National Labour. Perhaps his presence was a mark of Father's affection and admiration for Ramsay.

A caricature colonel – actually a neighbour who, though indeed a colonel, painted exquisitely, in water colour, scenes of rural England wherever he found it untouched by the twentieth century – said to me: 'Never go to the cinema myself, can't follow the story. You've been in Germany, haven't you, Alec? Don't like this fellow they've got. Daresay they deserve him, but don't care for him myself. Worse than the old Kaiser and he was no gentleman. Always at your throat or grovelling at your feet, that's the German.'

'Do you know,' said a very old don, 'when I was young, we used to have German civilisation held up to us for our admiration. They were a dreamy race of musicians and philosophers. And peasants, naturally. You got peasants all over Europe then. Except in Scotland. The Scots developed beyond that stage before anyone else, before even the Americans.'

'Don't care for Americans,' the colonel said, 'always putting a price on everything.'

'I saw Kipling in the club last week,' Father said. 'He's getting very frail, poor old chap. But you still feel there's a volcano simmering.'

'Kipling,' the don snuffled with aged malice. 'Well, his Empire's gone all to pot.'

It was a time when most British films were low-budget trivialities, made to satisfy the quota. The quota was some civil servant's brainwave, an ineffectual attempt to nurture a native film industry. It required that for every foot of foreign

– in reality American – film shown, there should be a corresponding footage of British film. The result was a series of shoddy thrillers and mindless comedies, dire adaptations of West End plays – at a time when Shaftesbury Avenue itself was at its least enterprising or imaginative. Anything disturbing was to be avoided. Nothing controversial had a chance of being made. In this way the British film industry faithfully reflected the ethos of the National Government. If the people no longer went to church, then film should supplant religion as their opium.

To his credit Alastair rebelled against this. His sojourn in filmland now seems an exercise in bitter comedy. Its failure confirmed his conviction of our national decadence. Just as Mosley's inability to make any real impression on British politics proved to Alastair that parliamentary democracy was, as he put it, 'a swamp that swallows up any noble enterprising ideas and drowns them', so the collapse of his British film hopes left him threshing about, contemptuous of 'the system' that had thwarted him.

His first ambition was to make a film about Caesar.

'Not Shakespeare's version,' he explained to me, condescendingly, over dinner at the Ritz Grill. 'That's a libel on a great man. No, I want to make the real story, to show the decadence of republican politics. I want to show Brutus as the self-righteous Liberal, the bag of wind he really was, a Baldwin of his time, and Cassius as a cowardly cynic who wants to keep things safe for the rich. Cassius, you see, is the symbol of the Jew.'

'But he wasn't one, was he?'

'That's obtuse, Alec. I want to energise the masses in the service of the Leader, and to show that if you don't succeed in doing so, then they will become dupes of the Red demagogues. That's it: on one side the corrupt old system, on the other Red violence; and in between, Caesar, the embodiment of true Roman interest, the man of Empire, the demigod. Nothing like it's ever been done.'

Nor would be.

Caesar was not the only project devised, elaborated, enthused over, and abandoned. A film to tell the story of Lawrence of Arabia – a friend of Father's, a frequent guest at Blankets, and Alastair's boyhood hero – was another.

'Don't you see, Alec, Lawrence is the true figure of our time, the last great imperial figure, the lost leader, the cold Romantic, the self-tortured victim of a rotten society. The real question to be explored is what we are to make of a nation that could let Lawrence slip. I want to start with Lawrence in the RAF, on his bed in the barracks – that's a wonderful scene – and then cut straight to the triumphant entry, Christlike, into Damascus, and then the petty politicking of the peace conferences which destroyed his faith. It's the true story of our time.'

Then, perhaps by a natural association, perhaps in confusion of Lawrences (but that was my unkind joke), he proposed a film of what I then called the other Lawrence's least coherent and least filmable novel, *The Plumed Serpent*.

'Rubbish, *The Plumed Serpent* is cinema in words,' he answered me. I think now he was right, but, for then, in England, the project was preposterous.

I have been remembering Malraux, whom later I knew in Madrid. Recalling him, I took my copy, never read through, of *Antimémoires* from the shelf and blew the dust off it. 'To reflect upon life – life in relation to death – is perhaps no more than to intensify one's questioning.' Does that mean anything, nothing, or everything? Alastair, for all his Etonian naivety – or because of it? – would have approved the gnomic dictum. Malraux, the anti-Fascist, has often seemed to me the authentic Fascist, in his addiction to the grandiose. He writes of 'an intellectual problem which interested me a great deal: how to reduce to the minimum the play-acting side of one's nature'. Again Alastair, with his burning sincerity, might claim to have done so – while, like Malraux, casting himself always as the lead.

There is that story Koestler tells of his first encounter with Malraux. He had gone to him in search of a donation to some organisation with which he was then connected – the Institute for the Study of Fascism or something equally bogus, Koestler then still being, I think, an agent of the Comintern. Anyway that doesn't matter. He was also, he says, 'a fervent admirer of Malraux', and he delivered his spiel somewhat nervously. Malraux listened in a silence only interrupted from time to time by one of his dramatic nervous sniffs (I remember these sniffs and the equally abrupt nervous reaction myself), followed by a sharp slap of his palm against his nose. Koestler talked at some length, ending, I assume, with the request for a donation or, perhaps better, the promise of a puff for his institute from the Great Man. Momentary silence. Then Malraux advanced on him, 'threateningly' Koestler remembered. '*Oui, oui, mon cher,*' he said, '*mais, que pensez-vous de l'apocalypse?*'

What indeed?

One cannot imagine an exact English equivalent of this question, translation so inadequately translating; yet it was the type of interjection in which Alastair delighted. There were few pleasures greater for him than to throw others off balance. His going to bed with Trude had had just that effect – intended? I think so – on me.

The Stuart-Styleses gave a dinner party to celebrate Vanessa's engagement to Alastair. It was January '36. The courtship – ridiculous word – had been brief, in best modern style.

'Really,' Vanessa drawled, 'one can't be bothered with the sort of games they used to require.'

The house in Belgrave Square, to me the dreariest part of London, was full of bad modern paintings and stripped furniture painted white in the deplorable style made fashionable by Syrie Maugham. Ronnie Stuart-Styles wore an apologetic look in these surroundings which reflected his wife, Honor's, taste and fortune. She was the daughter of a Pittsburg steel mill heiress. Now she talked, condescendingly but with some enthusiasm, of Mrs Simpson: 'A really nice woman, and from good Baltimore society, well, the best Baltimore can offer, nothing to all this, of course.'

Her husband, small, balding, pop-eyed, and pot-bellied, seemed an adjunct to her forceful personality, like the two cream-coloured pugs that sat surveying the company with appraising gaze. Honor had rescued Ronnie from the Foreign Office, where he was remembered, Hector said, for some faux pas, the exact nature of which remained veiled, in Istanbul. Now he wrote slim superior biographies. One critic had summed them up as 'Strachey-and-soda'.

There would have been six or seven courses. The food was commonplace. Nobody remarked on it. Now, and for some time, it has been usual for much of the conversation at a dinner party to dwell on the subject of food. Discussion of dishes, questions as to their composition and origin, are expected. It is thought rude to ignore such matters. This is natural enough; your hostess has probably cooked the meal herself, certainly devised and supervised it. An interest in food is regarded almost as a sign of good manners, even intelligence. It wasn't like that then. As a topic of conversation, it was as far off limits as religion. It was not even, I think, permissible to remark on the wine, though when the ladies had left us, commendation of the host's port or brandy was acceptable.

I was placed next to Vanessa. She was full of enthusiasm for the new reign in prospect. She recalled a speech the Prince of Wales had made to the British Legion advocating friendship with Germany.

'How wonderful,' she said, 'if he could lead us in a real national revival!'

There is a natural temptation to judge as stupid those whose views are repugnant. Vanessa, wonderfully bare-shouldered, with red-gold hair, swelling breasts, and her air of disdain, was, to my irritation, not stupid. Her education had been neglected. Her conversation showed a veneer of acquaintance only with the sort of writers who were known in Society – Vita Sackville-West (the Hungarian baroness's admiration as I remembered) rather than Virginia Woolf, for example. When I mentioned Wystan Auden, she looked gloriously blank. And yet, as we talked, I was made aware of a hard, determined intelligence. Moreover, the manner in which she shied away from those areas where her ignorance might be exposed, suggested not so much a complete indifference to whatever hadn't happened to come her way – which I might have expected – as a surprising vulnerability. And so, despite everything, I found myself liking her for that.

Worse, I felt her allure, to employ a word then much in vogue among those who would later be called publicists. The oyster-coloured gown, bare-backed but riding the ridge of her breasts, seemed to have been put on in order to be torn off by a male hand. And she had a way of inclining towards me, and then drawing half the same distance away, that spoke of her awareness of herself as a splendid, desirable animal. I couldn't avoid the thought that, while she and Alastair made a dazzling couple, it would require little to prise her loose. And she knew that, and felt my temptation, and delighted in the knowledge of her power.

'Tell me about Alfred Moss.' I didn't actually speak the words, then. It was hard in the sterile formality of that dining room to imagine the daughter of the house in the bed of that notorious old satyr. But then I had seen them together, Moss's rheumy eyes fixed devouringly on her, and could have no doubt. Even less than none now that, seated beside her, I had felt the pull of her sexuality.

The old King was dying, in the chill mists of the New Year. Kipling was going too. They would tell us that the King's last words were 'How is the Empire?' 'What's on at the Empire, more like?' Annie would say – not claiming the line as her own.

At the Stuart-Styleses' table we were between two worlds.

'I remember the Durbar,' Father said. 'It's the end of an era.'

Then, reverting to the King's dying, he recalled one of his favourite stories, of the old woman, a shepherd's widow (of course!) of Tweeddale, who tramped more than twenty, sometimes thirty, miles to see King George, and who, when asked why, answered: 'We maun aye boo to the buss that bields us.'

'There was more wisdom in that auld wife than is to be found in all the writings of our rootless intellectuals,' he declared.

His words, as so often, cast a gloom over the company, not lightened by the departure of the ladies. Vanessa paused to ruffle Alastair's hair as she passed behind him. He caught her wrist and held it a moment. She looked over his head at me, her eyes wide.

I am trying, with the difficulty of pain aggravated by the uncertainty of memory, with its dark caverns, to tell a story I do not understand. If I understood it, I would feel no need to tell. That is to say, I am writing primarily for myself.

But only primarily. Five years ago my niece Hattie, Kirstie's younger daughter, came to see me. It was a duty call. Hattie lives in Edinburgh, more than an hour's drive from here, and every six months or so she becomes conscious of neglected duty – not that I see it as duty, but she, being moral and well brought-up, does – towards her aged and, as she would have it, lonely uncle, and so descends on me.

'We are rather a remarkable family,' she said that afternoon. 'Only I hadn't thought of us that way. There's a young journalist, on the *Scotsman*, telephoned me' – Hattie never says 'phoned' – 'last week. He said he was wanting to write a play about Uncle Alastair. I didn't know what to say.'

'Best to say nothing then.'

'Yes, but, he's a friend, as it turns out, of Andrew's' – Andrew being her son, a nice boy – 'and I don't know what Andrew's been saying. I don't know what Andrew could know to say. But I don't want scandal starting up.'

'It's all dead ground,' I said.

'But for the children,' she said, 'they're even more ignorant than I am. I talked it over with Mother and . . . *you* must write it, Alec.'

'Write what?'

'The story of our family.'

'Oh that . . . I'm seventy-five. And you mightn't like it.'

IX

London 1936

Max said: 'I wish I'd known Berlin. Was it really wild? It must have been.'

'I don't know. It was wild by what I'd seen. I've never seen New York.'

'New York can be wild, but I'm sorry to have missed Berlin.'

'You wouldn't like it now. From what I hear.'

'No, I guess I wouldn't. I really guess I wouldn't.'

We were in Gaston's. It was late afternoon, February. The lights were on in the streets, but the alley below, with just one dim lamp at the corner, was veiled in rainy obscurity. We had been playing chess. Max had a good chess brain. He had mated me in fifteen moves.

I thought for a little of Berlin, of how it had been there, at this time of the afternoon, when the wind blew chill from the dark pine forests and sandy wastes of Brandenburg, coming all the way from the Urals, or alternatively the city was held for days, motionless in a hard frost, still as a stage set.

Zita brought us more coffee. It was brewed in a Neapolitan pot, the kind you turn upside down when the coffee has come through, and was strong, velvety and sour. Zita also sold Toscano cigars, and we had bought one and cut it in half, which was what, she said, you were supposed to do, and the way the coachmen smoked them in Florence.

'Did you ever know Barbara Jakobsen in New York?'

'I've read her, but I don't know her. She's good, isn't she.'

'She's good. She's so direct. She can't hear a lie without nailing it, and she's never deceived by cant.'

'She must be unusual,' Max said. 'I knew her brother though. He was a sweet boy. Then he killed himself. Don't ask me why. That boy had everything, looks and talent too. And they're loaded, really rich. That's why I think it's so great Barbara is what she is. But her brother killed himself.'

'There's too much of that,' I said, and took another sip of the Strega Zita had brought us with the coffee.

'Alec,' Max said, 'I'm worried about Hector.'

'We're all worried about Hector. Hector most of all.'

'It's not a joke, Alec.'

He pushed his face towards me. His breath was warm and creamy.

'You know we've split up, don't you? I couldn't take the scenes. It wasn't just the jealousy. It was like he resented the fact that we'd been close, as if he thought I knew him too well. I'm not making myself clear.'

'I understand. Go on.'

'But now he's taken up with a real bitch, a German boy, says she's a refugee, which she may be, but whatever she is, she's trouble. They were at Nancy's last Saturday, and you know how they talk there. Maybe you don't, but they do, and Fraülein Muffet was waggling her ass and looking like the cat that got the cream. Alec, it's not safe, Hector was safe with me, you know that, but now, it's like he's sent out a gilt-edged card saying "Blackmailers Welcome".'

His concern was genuine. It was clear Hector was living on his nerves, courting disaster perhaps in the hope that it would free him from responsibility. Yet, on the other hand, he continued to function with rare efficiency. It struck me that Max didn't realise that. It surprised him, for instance, to be told how highly regarded Hector was by his superiors. He couldn't be blamed for that. The Hector he knew was a different creature from the rising star of the Foreign Office, where – the Permanent Under-Secretary had told Father –

there was nobody of his rank, no one under the age of forty indeed, capable as Hector of drafting a minute that was as clear, elegant, showed such a grasp of the subject, and yet contrived to remain non-committal. The Hector Max knew was emotionally all at sea, tossed helpless on waves of lust, resentment, self-love and self-hatred; now proud, now abject; both cruel and sentimental, often at the same time. No wonder that Max couldn't understand that his man, who was tempted by thoughts of self-destruction and who was also possessed of a need to hurt those whom he nevertheless loved – this being the only manner in which he could forgive himself for the weakness that let him first desire and then make love to them – was also, intellectually, a precisely-registering fine instrument.

This contributed, too, to his emotional disarray, for his analysis of the political situation terrified him. He knew, as I was almost sure I did, that war was coming in Europe as winter follows autumn. It might not come this year or the next, but it was coming. He believed, of course, that an alliance between the Western 'so-called democracies' – as he styled them – and the Soviet Union could avert it, but he was also certain, with that grim and chilling certainty that comes to a man who has made it his business to assess unpleasant evidence, and to get that business right, that that alliance would never be made. There were too many people too close to Baldwin and Chamberlain who feared Communism more than Hitler, who, indeed, took Hitler at his word, or one of his words, and accepted him as a bulwark against the Red Terror. And nothing short of the reality to which they shut their eyes could change that opinion. So Hector worked in despair, framing his minutes in such a way as to try to nudge his superiors to the conclusion which he desired, but which he nevertheless knew they would never reach.

I didn't, even then, share his view as to the benevolence of Stalin. News was coming through to make me question whether the Soviet Union was actually Paradise Realised, but

I knew enough also to know that we could only beat Hitler if he was forced to fight a war on two fronts. I had talked with Barbara and others who knew France better than I did, and I was with them in thinking that the French army wasn't what it was cracked up to be, and that French politicians had no stomach for another war. They couldn't do it. No Frog politician, worse, no Frog general, Barbara had said, could write out an order of battle without thinking of Verdun.

Max said: 'I stayed here because of Hector you know, and now maybe I'll go back to New York. But I don't want to, I like it here.'

Behind him on the wall, shadowy in the dim light, was the mural Alfred Moss had made representing the Commedia dell'Arte. He had given Max, as Harlequin, the same forlorn – lovelorn – look that he now wore as he sat opposite me. But I thought: in the Commedia things always come right, because, no matter what tragedies occur, tomorrow the same characters will be improvising new variations on the same themes; the plot unfolds in the same old manner, and only the words are new every night.

I said: 'Was Vanessa really Alfred Moss's mistress?'

'Oh yes. She's marrying your brother, isn't she?'

'So they say.'

'If I liked girls I could go crazy for her,' Max said. 'So in this case I'm glad I don't. But with Alfred of course, it's easy come easy go. Zita cancelled his bar bill for the mural, you know. He's amazing, Alfred. I was with him in the Eiffel Tower one night, when they asked for his bill there, so he told them to clear the table and then took out a piece of charcoal and in half an hour had drawn a corner of the restaurant on the white cloth, and they took that as payment. There is something to be said for being a painter. Mind you, you've got to be careful with him. He tried to rape me one night. I had to hide behind dustbins to escape him.'

'She doesn't like Jews,' I said.

★

Honor Stuart-Styles told everyone that if the King had still been Prince of Wales he would have been happy to attend the wedding at St Margaret's, but since he was now King, protocol forbade it, which was crazy, wasn't it, it was one of the things that she was sure he would put right when he had had time to shake the stuffiness out of the Court.

But Mrs Simpson was there, the picture of enamelled elegance. The guests were divided between country neighbours who didn't know who she was, and those 'in Society' who were only too conscious, and ready, most of them, to pay court to her. Which goes to suggest that the Society friends of the Stuart-Styleses had more than a touch of the riff-raff about them.

Alfred Moss, shaggy and wearing his morning coat in a manner which made it look like a theatrical costume (and, indeed, he confided to me that he had often worn it in the amateur theatricals he adored) swayed up to me, a cigar in the corner of his mouth.

'Charming couple, ain't they. Wish I could say I'd slept with both of them, but you're his brother, ain't you, so I won't make that boast to you. Think it'll last?'

'To have and to hold, till death us do part.'

'Think so? Bet you don't.' He withdrew a flask from an inside pocket and tipped some brandy into his champagne. 'Thin stuff, wedding fizz. Like a spot? She's a bolter, you know.'

'A bolter?'

'Little Van. I was the first that had her, you know. Fifteen and already . . . well, you've just got to look at her. Matter of fact, saw you doin' just that, naughty boy. Always wondered if she might be my daughter actually. Does that shock you?'

'Not particularly.'

'You're a cool one then. It's an awful crowd they've got together, ain't it. Your side may be all right, can't say, look dull as the Royal Academy, but may be all right. But the other! See that chap there? The German Ambassador.

Whatever next? But you knew that, of course, you've lived in Germany.'

'Yes,' I said, 'I have.'

Leaving the office that morning, I had gone into the foreign newsroom, and glanced at what was coming over the wires. There was a two-line report from Berlin. It said that Professor Liebknecht, distinguished academic and vocal critic of Hitler, had died suddenly. A heart attack apparently.

I had tried to put a call through to Trude. Impossible. I sent a telegram. It was only a week since Father had reported that at last the invitation to lecture in Oxford was going to be extended to him.

Alfred Moss said: 'I've got cousins in Berlin, lots of them, you know. What's going to happen to them?'

'They ought to get out.'

'Course they ought. But they're sitting tight, like a hedgehog rolled in its ball in the middle of the autobahn. What should we have done when the little bastard marched into the Rhineland? Should have biffed him, shouldn't we?'

'Yes.'

'Not the Jewish way, biffing. But in the world today, you biff or get biffed.'

He drifted off. For a little I watched him. He approached Lady Markinch whom I knew to be violently anti-Semitic, and was soon – as they said in the captions to photographs in the *Tatler* – 'sharing a joke with her'. I drew close. He was telling her one of the Jewish stories for which he was famous.

'One of my compatriots, one of my rich compatriots, dear Lady Markinch – let us say Mr Goldstein, a cousin of mine – emerged from his house in Grosvenor Square one morning to be accosted by a poor co-religionist, what we Jews call a *schmorrer*. Now my cousin Goldstein is a generous man, so he gives the *schmorrer* half a sovereign and goes on his way to the City. At lunchtime, entering Sweetings as is his wont, for a couple of dozen oysters, he is surprised to find the same *schmorrer* sitting on the next stool eating a large plate of smoked salmon. "Aren't you the poor man to whom I gave half a sovereign this morning?" asks Cousin Goldstein. The *schmorrer* agrees that this is, indeed, the case. "So, why," asks Cousin Goldstein, with considerable indignation, "do I now find you here eating smoked salmon?" "Mr Goldstein," the *schmorrer* spreads his hands – in the manner of our race, dear Lady Markinch – and says: "So: ven I haf no money I cannot eat smoked salmon – ven I haf money I muss not eat smoked salmon? – so tell me, pliss, Mr Goldstein, ven shall I eat smoked salmon?" '

Lady Markinch laughed again, shaking, indeed, with laughter, and burbling: 'Really, Alfred Moss, you'll be the death of me, you will . . .'

She clutched him by the sleeve, as if her mirth was such that his support was necessary to keep her upright; and as she did so, he caught my eye, winked, and a look of enormous, pervasive contempt, embracing Lady Markinch, the whole gathering, and himself also, momentarily darkened his expression; then, collecting himself, he embarked on another anecdote, playing the Jew who sings to the Gentiles whom in the depths of his being he despises, to assure himself of the indulgence he also despises and yet knows he needs.

'You enjoyed my performance,' he said to me, 'but you ask why do I give it? To remind myself that I am not an Englishman, my dear. And there are other advantages. If I played the complete Englishman, they would say, behind my back when I was gone: "All the same, Millicent, I can't forget he's really a Jew. There's something just a bit oily about him." As it is, what do they say? They say: "Of course he's a filthy old Jew, anyone can see that, well he never allows you to forget it, but he's rather sweet all the same, and such fun, I can't help liking him." So, you see, it pays – and that's all that matters to the old Jew, yes? Nevertheless, England is the only country where a Jew can feel safe from persecution. Prejudice, yes, of course, that is everywhere, but persecution, no. Shall I tell you why, my dear? It is because we have an Empire. When you've black men to boss about, who cares about the Jew?'

He stood, magnificently waistcoated in pale rose-coloured silk, a thick gold watch chain stretched over the upper reaches of his Edward VII belly, and smiled on me.

'Your brother seems a charming boy,' he said again, 'but is he man enough for little Van? Just wondering, you know. How beautifully the English do these affairs. There's no nation like them – like us, shall I say? – when it comes to putting on a show. Compare the jingle-jangle of the Garde Republicain with the Household Cavalry – operetta to music drama. Do you know, I believe it's true: there'll always be an England. Someone should tell little Adolf, don't you think.'

He tipped his flask again over my half-empty glass of champagne, and then topped up his own.

'Women and wine should life employ, / Is there aught else in life desirous?' He hummed, and moved away, walking flat-footed, serene, towards a countess whose portrait he had painted with a bravura that did not altogether conceal his ironic awareness that she had once danced for Cochran, near-naked in the front line of the corps de ballet, and kissed her hand.

The assembly was of the sort which the illustrated papers would describe as glittering. There was no doubt that between them the two families had got a distinguished haul of guests. The list, published in the *Morning Post* (itself tottering through its last months of independent life, before being absorbed into the *Daily Telegraph*, an experience which one journalist would compare to 'being bludgeoned from behind while walking along quietly in the sunshine') would certainly be impressive. The young Foreign Secretary, immaculately dressed, looked, as ever, the very model of the English gentleman-statesman. Hector had expressed his doubts about him: 'He lacks the inquiring mind, I'm afraid. His father, you know, was a mad baronet, his mother a famous beauty. He takes after both of them. So the foreign policy of a great empire is in the hands of an hysterical beauty, while Germany and Italy are ruled by gangsters, and France by municipal adulterers. And then people call him brilliant.'

'He has a nice sheen to his hair, you must admit.'

Now, however, in approved Foreign Office mode, Hector was inclining his head, apparently all attention, to whatever banality his chief was imparting.

I felt a hand on my shoulder, and turned to see Colin Kilgour smiling at me.

'That was a rum old codger you were talking to.'

'Oh, you mean Alfred? He's a very distinguished painter.'

'What? The sort that puts both eyes on the same side of a person's nose. No thanks. Give me old Munnings. At least when he paints a horse you know it's a horse.'

'Alfred's not exactly modern. You might even like his work, Colin.'

'A Jew, isn't he? I'm never comfortable with the Chosen Race.'

Colin laughed. I hadn't seen him for a couple of years at least. His face was thinner. His cheeks had lost that bloom which had led Guy Holland to call him 'that beauty you brought to Blankets'. But his brown eyes had still that appealing look of a spaniel that doesn't understand why it isn't being taken for a walk.

'It's good to see you,' he said.

'Been too long.'

'I say, this is quite a show, isn't it?'

Kirstie approached us, smiling.

'I hate London weddings,' she said. 'I hate champagne too. What I would really like is a cup of tea. I don't suppose there's any chance . . .'

'Leave it to me,' Colin said. 'I'll go and forage for you.'

'Oh sweet,' Kirstie said.

'Well, he is sweet,' she spoke a little defensively as Colin cut his way through the throng, with an assurance he wouldn't have had when I loved him. I thought it was partly his diffidence that I had loved, his awareness that he wasn't, in his words, 'good at thinking'.

'I never said he wasn't. You know he's my oldest friend.'

'Yes, but . . .'

'But what?'

'But you don't have much in common now, do you, and so you rather despise him. Well, not despise, perhaps, but you haven't much time for him. You think he's limited.'

'We all have our limitations.'

'Don't be so philosophical. I rather think I'm going to marry him.'

There was something disturbing in the thought of marriage. Yet it couldn't be postponed indefinitely. George had cabled his intention of marrying the wife of a fellow-planter. It wasn't clear whether she was in reality a widow, or whether there would be a divorce. Her name, Elsie Laidlaw, suggested that she and/or her ex- or present husband were Scots. That was all we knew of the matter. Mother awaited a letter with some anxiety, which she had concealed sufficiently to put on a brave show at Alastair's wedding.

Annie shifted in the bed beside me, murmured in her sleep. It was only occasionally, now, that we went to bed together. I wouldn't have been there that night but for the troubled mood that was the result of Alastair's marriage. As it was, she had been reluctant to admit me. She had a new lover, a painter called Christopher. He was away in Cornwall, she confessed. So, 'Just this once then, for old times' sake.'

But I had never thought of marrying Annie. That wasn't itself a creditable reflection. There might even be a touch of the snobbery, from which I believed I had detached myself, to it. Now, placing my hand on her gently rising breast, I found myself thinking of Vanessa. That too was discreditable. I imagined myself undressing her, that rich hair falling loose about her magnificent shoulders, the slackening of eager limbs. Then I saw the 'adoring look' which Alastair had cast on her as they came down the stairs together. But how long would she be satisfied with that? The glance she had given me when I approached her at the reception had carried a note of challenge. Besides, some Russian writer – Lermontov? – says that adoring looks mean little to a woman. I could see that adoration wasn't really what Vanessa wanted. She could supply that herself. And would it be long before she found Alastair too ingenuous for her taste? Too untainted? Was there a taste for corruption there? That night in bed with Annie's hair tickling my cheek, I felt myself sufficiently corrupt merely to be imagining Vanessa as I did, stripped, quivering, urgent. The picture excited me, unbearably.

Thinking of Vanessa was a way of forgetting Trude. Forgetting is the wrong word. I have always had this problem: an inability to find words for the way my mind words. Lying there, listening to the night, I couldn't find Trude's face. It kept slipping out of focus whenever I tried to assemble it. It was as if at some level of my being, a level with which I couldn't communicate, I was willing myself to deny her, now, when her own world had cracked. I had walked with her by a lake, in autumn stillness, and heard her say: 'You laugh at me, Alec, for my devotion to Father. Well, I know his faults better than you could possibly. Nevertheless, what I love in him is that he is the very incarnation of the principle of virtue.' She could say something like that, without embarrassment, without an awareness that it might embarrass me. I could hear her voice, and yet I could not see her.

I thought: she has escaped me.

At last I slept, dreaming of turbulence in a ghostly city where I knew no one, and was yet, it seemed, recognised by all. Then the city of high towers was suddenly empty. The streets fell silent. I knocked in agitation on doors on the shadow side of a wide square. No one responded to my knocking, but thin laughter sounded from beyond the wall.

X

Spain 1936–7

The guns fell silent in the afternoon. That morning a shell had hit the man who sold watermelons at the corner of the plaza. He had been told it was dangerous to stand there, but that had always been his pitch, and he wasn't moving. If he was killed, well, that would be how it was. As it happened he wasn't killed, but he lost a foot, and lay screaming till the bombardment stopped. It was only a sporadic bombardment and it seemed as if the gunners were firing because they were bored rather than because they hoped to achieve anything. They fired their guns to remind us that they were there and to ward off their own fear. Nobody is brave under bombardment though you can get used to it and act brave. But you are not really brave. It is only that, because you don't know where the next shell will land, you might as well stay where you are as move. You might move to the place it will fall, otherwise. You just can't tell.

An American correspondent had told me there was a Terror in Madrid. He was eager to find out the details. Well, if there was a Terror I wanted to know about it too, so I investigated and found none. I was right to find none there, but there was a Terror later, in Barcelona, and because I had disbelieved the reports of the Terror in Madrid, I discounted the news that came in from Barcelona, thinking it was the same Fascist propaganda.

When the sun had moved round and the guns were silent, two boys in red shirts entered the square and lifted the melon vendor between them, each getting a shoulder under one arm, and half-dragged, half-carried him out of sight towards the first-aid post. It was good to have an end to the moaning and whimpering.

We went through to the dining room for lunch which we never took till the bombardment was over. We ate old mutton steaks and potatoes cooked in oil. The potatoes were good, and we drank Manchegan wine, and grumbled at the absence of news.

There was stalemate then on the Madrid front and we were in the wrong city.

A young English newspaperman whose name I always forgot was confident that the war was going to turn in favour of the Government forces.

'We've been given time to consolidate,' he said. 'The Fascists had to win in a big push, and they've failed. Now the tide will turn.'

'Balls.'

The speaker was Sye Barnton, a grizzled American whose experience of combat went back to the Spanish-American war of 1898 which he had reported for the man who made it, William Randolph Hearst.

Now, he said: 'There's one rule of war: that it goes to the side that can call on the mostest, and that's not always the good guys.'

As someone had explained to me, Sye was an unreconstructed Confederate, but that didn't mean he was wrong. It took me only a few days in Madrid to feel the way Lord George Murray did when he joined the Prince at Perth in September 1745: that he had to be there, but had attached himself to the losing side.

The day before I left London, Billy Hughes said to me: 'I had to fight to get the Old Man to send you. He thinks you're too emotionally committed.'

'But the paper's policy is to support the legitimate government in the face of Fascist aggression.'

'Of course it is. But we're old-fashioned. We try to tell the truth.'

'And he thinks I won't.'

'He thinks highly of you, but . . .'

I picked up my tickets from his desk and put them in my inside breast pocket.

' "What is truth?" said jesting Pilate,' I asked, and left the office.

It was a question that would lose its flippancy.

A few weeks ago I was invited to give a seminar to some students of journalism at one of the universities in Edinburgh. It is the sort of thing that occasionally happens to me. The tutor or lecturer in journalism was the son of a man I had recruited to the paper in 1946, and he invited me there, to be on show as it were: a specimen of the old type newspaper-man. People don't use that word now, I've noticed, but that was how we used to think of ourselves, as newspapermen. Now they talk of us as print journalists, or journos.

I spoke about Spain. I might as well have discoursed on the Napoleonic Wars. A few of the boys and girls had heard of the Spanish Civil War, but that was all – they had heard of it. Their Spain was a place for holidays.

Only one of them, a thin boy with a lop-sided face and spectacles, said: 'Didn't you all get it wrong?'

Later he stayed behind and asked me about it. He had had a grandfather in the International Brigade, he said, and he had been brought up on his stories, of how the first check to Fascism was given on the Guadaljara, and of how the war was the crusade of our generation.

'But then,' the boy said, 'I read Orwell – *Homage to Catalonia*, you know' – and blushed as if it was rude of him to suggest, even in the vaguest way, that I might not know – 'and that got me interested, and I read Hugh Thomas and other books and I did it as a special subject in my History degree, and it was never as simple or as good again as when my grandfather talked about it. In fact, it was bloody confused, and the more I knew, the less I understood, till I ended thinking that maybe it wasn't such a bad thing that Franco won; and so I found I couldn't talk to my grandfather about it, but he died last year. So what do you say? What do you really think?'

It would have been nice to have given him the answer that deep down he was hoping for, and to tell him his grandfather was right. But I couldn't.

I said: 'It wasn't as straightforward as it seemed to us at the time.'

Which it wasn't, indeed it wasn't. Back in London, in the office, the issue had been clear, especially to someone with a knowledge of Hitler's Germany. When I went to report the war in Spain, the doubts my editor had expressed to Billy Hughes were justified. He was afraid I would send them propaganda, and I left, despite my protestations, actually with that intention.

The issue was clear cut: good against evil.

But Spain wasn't the rest of Europe, and though there were Fascists and Communists in Spain, and I knew which side I was on in that battle, there were also animosities there that were foreign and remote, which belonged to the centuries we had put behind us, that yet lived in Spain.

So that made things different and difficult.

The Minister of Justice, a Basque called Manuel de Irujo, surprised me when I was admitted to his office. A crucifix hung on the wall behind him. It was about the time when the Conservative press at home was making great play with the murder, after rape, of nuns by the Republican soldiers.

'Yes,' the Minister said, 'these things happen.' He drew on his cigar. 'They are deplorable, but the Church, you must understand, is thought by so many to have failed the Spanish people. I do not agree, not altogether, but . . .'

Later, when he was called away, his assistant, a professor of law, Luis — but I forget his family name — sat in his place.

'You are sympathetic to us,' he said. 'We like that, but you must not make the mistake of thinking this a simple conflict. I myself have served in the army, but I declined to bear weapons because, you see, five of my six brothers are serving on the other side. Three in the Carlist Requetas, two in the Falangist forces. It is complicated, yes.'

The diary I kept during those months in Madrid was fragmentary, some days little more than an aide-memoire. Now, so many of the entries are meaningless.

'R. at the F., 6.30 — Govt stats fragrant.'

What can that mean? That the news was good, or that the government was painting too optimistic a picture. I suspect the latter, but I do not know. And who was 'R' anyway? The American correspondent whom I remember saying that the hair on Hemingway's chest was a toupee? Perhaps. (The line, I discovered years later, was not his own, but Zelda Fitzgerald's. It wasn't justified anyway. I scarcely knew Hemingway in Madrid, but I saw enough of him not to question his courage.)

'F.P. = C.C.'

That at least makes sense. C.C. was Claud Cockburn, F.P. standing for Frank Pitcairn, the name under which he wrote for the *Daily Worker*. Was that because he was still on the staff of *The Times*? Can't remember. I liked Cockburn, knew him well enough to have learned to discount seventy per cent of his information. Was he really, as he claimed one night when lit up by Fundador, a Comintern agent? I have always doubted it.

I had no doubts about an American called Jukes. In principle this didn't worry me. I thought we were all on the same side. But Jukes was the first to open my eyes to the way the Soviet Union was trying to take over the war and manipulate it for its own purposes, though that wasn't, of course, his intention.

Even Barbara Jakobsen distrusted Jukes, despite their common attachment to the Cause. Indeed Barbara, who had arrived in Madrid two months before me, and had spent much of that time, by her account – and Barbara, in these matters, tended to be truthful – in evading Hemingway's attentions, was the first to warn me against Jukes.

In Jukes I came to recognise something disturbing, repeated almost without variation over the centuries: the capacity of a cause to attract not only the idealists but the men who, while perhaps yearning – if one takes a charitable view – for the ability to respond to something noble, something beyond themselves, can in reality do no more than attach themselves to its outward semblance. Their inability to forget self, renders them, for the time being, more intense in their commitment, as if by displaying an extremism from which more moderate souls recoil, they prove, both to themselves and to the world, their own sincerity. But being ultimately incapable of any loyalty except to their own ego (which they can never for a moment set aside), their devotion is not to be trusted, depending as it does on the coincidence of the cause with their self-gratification. Yet, for the time being – that is to say, while this particular devotion lasts, which it does till the cause is felt to have failed them – no one is louder in protestations of commitment, or apparently more zealous in action. Again, because, it may be, that the depth of their unconscious is disturbed by the unspeakable knowledge of the nature of their loyalty, no one is more eager to discover treachery than the man, like Jukes, whose inability to forget self makes it probable that he will himself betray what he professes to love.

And yet Jukes was easy, fat, humorous, a man who appeared to possess an unquenchable spirit of gaiety. He radiated American generosity and openness. He was unaffectedly eager to show me the ropes, taking me on a tour of the outposts, to the front line above the Tremadura road where government forces were attempting to encircle and so snip off the salient which the Fascists had thrust into Madrid the previous November. The apex of the salient was the clinical hospital in University City, and Jukes, recognising, but sympathetically not dwelling on, my inexperience of combat, spelled out to me the tactical significance of what we saw. He chatted too in the most easy and friendly manner with the young militiamen who were waiting the order to attack the salient, and I found myself admiring and even envying the spirit of camaraderie which he so quickly established. It was obvious that they responded happily to his enquiries, that they enjoyed the feeling of admiration for their fortitude which he conveyed without committing the grossness of actually stating it, and I said to myself: 'This is the fraternity which I was seeking and which is the true meaning of what we are fighting for.'

'It's stalemate just now,' Jukes said. 'They can't advance. We can't drive them out. But things are gonna change. Come.'

He led me back from the lines, about fifty yards, to a row of little houses that had, most of them, lost their roofs. The windows were all blown in and the houses had been abandoned, all but one where an old woman still lived, refusing, Jukes said, to be moved. She had lived there all her life, her husband had died there, two grandchildren had been killed in the bombardment, and she wouldn't move.

'She's a typical Spaniard,' Jukes said, admiringly. 'They make mules look like they're co-operative.'

The Republican command had yielded to her.

'Real triumph of the will,' Jukes said.

He signed to me to go ahead of him into one of the ruined houses. There was a hole in the floor and steps had been cut into the earth. They went down a long way, to where they were swallowed up in the darkness. From out of the black night of the hole there crept the faintest illumination, the reflection of a distant light. Then there came a low thud.

'This is the way in,' Jukes said, 'the way some of them use as the easy way. But they bring the earth out by another route.'

'What is it? I don't follow.'

'No?' he said. 'But it's simple. It's a mine. Or the tunnel leading to the mine. They brought in miners from the Asturias and they're digging under the Fascist position. We keep up the shelling and sniping up there so that they learn to keep their heads down, and all the while we're preparing to blow their ass off. Neat, ain't it?'

He clapped the shoulder of a corporal who sat at a table in the ruined house as if it was his office, which in a sense it was, and who was there to prevent any unauthorised persons from descending into the depths where a surprise for the Fascists was being prepared.

'How goes it?' Jukes said.

He spoke in English and the corporal nodded and smiled.

'Boom!' Jukes said.

'Boom boom,' the corporal said.

'Boom when?' Jukes asked, pointing at his watch.

'Boom boom, yes.' The corporal smiled.

'Guess he don't know when,' Jukes said. 'Come on, boy.'

An early piece I sent gives, better than I can express them now, my feelings about those early months in Madrid.

Madrid, April 1937: When I wake in the morning I hear firing from the front line. It is like waking in the Ritz and hearing rifle fire in St James's Park. It is as close as that. And yet life goes on in the hotel the way life goes on in hotels all over Europe. Except for this: the servility of hotel staff has been abolished. The lady who still cleans my room and makes my bed addresses me as 'comrade'. We are equals each doing our job and she understands that my job helps her as hers does me, though she does not understand what my job is, or not really. But she takes it on trust. There is a lot of trust in Madrid, and waking in the morning here is like waking in the morning of the world made new.

But the rifle fire from, as it were, across the Green Park, is a reminder that we must fight to hold the idea that the world really can be made new.

There is fighting, and shells fall every day on the city. People have learned to live with that, the way they have always lived with poverty and hard work. You cannot be in Madrid now without feeling a warm glow of admiration for its citizens, and, for many of us foreign correspondents, that admiration has turned to love as well as a deep respect.

I had got the Spanish character all wrong. I had thought of it as volatile. We use the word 'Latin' and the phrase 'Latin temperament' too easily and too loosely. The Madrileños are as fixed in their determination as any Scot or Yorkshireman. There is a war to be won and they are going to win it. They will take what suffering comes their way, and still go on regardless.

It was the upper classes of Spain that were rotten. The working class is sound. They remind me of the old Scots Covenanters I used to hear of in the Kirk. But the Madrileños are not aspiring to a heavenly kingdom. They just aim to make Earth a better place.

How easily I talked then about 'the Spanish character', even though I questioned the common understanding of it. The idea that such a thing as national character exists and is identifiable may be a necessary myth. But it is all balls. Orwell was guilty of the same sentimentality – which is also intellectual laziness. In some essay he dwells on the innate gentleness of English life, as if this was a national characteristic, rather than a set of attitudes formed in response to the peculiar economic and political circumstances of a brief period. When I was young my father would talk fervently of the hard-headed practicality of the Scots. Where do you find that today?

Jukes took me to a hospital founded by the American Friends of Spanish Democracy which was behind the Morata front on the Valencia road. He said there were people there he had to see and it was a good place to learn the true stories of the war. He said you couldn't believe everything wounded men said, but when you had listened to a lot of them, you could form a better idea of what was true. I thought it was easier and safer to get news from them in their hospital beds than to risk your life at the front, but there was no question but that Jukes wrote good pieces as a result of his visits, which he made at least once a week, he said, and so I went along with him. It wasn't till a lot later that I heard that some of the men he spoke to were taken from the hospital and shot, as a result of what he had learned from them.

In the cool of the long ward, which orderlies tried and failed to keep clean, because there were never enough of them, there was not quite silence, even in the depth of the afternoon when the pitiless sun blazed on the courtyard, and shafts of yellow light were filled with dancing particles of dust. The hospital had been a convent before it was requisitioned, and the chapel locked – dust had already gathered on the chain that held its door closed.

It was a hospital for the International Brigade and as you passed along the line of cots, each covered with rough grey blankets, you heard mutterings and oaths in a dozen languages. But the cries of pain and misery all came in the same tongue.

A young man, with a thick bandage stained yellow with spots of red covering his left eye, beckoned to me as I approached the foot of his cot. He asked for a cigarette, and I held it to his lips while he drew on it. His accent was Scots and I asked him where he came from.

'Edinbro,' he said. 'Do you ken the city?'

'I'm a Scot myself.'

'But you'll no ken Gorgie?'

'No,' I said, 'but I've a friend who's a doctor there. Dr Macrae, you'll maybe have come across him.'

'No,' he said, 'I'd nae use for a doctor, till I landed myself here. How are things at home? What do they think of us over here?'

'Things at home don't change.'

'No,' he said, 'that's what brought me here. I wisnae unemployed, I had a good job in the brewery, and a wife and bairn. But I had to come. It behoved me to come. Do you understand that?'

'I think so,' I said.

I held out the cigarette again.

'Player's is it?' he said. 'You couldna leave me the packet?'

'Of course,' I said, 'and I'll bring you some more. Would you like me to write to your wife?'

'She didna want me to come. It was desertion, she said, and what was she to do for money to keep her and the bairn? She was right, I see that, but I was right too. I had to come. She doesna see that, but it was for the bairn I came . . .'

'Yes,' I said, 'but you can't blame her for not understanding that.'

'I dinna blame her,' he said, 'women aye see things a different road.'

'You'll be back with her soon. When your wound's healed, you can go home. You've done your bit.'

'Oh aye,' he said, 'I've done my bit. And for what? I'm no' so sure of the answer to that as I was when I came out here. And I'm maybe done for an' a'. I jalouse I've the gangrene though they winna tell me.'

'I'll write to her,' I said again.

★

But in my second letter I had to tell her that he'd gone. I didn't add that he had died for democracy. It didn't seem likely that it was the sort of thing she would want to hear. But I asked Toby Macrae to look her up, and sent him a cheque towards her support.

'OK,' Barbara said, 'so he died for an idea.'
'An old bitch gone in the tooth,' I said.
'Pound's a Fascist,' she said, 'don't quote a Fascist at me. People kill for democracy, they have to, so they have to be ready to die for it, too, that's all there is to it.'
'Democracy,' I said, 'a better world – and Jim Milligan's wife left a widow in a Gorgie tenement.'
'That's sentimentality,' she said.
'Is it?'

The brown indifferent rockscape of Castile rolled beyond us, under the implacable July sun, as the car lurched towards Valencia. We were on our way to the Congress of the International Writers' Association for the Defence of Culture. When we stopped to eat in a little village where the whitewashed walls of the house were pitted with bullet holes, we were cheered. The landlord of the inn, serving us cold tortillas and white wine, raised the clenched fist.
'Solidarity with the Republic.'
A boy who helped him pointed across the square.
'That's where we shot the priest,' he said. 'Good, eh? You should have heard him whine and scream.'

Report: Valencia, 4 July 1937.
The Congress, proclaiming 'the solidarity of the intelligence of all nations' was opened today by the new Prime Minister of the Spanish Republic, Juan Negrin.
Negrin is an essential figure of our time: a professor of law, an intellectual himself, who has been transformed by necessity and his own idealism into a man of action. His

address of welcome, recognising the commitment of the delegates to the cause of proletarian freedom, inspired in the audience a realisation of his sense of mission, and at the same time filled them with enthusiasm for the work they were capable of undertaking themselves.

But what was most impressive was the contrast between Negrin's appearance and the brave courage of his words. He looks as if he would be quite comfortable in the common room of an English provincial university. But the mood of Spain today makes heroes even of dons.

Those of us who had come from Madrid, where the war rages, to this temporary capital of the Republic, where the sea breezes blow as if in promise of better times, had arrived in a mood of scepticism concerning this Congress. For we questioned whether such a congregation of intellectuals could bring anything of value to the struggle. We were wrong for the war is not merely for Spain itself and the future of the Spanish people, but, we have come to realise, for the very soul of man, the spiritual health of Europe. Throughout the weeks in Madrid this summer, as the fighting continues in the very suburbs of the city, and even the main plazas are war zones where shells land every morning, it has been easy to lose sight of the wider import of this war as we have responded to the courage of the embattled people of Madrid. But now, on this first day of the Congress, which, it has been decided, will move itself to Madrid in two days' time in order to impress on the delegates the reality of the war, and on the world the reality of the delegates' commitment, we were reminded of what Spain means for Europe.

The French writer, Julien Benda, declared: 'The intellectual is perfectly in character in descending from the ivory tower of art to defend the rights of justice against barbarians.'

There are those at home who are still disturbed by the name 'intellectual', and inclined to scoff at the pretensions of those who style themselves as such. They should have been in Valencia today.

'I don't know if they'll run that,' I said to Barbara. 'My editor distrusts what he calls propaganda.'
'Change your editor,' she said.

Diary: July 4, Valencia:
All the same I'm not sure that Barbara is quite as taken with the first session of the Congress as I was. And she may be right. She has a distrust of abstract nouns, which is indeed her most pronounced Anglo-American characteristic. She can't see that they can have their own significance and force. I would like to think her scepticism is occasioned by her immediate preoccupation with Olura, a Basque reporter. But Olura has no time for this sort of thing. 'Later,' she says, meaning, perhaps, never. She is 100 per cent devoted to the cause; a Republican, secular, nun of war. In the hotel bar tonight Jukes was on good form. He told me with great delight that the Spanish writer, José Begramin, was going to denounce André Gide for the slanders on the Soviet Union which he has recently published.
I talked also to Ludwig Renn, once, till Hitler came to power, an officer in the Reichswehr, and an old friend of Barbara. To my dismay he was pessimistic. I say to my dismay because he has recently been made commander of the International Brigade. On the floor of the Congress he had asserted boldly that 'The role of writers fighting for liberty does not consist of writing stories but of making history' (shades of Marx and philosophers!), but now, drawing on a cigar and twirling a glass of brandy, he muttered: 'Even if we lose in Spain we shall have taught the world something of the meaning of Fascism. You know Germany, don't you,' he said. 'I was a guest at Goering's wedding. What a crew!'

He was a little drunk so perhaps his pessimism was to be explained by that. But I didn't like it.

Barbara is pessimistic too, for a different reason. She doesn't believe that the democracies – a word she always pronounces with scorn – want to know what is happening. 'Look at your editor,' she says, 'and that's supposed to be a Liberal paper.'

In the car, on the way back to Madrid, we quarrelled. I had been speaking of Trude, of how she had written to me that she might become a Nazi to protect her father, and how I wondered whether she had indeed done so.

'It might really have been a heart attack,' I said.

I had not heard from Trude since her father's death.

'Could she have made such a sacrifice?' I said.

Barbara stubbed out her cigarette, so hard that I thought she would really have liked to press it on my hand. Then she lit another and blew smoke in my face.

'You're hopeless,' she said.

'I'm sorry if you think that.'

'We're caught up in the great drama of the world and you keep trying to reduce it to the level of personal relations. They don't matter. You and I don't matter. We're not significant.'

'And Olura?' I said. 'Does she matter? Did Sophie matter?'

She hit me, back-handed. The rings on her fingers bit into my cheek.

Then she began to cry. I had not thought her capable of tears.

'I hate you,' she said, 'I really hate you, you and your damned English softness.'

'I'm sorry, I don't understand.'

'No you don't, ever. That's another thing I hate. England never understands. England will never understand till the Wehrmacht is goose-stepping down the Mall. God, there are days when I long to see that happen. And it bloody will,

133

don't you see that? No, you don't because you're blind. In the damn fog of that damned island.'

Away to our left, out of the deep blue of the sky, dark shapes emerged. Then sun glinted gold and they were aircraft. I watched them as Barbara sobbed. In the distance they looked like children's toys mysteriously in the sky. I watched them with detachment. Then they looked like birds of prey. They dived, towards us, and I heard the rat-a-tat of their guns. Earth flew in little spurts from the hillside beyond the road. Our driver swore. I put my arm round Barbara and covered her head with the skirt of my jacket. The driver accelerated. But we were coming near the top of the pass and the gradient was steep. Steam rose from the engine and the driver swore again. The planes were out of sight now, but I sensed they were turning above us. I still could not see them when they opened fire again. The car slewed across the road and crashed into the rockface that flanked it. I thought: if we had swung the other way, we'd be in the ravine. The driver was slumped over the wheel. He made no sound. The engine fell silent. Blood trickled through his white shirt spreading across his back. More blood oozed out of his mouth. I could see his mouth because his head was at an angle.

I opened the door of the car and stepped out into the road. The sky was empty. It was a big sky but there was no sign of the planes. They might come back but for the moment they weren't there. I took hold of Barbara's arm and got her out of the car.

'Are you all right? Are you hurt?'

'I'm in one piece, I guess. Is he dead?'

The steering-wheel had penetrated the driver's chest. I put my hand on his shoulder and shook him, very gently. There was no response.

'Poor bastard, poor Spanish bastard.'

I didn't say: He died for the Republic. I said: 'What do we do now?'

'We get off the road, that's for sure.'

We climbed maybe twenty yards up the hill. There was no cover. We sat on the hot rocks. There was still no sign of the planes.

'I don't even know his name,' I said.

'It was José. He wasn't even a nice boy. He was sullen and he didn't want to be a driver. He didn't want to be in the war, even,' she said.

'Well, he isn't now.'

I looked up at the sky. It was still silent and empty as the desert. I descended the hillside, and got back into the car in the front passenger seat. Very carefully, and with repugnance, I tried to ease his body off the wheel. I couldn't do it. Then I saw that he had placed his wallet on the ledge in front of him. I got that. It would have his papers and we could deliver them to someone in some position of responsibility. So we could report his death to authority and then it would be up to authority to tell his family. If he had a family. If we got to Madrid.

A little later, when there was still no sign of the planes returning, and only the wrecked car and the dead boy were there to assure us there really had been an attack, another car came along the road. We stopped it. It was carrying Jukes and Sye Barnton.

The next morning, as the delegates assembled for the first Madrid session of the Congress, I overheard Jukes describing his vain attempt to save our driver's life.

'If I had been on the scene sooner,' he said, 'I guess I'd have been successful, but the passengers he was carrying didn't know what to do.'

Then, looking up, he caught my eye. He laid his arm across my shoulder and gave me a squeeze.

'Hell, Alec,' he said, 'you did your best. And that's all we can do I reckon.'

★

135

Malraux spoke, nervous, impassioned, coherent in incoherence. He thrust his pale face at the audience, and dug his hands deep in the jacket pockets of a crumpled tweed suit – the cloth, even then I reflected, of a quality that would have dismayed my father and the tweed manufacturers of Galashiels. When he had finished speaking, we were all elevated, though few had a clear notion of what he had said, except that he had told us that in Hollywood, Lubitsch was making a film with Dietrich in support of the cause. But we felt we had been in the presence of someone for whom there was no gap between words and action.

What disturbed many was the news from Russia of a plot against Stalin involving high-ranking officers, chief among them Marshal Tukhachevsky. One after another, Soviet delegates rose to denounce them as 'enemies of the people' who had acted in collusion with Nazi agents and members of the German General Staff. A Spaniard expressed his horror: 'We believed that twenty years after the revolution the generals were marching side by side with the people. But now we see that even in the Soviet Union, it is the same as it is here in Spain.'

This discussion cast a gloom over all, not lightened by an idealistic speech from a young English poet, which wandered hopelessly into absurdity.

'*Quel con,*' Barbara said.

'Once a boy scout, always a boy scout . . . my dear, how charming to find you.'

I turned to see Guy Holland.

'What the hell are you doing here?' Barbara said.

'Oh,' Guy smiled, 'I too have seen the light.'

Barbara lifted her chin. The picture stays in my mind. It would be too much to say that I glimpsed then the woman who would be the severe inquisitorial star of American networks almost twenty years later, but now, looking back, it was that gesture which enables me to connect the Barbara I knew then, who entranced me, with the Barbara whom I

136

would never know except at a distance, through the denaturing medium of television, and found repugnant.

She said: 'I would advise you to have nothing to do with this man, Alec. He's a spy.' I was pleased to see Guy, all the more so because I was, in my best Anglo-Scot manner, embarrassed by Barbara's rudeness. With Guy it is not only that there is no need to be cautious, to think before speaking – as is always the case in conversation with foreigners, however close one feels to them – but I find he no longer disturbs me as he used to. This is because I find his homosexuality easy to accept, having so completely outgrown my own.

He was eager – Barbara distrustfully would say over-eager – to explain how he came to be there, how his political conversion had been effected.

According to him, it was love that had opened his eyes.

'Well, not love exactly, my dear,' he said, 'because I've never been in love, not since I was fourteen anyway and crawled with lust for Robin Maltravers – you remember him? Dishy little piece who came to Blankets with me. Poor Robin, the last I heard he was undergoing psycho-analysis in Zurich – decreed by his Gorgon of a Mamma in an attempt to cure him simultaneously of pederasty and dope. There was an unfortunate accident – you may have heard? – involving a Lower School boy – from Uppingham, can you imagine? – who turned out to be the son of a high court judge. My dear you could smell the stink the length of St James's. But,' Guy sighed, 'long ago in the summer half, after a year of bliss, Robin ditched me in favour of a lisping blue-eyed choir boy, and ever since I've taught myself that love is not my milieu. Fancying, yes, of course, but not true love, never again . . .'

Guy spoke in his usual exaggerated manner, emphasising the wrong word in a sentence, as if calling his own sincerity into question, but even as he did so I felt for an instant a pang of nostalgia for an English summer, deep grass under the willow trees by a river that scarcely moved except where it lapped the bank, ever so gently. He sipped his Fundador and resumed his tale.

He admitted – he couldn't very well have denied – that he had had a good many friends in the Nazi Party and had even been 'excited' – his word – by the movement. 'It was so agreeably operatic,' he said. The Night of the Long Knives had shocked him, for it was obvious then, that the Nazis had decided to stamp on homosexuality. The boy bars had already been closed and the first stories of homosexuals being sent to concentration camps were circulating. Germany was becoming uncomfortable for him. Still he lingered there, he couldn't say why.

'I wanted to see what happened, I suppose. After all, my dear, this was history in the making.'

And then, it seems, a boy he had known had been set upon by some Nazi thugs. In self-protection he had given them a list of his lovers. Two of Guy's friends, one Fritz Büchler the actor, were despatched to the camps for 'correction'. Guy himself was summoned to a department of the Ministry of the Interior, and given twelve hours to get out of Germany.

'So of course I did, scuttled like a rabbit. What I'm anxious about, my dear, is what has happened to Otto. You remember Otto – that rather sweet stocky blond? I'd taken him on as my house-servant – for his own protection, as I thought. But there was no chance of bringing him with me. I tell myself that he's tough and self-reliant, but I don't really believe it.'

Guy paused and lit a cigarette.

'Do you know,' he said, 'I never really believed in evil. Now I do. Evil's never seemed part of English life, has it, and yet I used to despise that. Oh dear, it's all rather a mess.'

'And now you are for the Republic?'

'Absolutely.'

All the same I am not really convinced. It's not that I

138

disbelieve Guy, but he is in a state of shock. And I can't be certain that Barbara is wrong to distrust him.

July 20: A tiresome letter from Father. George is apparently in trouble. He has been caught selling rubber to Chinese traders. The rubber, of course, belongs to the company that employs him, and so in effect he has been stealing from them. Father confused, but it appears that what George has done is quite easy to do. His employers don't intend to prosecute, because that would apparently be bad for the reputation of all White Men in the East. It's preposterous. They've dismissed him of course, but George refuses to leave Malaya. Instead he is urging Father to release trust money to enable him to buy his own rubber estate. (Apparently there are a few privately owned – that is, not by companies – and he has the chance of getting one from a Frenchman.) Father doesn't know what to do. It all seems so trivial here. The worrying thing is to find Father so indecisive. And yet should that surprise me? After all, isn't his state of mind characteristic of a ruling class that thinks it can make a deal with Hitler? Incidentally, Mrs Laidlaw has ditched George too.

July 26: I don't know that I am doing any good here. Of my last three dispatches, one was so heavily censored at this end that it was rendered too insignificant to use, and the other two have been spiked by London. Billy Hughes is not pleased. I gather I have put him in a difficult position with both the editor and the proprietor. So difficult, indeed, that I'll be lucky not to be recalled. I got through to Billy on the telephone. 'For Christ's sake,' he said, 'remember we're a Liberal newspaper, and the boss hates Socialism.' I almost threw it up on the spot. We're engaged in a struggle for the soul of Europe, and I'm working for a paper that doesn't understand anything since Asquith was in No. 10. It's futile. This although Ian Forbes was beaten up in Berlin two weeks ago. I suppose they will say he was 'imprudent'. That's a favourite word. It makes me sick. To cap it all, Guy got in a fight with Jukes last night. He lost too. Barbara in a morose state. She really is in love with Olura, who isn't at all interested. As a matter of fact, Olura has sent me signals which make it quite clear she would welcome a pass. And I'd be happy to make one – if it wasn't that I'm really fond of Barbara. What a mess.

Madrid remained a city under siege, and yet nothing happened except in our private lives. It wasn't like that for the Madrileños of course, but even their situation wasn't as straightforward as I had idealistically supposed. That's to say, they weren't all good Republicans. Indeed, Guy was soon frequenting circles which, however appealing they might be to him socially, were politically suspect. It was Barbara, of course, who drew my attention to this. She remarked too that it was very strange that Guy was in Madrid as the representative of a paper whose proprietor took a friendly view of Fascism. I argued that he was really a political innocent.

'Innocent? Him? Who do you think you are kidding, Mr Allan?'

There was suspicion everywhere, and I came to believe that we journalists were regarded as vehicles by means of which propaganda could be disseminated. When I put this to Barbara she denied it so vehemently that I was sure I was right. She drew her brows together in a manner that recalled the way she had looked when Sophie first responded to the Hungarian countess. It was a gesture that said: this can't be happening. But it was.

I said: 'Do you know what we are? We're "useful idiots".'
She didn't like that, not a lot.

The militiamen who woke me before it was light on the

morning of 1 August, and told me to dress, had none of the happy spontaneity I had associated with the Republican soldiers. They had close-cropped hair, and faces that said nothing. They were polite, but only just, in their insistence that I accompany them. They refused to say anything more. Perhaps they knew nothing. That was probably the case, for when I had dressed, and stepped out into a morning that still had a touch of night coolness, and even hinted at the coming of autumn, they drove me to a block of government offices, without speaking, and then for the first time relaxed when they handed me over to the care of a white-faced man in a shabby suit. I tried him in Spanish and he made no response.

'So what do you speak?' I said in English, but he just shook his head, and led me along a maze of grimy passages to a door, the top half of which was made of clouded glass. He knocked and ushered me in.

The two men sitting at the table looked as if they had been up all night. I knew one of them; he had been a junior minister when I arrived in Madrid, and then he had briefed me on the military situation. He was called Miguel, and was a doctor of medicine. I had liked him for his resigned courtesy, but he hadn't filled me with confidence. Despondency hung over him like a bad conscience. Perhaps that was why he had lost his ministerial post.

Now he waved my escort aside and gestured to me to sit down at the table which was bare except for three overflowing ashtrays and a couple of tiny coffee cups.

'It's very difficult, Señor Allan,' he said, 'very difficult and disturbing.'

He closed his eyes.

'I had no wish to bring you here, you must understand that,' he said. 'It would be nice to have some coffee, perhaps.'

It was evidently a hope not to be answered. His companion picked at the cuticle of his left index finger. He was bald and sweating in a thick dark suit of coarse worsted.

He ran a stubby finger round the inside of his dirty shirt collar, and lit a thin yellow cigarette.

'We accepted you here,' he said, 'in good faith.' He spoke in English with an accent I couldn't place. He opened a drawer in the table and fished out some papers.

'We thought you were a friend to the Republic. And now we find you write this.'

He pushed the papers towards me. I recognised the dispatch I had been prevented from sending.

'You speak of dissension,' he said, and sighed deeply. 'Why do you suppose there is dissension in the Republican command? And even if there was, which I categorically deny, is it a friendly action to say so?'

'I'm a newspaperman,' I said. 'It's my job to write as I see things.'

'Even when what you write is a slander?'

He tore the sheets in two. His hands were very hairy, and he held them aloft as he let the torn sheets fall away.

'And this,' he said, producing more paper. 'This account of the proceedings of the International Congress. Reading between the lines – that is the correct English expression, I think? – it seems that you cast doubt on the veracity of the Soviet delegates. Is that a friendly act?'

The Spaniard, Miguel, shifted his gaze to the ceiling. 'I am sure Comrade Allan has an explanation.'

'I am sure he has, but so do we. And that explanation is that Comrade Allan is no friend of the revolution. You have lived in Germany, Comrade Allan? Yes? And were acquainted with Professor Liebknecht? Yes? On intimate terms with him, I think.'

'Look,' I said, 'I don't understand this, any of it. And what has Professor Liebknecht, who is dead by the way and perhaps murdered by the Nazis, to do with anything?'

'A Social Democrat hyena, and you ask what he has to do with your case. We note that. Then you are a friend of the

Englishman, Holland, I think. Who is a degenerate. You keep nice company, Comrade. And what do you say to this?'

He withdrew a newspaper cutting from the drawer and pushed it across the table towards me.

I read: 'Why Franco Must Win'. The by-line was Alastair's.

'Your brother. I think.'

'My views aren't his.' I appealed to the Spaniard. 'You must know how here in Spain families are divided. It is the same in England. My brother is very young. And uninformed.'

Miguel shook his head, not seemingly in denial.

'You understand,' the other said, 'that this is an informal conversation, Comrade. Your case is only at an early stage.'

'I didn't know there was a case.'

'Nevertheless, there is. Your friend Señor Holland now. He too has lived in Germany where he associated with leading Nazis. And he is a degenerate, a homosexual. You must see that to associate with such a man is itself suspicious.'

'You say this conversation is informal. Then I take it I am free to end it.'

Why do I, half a century later, recall this inconclusive and, it seemed then, pointless conversation with such clarity, so that even as I type these words, I catch the odour of corruption mingled with the acrid smell of those thin yellow cigarettes that emanated from the bald man?

Because in that moment I felt out of my depth, an Anglo-Scottish amateur trapped in a cage of carnivores?

Because reading Alastair's naïve and earnest article, I felt a premonition of dread?

Because, in the despondent subservience of Miguel, I understood the real betrayal that the Spanish Republic was enduring?

I went straight to Guy's room where I found him still in bed.

His companion was an American boy, a Quaker, who had come to Spain to drive ambulances, which he did with a courage that was all the greater for the terror that he experienced when under fire. I had been with Guy when the young American confessed this, and that was the moment when Guy began to lust for him. Now the young American rubbed sleep from his long-lashed eyes, and looked guilty and embarrassed by my bursting into the room. His look made me ashamed, and I thought my alarm on Guy's account exaggerated. Yet when I had apologised and explained why I had disturbed them so early – for to my surprise my interview had taken less than an hour – Guy's own immediate apprehension was such that, unwillingly, I wondered whether the distrust of him that had been expressed to me was in reality justified.

'Timmy,' he said to the boy, 'you'd better go.'

The boy looked at me. I turned away. In the mirror I watched him slip from the bed and bend to pull on his briefs. Then he sat and his hands shook a little as he worked at getting his socks on. It could have been hangover. A bottle of brandy, three-quarters empty, stood on the table. I lit a cigarette and turned round. He had his trousers on now, and a blue shirt. It was unbuttoned and there was no hair on his chest. He gave me a half-smile, then slipped his feet into shoes, leaned over and kissed Guy on the cheek. He straightened with a touch of defiance and left the room. He hadn't spoken a word.

'He's a nice boy,' Guy said as he got into a silk dressing-gown.

'Why did you come here, Guy?'

'Why do I go anywhere, dear boy? I hoped I would find something here. I haven't of course. Don't worry. I'll be on my way. I don't want to queer your pitch.'

He poured himself a glass of brandy, and drank it.

'I rather envy you, Alec. Damn you.'

He gave himself some more brandy and sat by the window with his back to me.

'I think I hoped to find something here. A cause, I suppose. Do you imagine I don't feel the futility of my life? I have just the wrong amount of money, you know – not enough to do anything with, too much to require me to make anything of myself. And perhaps I couldn't have done so anyway. Dear old homosex, you know. It's a fairly pitiful sort of rebellion, isn't it? To be a pansy rentier. I'll be thirty next year. Sad. It might be different if I was an artist. But I'm not. Or really intelligent. But I'm not. I'm only an average sort of fellow – with tastes that the average man despises and resents. And they're not going to change. Timmy's a nice boy. Have I diverted him from his natural course, corrupted him? Go on, tell me I've corrupted him. I'm sure his mother would think I have. Do you know I often think of killing myself. But it would be an empty sort of gesture. I mean, who would care? But what am I saying? And at breakfast too.'

He raised the glass of brandy.

'*Non moriturus*, ducky, *te saluto*.'

Guy left Madrid the next day. He took Timmy with him.

In the weeks after his flight I was prey to unlocated anxiety. I woke in the morning filled with such apprehension that it required a moral effort to rise from my bed. I listened to the sound of the guns and felt nothing but reluctance to dress, leave my room, and talk with others. I found myself, who ignored the guns, starting if suddenly addressed. I drank too much, and became agitated rather than soothed.

Seeing my interrogator – the bald man in the hairy suit – sitting in the hotel bar, alone, three evenings in succession, for hours over a single glass of beer, alarmed me – partly because he made no acknowledgement of my presence, though I felt he was recording the number of times I called for another drink. Barbara told me his name was Oskar, a

Bulgarian, imprisoned several times on account of his Communist activities, now an agent of the NKVD.

'Why doesn't he speak to me?'

'If you're so worried, why don't you speak to him?'

The war had turned against the Republic. In Barcelona the anarchists were being purged. Idealism was dying on me. It was impossible now to believe that we were preparing the way for the young poets exploding like bombs and the bicycle rides in the suburbs on summer evenings.

In a few years Auden would write new lines that better caught the mood of these last weeks in Madrid:

'Intellectual disgrace/ Stares from every human face,/ And the seas of pity lie/ Locked and frozen in each eye.'

'How will we remember this time?' I asked Barbara, who for days on end was my constant and only companion, as we sat soaking, the war receding, sucked away by the brandy, like water finding its way along the gutters to the drain.

'Closing time in the Last Chance saloon,' she said – the first time I remember hearing that expression which, years later, was to become a tired journalist's cliché.

'When England and France voted for non-intervention,' she said, 'they got out the paper on which they would write their own suicide note.'

'So it's time to get out?'

'It's time to get out, I guess.'

'Will you go back to the States?'

'No, I'm a good American. I'll go to Paris.'

'And Olura?'

'She doesn't know yet that she can't stay in Spain. I'll wait for her in Paris. If she wants to come. There's not going to be a lot of time or place for that sort of personal happiness for any of us for a long time. You've got to understand that, Alec.'

I lit a cigarette, watched Oskar not watching me, and felt again that tremor that alerts you to the perils of the forest.

'I've no guide,' I said. 'I wish I had your faith.'

'Oh,' she said, 'it's not that comfortable. It's an abstract sort of faith, you know. History will fulfil its destiny, sure, but we can't any of us tell if we'll still be on the train. And it's a hell of a journey. You think of me as I'm not. Sometimes I seem schizophrenic. I can believe two opposing contradictory things at the same time.'

'That's said to be the mark of a first-class brain.'

'Oh, is it? I can't forget the way that boy José looked. In the car. He was so, like, surprised and resentful.'

XI
England 1937–8

Could there be, I thought, a more agreeable contrast to that idea of 'Historical Reality', of which Barbara used to speak with such decisive approval, than an English country wedding on a soft October day? Kirstie, to please Mother, had surrendered her wish to be married in Scotland, where Mother was never comfortable, though she tried to conceal this from Father; and the parish church (part Norman, part early English, with an ornate Victorian rood screen, the original having been destroyed by Cromwell's troopers) spoke of that decorum and sense of tradition which Mother valued so highly.

'A girl should be married from her home,' she used to say. 'Anything else is vulgar.'

By 'vulgar' – perhaps her favourite term of condemnation – she meant whatever went out of its way to draw attention to itself. Though she had not said so at the time, Alastair's wedding to Vanessa had been in her opinion 'vulgar'. Indeed as I ushered her into the church, towards the front pews reserved for family, I realised that, in Mother's eyes, Vanessa, magnificent in an amber-coloured dress that emphasised the lines of her body in dramatic and seductive fashion, was unquestionably 'vulgar' herself. So, even, was Alastair. Perfect in Father's opinion and to be forgiven anything by him, he was viewed more critically by Mother. Admitting – who could deny? – his charm, beauty, and vitality, she nevertheless classed him as 'unreliable' – a grave sin in her eyes, compounded by the distaste which his ready recourse to the immediate and convenient lie aroused in her. Mother's moral standards were perhaps no higher, or – to put it in a way that may be more easily appreciated by the young – no more narrowly demanding, than Father's. Indeed they agreed in their criteria. It might even be argued – was, indeed, on occasion by Kirstie – that Mother was actually, though retiring and disliking the society of any but family and old friends, more worldly than Father in as much as her judgement was free of that sheen of Romanticism which allowed him to respond to the glamour of the Great World, of ideas, and of his own peculiar view of the influence of the past, and which led him to conclusions which she regarded as sentimental.

There could be no doubt that she approved of Colin. The boyish lack of self-confidence, arising from that awareness that he was 'not good at thinking', had never quite left him, but had been converted into an agreeable modesty and reticence. His unwillingness or inability to express any opinion but the most severely conventional appealed to Mother as a manifestation, rare in his generation, of true gentlemanliness. She was not mistaken in this. Devoted to Jane Austen's novels she saw Colin as just the sort of young man to marry an Austen heroine. Kirstie would supply any spark that he didn't have; in return he would provide her with a husband who could be relied on to do the right, the honourable, thing.

For my part, to pursue the literary comparison, Colin seemed more like a Scott hero – Edward Waverley, to take the most obvious example – an agreeable and – yes, there was no escaping the old-fashioned word – honourable young man adrift in a world he could not understand.

What made Colin most lovable was his air of vulnerability. He might, as Mother supposed, be relied on to do whatever was proper, but, as I had felt at school, it was as if his doing so was prompted not only by a sense of duty and an awareness

149

of what was expected of him, but by the need to wear armour to protect him in a world that seemed alien and hostile. Though he had moods of low spirits which expressed themselves, surprisingly, in truculence, as when, for example, on one of my boyhood visits to his mother's house, he had after some apparently trivial criticism directed at him during breakfast, refused to speak to his mother for the remainder of my time there, or on another occasion at school disappeared into the hills, all day, missing chapel, and being caned for doing so, yet even the usual sunniness of his demeanour had something defensive in it. He had always seemed in need of my protection, and to that extent, I was the stronger, though elsewhile Colin's careful conventionality made it appear otherwise.

Well, I had abandoned the role of protector long ago, and what remained was a half-guilty affection. Now Kirstie could take over that part in full.

Mist hung gentle around the yews by the churchyard wall. Colin and his groom's man, a brother officer, waited straight-backed before the altar. The last latecomers hurried up the path. Then the Daimler drew up, and I went to help Kirstie out. She smiled, happy and confident, behind the veil. Father gave her his arm.

Compared to Alastair and Vanessa's wedding, this one was impressive in the picture it offered of the coherence and solidity of our society. This was not just because of the absence of people like Alfred Moss, or because there was nobody in the church to whom Father was likely to apply his favourite 'rastaquouère'. Eccentrics were not absent; they never are. But those who fell into that category, such as, for example, Colin's Uncle Hugh, whom I observed taking a quick swig from his flask during the Voluntary, fitted comfortably within the pattern. And, I had thought, as I ushered the Haskins family to their pew (Frank muttering that he hoped to have the chance of a word with me about Spain), the pattern accommodated a range of classes. Mrs

Haskins beamed on me, and on the occasion. Kirstie and she were old allies, and she had taken to Colin from his first visit to Blankets. (She had made her disapproval of Vanessa clear, giving a deep sniff when compelled to mention her.) She had protested that she couldn't possibly come to the church 'what with the reception to see to', but Kirstie had told her not to be silly. If Mrs Haskins wasn't there, she wouldn't be either.

'Alec,' Toby Macrae approached me as we left the church.

'It's good of you to come down. Kirstie was awfully keen that you should.'

'Wouldn't have missed it for words. You're bearing it well for a jilted man.'

'Stiff upper lip, the old school, you know.'

'It's nice to be here again. Long way from Gorgie.'

'A long way.'

'What news of brother George?'

'Not the Kipling character we hoped for,' I said. 'More a Willie Maugham one, perhaps.'

'Adultery, embezzlement and opium dens?'

'That sort of thing.'

'Don't underestimate George,' Toby said. 'I've always said old George will surprise us. There's a rich streak of lunacy there, which makes him peculiarly fitted for the modern world.'

Toby himself looked as if the modern world was treating him harshly. Later, back up at the house, he began to talk of social conditions in Gorgie, of the manner in which unemployment and poverty not only destroyed his patients' health, which was his immediate problem, but corrupted sensibility, which was Society's.

'Of course,' he said, 'there's an inherited Calvinist dourness and tenacity that sees most people through, even, God help them, in good spirits, but it's pitiful to see the lives of ordinary decent chaps being thrown away, and to see their womenfolk look forty at twenty-five. And Edinburgh, you know, has suffered less than other areas of Scotland. But you do know all that of course. I still remember those articles you did on the Distressed Areas. They were your best work. I don't say Spain isn't important, but there's sair wark in oor ain midden, Alec. Dr Pangloss has disowned me, you know, forbidden me the house on account of the deleterious influence I might exert on young Torquil. You scarcely knew him of course – my little brother, you remember. Dr Pangloss is quite mistaken if he thinks anything I say could have any effect on Torquil who's a chip off the old block, and already heading to be a proper little Edinburgh WS – wears spats and speaks in a pinched voice. But Dr Pangloss has concluded I'm a red-hot Socialist, even a Bolshie, and a disgrace to the family scutcheon. I, on the other hand, regard him and wee Torquil as a disgrace to our common humanity. So there's at least a measure of agreement. I say, is there any whisky? I've developed an ideological objection to champagne. That's to say, I really don't like it.'

Directing him towards father's library, where he could find a tantalus offering a choice of whiskies and brandies, I watched Kirstie and Colin greeting the line of guests. There was, it couldn't be denied, something impressive in the complacency of the gathering. Mother's side of the family offered the spectacle of the utterly assured England of the shires. Duty had called them here, and they had responded, depriving themselves of a day's fox-hunting in good scenting conditions, or pheasant shooting on a perfect, still, windless afternoon. Theirs was the England, I thought, whose indifference to foreigners was matched only by foreigners' inability to understand its placid and unassertive self-confidence. It was an England where I too would have liked to feel at home. Toby had once, years ago, said to me: 'I really love the south of England, it's almost my favourite foreign country, but I can love it only when I remind myself it is foreign.'

The sight of Kirstie and Colin made me reflect again, as I had on Alastair's wedding day, on the question of marriage.

Certainly I was no nearer to it now than I had been then. I felt about it rather as I did about England: that it was an admirable institution which I would like to belong to, but which something indeterminate held me from applying for membership of.

Nor was there any candidate. I had heard nothing from Trude since before going to Spain. Annie, playing in some repertory company in the north of England, had drifted off into the limbo of Bohemia.

'You're looking very thoughtful, not right at a wedding.'

'I was brooding on marriage.'

'Sheer hell, darling,' said Vanessa. 'It's not that I don't adore Alastair. I do, of course, it's just the thing of being married that is hell.'

'Yes, I can see it might be. All the same, it's an experiment that I was thinking it is time I made. Pity you're already tied up.'

'As to that, I was just wondering if it was time to take a lover.'

'Be in rather poor taste, you and me.'

'I adore poor taste.'

'Where is Alastair, anyway?'

'How should I know? Not, I think, having it off with one of the bridesmaids, though I caught him looking hungrily at the peachey blonde one. Who is she anyway?'

'A cousin. Lucy Pelham-Grey. No competition for you there, Van.'

'Not so sure. She looks as if she should still be at school. That's always competition. Have you seen Alfred since you got back? She would be just his type, don't you think? That innocent look. He can never resist that. He couldn't resist it in me. Then I lost it.'

'Can't picture you as innocent, Van. Sorry.'

'Look,' she said, 'seriously, there is something I want to talk to you about. I can't here. It's about Alastair really. No, not sex. So you don't need to be embarrassed. But it's important, or at least I think it is. So why not come to lunch one day next week, just the two of us? Say you will? Sweet. I know you think I'm awful, but say yes.'

She darted forward and kissed me on the cheek. I caught a breath of sexuality; it came to me like music, Bix Beiderbecke perhaps, played in the distance on a summer night, unsettling, inviting, melancholy. As she turned away, I saw Mother's eyes fixed on us.

Alastair himself, I now observed, had joined a group of young people gathered about Father. Among them were a couple of Colin's brother-officers, lean, respectful men pleased, perhaps, to have this opportunity – rare in their experience, for Colin's was not a smart regiment – of listening to someone who had been close to the seat of power where their own future was determined. I had noticed one of them earlier, in deferential conversation with the Prime Minister, a welcome guest despite his decision, taken reluctantly he stressed, to omit Father from the Cabinet he had formed when he took over from Baldwin earlier in the year.

Now Father was holding forth. There was nothing he loved better than an audience of the young, and not for the first time I thought that he should really have been a don. But perhaps his pleasure was all the greater for this opportunity being occasional and divorced from any professional duty. I approached the group.

'Europe,' he was saying, 'dismays me. When I survey the continent I see a combination of a loss of nerve and a surrender to the threats and promises – promises which are inherently false for there is no reverence in them – of ignorant and arrogant demogogues. It is profoundly unhealthy, for the European tradition, which sought the *via media*, has been corrupted by men with no understanding of the estate they have annexed. There is, everywhere, an ugly pathological savour. It is as if a mature society has been invaded and dominated by diseased and vicious children.'

'So war is inevitable,' one of the young officers said. Father shook his head.

'How can we contemplate another war when we know its destructive nature? The Great War poisoned the rich stream of European civilisation lovingly constructed over the long centuries. Can we really bring ourselves to engage in a new conflict, the consequences of which will certainly be still more deleterious? Can we again ask decent young men of all the nations to re-enter the Inferno of the Apocalypse? It is unthinkable. So what is to be done, for that is always the great question of life. What is to be done? We must place Europe in quarantine, leave the diseased Continent to its fate. It maun dree its ain weird, as we say in Scotland. And meanwhile we must devote ourselves to those parts of the world where sanity still maintains its hold: the United States of America, the Dominions and that great Empire for which we have assumed the noble role of trustee. The policy we have adopted towards the madness of Spain – the noble policy of non-intervention – we must extend to the whole diseased Continent before we too catch the infection and perish of the plague . . .'

So he went on, and on. Though he rarely set foot on the Continent after the Great War – a couple of sojourns at Aix-les-Bains with the Baldwins and one tour he made with me of the French cathedrals, being about the sum of it – yet no one I have known was deeper and more reverently (to employ that favourite word of his) rooted in European civilisation. As classicist, turning in leisure moments so often to the Odes of Horace (half a dozen of which he rendered into Scots verse, or 'the Doric', as he liked to call it), and as Calvinist – if, like his mentor Stevenson, Romantic Calvinist – he was consciously the heir of all that was in his view finest in the European achievement. Moreover, like Stevenson again, his love for France was profound, warmed by the last flickering fires of the Auld Alliance with Scotland. And this held, even though he disapproved so vehemently of every

French political impulse since the days of Richelieu. I once found him standing a quarter of an hour before a Monet and murmuring: '*Oh, la belle France, la belle France*'. Yet in his urging that we should avoid any Continental entanglement or commitment, his sincerity was evident. It was as if he looked on the faces of the young men surrounding him and saw the graves of their fathers, as if he glanced across the room to where Colin, head bowed and cup and saucer in his right hand, was listening – with a courteous attention, which was unlikely to be warranted by whatever was being said – to my intolerably prolix Great-Aunt Charlotte, widow of a former Bishop of Bath and Wells, and addicted to the minutiae of ecclesiastical gossip, and saw in the young man doing the duties of a newcomer to the family his hero father, with whom Father himself had shared a beat on the Tweed; having first got to know him as a subaltern, riding miles with him on the High Veld, in his golden years after the South African War, when as a junior member of Milner's Kindergarten, he had been given the glorious opportunity of setting the world to rights, an experience which he referred to often as 'the making of me'. It was very probable. There were times when we were all ghosts to Father.

Alastair and Vanessa lived in a rented house in Hertford Street, a narrow skimpy place with awkwardly-shaped rooms. 'The address is all right,' Vanessa would say, 'and the situation. Alastair doesn't care where he lives. So we might as well be here as anywhere.'

She had forgotten I was coming and looked sulky. This suited her. Nineteenth-century novelists – Trollope and Thackeray, for instance – were well aware of the attractions of the bored and bad-tempered beauty, all the more seductive for being apparently indifferent.

'I wasn't going to have lunch,' she said. 'I suppose you want some.'

'I usually eat something about this time of day.'

'Have some gin anyway, since you're here.'

'All right.'

'We could go out to the pub later, I suppose. I rather like the market pubs. You never see anyone you know in them, except the local tarts. Some of them are quite interesting.'

'You surprise me.'

'I surprise myself sometimes.'

Then, downing her gin and bitters and giving herself another, she began to talk of Alastair and the disappointment of her marriage. She didn't, she admitted, know precisely what she had hoped for. Unlike many girls of her class and generation, she wasn't ignorant about sex. Well, I knew, didn't I, that she had been Alfred Moss's mistress. She hadn't tried to hide it. Why should she? She didn't expect her husband to be a virgin, nobody did, so it was fair enough that she should have had some experience too. And Alastair hadn't minded that. She wanted to be fair to him.

'Sex is all right, actually,' she said, 'or was.'

'Was?'

'So soon, you think? But yes, was. We're bored by each other. I hadn't realised, you see, that he's only a child.'

'What do you mean?'

'I hate being asked what I mean.' She made a face, thrusting her lips towards me in a pout that strangely resembled the characteristic gesture of that bar boy in Berlin who always seemed about to kiss you.

'You must know he's a child,' she said.

'Yes I do, but I'm surprised you've found it out so quickly.'

'You've always underestimated me.'

'Have I? Perhaps I have.'

She rucked up her skirt and scratched her thigh.

'Admit it,' she said.

'Admit what?'

'You like looking at me.'

'Who wouldn't?'

157

I saw how the afternoon would be spent. I had felt desire rise when Vanessa first stretched herself on the sofa, the too perfect beauty of her face clouded by her ill-temper, giving me also a fore-glimpse of how it would look when gin and disappointment made it puffy and coarsened her features. Now, it was a relief to know that there would be no need to crank the tired mechanism of seduction into action.

'It's not just because I'm your brother's wife, is it?' she said later.

'No,' I said, thinking of Trude, 'not at all.'

Later we went out and ate oysters and drank Reid's stout.

'I said I'd tell you why you think I'm awful, and I haven't.' She giggled. 'You did think I was awful, didn't you?'

'I couldn't have told you so before, but yes I did, that first time we met at Gaston's. It was something you said.'

'You thought I was an ignorant upper-class bitch.'

'Something like that.'

'It's not my fault. It's all I know.'

'You're laughing at me.'

'If you like.'

'I didn't think you had a sense of humour.'

'No, you just judged me. And condemned me.'

'I was wrong. Clearly.'

'I wish to hell you were. I know I'm not nice. Most people who aren't nice don't know it. But I do, always have done. There's nothing I can do about it. It's something chemical, I daresay.'

'Never mind. I quite like you now.'

'I don't like myself much. I'm crazy about myself, I can see that, but I don't like myself. It's not the same thing you know – self-love and self-liking.'

Often in the next months I told myself, stepping away from Hertford Street, or hearing the door close behind Vanessa when she had come to me (as happened more often) in my

158

flat in Fitzroy Square, that that was the last time, it was all over between us. But I had only to hear her voice on the telephone, the brisk assured 'it's me', which was her habitual opening, to be drawn back. What's more, if, for any reason, a couple of weeks went by without there being a chance for us to go to bed together, I was tormented by fantastic dreams, and made miserable by jealousy. Once, in February, I stood for three hours in a doorway opposite the Hertford Street house, watching to see who would emerge, before eventually arousing the suspicion of a constable and being obliged to move on.

Jealousy thrives on uncertainty, and I told myself I had no cause for it, if only because Van never allowed me to suppose I was her only lover. Indeed she took pleasure in making this clear to me, even going so far as to tell me how one afternoon she had picked up a middle-aged businessman who had assumed that she was a professional.

'I didn't disabuse him,' she said. 'After all money's money and I was curious to see what he thought I was worth. Do you think that's depraved? You do, don't you.'

'Up to a point.'

'But you've picked up tarts yourself. Why's it different? Or from Hector picking up guardsmen?'

'I don't really think he does, you know.'

'Don't you?'

'No.'

'Alastair says he does.'

'Guardsmen aren't his type, that's all.'

'He was quite nice, my businessman. "Thanks very mooch," he said. You do think it's depraved, don't you.'

'So how much did he pay?'

'Not telling.'

Hitler marched into Austria. The Anschluss was effected. Ninety per cent voted for it in a rigged referendum. I begged

159

Billy Hughes to let me go there to report. 'The Boss says "no",' he replied. I thought of resigning, didn't.

'War's certain now,' I told Vanessa.

'Austrians,' she said, 'they don't mean much, do they? After all, they're all the same people. I don't see that it matters.'

'Ask Alfred if it matters for Austrian Jews.'

'Oh, Jews,' she said. 'I don't think of Alfred as a Jew.'

We spent Easter at Blankets. Mother eyed me askance. 'She knows about us,' I said to Vanessa. But Mother said nothing. I thought: Mother's like Chamberlain; she thinks that if you ignore a problem, it'll go away.

'I hear you and Vanessa are having an affair,' Hector said. 'You'd better be careful. We don't want a scandal.'

'Quite,' I said.

'It took some effort to hush up George's business, you know. Where is Alastair anyway?'

'In Germany, Van says. Someone's put up money for a new film company. Van thinks it's German money.'

'They're not going to divorce, are they?'

'No, why should they? Van says he's got a Fraulein in tow. I don't know where she gets her information.'

'I didn't think you even liked her. I thought you disliked her as much as I do.'

'It's not a matter of liking. I'm crazy about her. That's the way we live now. There's not much time left, is there?'

Then we talked of Hitler's next move. There was no support, Hector said, in the FO, for standing up to him.

'The fools are more afraid of Communism than of Hitler.'

Father was short of breath, but insisted that we walk through the oak wood to the high downs. He voiced his confidence in Chamberlain. I reminded him of how he had spoken the day of Kirstie's wedding, about the state of Europe. He smiled like a sly old lady: 'I do get carried away,' he said.

'I don't think Hitler is a vain man,' he said. 'And that's important. Rhodes said to me once: "You can make your book with roguery, but never with vanity, for the vain man is incalculable." That's true. I worry about you boys, not you, Alec, for you had a wise head on young shoulders when you insisted on being schooled in Scotland. But I sometimes think I erred in sending your brothers to Eton. It's the greatest of schools, and yet Hector and George are both *déraciné*. Strange. When I'm gone, I'd like you to keep Blankets. It's been my Sabine farm – "*ille terrarum mihi praeter omnes angulus ridet*". But perhaps you think it won't be possible. You think war's inevitable, don't you?' I had never known him so jumpy. Usually, he would abide by the advice of his beloved Horace and strive: '*aequam memento rebus in arduis servare mentem*'.

Now he hammered the ferrule of his blackthorn stick on the turf.

'I simply don't understand it,' he said. 'I don't understand the will to destruction that has been let loose on the world. "They grope in the dark without light, and he maketh them to stagger like a drunken man." Do you recall, Alec, the words of Job's wife: "Dost thou still retain thy integrity? Curse God and die." That is the madness that sounds in my ears.'

He inveighed against George – 'that a son of mine should stoop to such dishonesty' – and against Hector – 'great gifts, but will he make anything of himself? There's a lightness there I cannot like' – but said nothing of Alastair, though I guessed that anxiety concerning his Benjamin was the cause of his present distress.

When we returned to the house, his mood shifted. He became his habitual self, talking at great length to Vanessa about the battles of the American Civil War, the book that he was currently engaged in writing.

'I would say God send us a man like Abraham Lincoln,' he remarked, 'if it were not that I believe he has indeed vouchsafed us his match in President Roosevelt. Of all the leaders of great nations whom I have been privileged to know, none has impressed me more. He is wise like an old dog, and yet has the heart of an ardent youth.'

'Do you think he knows about us?'

Vanessa, at the corner of the stair, with light from the pre-Raphaelite stained glass rosy on her cheek, placed her hands on my shoulders, and looked down from the upper step.

'I'm certain he doesn't.'

'I think he has suspicions.'

'That's not the way his mind works.'

'You were right.' She laid her finger on my lips. 'Your mother does know.'

'She hasn't said anything, has she? No, she wouldn't have. She never speaks out.'

'Come to me tonight.'

'Better not.'

'I want you.'

'I want you too.'

'Damn you. I didn't mean to feel like this. I don't like it.'

Her tongue touched her upper lip and for a moment she looked vulnerable, lost, beauty in distress.

'It's awful,' she breathed, and turned away. I followed her to the door of her room and took her hand.

'We'll go tomorrow,' I said. 'Church is obligatory, but after lunch.'

Hector extended himself across the billiard table, only one toe on the floor. He held the pose a long time before playing the shot.

'Damn,' he said as he missed the cannon. 'I concede.'

'I'd better complete the formalities.'

He mixed two whiskies and soda and handed me a glass.

'Guy's back,' he said, 'did you know?'

I shook my head, put the cues in the rack.

'You saw a bit of him in Madrid, didn't you? How was he?'

'Unhappy.'

'Yes. I had lunch with him last week. I've made a decision. To be celibate. Chaste. It was meeting Guy did it. I used to admire him awfully, you know, envied him really.' He slipped his whisky, and swirled the liquid round in the glass. 'He had such style, such panache, and the confidence in being what he is that I didn't have. And then the other day, in the Grill, I saw the way people looked at him, even the waiters, one of them especially — rather a juicy little piece — and I could see they all saw him as just a queen. Not an old queen yet, of course, but on the way to that, and his voice is changing to fit that picture. And I didn't like it, hated it actually.'

'Nobody would mark you as a queen, Hector. You're far too buttoned-up.'

'Thanks. But all the same. I took a look at myself in the mirror.'

He stood up to do so again. The narrow intelligent face, with the long nose and high cheekbones, always seemed to call out for an Elizabethan ruff below the chin, for he had the air of one of those sixteenth-century types, given to profound melancholy, and perhaps fated to end his life on the scaffold.

'I've a choice. Either I make something positive of my life or I degenerate. And so, chastity, self-denial. It's a sacrifice, but a sacrifice that will strengthen me for the work I have to do.'

'Poor Guy.'

'Poor Guy. I never thought I'd find myself thinking of him like that. But poor Guy, indeed. The Continent will soon be closed to him, and here in England, there's the constant danger of blackmail. It's an intolerable existence, and not for me.'

Even then I wondered whether it was really that lunch

with Guy which had prompted Hector's decision – a decision that I thought I knew him well enough to be confident he would abide by, whatever strain it imposed on him. I couldn't think meeting Guy again was more than the final determining factor – as if Guy was Hector's personal portrait in the attic – and it occurred to me that very probably Hector himself had been the victim of the blackmail he envisaged as Guy's lot.

Throughout those months leading up to Munich, that city whose name tolls like the funeral bell of Europe, I was irked chiefly by the refusal of my paper to employ me as I wished. Every request for a foreign posting was turned down. Billy Hughes insisted that, on account of my experience and connections, I was invaluable on the foreign desk in London.

'I prize your discriminating talents,' he was wont to say. 'You have that essential requirement of the foreign editor, a nose for what is really significant. So bear with me while I thwart your desires. "They also serve who only stand and wait", and you do a hell of a lot more than that, laddie.'

He was a kind man, if out of his depth.

I acquiesced, partly because no feelers I put out, carefully, to other papers promised what I wanted, principally because of Vanessa. Alastair continued abroad – occasional postcards came from Germany, from Hungary (I wondered if he had encountered Sophie's Countess and whether she was indeed still that), Italy and the South of France. They gave little information as to his doings, were indeed no more than a record of his geographical progress. Vanessa made it clear that their marriage was at an end. She now spoke of Alastair with a dislike that was tinged by contempt. It was natural. Nobody had previously rejected her. I think in her way she loved me, and did not value me only as a trophy. God knows she could have had more splendid ones. Taking her, for instance, to the Savoy Grill after the theatre, I was proudly conscious of the greedy looks she attracted. We came that summer to be accepted as a couple; the mildly scandalous nature of our relationship giving us, in some circles, a certain cachet. Even her mother seemed to approve, telling me that she did wish Vanessa had got to know me before she married my brother.

I have been so long a stranger to passion, it is hard to recover its intensity. How can that which enslaves also enrich? By the midsummer of 1938 I found I became irritable and at a loss if a day passed without Vanessa. Knowing her power, she saw to it that such days were frequent.

Recently I came on an envelope full of old photographs which I had no need to examine since each was imprinted more beautifully on my memory; and yet, for hours, I gazed at them, seeing those flat surfaces rise into flesh, catching, in one particularly, taken unawares in a garden, with hollyhocks behind her, that cat-like half-smile she gave when she thought herself unobserved and simply delighted in her own being.

Vanessa was twenty-two in 1938. I was twenty-eight. We had come to love each other (in as much, I thought, as either was capable of doing so). The passion was necessary. The thought of her was enough to set my senses running. The angle of her head . . . no, I can't go on. Enough that that summer at least, for the only time in my life, I experienced what Stendhal called '*L'amour-passion*'. And I think, though she was unfaithful, she did also.

'It's me.'

'Have you had breakfast?'

'Eating it.'

'Last night was awful. Lonely, without you. Tell me a joke.'

'Don't know any. Alastair's coming home. Telegram: "Expect me supper." What shall I do?'

'Come out with me.'

'Can't. You come here.'

'Should I?'

'Needing.'

165

'Really?'

'Really needing.'

'If he sees me look at you, he'll know. Bound to.'

'Don't care. Needing. Seven o'clock.'

'What will you do till then?'

'Have a bath. Admire myself . . .'

'So do I . . . love you.'

'Love you too.'

Alastair was alone in the drawing room in Hertford Street when the maid showed me in, not before she had given me a conspiratorial wink. He leaped up, apparently delighted to see me. He was thinner, had lost a touch of his boyish look, still had the air of the Captain of the First XI.

'Super to see you. Awfully clever of Van to invite you.'

'I was having dinner with her in any case.'

'Been doing much of that?'

'A bit.'

'I'm grateful. How are the old folks? Thought I'd run down to Blankets tomorrow. No, not tomorrow, got something on, next day. So how are they? Forewarned is forearmed I always say.'

I told him how they were, pleased to see that he was nervous and talking too much.

'Girls'll be down I don't know when.'

'Girls?'

'Didn't Van say? Not alone. Got a friend with me. Girlfriend actually. You'll like her. Thought we'd all go out to a restaurant.'

As it happened, when Alastair's girl, Yvette, appeared I did rather like her. She wasn't the Valkyrie maiden I had expected: Yvette was in fact a Breton, small, dark, with short, straight hair, expressive brown eyes, and a laughing manner. Van seemed to have taken to her also. I was impressed by Yvette's ease. Then I thought: is it possible he hasn't told her Van is his wife? Yes, it was only too possible.

We went to a little French restaurant in Soho, the Trouville perhaps, or Chez Victoire.

'I want to show Yvette that you can actually eat well in England. We both agree you can't in Germany, which is sad.'

Alastair was in radiant form. He made fun of the rivalries between the Nazi leaders, relayed jokes about Goering's appetite – 'They say he'd swallow up all Europe, if only it was on the menu which it may be, who knows?' – and about Goebbels' passion for blondes – 'If he saw even your photograph, Van, he'd be all over you, pity he's such a squirt of a man . . . of course the Fuehrer loves blondes too, and has a passion for the Mitford girls, though since he's very moral it's only Unity he lunches with alone, now that Diana's married to Tom.'

Why did I listen to this sort of talk? Because Alastair sounded like a Lower Sixth boy recounting House scandal.

'Are you sure Father's all right, Alec? He sounds so sad and tired in his letters, he never used to sound like that. Of course they're still full of sterling moral advice. Not a letter ends – not a letter did I say? – not a page passes without its copy book moral.

'You're all wrong, you know, Alec, in thinking there's going to be a war. The Fuehrer doesn't want war, does he, Yvette? You've heard him say he doesn't, haven't you? I mean, all that hysteria – it was hysteria, Alec – about the Anschluss. What on earth does it matter to us if Germans unite with other Germans? If all the Germans outside the Reich were added to those within – and the Sudetenland ones will have to be, the Czechs have treated them abominably, some of the stories I've heard would make your flesh crawl – even so it would give Germany a population of only 80 million. What does it matter to us, I'd like to know?'

He called for more champagne.

'You do like this place, Yvette, don't you, it's really quite good isn't it? You really should come back to Germany,

Alec. That reminds me – I've a letter for you from Trude. Here it is, don't read it now. How is she? Blooming, I should say. Still very sweet, too. But you know, Alec, the transformation since you were there is tremendous. You really should come back and see, and see some of your old friends of course.'

'I'd find most of them dead, in camps or in exile, I'm afraid.'

'Oh that's all balls. Hitler's the most popular leader in Europe. I don't say he hasn't been a bit hard with some of the trouble-makers, but that was necessary. And, you know, he's tremendously pro-British, he really is. The Duke of Windsor's visit last year gave us the most enormous boost. Of course nobody could understand how we had come to let him go. They all thought the fuss about Wallis absurd. If only relations between the two countries could be as they should. I think that's my mission in life: to promote understanding. And film's a wonderful way of doing it, isn't it, Yvette? We're about to start work next month on a movie about three old soldiers of the last war – one German, one Frenchman and an Englishman. Yvette's playing the French-man's daughter, and it's going to show the madness, the stark raving insanity of another war. The Fuehrer doesn't want it, for heaven's sake he fought through the last one, like Tom. If only we could get gouty old has-beens like Winston to shut up . . .

'Mind you, not all the Nazi leaders are out of the top drawer. I think that's what Father distrusts about them. Ribbentrop's what he would call a bounder and I wouldn't dispute it. All the same Goering's great fun as well as being remarkably able. Why don't we ask him to shoot at Sandringham? He'd love it. And the Fuehrer really wants an alliance with England.

'But you know, even if they're not all out of the top drawer, that's really one of the attractive things about the Movement. It's swept away all that class nonsense. I know

Tom thinks England's doomed unless we do that here too. And you really must agree, Alec, after what you've seen of the Distressed Areas. Ascot and all that, we've got to be done with that foolery.'

'What about champagne?' Van said.

'I don't see why I shouldn't drink champagne just because I want to see the end of the class system. That's a typical woman's argument. I want everybody to be able to drink champagne.'

'There isn't enough to go round,' Van said.

When, at last, the waiters were removing the cloths from the other tables, and hovering, weary-eyed and heavy-footed, Alastair accepted the evening must be interrupted, end or move on. He paid the bill, and tipped lavishly.

'Where shall we go now? What's the best new night club, Van? You always know that sort of thing.'

She gave him a name.

'But you go on,' she said, 'I'm tired. Alec can take me home.'

'Sure? It's not like you. All right then. Look after the woman, Alec, will you?'

He kissed his wife, lightly, and turned away, putting his arm round Yvette.

In the taxi Van said, 'Your place, Alec,' and kissed me, thrusting her tongue between my lips.

Moonlight and movement awoke me. I stretched my arm out and found the bed empty. I got up and, looking through the open doorway that led to the sitting room, saw her on the window-seat, in profile, her knees drawn up and her arms clasped about her legs. I went through to the little kitchen and made a pot of tea and joined her. Only when I passed her a cup did she become aware of my presence.

'It's all right,' I said, remembering now how, as never before, she had wept in my arms when we had made love.

'You've done something to me, Alec,' she said. 'When we

169

first met, you didn't like me and I said I would tell you why you didn't, but I never did, did I? Not really. You thought I was a Fascist, didn't you, even if I was with Alfred Moss.'

'I thought you spoke like a Fascist,' I said, 'and yes, I thought you were fairly awful. But it was a long time ago.'

'I was excited,' she said. 'It's not nice, there's a part of me that is still excited by that sort of thing, men in boots, ruthless men, cruelty – maybe always will be. I was excited by Alastair this evening, hellishly, I had the hots for him, it's hopeless. But I'm glad he has that girl. Otherwise. I know I shouldn't, but Alec, Alec, please . . .'

I held her in my arms, and in a little, drew her back to bed. We made love – I recall sadly – with a tenderness there had never been before. But she still wept again afterwards, and when she slept her cheek was damp with tears as it rested on my chest.

It was not till the next morning that I remembered Trude's letter.

Dearest Alec,

It is very curious that I entrust this letter to Alastair because my sentiments are so different from his, and yet I know that I can trust him to deliver it safely. Is it not terrible that I should find myself writing in such a way?

My life has not been easy in the two years and more since Father was killed.

Yes: I write 'was killed', not 'died', though I cannot prove it.

It is not in the external circumstances that I have found difficulty. These have been sufficiently comfortable. I have enough money. I had not realised that Father was quite wealthy, because, of course, he himself gave no thought to such matters. So I do not have to work. This is good because the Fuehrer prefers that women should stay at home. He particularly prefers, I believe, that intelligent women should stay at home.

So I have done so, and have engaged myself in writing a novel, though I do not imagine it will ever be published.

You ask if I know enough to write a novel, and I must confess that it is probable that I do not.

I am afraid my English is rusted. But it is a pleasure to try to write in your language.

Alastair tells me that you have not married. Perhaps that is wise. If one marries, then there are children, and this is not, I think, a world into which one should wish to bring children. So, I expect I shall soon be classified as an 'old maid'.

Shall I write about the political situation? It is too painful. There is no question but that Hitler is a popular leader. Even many of my friends – Gunter and Oskar, for example, if you remember them – have learned at least to simulate enthusiasm. They shrug their shoulders and say: 'We are Germans, we must live here, and things aren't going to change. So we must make the best of it.' I do not blame them, though I am sad. I think that if I was a man I might shrug my shoulders also. Fortunately I am not a man.

So we must hope for better times.

But, Alec, you must not believe what is written about the rape of Austria. Alas, it was not like that. The Viennese were crazy to live under the swastika. And what can we do about it?

Meanwhile I have had a proposal of marriage. Does that shock you? Peter is a banker. He says he knows you, and believes you will remember him. He is also a friend of Barbara. But I do not know if I shall marry him. I do not love him. On the other hand, to be an unmarried young or not so young, alas, woman in Germany today is to be regarded as a little odd. Like Barbara's friend Sophie – you remember? – who has returned from Budapest, and who is not happy.

This is a long letter and it is nice as if I was chatting to you – with what pleasure I recall so many of our talks, especially those in the mountains – but I have not yet dared to approach the main purpose of my letter. So, I clear my throat:

Alec, you must please persuade Alastair not to return to Germany. Perhaps your father will forbid it? It is for Alastair's sake I write. He is charming but, I now find, foolish. He lacks the critical sense. And if he returns here he will come to harm. Of that I am certain.

It seems to me that I am in a sense a traitor to send this message by his hand. Nevertheless I do so.

If we had either of us religion I would say pray for us both, for we are entering terrible times. But I do not have that faith, and nor do you, unless something has happened to change you. And I do not have either the faith that I think Father had – and perhaps yours also, dear Alec – in the upward and onward progress of humanity.

It is strange. Writing this letter has enabled me to make up my mind. I looked out of the window just now. It is four o'clock in the morning and there is a beautiful, large summer moon becoming pale. The leaves of the chestnut trees are touched with the faintest pink of a new light, and it is very calm. It is the most beautiful calm, Alec, as if God really had made the world and made it good. We know that is not true, of course, but there are, nevertheless, moments when it seems to be true. Ah, if I could quote Nietzsche, but my memory is so inexact. I refer to his insistence that the truly strong person is joyful. There is something about a new fragrance, bringing salvation – and a new hope. You remember? Yes, here it is, coming pattering like the footsteps of a little child through my memory . . .

But it is only when one is alone, in the first light of day, that this seems believable. And if it is ever to be so, then I fear we must first pass through the shadows, the valleys of death and humiliation.

I have been diverted from what I intended to say about the decision I have just taken: I shall marry Peter.

There! That will disappoint you, not, of course, because I am foolish enough to suppose that you still love me, or think you love me – for in reality I knew that you loved an idea which I represented. (Perhaps, you will say: but that is all love ever is, or can be – the loved person a representation of whatever virtue the lover at that moment most prizes, most ardently aspires to. Perhaps you will say that, and perhaps you would be right.)

In any case, even if I am wrong, and you did really love me, it is impossible that you should have gone on doing so as anything more than a sentimental memory. It is so many years ago. We have both grown and suffered and experienced so much in the meanwhile!

No, you will be disappointed precisely because I have already told you that I do not love Peter – and, indeed, I could never love him, and do not even respect him. So you will say: Trude is less than she was. And you are right to say that. I am less than I was, less healthy (I mean in spirit, my bodily health is excellent). But I am also more: more wary, more knowledgeable. And it is exactly because I do not love Peter that I shall marry him, because I have been hurt too much and do not, cannot, entertain the idea of being hurt further than the world is already destined to hurt me, and all of us.

So, why marry? You ask that – I can see you, furrowing your brow as you do when you are puzzled.

Because he offers me the protection which I need.

That is why.

So, I am a coward? I do not think so. You will remember that Nietzsche praised Thucydides at the expense of Plato (who – it is clear today – is the spirit of our times, preferring the idea of things which dazzle mankind and allow terrible actions to be performed because the idea justifies them). But Nietzsche said that Thucydides displayed courage in the face of reality, and that Plato was a coward who fled from reality into the ideal . . .

So, in agreeing to marry Peter, who loves me in his tepid lukewarm banker's-minded manner, I am accepting reality. We are on the verge of the Inferno, my dear Alec.

Do not write. It will not be safe. And persuade Alastair that Germany is no place for him. Bind him to England, for his sake.

Do not write, but keep a corner of your heart for me, and do not forget . . .

I send you all the love of which I am capable, and it is now a poor thing.

Trude.

'So, has she written a complete bloody book?'

Van passed me a cup of coffee and lit a cigarette. 'Were you in love with her? Or the other way round? Should I be jealous?'

'Here,' I said, 'read it for yourself.'

'You know I can't read German.'

'It's in English. She likes to write in English. And yes, to answer your question, I was in love with her but she was never quite in love with me. She slept with Alastair, actually.'

'Is that why you go to bed with me?'

'Of course. Read it.'

She bent her head. Vanessa always read slowly as if it was not natural to her. This was somewhat deceptive. It was true she didn't read often – to that extent certainly wasn't a natural reader, not the sort for instance who would rather read the back of the cereal packet than not read. But when she did, she read very thoroughly and absorbed the matter. So, to offer another contradictory example, I had been

174

amazed to find that she had in the last months acquired a considerable knowledge of George Eliot's novels, not then likely to be known by the sort of people among whom she habitually mixed, nor, indeed, the sort of stuff she had previously been attracted to.

She took a long time over Trude's letter. I sipped my coffee. Her hair hung loose and obscured her face. The sunlight played butter-coloured on her naked magnificent shoulders.

It wasn't to be expected that Van and Trude would like each other. They were serious about such different things. Together they might form my ideal woman, except that it was inconceivable they should be put together. Perhaps life would be more endurable if we were allowed two wives – and excused domesticity, except at rare moments like the present.

Trude and I had been, I saw it, so young, so very young, caught in a moment of adolescence, that period of life when it is natural to believe in perfection – when it is natural too to be introspective. Van perhaps had never been adolescent. She had moved straight from a (corrupt?) childhood to adulthood without illusions. Was that what Trude was now aiming for? Was Van already ahead of her in being like Nietzsche's idea of Thucydides, in control of herself, consequently in control of things. I saw Trude tossed on the waves through which Van determinedly cut.

'She does go on,' Van said.

'I suppose so.'

'You'd have found her an awful bore if you had married her, but I can see that a letter from her is a treat, just up your alley. Will she marry this chap Peter?'

'It sounds like it.'

'Sounds grim, too. But who am I to speak? I've made my own mistake.'

'I can understand why she might marry him.'

'Oh, yes. You will speak to him, won't you?'

'Who?'

'My mistake. Alastair. You'll speak to him as she asks, won't you. Was she in love with him?'

'No, attracted.'

'Like me. Maybe not. In a way I was in love with him. Anyway I thought I was. Doesn't matter. But you will speak to him? This German mania frightens me. Do you know something? I don't really like foreigners. They never seem to make much sense.'

When I got to Blankets on the Saturday afternoon, it was to find a house party taking tea on the lawn. There was a junior minister and his wife, a couple of back-bench Tory MPs, one also accompanied by his wife, the other not, which didn't surprise me since I knew that Edwin Pringle's marriage was very much of convenience, to still rumours and satisfy his constituency chairman, or rather his constituency chairman's wife who was known to view with disapproval anyone over thirty who was not provided with a wife, suspecting them – correctly it would have been in Pringle's case – of what she deemed to be unnatural vice. There were also a clergyman and his wife and a couple of Oxford dons, accompanied by an undergraduate whom I didn't know, and who might, indeed, have come separately. It was not the sort of company that Mother cared for, though she always disguised this from Father.

It wasn't long before she disengaged me, which she did in her usual manner, unobtrusive but irresistible, and led me to her own sitting room where, it was understood, guests were welcome only on the sort of oblique invitation which had brought me there. This sitting room had, for all of us, associations less pleasant than the actually charming south-facing room with its faded chintz, Morris wallpaper, and agreeable water colours, themselves the work of Mother and her sisters, perhaps an aunt also, would have suggested to someone seeing it for the first time. This was because it was the stage setting for what we called 'Mother's little talks', exercises in assertions of moral superiority which George alone among us had been able to defy. Even so, it has occurred to me several times that the real reason for George's flight to the East was to be found in a determination to escape that sitting room.

'I'm well aware,' she said, motioning me to a chair, taking an oval Egyptian cigarette (Sullivan & Powell's Khedive brand) from the mother-of-pearl inlaid cigarette box which was filled every morning, the unsmoked cigarettes being first removed in order to be relaid at the top, then waiting for me to leave the chair where I had just, at her silent insistence, placed myself, in order to take the lighter from the same table to the right of her chair, and hold the flame towards her. 'I'm well aware that things aren't just as they were when I was a girl, but it was a touch embarrassing for me when Hortense Ladiwick, tiresome I grant you, told me that she had seen you lunching with Vanessa at the Savoy Grill. Now of course there is no reason why you should not take luncheon in a public place with your sister-in-law, and I would expect even Hortense to realise that. Which of course she does. So the fact that she felt obliged to give herself the pleasure of bringing it to my notice suggests that there was something disturbing about the manner of it, the suggestion of a greater intimacy, perhaps, than is altogether suitable. You know what Mrs Patrick Campbell said.'

'Do I?'

'Don't pretend to be stupid, Alec, it doesn't become you. There's one unforgivable vulgarity, and that is to give rise to talk. But you all seem determined to do so. I wonder why.'

'Conventions change, Mother.'

'I never thought it a suitable marriage. Honor Stuart-Styles has been committing that particular vulgarity since her second Season. They're not intending to get a divorce, are they?'

'Naming me as co-respondent? No, they're not.'

'Your father wouldn't know where to hide his head. He sees nothing of course. So he feels things more deeply.'

She dropped her cigarette into a bowl in which rose petals floated. ('It doesn't look pretty,' she was wont to say, 'but it's preferable to the nasty smell of a used ashtray.')

'Discretion, please. In any case, you'll be tired of her before long. Any intelligent man would be.'

I whistled up Lucy, one of the spaniels, and set off through the woods. As usual, Mother had implied much more than she had said. As usual she had left me in a condition of moral discomfort. Without Father's Romantic attachment to the days of their youth, which led him, despite his undoubted love for his children, to the sad conviction that we were less than his generation had been, and therefore required, Alastair especially, to be protected against the contagion of the times, Mother, even in her reticence, expressed a sort of contempt for our weaknesses. It was as if we had failed her in conforming to the standards of the world we lived in. Yet, in childhood, it had been difficult for all of us to be quite certain how she expected us to behave. That, I said to myself, was surely her failure.

Passing beyond the trees, among which the spaniel still industriously searched, I came on to the open downland. There had been an Iron Age settlement here. Then it had been abandoned, the hillside reverting probably to scrub in Saxon times. The monks of the abbey, first established in the eleventh century, half-way down the hill, had turned the downland to sheep farming, bringing prosperity. The three or four church towers visible from where I lay – the number depending on the season of the year – testified to medieval wealth.

The spaniel came and lay beside me, mouth open, tongue hanging out, and I placed my hand on her soft heaving shoulder, and felt at peace. History was very quiet on that hillside.

★

At dinner, Alastair got in an argument with one of the Oxford dons. Mother suppressed it, but it revived when the ladies had left us to our port. The don took the view that if Hitler pressed demands on Czechoslovakia, we must resist them.

'Our natural ally is the Soviet Union,' he said.

'Would you let Bolshevism loose on Europe?' Father asked.

'I am not so sure that the Soviet Union should still be considered Bolshevik. In any case, it's common sense. If we are not to see Hitler destroy the states established by Versailles, then we must compel him to fight a war on two fronts.'

'Can we really contemplate another war?'

'I trust it won't be necessary. The prospect of a war on two fronts would be enough, I believe, to deter him.'

'Versailles,' Alastair said, 'is the cause of whatever trouble there is in Europe.'

He spoke with a cool insolence that dismayed me.

'Is there really,' he said, 'any reason on God's earth why the decent hard-working Germans of the Sudetenland should be ruled by Czechs? It's madness. Versailles was the crazy and vindictive settlement of the victors. We have to get rid of it. Then there will be a chance of peace in Europe.'

The same argument, no doubt, was echoing round a thousand dinner tables, sounding in innumerable saloon bars and roadhouses. Here, where there was some pretence to true knowledge of the circumstances – the weakness of our defences for instance, our terrible lack of military readiness – it remained as confused, as corrupted by private fears and prejudices, as it was amongst those whom almost everyone at our table would have dismissed as uninformed.

'I don't mind confessing,' the other don, a historian, said, 'that I dread another war. I saw enough of the last one to have reason for that. We've never recovered. France is half the country it was in 1914.'

The party had dispersed, some returning to Oxford, others mounting the stair to bed. We lounged in leather armchairs in the billiard room, with cigars.

'Father's failing,' Alastair said, 'it's sad to see.'

I threw a couple of logs on the fire. The spaniel, disturbed by the spark of flame, looked at me resentfully, then settled herself to sleep again.

'Van told me about you and her.'

'Did she now?'

'Yes. I should be angry, I suppose.'

'I don't think you've the right to.'

'No. Doesn't matter anyway.'

'She's still fond of you. She's worried about you. We all are. Father most of all, though he can't find the words to express what he feels.'

'That's not like him.' Alastair drew on his cigar. 'Or perhaps it is. I don't know. At this time of night I don't know anything.'

'Good.'

'What do you mean, good? Never mind. Listen, there's the owl. Jolly.'

'Yes, jolly.'

'I used to like lying awake in bed when I was a boy and listening to the owl. Funny how we go for the same women. I think Van would like a divorce.'

'She hasn't said anything to me. It would kill Father.'

'Oh,' Alastair smiled and waved his cigar negligently, 'I'd supply grounds. No difficulty there. You wouldn't be named. Don't worry.'

'It's not that that worries me,' I said, 'or Van, come to that. We neither of us like the way you're heading.'

Alastair opened his eyes, very wide.

'But I'm serious,' he said, 'it's not a game. I really and truly believe that our only hope is an alliance with Germany. Otherwise, it's an end – to all this – to all we love and value and stand for.'

'An end to the owl on a summer night in England?'

'An end to the way we feel about the owl, an end to our sort of sensibility. We need a united Europe – Britain and France and Germany standing together, against the barbarism of the East. The new Germany holds the gate, just as it did in the days of Teutonic Knights. You can't allow a little country – an artificial little country – like Czechoslovakia, to stand in the way of a new order in Europe. It's the only way, also, we can save the Empire. I'm not a politician, Alec – I'm a film-maker – but I can see that.'

'And you're going back to Germany? You're determined?'

'What's the drama? I told you I'm going back to make a film, just as soon as the financing's complete, which isn't easy, I can tell you, unless you're prepared to put yourself in the hands of the Jews, which I'm not, of course; but yes, when that's complete and fixed, I'm going back. But if it's any comfort to you, we'll be filming in France, mostly. I wish you weren't so blind, Alec. About Germany, I mean. You can tell Van I'll supply her with what she needs, if she really wants it. But I don't see the point. I'd have thought things were quite happily arranged as they are. I don't expect you want to marry her, after all?'

When I was dressing a few hours later, I saw the Lagonda roar off up the drive. Father was unusually silent at breakfast. Later I accompanied him and Mother to church. The parson took as his text, 'The Kingdom of heaven is like a grain of mustard seed', and told us about the quiet working of God's purpose for the world. He had been a field chaplain on the Somme, but his faith was Early Victorian. The same sermon, if somewhat longer, might, I thought, have been preached

181

from the same pulpit a century earlier, twenty years before Darwin published *Origin of Species* and called the idea of an anthropomorphic deity into question.

On the way back from church I called, as I often did when at Blankets on a Sunday, at the Haskins' lodge. Frank was away, training with his Territorials. Old Haskins shook his head.

'Frank says we're heading for another war. It makes no sense to me.' He looked on his son with a certain wonder. Though Haskins himself had an innate dignity (characteristic, in fact, of so many whom social scientists would consign to the servant class) which made him regard every man as his equal before the Almighty; his understanding of society – a word he could never have employed – was comfortably hierarchical. He was a little perturbed when Frank, having moved from childhood equality through a certain adolescent stage of rebellious resentment, began to converse with me, and to a lesser extent my brothers, on level terms. Old Haskins was even offended when he saw that I accepted this as natural. I think he felt it falsified his own relationship to the gentry. It seemed even more wrong to him when Frank became a Labour councillor in Oxford, and revealed his aim of being adopted as a Parliamentary candidate. Such things, his father thought, weren't for the likes of them. His attitude puzzled and irritated some of Frank's acquaintances, but not Frank himself. On the other hand he took a gently malicious pleasure in teasing the old man by remarking that I was considerably further Left than he was himself.

'What Mr Alec thinks is his business,' his mother said. 'I'll thank you to remember, young Frank, what you were brought up to believe.' These differences did nothing to disturb the love and trust they all felt for each other.

XII
London 1938–9

The night Chamberlain came back from Munich with his piece of paper, Alfred Moss gave a party.

It was coincidental, being his birthday, and the party arranged for some weeks. But Chamberlain changed its mood. Even the day before, everyone would have been on edge, fearful, thinking in many cases – mine certainly – that we shouldn't be there, that it was unforgivably frivolous to go to a party when bombs might fall on London in a couple of days. ('Oh I don't know,' Van said, 'think of the Duchess of Richmond's Ball.') But now, even those of us who felt most ashamed and swore it was a terrible and disgraceful sell-out, couldn't conceal our relief. We were all giddy-headed; it was like being given an unexpected holiday at school.

'Now I know what the condemned man must feel when they tell him his execution's put off because there's been an electricity strike,' Max said. 'And look at Alfred, he's a dozen years younger. On his birthday too!'

This wasn't quite accurate, perhaps because Max was too excited to be observant. Alfred certainly looked splendid. He wore a suit of plum-coloured velvet with a silk shirt and rings on his fingers. His hair – not cut for several weeks – hung in brilliantined ringlets. But it was the expression of weary disdain that gave him the look of Disraeli; he was one who has seen and suffered all, and as he moved through the throng, bestowing a kiss here and a pat there, his demeanour said that, while he was delighted that Chamberlain should have given his birthday party a mood of irrepressible levity, he wasn't deceived. Tomorrow would still come and reality prevail. Meanwhile, on with the motley.

I hadn't seen Max for months, only once – briefly, in a theatre bar – since my return from Spain. It was necessary, first, to catch up on what had happened to Annie – working still in the North, it seemed – and other friends. I said I was surprised to find him still here himself. Someone had said he had returned to the States. In any case, I had often wondered, never got round to asking, and this was as good a time as any, how, in view of Equity's attitude to American performers, he contrived to work here so much. He opened his eyes very wide.

'But of course I've an Equity card, sweetie.'

'How come?'

'Because I've a British passport, didn't you know? I was born here, Dad was English, and though we went to the States when I was a baby, I've clung on to British nationality, clung like ivy. In fact, but don't tell anyone because I don't think one's supposed to, I have two passports, British and American.'

'So what happens if there's a war?'

'Sweet Mr Chamberlain's prevented that, hasn't he?'

'Come off it, Max.'

'War postponed, honeychile, is war that may never happen. But if it does' – he struck a martial or at least military attitude – 'this boy will do his bit, whatever that is.' Then, dropping out of his camp manner, he asked how Hector was.

'But he's in Bucharest, didn't you know?'

'I've heard nothing of him for such ages.'

No, I thought, he's cut you out. Well, that happens when love has died. All the same, Hector, Max had – has? – a disinterested affection – even love – for you; and that is something you deny yourself at some risk.

'You heard he's taken a vow of chastity?'

'Poor Hector. More than you have, Alec, from what I hear.'

'You probably hear right. And how's your own love life?'

'Sad.'

Edwin Pringle approached us, clutching a plate of lobster salad, which he had some difficulty in controlling. He began to talk of Chamberlain's triumph, and reminded me that he had said at Blankets – 'and how I love visiting that place, such a pity your father has decided he is past it, I'm sure he isn't, but he says he is writing his memoirs: wonderful' – that we would not go to war over Czechoslovakia. It was not that he had anything against Czechoslovakia, he was a true friend of democracies everywhere, but all the same, to go to war in order to compel the Sudetenland Germans to remain part of a Republic which they didn't wish to belong to – that made no sense? And as for the idea that we should form an alliance with the Bolsheviks – perish the thought. 'You may think me narrow-minded, Alec, but I can't forget I'm a very rich man.'

All the time he was speaking, he was eyeing Max, and he made this last statement about his wealth with an unusual emphasis.

'Do introduce, please,' he said, 'I'm sure I've seen your young friend before, I mean I know I have – I couldn't forget, honestly, but I know we haven't met. So do introduce please.'

I did so, reluctantly, and added: 'Is Linda with you tonight, Edwin?'

'A dancer?' Edwin said, ignoring me. 'On the stage? In revue? "Three's a Crowd", was that it? Of course it was. I really loved it. Well, this is a treat.'

He took Max by the elbow and guided him towards the buffet. Max glanced back and raised his left eyebrow.

'That looked like a brush-off, darling.' Vanessa, coming up from behind, kissed me on the cheek below my left ear.

'Poor Max,' I said, 'I've seldom seen Pringle so excited.'

'Max can look after himself, pansies always can. I've just been enduring being undressed by the eyes of a man who says he's a great friend of yours. He's talking to Mummy now. I should say he was once a good deal more than a great friend of hers.'

I looked to where she indicated. Jukes had his arm round Honor's waist, and was leaning towards her, his mouth open in laughter.

'He says he saved your life in Spain.'

By the time we had made our way across the room, where half a dozen couples were now dancing, Alfred Moss had joined Jukes and Honor.

'So, Jukes,' he was saying, 'you have been denied your war?'

'I guess where things are hot, you'll find me there,' Jukes said. 'Hi, Al, good to see you, boy. Al here knows, we went through some tough times in Spain, didn't we, Al?'

'As you say . . .'

Alfred Moss smiled.

'We'll all soon know what you call tough times.'

'Surely not?' Honor said. 'Herr Hitler has given his word to the Prime Minister.'

'Sure,' Jukes said, 'the umbrella man has chickened out, and bought you a month or two, but speaking for myself I would no more trust little Adolf's word than I would drink water straight from the Hudson. Or the Thames.'

'You're just trying to frighten me,' Honor said.

We have all read accounts of the London Season of 1914, how it was the most glittering and extravagant of all, as if half-consciously preparing splendid memories which would throb like a macabre drumbeat through the hell into which Europe was about to plummet. Alfred's party couldn't compare. Magnificent in its way, undeniably lavish, no expense spared (itself something that would cause Alfred trouble when the Inland Revenue came to compare his stated income with his expenditure, so contributing to his descent into bankruptcy a couple of years later), it neverthe-less failed to quell the sense of foreboding which, from a few months previously, and right up to the actual outbreak of war the following September, hung over us: a mood which made everything we did – including my affair with Vanessa – seem merely provisional, a temporary arrangement which we couldn't hope would endure.

For me, the presence of Jukes sharpened this feeling of apprehension. His arrival in London was like the circling of vultures. The eternal spectator, he was also the harbinger of horror, made all the more disturbing by his invariable air of cynical and malicious authority scarcely masked by the pretence of being a good fellow.

'So,' Alfred said, 'there is going to be a war, all the same, eh Jukes. And what will America do?'

'There'll be a war,' Jukes said. ' "The statesman who, knowing his instrument is ready, hesitates to strike first, is guilty of a crime against his country." That was the Freiherr von der Goltz, author of *The Nation in Arms*. Well, the German nation is in arms, and waiting the right moment. That's all. As for us Americans, I guess we'll sit this one out.'

'You think so?'

'Sure, why wouldn't we? Mr Baldwin and Mr Chamber-lain stood for non-intervention in Spain, and so did the Frogs. I guess we'll non-intervene in Europe as a whole. So don't fool yourselves. This time the US Cavalry will stay the other side of the Atlantic.'

Vanessa tugged my sleeve, drew me away.

'That man's horrible,' she said. 'Did he really save your life?'

'No.'

'Good. I thought maybe he did, but you just didn't want to admit to having your life saved by him. I wouldn't.'

As winter approached Vanessa found she was pregnant. Probably, the child was mine. She said it was certain. She had been to bed with no one else since Munich. Munich, she said, had convinced her that we might have only a short time together, and she found that she didn't want anyone else. She enjoyed the idea of being faithful to me, she said. I believed her, or almost. In any case, I liked the idea that she was carrying my child. And I thought – still think – she was telling the truth.

Fortunately, we had spent a few days in Paris in October. I had gone there for the paper, and she had come because it might be the last time she would see Paris. Since we had allowed it to be understood at Blankets that Van had accompanied me with a view to spending a few days with Alastair before he started shooting his film, Father didn't doubt that Alastair was the father of the prospective grandchild. I don't think Mother was deceived even then, but she preferred to exercise tact and pretend she was. Father was delighted. It would have been cruel to deprive him of his happiness. It wouldn't be the first grandchild: Kirstie and Colin had had a daughter, Jean, in the autumn. But Alastair's child would be special, and the thought warmed Father's heart, convincing him that he had only imagined the troubled state of the marriage. The suspicion with which he had viewed Vanessa – suspicion we both recognised though he tried to hide it – was dispelled. Now she could do no wrong.

As a consequence, divorce became unthinkable. It took me some time to persuade Van of this. She was indignant as well as puzzled.

'It's your child,' she said, 'don't you want to acknowledge it?'

'It's my child,' I said, 'whether I acknowledge it or not. But we can't do this to Father. He dotes on Alastair.'

'You're impossible,' she said. 'I hated him in Paris. I never want to see him again. Doesn't that make a difference? Don't my feelings count?'

Nevertheless, she acquiesced. The word 'noble' has a

strange and unconvincing ring to it now, but still this was the noblest act of her life.

XIII

What I have been writing tends, I see, to the personal, as if I was attempting autobiography. To a degree this is unavoidable: direct experience had, can even retain, its freshness, which the reported experience of others lacks. I had thought to repair this by means of the imagination, even to the extent of invention. But when I have essayed this, I have torn up the pages in disgust. It seems to me frivolous, reprehensible, dishonest, to make of people I knew characters in a fiction – or even a 'faction'. So, much of the time therefore, I am thrown back on myself.

And yet it is not the story of an individual that I am trying to tell. It is not even the story of a particular family. The more I write, even when I am penning memories of love-making, or reconstructions of conversations dimly remembered – the reconstructions being sometimes prompted by a note in the journal I continued to keep, though its scrappiness and banality preclude its direct use, most of the time – I am conscious that what I am really attempting is the anatomy of a moral failure. It is not the failure of an individual. Indeed the failures of particular individuals are, it seems, determined by the wider failure of a class. I began by recalling the success, in various guises, of Father's fictional memoir, *Corners of Foreign Fields*, the original book, for all its purple passages, too easy nostalgia, lapses into sentimentality and so on, nevertheless opening the question which is at the heart of my own scribblings. Put simply, it is: what caused the demoralisation of the British Establishment? That puts it perhaps too simply. It might be better to ask: what causes led us, as the century advanced – and that 'us', be it noted, includes me among those charged with the failure – what causes then led us to develop a disinclination to look reality in the face?

I come back, inevitably, to that passage from Nietzsche which Trude quoted: to his preference for Thucydides over Plato, on the grounds that Plato is 'a coward in the face of reality'.

And wasn't that our situation precisely? Hadn't it been that, at least since the moment when we turned away from the reality of the dictators into dreams of a gentler future? Could one, to take an extreme example, imagine the Duke of Wellington behaving as Chamberlain did?

But – I remember Kirstie objecting once, years ago, when I developed this argument over her dinner table at Tully-moran – what about Churchill? To which I could reply only that if Churchill faced one reality, he could not bring himself to confront the other: which was that his policy – necessary as it no doubt was and certainly seemed to be – was itself evasive. He did not come to power to preside over the liquidation of the British Empire! Oh, no! There are times when de Gaulle seems to me to have been as superior to Churchill as Nietzsche found Thucydides superior to Plato – and for the same reason.

It took me a long time to come to this conclusion. In the summer of 1940 I surrendered to the magic of Churchill's rhetoric. So did Father, who had distrusted him for years as 'a brilliant child who has never grown up, and doesn't want to'.

In the months before the child was to be born, we sometimes quarrelled. We were not sharing the flat in Hertford Street and this made our quarrels easier to sustain and yet to recover from. We could avoid meeting and nurse whatever grievances we had. On the other hand each meeting was like a new beginning. I sometimes thought: this is the best way for couples to live. That was because it was the only way I could live as part of a couple.

But it was not – this was at the heart of the problems – the way Van wanted us to live. Admitting, as she did, sometimes, her incapacity for love, at least of another adult who, being adult, inevitably invaded the space she prized, she was nevertheless that spring and summer, as completely in love with me as she was capable of being. It was no longer just sexual desire, and this in turn made me uncomfortable. She was demanding of me what I was unwilling, incapable, of giving. We were in this respect too much alike. Except in bed, neither was able to surrender a flinty and private arrogance. So we quarrelled. About what, I mostly can't remember. Trivialities, I suppose.

Yet there are, perhaps, no trivialities in relationships between a man and a woman. The look of irritation or boredom is not a triviality, being an act of rejection. There were moments when I welcomed such rejection. I said to myself: the world is about to crack, like an egg, and it is intolerable that I should be concerned with the fact that Van is late for an appointment or that I forgot to telephone her yesterday. Sometimes I admitted to myself that I hadn't forgotten. I had instead sat, drinking whisky, beside my telephone ready to call her, and then flinched from doing so. At that moment I knew that this was the last thing I wanted to do. That was because I wanted to escape. I have always wanted to escape from anyone who held me close. I would have wanted to escape from Trude if she had permitted me to get into a position where she held me close. It was the fact that she denied me that which drove me to demand it.

So I was unjust and unkind to Van, and it was no justification that she was unjust and unkind to me. Though it sometimes seemed like a justification, especially if I was a little drunk, as I often was that summer. It was no justification either that all our friends felt their nerves on edge. The converse was true. Because we might all be dead in a year's time, or in a concentration camp, there was an obligation to be kind.

I often thought about being in a camp. It seemed quite probable that I would be. My writings, not very well known, were nevertheless conspicuous enough to have me on a Nazi Black List. Not the number one list of course – I wasn't so conceited as to imagine my name might be there – but a subsidiary list.

It angered Vanessa when I talked of this. Of course, it was folly to do so. I knew she detested that sort of speculation. She had a lot to say about not crossing bridges till you reached them. 'You're not Jewish,' she would say, 'don't give yourself airs.' And I could understand that that was indeed what she thought I was doing, and why it irritated her. Nevertheless I continued to play with the idea and torment her, even though it frightened me.

It was much easier and pleasanter, being less demanding, to spend evenings with Barbara or Max. We would often meet in a pub in Soho and do the rounds of the bars there and in Fitzrovia. Often we would end up at Gaston's. The pubs were full of men and women trying to talk their apprehension away. They spoke of poetry and of who was sleeping with whom. It should have been comforting.

Sometimes, on evenings when I was with Max, I thought that life would have been simpler if I had stuck with boys. I thought this, even though I knew it was a lie. It was just that I liked playing with the idea.

One night, at Gaston's, half-cut and still drinking brandy, I gave him an embroidered version of my schoolboy love for Colin. He said: 'The trouble with you, Alec, is that you're a Romantic. There's no room left for Romantics in the world.'

'I don't know about that,' I said. 'What is Fascism but diseased Romanticism?'

'Is Alastair really a Fascist?' he said.

'He may be. He's never grown up, you see. Fascism is a creed for boys who never grew up.'

'Unlike Marxism,' he smiled.

I went into the office towards noon on a sunlit morning in May. I had walked across Green Park and St James's Park and stopped for a Guinness in Ward's Irish House in the Strand. It was a day like a Fats Waller record, which let you think there might be no war.

Billy Hughes said: 'He wants to see you, he's not happy.'

'When is he happy?'

Harbottle didn't like me. He didn't approve of me either. This was understood by both Billy Hughes and myself. I had often wondered why he didn't sack me. There were plenty of other journalists who could do what I did, with more consistent competence.

'It's the flashes of brilliance,' Billy Hughes said, but he didn't convince himself.

The truth, I think now, is that Harbottle was a snob. He valued my connections. Things have changed now, of course. Today the editors of newspapers are more likely than Cabinet ministers to have gone to Eton. But Harbottle had come up from the provinces as a young reporter. His father kept an ironmonger's shop in Smethwick. He was still uncertain with those he had been brought up to consider his social superiors, whom, however, he admired rather than resenting. An invitation to lunch with a Cabinet minister at his club gratified him, but still he couldn't leave the table without wondering whether he had committed some solecism.

Now I found him staring at the big globe on his desk as if the existence of all these foreign countries was a source of puzzlement and irritation.

'This piece you've written,' he said, 'about the guarantee to Poland. What do you mean by it?'

'I'd have thought it was clear enough.'

194

'Oh it's clear, certainly, horribly clear.'

'Well then.'

'As I understand it . . .' Harbottle paused to fill his pipe with a deliberation that couldn't disguise the trembling of his hands. 'You suggest that we should publish the argument that the guarantee offered by His Majesty's Government, in accordance with that of France, isn't worth the paper it's written on.'

'More or less that, yes.'

'And what do you expect our readers to make of that?'

Harbottle's consciousness of our readers' expectations was legendary. Nobody, it used to be said, had ever seen him with a reader. Perhaps he met them at home, but it seemed unlikely. The people he met at his club, where anyway he was scarcely gregarious, were not likely to read our paper, preferring *The Times* or even the *Telegraph*. His holidays were spent in a cottage in the upper reaches of one of the Yorkshire dales, where he indulged himself in the pleasures of hill walking and bird watching. I always thought his desire for solitude (intensified since his wife's early death three years previously) was one of the more attractive features of his not, generally, engaging character. Yet he claimed an infallible understanding of what our readers wanted, and his certainty had grown in the fifteen years he had edited the paper. Irritatingly, its more or less unvarying circulation suggested that he was right. Making the paper to suit himself, Harbottle created something that perfectly expressed the opinions of a swathe of the middling to lower-middling classes of England.

'You're suggesting, too, that the Government knows this, that the guarantee is a bluff?'

'I would put it more strongly.'

'Not in my paper you won't.'

He had got his pipe alight at last and blew smoke across the desk.

'Let's suppose,' he said, lengthening the 'o' in such a manner as to indicate his contempt for what was about to be supposed. 'Let's suppose that you are right.' He puffed again. 'I'm not saying you are, because to say so would be to suppose that Mr Chamberlain is practising a deliberate act of deception, but let's suppose – for the sake of argument' – something that Harbottle felt a distaste for, and so shunned – 'that you are. What follows, my lad? I'll tell you. It follows that the deception is aimed at Herr Hitler. Doesn't it? That its intention is to deter him? And so, if we publish this . . . stuff . . .' – he picked up the offending piece and let the pages flutter to his desk – 'we are saying to Herr Hitler: "Don't you worry about the British guarantee, the clever young men of England" – meaning you, Mr Allan – "can assure you it's worthless." That's what we'd be saying. For me to publish this would be tantamount to saying to Herr Hitler: "Go ahead, march into Poland, there's nothing we can do, or intend to do, about it." Is that – I ask you now – a fitting message for us to give?'

'It might be something like the truth. But there's more to my argument than that.'

'Oh, yes.' Harbottle puffed again. 'Oh, yes, there's more to your argument than that. Indeed there is. You tell the Government – you, that is, young Mr Allan – tell His Majesty's ministers that it is their duty – their duty no less – to come to an understanding – no, I'm wrong, more than an understanding, to a firm alliance – with the Soviet Union. Mr Allan, do you know what our readers think of the Soviet Union?'

'They don't like it, I suppose . . .'

'You suppose' – long 'o' again – 'correctly. Not only do they not like it, it represents everything they fear and detest – atheism, socialism, tyranny. What do you suppose they will say to the suggestion you make?'

'I'm not sure I care for the Soviet Union myself,' I said. 'But isn't the issue more important than whether our readers approve of the Soviet Union? We're talking about the peace of Europe.'

'Indeed we are. That is why Mr Chamberlain has given a guarantee to Poland. It is why France has given a guarantee to Poland. Mr Allan, do you know anything about the current strength of the Russian army? No, don't bother to answer. I was talking to a general – a very senior general – in the club only yesterday, and he assured me, gave me his word, that the purges Mr Stalin has carried out, purges which have decimated and demoralised the officer corps, have rendered the Russian army inoperative. Inoperative – his exact word. In his opinion it will take that army ten years to recover from the attack made on it by its political masters. Now, are you going to maintain that your judgement is better than that of one of our senior generals – one of our most senior and experienced generals?'

'Judging by the performance of the General Staff in the last war, I could very well be right if I did.'

'Don't be impertinent, Mr Allan.' He paused and twirled his globe. 'Tell me, have you discussed these views of yours – these peculiar views of yours, if you will allow an older man so to describe them – with your father?'

'I have.'

'And does he agree with you?'

'No. He's of your opinion, or what I take your opinion to be.'

'I am very glad to hear it. I have a great respect for your father. He is not one of those whose words are like the crackling of thorns under a pot. I revere him. And would you set your views up against his? Shame on you, laddie. Mr Allan, you're a young man of considerable talents, but you've a lot to learn. I am very pleased to have you on my staff, you've done good work for us, and Mr Hughes values you. But don't think you can be allowed to debauch my paper with Bolshevik propaganda. I'll not have it.'

'So how was the great man?' Billy Hughes asked.

'He thinks my words are like the crackling of thorns under a pot.'

'I haven't heard that line from him for some time. Ah well, things must be as they may. There's a despatch from Freddie Beshore in Rome I'd like you to cast your eye over. We have to be careful what we say about Musso, you know.'

Our child, a girl whom we called Rose, was born on midsummer's eve. Vanessa, tired and often tiresome in the last weeks of pregnancy, said first: 'Poor little beast to come into the world we've made for it.' The birth had been difficult which can, I believe, turn a mother against the baby, but soon it was clear to me that Van's offhand manner and disparaging remarks couldn't disguise the fact that she doted on the child. We both did. I found that I wished we had been honest and acknowledged I was the father. But then, when I went down to Blankets and found my own father fretting at Alastair's absence, and trying to find excuses for his darling's indifference, I couldn't regret the deception. I wired to Alastair to come in order that he might put on a show which would ease Father's unhappiness, but all I got in return was a message of 'good wishes and love to Van' and the plea that he couldn't abandon his film project at this delicate stage. I conveyed this news to Father in what I hoped was an emollient manner.

'Well,' he said, 'men must work and women must weep, and there's an end on't.'

He was soon distracted, however, by a letter from George. Reluctantly, persuaded by Hector, myself, and more effectively by Kirstie and our mother, he had got the family trust to advance money to enable George to buy a rubber estate, though he had done so shaking his head and muttering that no good could come of it, since George had shown himself to be dishonest, and a dishonest man in the East was on a downward path that couldn't be checked.

'Kipling,' he said, 'remarked to me once that when the

198

corruption of the oriental races has entered a man's heart, there is nothing to do but cut the painter that attaches him to his fellows.'

Now George wrote to say that he had taken to himself a Malay wife, and Father sighed at this latest evidence that 'poor George' was irretrievably heading for the dogs.

'He has no principles,' he said, 'and no dignity either, and for the man that lacks such, we may prophesy a speedy voyage downward.'

Mother thought differently. She said marriage would be the making of George. More surprisingly, she remarked, tartly, that as far as she could see if the Empire to which Father was so devoted was to survive, marriage between the races was an essential.

'Some of these Malay girls are very pretty, I believe, and they probably make good wives. But that's not really the point. Since we can't keep the subject races in subjection for ever then it is better if we mix with them.'

'Surprising sentiments, Mother,' I said.

'Only to those who won't look the length of their nose,' she replied. 'In any case, people used to say that Kipling himself was of mixed blood. He certainly had a dark look. I never cared for him myself.'

I had long outgrown my youthful love of Kipling's verse, and had learned in the manner of my generation to disparage him. Ferguson, the headmaster of my private school, had been accustomed to quote him, with tedious frequency, and Father bowed his head to what he called 'Kipling's gnomic wisdom', but for years such lines as stayed in my memory struck me as either comically inapposite or repulsive. I remember at Cambridge we used, when in wine, to chant derisively, the verse about the effects – clearly to be viewed admiringly – of the Norman Conquest:

England's on the anvil – hear the hammers ring –
Clanging from the Severn to the Tyne!

Never was a blacksmith like our Norman King –
England's being hammered, hammered, hammered into
    line!

And yet, that last drawn-out summer of peace, a summer of
afternoons on the lawn drinking Pimm's, or walking with
Van up to the ridge top from where we could, in the full-
leaved glory of the trees, see only one of the towers or spires
that winter disclosed, I found that 'The Gods of the Copy-
Book Headings' – though still a risible title – spoke my
thoughts:

As it will be in the future, it was at the birth of Man –
There are only four things certain since Social Progress
    began: –
That the Dog returns to his Vomit, and the Sow returns to
    her Mire,
And the burnt Fool's bandaged finger goes wobbling back
    to the Fire.

'Chamberlain to the life,' I said.
    'Oh stop it.'
    Van got to her feet and walked away, to the low, broken-
down wall of a sheepfold. 'Why must you?'
    'Because . . .' I said, 'it keeps breaking in.'
    'I prefer to keep life in compartments. This one will do for
now. But I sometimes get the feeling that you are really
looking forward to it.'
    'No,' I said, 'it's not like that. Or not exactly. It's more
that I can't rid myself of the feeling that life's on hold till it's
over.'
    'We've a child. That's not on hold.'
    'No, of course not . . .'
    But, at the back of my mind ran other lines, which, in
Van's mood, I dared not speak:

What is a woman that you forsake her,
And the hearth-fire and the home-acre,
To go with the old grey Widow-maker?

XIV

Paris 1940

On the afternoon of 9 May 1940, there was no news for me to report. Things were as they had been through the long months of what the French called the '*drôle de guerre*'. It was a perfect Paris day and the crowds in the streets went about their business or their leisure smiling in the sunshine. A lot of the men wore straw hats, for you could persuade yourself that spring had already given way to summer. In the evening I was going to see Garbo in *Ninotchka*, and I had some hours to let slip after lunch. So I strolled to the little park at the head of the Ile de la Cité, just below the Pont Neuf and the statue of Henri Quatre, and sat in the shade of the chestnut trees watching the fishermen.

They fished with long cane poles and fine leaders and feathered floats. When I first came to Paris I had thought they looked amateurish, and compared this style of fishing with the fishing in our Scots lochs and rivers, to its disadvantage; but now that I had watched them a good many afternoons, I knew that they were skilled fishermen, most of whom rarely went home without something for supper. It was restful watching them and feeling no inclination to do anything else. The fish they caught were plump and sweet like good fresh sardines; some of the quayside restaurants served them fried whole, in olive oil. The fishermen were mostly old or middle-aged, and they were all men. I never saw a girl fishing there, and only a few young boys. Many of these fishermen were veterans, some doubtless of the terrible

202

battles at Verdun, or of the first Marne, where they had saved the Republic. Now their sons or grandsons were in the trenches, preparing to fight their battles over again.

Sometimes I talked to the fishermen about their war. A number of them were pensioners, the '*Mutilés de guerre*', who occupied a privileged position in the French imagination. Some were Communists, and if you mentioned the present war which was not yet being fought, they shrugged it away in contempt or perhaps embarrassment. On the day war was declared, they had turned their backs on it. The Soviet ambassador had recently been expelled. In a telegram to Stalin he had denounced the French and British as war-mongers.

But that, I thought, was far from being our mood. I had covered the French mobilisation, and the phrase so often repeated that stuck in my memory was '*il faut en finir*'. It was impossible to imagine less ardent soldiers. They didn't like Hitler. Most liked nothing about him. They saw he had to be stopped, and regretted only that it had fallen to them to do so. A few were bitter about the politicians whose feebleness (as they saw it) had brought things to this point when they had to throw up their jobs, abandon wives and families, and trudge north. Back home Churchill and others echoed the old cry that France had the finest army in Europe, and therefore the world; but no one who saw the mobilisation could share this confidence. When I suggested this, my article didn't appear.

Norway was already a disaster, but the sun shone on Paris, the fishermen waited for a bite, and nothing happened. At the far end of the little park a band began to play dancing, mocking music, Offenbach I thought.

Barbara and I came out of the cinema smiling.

'All the same,' she said, 'the reason they like it so much is that it allows them to forget their fears of Communism. Russians as figures of fun, that's comforting. But at lunch today a lawyer's wife said to me that if the Germans attack there will be a Communist uprising and butcheries in the streets of Paris. She has laid in a store of gasoline so that she can leave for the South at a moment's notice. What can you do with people like that?'

They were the sort of people who had been talking all winter of the need for a negotiated peace. After all, they said, we don't really have any quarrel with Germany. Even some who thought we had reason to quarrel, nevertheless favoured negotiations. The novelist, Philippe Torrance, a friend of Alastair's, said to me one day: 'We went to war to defend Poland. And now Poland's occupied. So what are we fighting for? Can anyone answer me that?'

'Do you know,' Barbara said, 'French armaments production is based on the assumption that there will be no German attack this year.'

'So I've heard. I can't believe it.'

'Doesn't matter what you believe. It's true.'

I always envied Barbara her ability to look reality in the face. But then she enjoyed doing so. It was in her nature to take the dark view of things.

'What happened to that friend of yours, Trude?' she said, changing direction.

'The last I heard from her she was planning to marry a Nazi banker.'

'I always knew she was a sensible girl. All the same, she'd have done better to accept my invitation.'

'Too late now.'

'Yes, too late.'

The sirens sounded at dawn on the 10th. Watching from my hotel window across the Place Louvois, it was like an Elizabethan theatre with tiers of spectators at every level. But, instead of looking down on the stage, their gaze was fixed on the sky. You couldn't tell if the dots of planes were French or German. Guns barked from the other side of the river. The little chambermaid I encountered in the lobby was in tears. She was a girl from the Auvergne, and she had been in Paris only a couple of months. She wept, she said, for her brother who was at the Front.

Later in the morning I met Barbara at the Dôme. At neighbouring tables people were all saying the same thing. 'Finally, it's started.' We had got the news that the Germans had crossed the frontier into Belgium, violating Belgian and very soon Dutch neutrality. A member of the National Assembly, a Breton called de Kérilles, put his hand on my shoulder.

'So,' he said, 'the waiting is at an end. Good. In a month we'll be in Berlin or the Germans will be here in Paris. This is not just a battle. It's the decisive moment of the war.'

'They won't be in Berlin,' Barbara said when he had moved on.

She spoke in English, but loudly and clear enough to attract angry glances.

She said: 'The French think we'll step in. That's Bullitt's fault. He's too committed to be a good ambassador. The truth is that Congress won't let Roosevelt move, and anyway I'm not sure he wants to.'

I tried to telephone London, first the office, then Van. It wasn't possible to make a call. We didn't have an office of our own in Paris, so I accompanied Barbara to the offices of the *Herald-Tribune*, stopping first at my hotel to see if there were any telegrams. Paris was running normally, but no telegrams had come for me, the concierge said.

Certainly it all looked normal. The old women in black dresses were doing their shopping at the markets. Children were in school. The war hadn't yet disturbed anyone.

At the *Herald-Trib* they told us there was a press conference scheduled for five p.m. at the War Office. 'Maybe,' they said.

At the Press Club there was talk of a French counteroffensive. It was strange to be in a war and yet not in it. It didn't yet feel like Madrid. It didn't feel a bit like Madrid.

The press conference was uninformative. Things were going according to plan. 'Like a straight bootlegger they are,' Barbara said. 'There's a nasty whiff already.' Then she left me, to meet some of her banned comrades. When she had gone, another American correspondent said to me: 'It does you no good to be seen with that moll, fellow.'

At the bar of the Hotel Meurice, the first person I saw was Jukes. He was talking to a fat French pansy, a Marquis of some sort, and at first I thought I could move on without him seeing me. But Jukes missed little. I heard my name called, felt his restraining grip.

'Good to see you, old sport.'

'It's disgusting,' said the pansy, who was called Patrice. 'Have you heard what the Reds are saying? I've been listening to their so-called Radio Humanité. They are stirring up the *canaille*. They tell them there is no danger from Germany, only from French capitalists. They should be taken out and put up against a wall and shot.'

'Not easy, old sport,' Jukes said. 'They're broadcasting from German territory. Neat, eh? Friend Goebbels doesn't miss a trick.'

'You mean it's propaganda?' Patrice said.

'Sure.'

'All the same, I have it on good authority that if the Boches come within twenty miles of Paris, the Reds are ready to revolt. It'll be the Commune all over again.'

'Maybe it will.' Jukes smiled. He was enjoying his friend's agitation.

'Well,' I said, 'the trains are still running south.'

These days come back to me in snatches and snapshots. Is it possible that the next day, the Saturday, which was the first of the Whitsun holiday, I should have found myself at Auteuil and winning a packet on a three-year-old filly? Was this a way, I thought even then, to start living a war? There were parachutists over Rotterdam that morning, but the jockeys' silks fluttered bravely in the sunshine. There was an atmosphere of total calm, just as the newspapers said. 'Hitler's overreached himself at last,' was the phrase one heard time and again. 'He'll soon find we are Frenchmen, not Poles or Norwegians.' Of course he had gained ground at first, but 'I have it on good authority we were not surprised. We are retiring only to leap back at him.' The number of people who had things on good authority was legion. An American journalist said to me: 'People are obsessed with March 1918. Have you noticed? But there's no Foch this time, is there?'

My job was to report from the French capital. Harbottle had emphasised that I was not a war correspondent. 'What he wants is analysis,' I said to Barbara, 'which he won't use. He's determined, you see, that all must be going well. So the only stuff I can send that he'll print are morale-boosting pieces about the calm in Paris. Calm and determination. If I write that half of them are reconciled to defeat and the other half are indifferent, it'll be spiked. I can't do any good here.'

'It's going to be a long war,' she said. 'This is just the overture.'

'I thought the *drôle de guerre* was the overture.'

'All right, it's Act I, Scene I.'

On Wednesday 15th German troops crossed the Meuse and opened a fifty-mile-wide breach in the French defences. At the Dôme I was told that General Corap's 9th Army had collapsed. Its battalions were said to be full of Communists who had thrown their arms away; some said they had gone over, en masse, to the enemy. At the Ritz I heard that Corap had shot himself; at the Crillon, that he had been arrested by order of Gamelin and was to be court-martialled. 'There's nothing now between the Boche and Paris,' was the cry.

They were burning the archives in the gardens of the Foreign Ministry on the Quai d'Orsay.

There was talk of a mutiny at Compiègne by a regiment made up of Communists from the industrial suburbs of Paris. They had seized the town and were ready to surrender it to the Germans. I applied for permission to go north, was told 'the matter was in hand'; but journalists were barred from that zone. In the evening came assurances that the mutineers had been disbanded by loyal troops.

The police were patrolling the streets with rifles. Jukes told me of a Japanese embassy attaché he had met who said it was good to be Japanese now; not even a policeman would suspect him of being a Nazi paratrooper. I had no idea that was the sort of joke the Japanese liked.

On the Saturday, 18 May, I visited the Gare du Nord to see the Belgian refugees arrive. The Red Cross had set up a soup kitchen. A nurse said to Barbara: 'You're American, yes? Then tell me who has betrayed us? Is it the Reds or the Jews?'

'You think the Jews would betray you to the Nazis?' Barbara asked.

'Oh, yes, they are not true Frenchmen, you see.'

'But the Nazis are persecuting the Jews.'

'So they say . . . nevertheless . . .' She turned away to comfort, very gently and sweetly, a crying child who had lost her mother.

The Cabinet reshuffle was announced. We heard it at the Ritz bar. Mandel became Minister of the Interior. 'Good,' said Barbara, 'that may put some stuffing into them.'

'Mandel?' said the marquis, Patrice. 'It's logical. For a Jewish war they need a Jewish Clemenceau. Nevertheless, how much better to have a French one. If we have to continue the struggle, which I doubt.'

The return of Pétain was approved.

'They say he's only deputy Prime Minister, but he's the real strong man in the Government.'

'How old is he?' Barbara asked. 'Eighty if a day, isn't he?'

'Eighty-four, but you know, still virile. His mistress is less than half his age.'

'So is Hitler,' Barbara said.

I thought: Father knew him in '18. He said he was a defeatist even then.

'Come,' said Barbara, 'let's go and see Ilya.'

I don't suppose anyone reads Ehrenburg now. The young probably don't even know his name. Actually, in this memoir I see that I have been scattering names of which the young are altogether ignorant. For them, I am recalling a world as remote as Atlantis. It can't be helped.

Ehrenburg was then the Paris correspondent of Iszvestia, the recipient of Stalin Prizes, a Jew who survived Stalin's anti-Semitism, scarcely less virulent than Hitler's. He was an active anti-Fascist, a figure of the Writers' Congresses, who, nevertheless, forced himself to swallow the Nazi-Soviet pact. Barbara had known, liked, and admired him for years.

We found him at his desk in his apartment behind the Gare de Montparnasse.

'So,' he said, 'you are still here in this Paris which has been transformed into a deep forest where all are strangers. We must have some tea. I was told today that there are 40,000 German soldiers walking round the city in disguise. People will believe anything when the props of their existence are knocked away.'

He tugged at his beard. In his brown velvet smoking jacket he looked like a literary man of the end of the last century.

He said: 'It's happening faster than I thought, this débacle. We tried to buy time but time is the tide that is going out.'

'Will you stay in Paris when the Germans come?' Barbara asked.

'Naturally,' he said, 'it will be interesting. I shall write a novel to be called *The Fall of Paris*. It's ironical. As a respected Soviet citizen I am the safest Jew in Paris.'

I resumed my diary.

May 20: An editorial observes: 'The more the Germans advance, the more they enter danger, for they are distancing themselves from their bases, while, on the contrary, the more we retreat the better our condition, approaching our own bases.'

'Swell,' said Barbara, 'let's retreat to the Pyrenees, that'll finish Hitler off.'

When I tried to send a dispatch today, the censor cut out all reference to the bombing of Le Havre.

I said: 'Does that mean it didn't happen?'

'Please,' he said, 'no jokes. It is not the time for your English sense of humour.'

Le Figaro publishes a recipe for stuffing artichoke hearts with leftovers. Ration cards are being distributed. There is already a shortage of bread.

At my hotel I found a letter from Van: cool and, as it were deliberately, uninformative. She doesn't mention Churchill, but tells me the baby has a cold. She doesn't ask about Alastair.

May 21: This morning I didn't want to get up. The sun streaked through the half-closed shutters and there was a smell of new-baked bread in the air. Lying in bed, watching the changing pattern of the ceiling, it felt like a good Paris morning. There was that sentence of Hemingway's – 'The war was always there, but we did not go to it any more.' For a little the war was not coming to us. The world was private once more. I read Van's letter again, and thought of her in bed with me.

When, after all, I got up and dressed in a light grey

summer suit and felt like a boulevardier with the war still in another time, I left the hotel and strolled through narrow streets to the river, and it was peaceful. I bought a paper and went to a little Breton restaurant and ate lamb from the salt marshes and drank a half-litre of red.

But in the streets the people looked different. The bones of their faces were sharper. It wasn't hunger. That, I suppose, will come later. It was anxiety.

At the Senate, Reynaud was to speak in the afternoon.

He spoke well, with energy. But the energy was not transmitted. It was as if he threw his words into the empty air. He admitted mistakes had been made, they had overestimated the extent to which the Meuse would prove a barrier, they had failed to blow up its bridges ahead of the Panzers, they had had to reply on 'sparse divisions badly led, badly trained, and badly supported.' But now things were being put right. That was why he had recalled Weygand, Foch's lieutenant, to the command.

Too late, some muttered. Too old, said others.

'France cannot die.' Reynaud extended his arms, a gesture that made him look like a pouter pigeon. 'And if one day I was to be told that only a miracle could save France, then I would at once say: "Very well, Gentlemen, I believe in that miracle, because I believe in France." '

But the French do not believe in miracles. Talk of miracles cast a depression over the Chamber, which, after all, is full of anti-clericals who have outlawed miracles.

Nevertheless, the dispatch I wrote and telegraphed to the paper was optimistic. I praised Reynaud's 'indomitable fighting-spirit'. It's what Harbottle wants to hear. And there is something splendid about the little man. He represents everything that is good and fine about the individuality of provincial France.

Only, when I compare this essentially civilian and civic figure with the gangsters to whom he has opposed himself, I feel despondent. There's this, in contrast, to be said for

Churchill: he's a sort of gangster himself. Yet gangster isn't exactly the word. He's a seventeenth-century figure, you can imagine him as a Cavalier general. Of course the Cavaliers lost.

May 22: Some of my colleagues – Sye Barnton, for instance – are packing in readiness to return to London. That's where the story will be coming from very soon. But I hesitate. There's a fascination in this Paris that is so tranquil and beautiful on the surface; what nerves are trembling underneath?

I went this morning to the church of St Etienne-du-Mont, behind the Pantheon. It's late Gothic, very fine. I'd never entered it before. But I went because they are starting there a four-day cycle of prayer. Parisians who haven't, by the look of them, prayed in years – except perhaps for a win on the tierce or for a new spring outfit – filled the church. It's been chosen because it houses the tomb of St Genevieve, whose prayers caused Attila and his Huns to turn away from Paris.

'It'll take more than prayers to a dead woman who may never have existed to get Hitler to turn away,' Barbara said. She thought I was crazy when I said I had been moved by the service. The priest urged the congregation not to blame their leaders, but to give them full confidence. A difficult demand, though I do trust Reynaud. That's to say, I trust his intentions.

A press release: 'Despite present business conditions M. Mitty Goldin, director of the ABC Music hall, thinks it his duty, for performers and staff, regardless of reduced and even negative receipts, to continue performances with the entire cast. From Friday, at both matinées and evening performances, there will be a new comedy show featuring French songs, both patriotic and sentimental, and some of the most celebrated stars of the cabarets, who represent the indomitable spirit of France and our beloved Paris.'

So that's all right.

Weygand was back in Paris this morning. He arrived straight from the front and marched into Reynaud's office without having taken time to wash or shave. He is reported as being full of optimism and élan. The official line is that 'his entire being gives off energy and decision'. He plans the counter-attack – to involve the BEF which, of course, he doesn't command. But, if the battle is truly lost, then our aim must be to secure the Channel ports, so that we may evacuate our army.

Remembering what Barbara said about Pétain's age compared to Hitler, I can't forget that Weygand himself is over seventy. When Napoleon destroyed the Austrians at Austerlitz and the Prussians at Jena the next year, it was the other way round. Nap was just thirty-six and the Austrian and Prussian commanders were more than twice his age. Hitler is fifteen years younger than Churchill too.

When people talk of Weygand, they are really pretending he is Foch: 'My centre is giving way, my right is in retreat; situation excellent; I shall attack.'

If only it was as simple as that. Foch had something to attack with, and the German army had exhausted itself.

Refrain of French journalists: 'Why are you English holding back your planes?'

You can't give the honest answer: 'Because we don't believe in the French will to fight.'

Waiting for Barbara in the Ritz bar this evening, I heard my name called. The voice, a fluting alto, brought with it intimations of summer at Blankets, of lazy afternoons in the shade of the elms. For a moment I did not recognise the speaker. Then I saw it was Robin Maltravers disguised as a captain in an unidentifiable regiment.

'My dear,' he said.

He wore the uniform, wasp-waisted, in a manner that suggested he had a supporting role in a Viennese operetta.

'What are you doing here, Robin?' I said. 'I must say one does see the most surprising people in uniform.'

'Well, I never could resist, could I?'

'I suppose not.'

'So, of course, the moment the old country was in danger, I answered the Call. "I 'listed at home for a lancer – oh, who would not sleep with the brave?" Not that I have seen much sign of bravery, my dear. I'm on our former King's tiny staff, and I have to say that HRH is in the most shaming flap. The Duchess has gone south, and the only thought in that inadequately stocked mind is how and how soon he can join her. Really, it's contemptible, the little man might as well be French. So I doubt if I shall stay with him much longer. I'm pulling every little string I can lay my delicately-manicured hand on to get transferred. The Lancers would do very well, I've always found Guards officers so stuffy and bogus. How they come to command such charming young men I shall never understand.'

Curiously, his attitude didn't surprise me. I don't know why I write 'curiously'. There's nothing curious about it. Robin's particularly open flamboyance has always required a deal of courage to carry it off. He'll probably end the war with a DSO.

'I saw your little brother the other day,' he said.

'I didn't know he was in Paris.'

'Oh yes, he's quite a pet of HRH, and of some of his seedy and disreputable millionaire chums.'

'Disreputable, Robin? I'm surprised to hear you use the word.'

'It's the war, ducky. It's made me ever so old school. I catch myself sounding just like my Ma.'

I tried to find out from him where Alastair was lodging. But he was vague. Unlike him.

Thursday, May 23: Calm, beautiful and sunny Paris – an

214

afternoon on which the young Marcel might have watched Gilberte playing shuttlecock in the Champs-Elysées. It was strange to see workmen repairing the pedestal of one of the statues on the Pont du Louvre. Perhaps the Fifth Column are smartening the city to welcome Hitler.

The absence of hard news is agonising – but it looks as if we are retreating to secure the Channel ports. If so, the War Office has concluded that the Battle of France is lost.

In the evening, Barbara and I went to see Ehrenburg again. He had telephoned Barbara asking her to call on him. He looked doubtful when he saw me, then made a vague gesture with the hand, to suggest he was sweeping reservations aside. First he told us he has been having trouble with the police. There is a danger he may be expelled. On the other hand, this afternoon he was summoned to the office of Anatole de Monzie, the Public Works Minister.

'Monzie's an old friend, acquaintance anyway. To tell you the truth, I have never been certain of his political position. That didn't alter the fact that the summons aroused my keen interest. He was sitting behind his desk smoking his pipe. If the intention was to impress on me his calm, well it failed. He was decidedly agitated. And no wonder. He didn't waste any time. "Listen," he said, "the situation is critical. That's why I've been empowered to speak to you. The Government is divided. Pétain and Baudouin and others want to surrender. Reynaud refuses. So, of course, does Mandel. But we have very few tanks and even fewer planes." Then he paused. I asked him why the Government continued to persecute good French Communists. Wasn't it folly to anger the working class on whom any effective resistance depended? He couldn't deny that, but he obviously regarded it as a diversion. Then he came to the point. France was prepared to restore

215

diplomatic relations with the Soviet Union if it got planes in return.'

'They really are desperate then,' Barbara said.

'This is in confidence, you understand,' Ehrenburg said. 'I went straight to our embassy, and after consultation with Ivanov, who's the chargé d'affaires, drafted a telegram myself. It will go direct to Stalin.'

'Why do you think he told us that?' I asked Barbara as we turned away into the soft night. 'Covering himself in some way?'

'Warning us that France is beaten. Stalin won't send planes. How can he?'

'But is it in the Soviet Union's interest that France should lose the war?'

'It could be. Depends on the form of the Peace.'

May 24: I cabled the paper last night saying there was nothing useful I could do here now, and suggesting I be recalled to London. It made me feel shabby to do that. Yet it was true. The radio speaks of heavy attacks for the Amiens salient, but we don't know the outcome. The franc has moved up against the dollar. God knows why. It's impossible to believe that the Germans may be here next week. And yet we know they may. I had lunch at the Racing Club in the deep peace of the Bois de Boulogne. There, it still seems like the *drôle de guerre*. Back for a press conference at the War Ministry, full of lies and evasions which nobody cared to question. Should I have asked difficult questions? Yes, of course.

At my hotel I found a note from Alastair's friend, the novelist, Torrance, suggesting dinner. It was urgent that he spoke to me. I couldn't think why. All I know of Torrance is that he was one of the writers whom Alastair had engaged to work on the script of his film about the three veterans of the other war – a film that can't, surely, be made now. Or has it been made? I don't even know that.

All the same I'll go. Of course I will.

The diary peters out there. As a matter of fact I left it in my Paris hotel, and one evening in 1946 when I stopped there for a night en route to . . . I can't now remember where . . . the hall porter presented me with it, as though it was something of great value; he had found it and kept it for me, and now waited for thanks and, of course, a tip. Which I gave him, in dollars, it being a time when the Treasury forbade us to take more than a very small quantity of sterling out of the country – a fact which will seem inconceivable to the young who cherish the illusion that money is theirs absolutely, and have not yet learned the great truth of modern life: that it is merely hired them by the State.

But I do recall something, snatches like distant music, of that dinner with Torrance. Again, the name will mean nothing to anyone under the age of fifty or perhaps sixty. Torrance's vogue was brief. Young enthusiasts for the cinema may have seen the film of his novel, *A l'ombre du futur*, which those who know about such matters declare one of the masterpieces of French cinema in the years before the '*nouvelle vague*' broke – limply, I've always thought – on the shore. It had a certain charm, which is more than can be said for its *auteur*. And yet, though I couldn't like him, and indeed found something reptilianly repulsive in his manner, it is perhaps fair to say that the unquestionable charm of this little story of the love between – I'm sorry, the doomed love between – the wife of a Vichy official and the idealistic schoolmaster–novelist represents the best of its author; I am not speaking as literary critic, for I have read little of his work, but rather I mean that whatever there was that was good and noble and generous in Torrance was present in the film. Of course its success was principally the result of its profound self-pity, but that may be said of most works of literature that achieve popularity. Isn't self-pity the reason we are drawn to Hamlet or Anna Karenina? Not to mention Scarlett O'Hara.

But the impression Torrance made on me that day was disagreeable. He was in a funk.

His funk held him from approaching the reason why he had wanted to see me. Instead he talked of literature, or rather of himself in literature. It did not seem the moment for that. I asked him about the film that I supposed he had been writing for Alastair or helping him to write.

'It's impossible,' he said, 'this war has made it impossible. This foolish war.'

I told him I had been surprised to hear of his association with Alastair.

'I've read some of your pieces,' I said, 'and thought you were on the Left.'

'The Left is impossible,' he said. 'It is impossible for an intelligent man to remain there. War is folly, and the Left has encouraged it.'

'Do you have a message for me from my brother?'

'Why should you think that?'

He crammed his beefsteak into his mouth, and then took a piece of bread and mopped up the gravy juices. He had declined wine, being, I guessed, one of those egotists who fears its relaxing effect. Then he launched himself into complaint. The world had treated him badly, my brother in particular. He had put aside important work to write this script, and now he was cast aside. It wasn't fair. Moreover, Alastair owed him money. Moreover, Alastair had taken the girl, Yvette, from Torrance. 'She was my discovery,' he told me, repeatedly. It seemed that he was expecting me to recompense him. He traced a political parallel between Alastair's abandonment of him, and the retreat of the British army to the Channel ports. 'The truth is, you are not Europeans,' he said, several times, 'and it was folly to have trusted you.'

I merely replied that individuals must expect to be

218

damaged when the world cracked. He didn't like that. It was quite wrong that the breaking of the world should hurt him.

Our encounter was disagreeable, boring, barren. That isn't why I recall it now. It is because the sour whiff of resentment and self-pity which he emitted carries with it, over the years, the quintessence of Vichy, though in fact Torrance would, I learned later, disengage himself in good time from Vichy too, and re-emerge as a veritable hero of the Resistance. The long best-selling novel he was to write about the Resistance – a candidate for the Prix Goncourt in 1948 or '9 – couldn't, when I read it, efface the memory of that dinner and his self-pity like a nasty smell. I read in him, even then, the corruption of the French spirit. During the war years, whenever I thought of Pétain's National Revolution, I thought of Torrance.

Finding Torrance disgusting, I thought less of Alastair. That was ungenerous, and it did not occur to me that the Torrance who presented himself to my brother, at whose hands he hoped for benefits, would have appeared very differently from the tiresome complainant who had forced himself on me. It is possible, indeed, that he might have caught something of Alastair's gaiety, and something of my low spirits. We judge people as we find them, and that is natural, there is nothing else we can do; yet in making that judgement we should, if we were wise, strive to remember that we are judging only one aspect of a person, that which he chooses, not necessarily consciously, to display in our presence or in other episodes of his life of which we may learn. Furthermore, such knowledge as we have is partial and dependent on what is transitory. It cannot take account of how the person under consideration thinks of himself; and even those with little self-knowledge must have more knowledge of themselves than others can.

In his own view Alastair, I'm certain, was indeed the daring figure that he presented to the world, or thought he presented. But weren't there moments when he questioned his capacity? Weren't there moments when he felt insignificant? Van used to deny the existence of such doubts in him, but then Van saw people so clearly that she could never take account of any complexity.

XV
London 1940

'I still think it odd that you didn't try harder to see him.'

'But it was odd in every way, there.'

Sunlight, flooding across Park Lane, lay golden on Hertford Street. It was a Sunday afternoon. The peal of church bells drowned the throb of aeroplane engines. Rose slept in the Art Nouveau bassinet, a gift from Van's mother. Now Van passed me a cup of Fortnum's Lapsang and said again: 'Of course, I know now I've never understood him, but I thought that was because he was still a schoolboy, and so unfathomable. But now I find that I don't understand you either, and you're not a schoolboy.'

'Well,' I said, 'there it is. Somehow we didn't see each other, and I don't know where he is now.'

I was thinking I should like to attend Evensong. That wasn't or wouldn't be to Van's taste. So I didn't mention it. But the words of the *Nunc Dimittis* ran through my mind, and evening chapel at school in summer with the west window burning, and streaks of rich gold and purple dancing on Colin's hair. Colin was missing, believed killed, at St Valéry.

It was on my second night back from France that Van told me she had slept with Jukes. It wasn't a confession or apology; just a statement. He had called to see her, to give news of me, she said, and they had had dinner, and then . . . it seemed natural.

Didn't it worry her that he had been her mother's lover? That she herself had pronounced him 'horrible'?

Not at all. She wouldn't say it added zest; it just made no difference.

'He's quite an attractive man, you know.'

'He's a skunk.'

'Doesn't stop him from being attractive to women. Besides, I didn't know if I'd ever see you again. You were very thick with some girl in Paris, it seems.'

'Is that what he told you? The girl was Barbara. I've spoken to you about her. I might as well be jealous of . . . oh, say, Max as you of Barbara.'

'You're naive, Alec, do you know that? There's more reasons than bed for jealousy. Not that I was jealous. I didn't care if you were having it off with her or not. I just felt like going to bed with Jukes.'

'Once, or more than once?'

'Once, so far. You don't own me, Alec. We're not even married. You chose that we shouldn't be, remember?'

It was surprising to find no one staying at Blankets. I had not realised how completely Father was out of things. He sat on the lawn, a rug round his knees to guard against evening chills, and a volume of Horace on his lap. The book lying on the table beside him was Dorothy Sayers' *Busman's Honeymoon*, and it seemed likely that he had been giving it more attention than the Horace. And why not?

He held out his hand. I grasped icy bones, and laid my hand a moment on his shoulder.

'I've been fancying I could hear the guns,' he said, 'but there are no guns, are there?'

He was silent throughout dinner. Mother kept the conversational ball rolling with news of county neighbours, and local chit-chat. Family matters were not raised. Even Kirstie's loss passed unmentioned. I wasn't asked about Van or Rose; nor about my time in Paris. Father ate little of the fish, and less of the gigot of lamb; but he drank perhaps half a bottle of claret. When Mother left us, she said: 'Don't be long, he tires easily.'

'She thinks I'm failing,' he said. 'Perhaps I am, like civilisation. Two wars in a generation, no wonder the French collapsed. Have you heard aught of Alastair?'

The out-moded Wardour Street phrasing seemed to distance him from what he feared might be.

'No,' I said, crossing my fingers under the table.

He sipped whisky and soda. His cigar went out. He had difficulty in relighting it.

'Tell him he should come home. Tell him everything's different and he should come home.'

What did he mean that everything was different? It could of course be taken as the vain wanderings of age, which indeed does find, as I have now discovered, everything standing at an odd angle to experience. But I think his meaning was more exact.

He didn't want to know what Alastair was doing, because he suspected he knew the answer. But he was harking back to old heroes of his – Jacobites who had served in foreign armies, who had fought for France at Blenheim and Fontenoy, and been able to do so with honour; but there was no possibility of honour in doing something of that sort in a war in which nation was ranged against nation, not king against king or pretender.

Then he said: 'I wrote to Winston, you know, offering my services, in any role. I suppose I must call his reply generous, but he held out no encouragement. He said it was time for my sons to carry the baton. My sons – not one of you in uniform – I except you, Alec, for reporting's war work of a sort, but . . . Hector a degenerate, George a common thief, and Alastair – where is the boy and what is he doing?'

'Perhaps,' I said – and God forgive me the *suggestio falsi* of my words – 'he has good reason for not being able to send you any information as to his activities.'

*

Mother was not dismayed by the absence of guests. She had never, I thought, taken much interest in them. She accepted that public life demanded their presence, and that it was proper that Father should be engaged in affairs of state, but she couldn't, herself, take them with great seriousness. She was happier talking with Haskins about the vegetable garden or greenfly on the roses, and with Mrs Haskins about the affairs of the village, than with politicians or dons. And she was, perhaps, happiest on her own, and not required to talk at all.

Now, sitting upright as she had been taught to sit, she drew on her cigarette, and said: 'Tell me the worst.'

I pretended not to understand her, but she brushed that aside.

'What is he up to?'

'If I knew for certain I would tell you.'

'Your father daren't ask. Old age has made him a coward. I was afraid it would. It's made me bold. In the end I would rather be wounded than fobbed off. Do you see that?'

'Yes,' I said, 'it's the revenge we take on our parents, to keep things from them as things were kept from us as children. But, truly, I know nothing. All I can say is Alastair is in with what you would call the wrong set.'

'We've been privileged,' she said. 'We've lived easy. I've always known that. But I've accepted it, willingly – I wouldn't have liked to live otherwise – because, fundamentally, I have always accepted that in times of danger and hardship we would place ourselves in the front line. As my brothers did. As Colin has done.'

Yes, I thought; but perhaps it is not so simple. Perhaps your generation was fortunate to be granted the belief that it was simple, that patriotism was once as clear and certain as a winter frost. But it isn't like that now. It's more like Tudor times, like the reign of Elizabeth and Mary Stuart. We live in a world where the frontiers are ideological, and in which patriotism means different things to different people. And whatever he does, I don't question that Alastair is, according to his understanding, a patriot. So don't let's pretend that this is 1914, Mother.

But I said none of that. I merely repeated, coward-fashion, that, truly, I knew nothing; and then asked her what Kirstie's plans were.

'Do you think she can make plans?' she said.

The sun shone and they laid barbed wire along the beaches. The Third French Republic ceased to exist. Pétain was installed as France's Hindenburg: a vain, proud old man, verging on being what Scots call dottled, but with, nevertheless, a peasant thrawnness.

One day Harbottle said: 'I don't trust Winston. Everyone can see how he loves power, and war.' Harbottle, I realised, would welcome a compromise peace. At heart he was still a Chamberlainite, and regretted that Halifax had not become Prime Minister when his hero was forced out.

I made moves to accelerate my call-up, to Van's displeasure.

She continued to see Jukes, even while admitting that my judgement of him might be right.

'Can't help it,' she said, 'sorry.'

When I repeated, for what must have been the forty-second time, my analysis of his despicable character, she threw a gin bottle at my head, cutting me just above the left eye as I turned away. Meanwhile the wireless told us of a great air battle over the Channel. Fifty-three enemy planes shot down. We paused in our quarrel, kissed, held each other close, and her tongue licked the blood that ran down my cheek.

It was like that: storm, reconciliation, obstinate refusal to deny Jukes her bed.

Barbara arrived in London, by way of Portugal. She spoke of the long trail of French refugees returning north now that the fighting had stopped; of Vichy's lust for revenge on those accused of demoralising France – Jews and schoolteachers, she said; of rich English in Lisbon which was full of Nazi agents; of how, back in Paris, the shopkeepers were doing well out of the occupation army.

'It's almost amusing,' she said, 'one day a Frenchwoman protested at the law which forbids her to buy more than one pair of silk stockings while at the same moment in the shop a German officer was buying a dozen pairs to send home to his wife. So he turned to her and shut her up: French legs, he said, had been dressed in silk while German ones had had to make do with cotton. So it was now, as a matter of philosophical principle, justice, and moral evolution, the turn of German ladies to wear silk. You don't often see a smart Frenchwoman silenced, but that did it. So, where's it happening here?'

We went to the Café Royal, then in its guttering candlelight of fame, where I could be sure there would be people we knew whose presence would delay the news about Alastair, which I sensed Barbara had and was half-reluctant, half-eager to impart.

Alfred Moss was there, with Max and Guy Holland and a lean, dark American I did not know. Aware of Barbara's dislike of Guy, I would have passed them with a casual greeting, but she settled herself at the table without a word, taking the American briefly by the hand and nodding at Alfred in a manner that showed they were old acquaintances.

Max was in the uniform of an aircraftsman. He looked like a schoolboy in the Cadet Force.

'I'm on a pass,' he said.

He was stationed at an aerodrome in Essex. It was further out on the Central Line than he had known the tube extended. If the trains weren't running, the bus service wasn't too bad.

'I'm enjoying it,' he said. 'It's a surprise. And the boys are

226

so sweet. It's nice for an old whore like me to feel part of things.'

'Come off it, Max.'

He spoke with awed enthusiasm of the heroism of the young pilots.

'I'm in love with them, collectively,' he said. '*Amour fou*, I tell you – just what you used to talk about when you were writing that Stendhal thing. Did you finish it? No? Pity.' Love was in the very atmosphere of the station, he said. They had such an uncertain grasp on life. Even the ground staff felt that. Any drome was after all a prime target for the bombers. So there was a mood of gathering rosebuds. 'And some of them are very sweet.' All the same it had been embarrassing when Edwin Pringle had descended on the station in a Rolls-Bentley overflowing with flowers and hampers from Fortnum's, and insisted on taking Max out when he came off duty. 'He'd discovered when that was too, so I really couldn't say no, could I? All the same the CO has been eyeing me a bit askance ever since.'

'Probably fancies you himself.'

'Not so, I think. But my staff sergeant has been ever so sweet about it.'

The Café was filling up. Perhaps half the men were in uniform. So early in the war, liquor was not yet in short supply. Several tables had ice buckets of champagne beside them. The mood was cheerful. People had not yet acquired that tired, careworn, 'Britain-can-take-it' expression that I associate with the war years. At the next table was a group of Frenchmen. They had come to join de Gaulle, of whom, it was apparent, few of them had ever heard before his famous broadcast of June 18. Now they toasted 'Moi, Général de Gaulle' not without a suggestion of irony.

Guy called for another bottle, and a large brandy for himself.

'Yes,' he said, 'I'm in a funk. I can't sleep at night unless I'm at least half-cut. Then I don't mind if a bomb takes me.

I've failed my medical, you know. Perhaps I should have gone into the Foreign Office. Then I could be safe in Bucharest like Hector.'

'I don't think Bucharest's going to be safe for long,' I said.

Alfred Moss had embarked on one of his Jewish stories. The lean, dark American looked embarrassed. I wondered if he was Jewish himself.

Guy said: 'Timmy left me, you know. You remember Timmy, in Madrid? He's gone back to the States. There was some talk that I should go too, but then, I thought, no. I said to myself: you're not a Left-Wing poet who's been calling for an anti-Fascist Front. There's no cause for you to skedaddle, sweetie. I hear you saw Robin in Paris, and that he's a hero now.'

This waspishness was new.

'I quite agree, dear, I have become the most frightful old bitch,' he said.

Barbara interrupted Alfred Moss.

'Do you think it's quite the time to be telling that sort of story?' she said.

Alfred spread his hands, playing the caricature of the Jewish pedlar.

'Vy not?' he said. 'Vot's new? Hitler? Always ve Jews have been persecuted . . . so vot can ve do but laugh?'

'I should have thought it was a time for solidarity,' Barbara said.

'You mean' – Alfred resumed his normal English voice, the voice which reminded you that it had been his grandfather who came to London from the ghettoes of Central Europe to set up as a merchant in the City of London, with a success to which his son's Surrey estate, knighthood, membership of the House of Commons and friendship with Edward VII bore witness – 'you mean,' Alfred said, 'that we despised Jews should conceal our Jewishness and pretend that we are Gentiles – for self-

228

protection? That we should do this in England? Miss Jakobsen, you surprise me.'

'That's not what I meant at all,' Barbara said. 'You know quite well that's not what I mean. But it's in poor taste now to tell that sort of Jewish story. That's all.'

'And what sort of Jewish story should I tell, dear lady?'

Edwin Pringle, cigar in mouth, bow-tied, striped-suited, pink carnation in buttonhole, had approached our table during this exchange. He squeezed Max's shoulder.

'What a becoming uniform. But it's Alec I was seeking. Your presence, dear boy, is an unlooked-for bonus. But I must have a word with Alec first. D'you mind? It's private.'

We moved to one of the few unoccupied tables, in the window, shielded by the net screens from Regent Street where the sun still lay warmly on the stonework.

'They told me you might be here. I'm so glad to have found you.'

We settled ourselves. Pringle beckoned to a waiter and ordered whiskies and soda. For a moment he said nothing, but looked round the room; his gaze settled momentarily on Max, who was now laughing at Alfred's dogged conclusion of his story, which, probably, Max had heard more than once already.

Pringle puffed at his cigar. Then, when our drinks had been brought, he said: 'I'm a great admirer of your father. I think you know that. It's why I've sought you out. Trouble. There's going to be a question in the House about your brother.'

'Alastair? What do you mean?'

'Essentially the question is seeking information about those of His Majesty's subjects in occupied or unoccupied France, but there's a sting in the tail, specifically mentioning your brother, and asking whether there is anything known about the possibility that he may broadcast on French radio. Have you heard of that?'

'I've had no contact with Alastair for weeks.'

229

'Has the news reached your paper?'

'Not as far as I know. But I'm not encouraged to go there often.'

'Well, you'll appreciate there's nothing I can do to prevent the question being asked, but I think you should warn your father. Whether the broadcast happens or not, the mere fact of the question's going to arouse a lot of interest – on account of him. Bloody young fool, your brother, I'm afraid. The FO aren't too happy, as you may imagine.'

'It's good of you to have told me. He's an idealist, you know.'

'Yes. They cause a lot of trouble, idealists. Now I must have a word with young Max before he's whisked back to his unit. Pretty game of him, isn't it – he could have sloped off to the States easily enough.'

Some years after the war, during Maxwell-Fyfe's regime at the Home Office, when Guy was arrested and charged, along with two others, one a journalist whom I knew, with having had sexual relations – committed gross indecency, whatever the exact term was – with two young national servicemen, who had admitted the 'offences' and were to act as witnesses for the Crown, he told me that when the police arrived at his flat, and he knew from their expressions that this was not another questioning session, but that they had a warrant for his arrest, he felt a wave of relief flooding over him. It was, he said, the moment that he had expected and feared since he first knew his own nature. He almost welcomed it. 'I don't know why,' he said, 'it was just, I suppose, that it was the right shape, I mean dramatically.' He told me this a couple of years after his release when we met, by chance, in Rome. We were sitting over Negronis outside a bar on the corner of the Campo di Fiori. It was early evening and still warm. The smell of melons and peaches from the morning market lingered. Guy's Italian boyfriend had gone off on some errand, a little breeze puffing out his thin cotton shirt. Guy drew on his Toscano cigar and the smoke drifted up into the soft golden light tinged with grey at the edges, and he said: 'I often thought you must have felt like that when you heard that first broadcast of Alastair's.'

'I never actually heard it, but, yes, by and large, the feeling was the same.'

'The worst news is good news in a curious sense. It's such a relief that it's actually there. I knew you'd understand.'

'Yes,' I said. 'It killed my father though.'

Before catching an evening train to Oxford, I went to the Commons to hear Questions. The press gallery was only half filled. Van had wanted to come too, but I had dissuaded her. 'It would only draw still more attention. We'll meet after,' I'd argued.

'I could shoot him, I really could,' she said.

Some of my colleagues eyed me disapprovingly, as if whatever guilt Alastair had incurred, stuck burr-like to me also. Jukes was there. He said: 'What was it Dr Johnson called patriotism?'

'The last refuge of a scoundrel.'

'That's right.'

The question was being put by a Tory MP, Sir Frank Loochy, himself suspected a few years back of a flirtation with Mosley. Certainly he had been close to him in the days of the New Party. Now he was trying to distance himself from that past. That was my first impression. Loochy was greeted with catcalls from some Labour backbenchers. He had never been a popular member. The question was answered with elegant circumlocution by Rab Butler, then under-secretary for Foreign Affairs, and, since the Foreign Secretary, Halifax, was in the Lords, the chief FO spokesman in the Commons. He was already a master of saying nothing at some length. His reply cast a misty doubt over events. He made it sound as if whatever Alastair might or might not be doing, His Majesty's Government, though not apprised of the situation, accepted that its motivation might well be, on the available evidence, both honourable and patriotic, even though it could not receive official approval. He didn't, of course, use those words. Indeed you could have analysed his reply and reached a different conclusion as to its meaning. The intention was obfuscation. Butler was committing nobody to anything. All the same Jukes dug me in the ribs and said: 'So, appeasement's still in the race. That's not going to please Winston. He's no time for Butler anyway, you know.'

Edwin Pringle, a close friend of Butler's PPS, Chips Channon, had arranged for me to see the Minister in his room after Questions. Pringle collected me at the bottom of the staircase leading to the press gallery.

'That didn't go off as badly as I'd feared,' he said.

'You didn't tell me it was Loochy who had put down the question.'

Pringle took me by the arm to guide me through the corridors.

'That was odd,' I said, 'wasn't it?'

'What?'

'That you didn't tell me.'

'You didn't ask.'

'No, I assumed it was a Labour man. I don't know why. But it puts a different perspective on things.'

Chips was waiting in Butler's room, a cocktail shaker in his hand.

'I thought Rab handled that very nicely,' he said. 'He's a great respect for your father, you know. So have I, of course. You will give him my love, won't you? He's always been charming to me, and when I was young he was very sweet about a novel I wrote. Did you know I set out to be the English Proust? Another dead ambition. I hope you like this, it's my own invention, I call it 'The Bishop's Kiss', and I've laced it with the tiniest dash of Benzedrine.'

Edwin said: 'Wonderful, Chips.'

The cocktail was actually rather nasty: too sweet, but welcomely strong.

'Did you hear Maggie Greville's crack about Mrs Keppel?' Chips said. 'Circe Londonderry told me it. Maggie said: "To hear Alice talk about her escape from France, you would think she had swum the Channel with her maid between her teeth." Delightful. Maggie can be a venomous old toad, but she has a turn of phrase you can't help enjoying. Rab's always late, I'm afraid. He's really very strange, you know. Just the other day, he had an appointment for lunch with the Egyptian Ambassador, and insisted on travelling by bus, even though he was late already. And it's not as if he's a poor man. I'm talking too much. I think the House is already getting tired of Winston, what do you think, Edwin?'

'I was talking with L.G.,' Pringle said. 'He's never liked me of course, so he took pleasure in suggesting that I shouldn't have changed horses, as he put it. He says that after Winston's first great blunder – which, I quote, "from my long and deep knowledge of him will not be long delayed" – the country will turn against him and remember Gallipoli. Poor little Neville's not well, I hear.'

'Poor Neville. Some day people will appreciate his heroic efforts for peace. That was a charming boy you were with the other night, Edwin.'

'Max?' Pringle said. 'I've Alec here to thank for him.'

'Really?'

Channon cocked an eyebrow.

'Really?' he said again, and, extending the shaker, refilled my glass.

At that moment Butler appeared, entering the room as if it wasn't his, and we might question his right to be there. Introductions were made, regards for my father expressed, enquiries about his health. I thanked him for what he had said, or rather the tone of his answer. He was apologetic, evasive.

'Do we know how Loochy came to put the question?' I said.

'He's rather a loose cannon,' Butler said.

Then he began to question me about Alastair. I was at once aware of a penetrating and sceptical intellect, which his soft appearance and hesitant manner seemed intended to disguise.

'Of course, we're all patriots,' he said, 'but that doesn't help much, I'm afraid. You were in Paris before the invasion, I believe.'

'Yes.'

'It must have been difficult. It's a mistake to pretend we can understand the French. England's so different. Does your brother know that?'

I tried to find out if they knew exactly what Alastair was supposed to have said, or to be going to say, for there seemed to be some doubt − wasn't there? − as to whether the broadcast had actually taken place.

'What you might expect,' Butler said, holding his withered hand in front of his belly, as if to show me that he was not a man of war. 'The Red menace to European civilisation, the need for a negotiated peace, that sort of thing, I imagine. Awkward of course, don't you think, when "Grand Politics" come up against morality? Or do you think morality can have no place in the scheme of things? I'm sure you don't. We're doing splendidly now of course, but *c'est magnifique, mais ce n'est pas la politique*, eh Chips − that's your line, isn't it? Your father will be alarmed and distressed. I wish that could be avoided. I'll do what I can, tell him. But I don't expect to be here much longer. Of course, the job I would really like is as the last Viceroy. But that's not probable, I'm afraid. Whatever happens, nothing will be the same after the war, will it? You understand that, I think. I've read and admired your articles, you know.'

I have condensed into one speech the gist of a conversation that rambled over some three-quarters of an hour. Butler

234

was – it was clear even then – a considerable figure. The naivety of some of his conversation was calculated. Without my realising it, he extracted from me all that I knew about Alastair, and led me to voice fears and suspicions that I would have preferred not to speak about. I sensed a certain sympathy for Alastair's position, if not for what he was doing.

'Of course,' he said, as we parted, 'we must never forget we're a sea power, the island race. We've never achieved anything on the Continent without allies. Your father makes that point in his biography of Castlereagh, I remember.'

I strolled across St James's Park to meet Van at the Ritz. I thought of my walk there, years ago, with Hector, and of his fears. He was well out of things at present. A nanny with two small children was feeding the ducks. She wore a black straw hat, like a French abbé; the children laughed as ducks squabbled over the pieces of bread that were tossed to them. They were nice-looking children. Would they grow up under Fascism? And when would the ducks be taken for food? The soft English evening made my questions feel foolish. And yet, only the other day, meeting Eric Blair (as I then thought of Orwell) at the BBC, he had told me, eyebrows beetling and that thin voice trembling with, I supposed, contempt, rather than rage, of how the English Left intelligentsia – the pansy-Left in his terms – were now completely defeatist, looked on the war situation as hopeless and were almost eager to surrender and lick Hitler's arse.

'Well,' he said, 'you were in Spain, Allan, so you can't be surprised. All the bawlings about the need for a Popular Front, and now, when the real show begins, they behave like French politicians.'

The Palm Court was animated. It held several acquaintances, none, fortunately, known sufficiently well for it to be discourteous of me to offer only a nod of recognition. I found a table at the end of the room, under the bronze nymph whose nakedness was respectably devoid of any erotic suggestion. Van was of course late. Like many egoists she was habitually unpunctual, a trait of character expressing not only her impatience, but a need to be the central figure in whatever might have been arranged. Only a few months previously, I had found this more touching than irritating. It seemed an expression of her vulnerability.

Chips's cocktails had been disagreeably strong and cloying. I ordered a pot of Darjeeling. I knew it was my duty not to miss the early evening Oxford train. I mustn't arrive late at Blankets. All the same I was, on this occasion, not sorry that Van hadn't yet arrived. A period of solitude was agreeable. Two progressive novelists were entertaining a blonde girl at a nearby table. She was very pretty and her little-girl voice floated over the general murmur of conversation. She was clearly in a state of sexual excitement; as if she was offering a challenge. She was, I feared, wasting her time, dissipating her energies; these two mild products of the English public school system were no more interested in her than in the bronze nymph herself. It seemed strange that she shouldn't have realised that. Van would have known it straight away and made them feel her scorn.

She arrived, eclipsing the little blonde, and settled herself without apology for being late. I poured her a cup of tea. She radiated discontent, but said nothing. When I began to tell her about the Commons and my meeting with Butler, the line of her jaw tightened. It was impossible to believe that our lips had met in eager kisses. An immense weariness assailed me.

'You don't seem very interested,' I said.

'Why should I be? I've written him off.'

'But you wanted to come to the House.'

'You prevented that, didn't you? It's nothing to do with me.'

Silence formed, like mist filling a valley. We had never been more distant. Sentences turned themselves over in my mind, went unspoken. Communication with the nymph could have been no more difficult. The blonde girl laughed, failing to stimulate a response from her companions. The futility of the hours we had spent together, even in bed, lay heavy upon me. Van stubbed out her cigarette.

'I shouldn't have come,' she said, 'but since I'm here, it's decided me. Jukes wants me to move in with him. I'm going to say yes. You had your chance, Alec. Now it's gone.'

'It's like that, is it?'

'It is.'

'There's no use asking why, is there?'

'None at all.'

'These things happen. I'm sorry. You know he's awful, don't you?'

'I'm a bit awful myself. I've told you so. Anyway he's what I want now.'

'And what about Rose?'

'She'll come with me, of course.'

'I'm her father.'

'Not legally.'

My scrap of a diary (which I have been using as an aide-mémoire, unnecessary for scenes like that in the Ritz) reminds me that I encountered Frank Haskins on the Oxford train. He had heard about the Parliamentary Question from one of his Party friends, just by chance, he said.

'He never had a head, Alastair, did he? You know he's no Fascist, I know he's no Fascist, but he walks and talks and smells like a Fascist, so you can't blame them as thinks that's what he is.'

'He's a bloody fool, I'm afraid,' I said.

'There's no doubt about that, but what you and I know to be foolishness, knowing him, others see as something a lot worse. Well, it's going to be a long war, Alec.'

'I suppose we have to hope so.'

Frank was on leave. He was just about to be commissioned into the REME. They had tried to insist that his civilian occupation was reserved, but he wasn't having that. Thanks to his Territorial experience, he had managed to get called up soon after the outbreak. Unlike almost everyone I knew, he was an enthusiast for the war. He saw it as the means of effecting a social revolution.

'Nothing bloody, mind, that's not the way we do things in England, but we're going to realise that we can only win this war through Socialism. It's not just that it's being fought to make Socialism possible. It can't be won unless we socialise the nation. So there's a lot to be got rid of before we can fight effectively. Starting at the top. Starting at the top. That paper you write for, Alec, 's full of defeatists. You'll find more defeatism in your London clubs than in the people's pubs.'

'I wish I'd your confidence, Frank. Maybe I spend too much time in the clubs you're talking about. But I was in Paris, you know, and that experience doesn't make me confident.'

'No,' Frank said, 'but we're not French, are we? So we'll beat old Adolf. You'll see.'

'I hope so.'

'If only these bloody Reds would work, and listen to Ernie Bevin and not Joe Stalin.'

'It does me good to hear you, Frank, it really does.'

We took the bus from Oxford to the village. (Mother had told me on the telephone that Father was nervous about the petrol situation and reluctant to send old Haskins with the car: 'Such a lot of nonsense.') Then, after a pint in the pub, where Frank was received with that mingled respect and irony that the English villager extends to local boys who have risen in the social scale, we walked through the soft evening to Blankets, cutting across the meadow, our shoes soon wet from the heavy dew. A heron rose from the stream. The heat of the day lingered and beyond the church a field of stooks glowed golden. The last rays of the sun lit up the squat Norman tower.

'Not so hard, is it, to think of England as worth fighting for, on a night like this?' Frank said.

'Not so hard.'

He paused to relight his pipe. An owl hooted and a little moon crept over the beech wood.

'And yet,' he said, 'there's tens of thousands of lads 'll fight just as hard for England as you and me, lads as have never known the sort of peace we know here, lads that have never heard an owl or seen night fall without the streetlights coming on. "If England was what England seems / And not the England of our dreams, / How quick we'd chuck her. / But she ain't." You can't beat old Chesterton.'

'Or Kipling, Frank.'

'Kipling, was it? I don't know as I like to be quoting Kipling.'

'Bad marks at the Party summer school if you do.'

'There would be, aye.'

Mother met me in the hall.

'If you haven't eaten, there's cold mutton and pickles. But we thought you would be here earlier. He's been fretting. Go through to him, will you?'

'I walked up with Frank. We stopped off at the Fox & Hounds.'

'Oh, Frank . . .'

Mother, perfectly at ease with Frank's parents, whose company she preferred to most outside the family – indeed she thought of them as being part of the family – was uncertain with him. In principle, as a good old-fashioned Liberal, she approved of his determined self-improvement. In practice, perhaps not surprising in one who had never really been able to accept Lloyd George as the sort of person you might have to dinner – certainly not to stay – she was made uneasy. She didn't quite know now whether Frank should come to the front or the back door.

'This is a bad business,' she said.

'How much do you know?'

'There are always friends quick to relay painful news.'

In the last couple of years Father's library had ceased to have the look of a work room. So I was surprised to find him at his desk, and writing. He had never learned to use a typewriter, relying on his secretary, Mrs Clarke. Some of his last books had, I fancy, been dictated to her. But now, perhaps as a distraction, he was at work.

He rose at once, hesitated, as if for a moment he was about to embrace me. But he had never been a man who relished physical contact. I had never seen him kiss my mother, though he would extend his cheek to Kirstie, and also to Alastair. There had been nothing more than a handshake between us since he left off kissing me on the forehead when I was at my private school. This behaviour was, of course, unremarkable in his generation, and seems worth mentioning now only because I observe manners have changed so completely in this respect.

'Do you remember my grandfather?' he said.

'Yes, of course.'

'"*Heureux qui, comme Ulysses, a fait un beau voyage.*" I've been attempting a memoir of him. Uphill work for a weary mind.'

'He told me to make things,' I said. 'I've failed him.'

The siphon squirted. He handed me a drink, gestured towards a cigar box, applied a match to his pipe, and crossed to the window to gaze on the darkling Tennysonian lawn and the rich shape of the elms framed against a sky from which all colour was departing. The smoking jacket hung loose upon him and the thinning hair, usually disciplined by brushwork and Trumper's Eucris, floated in stray wisps.

'Have you come to offer comfort?' he said. 'I want none of it.'

'I don't know how much you know.'

'Too much. More than I would choose.'

Like many Scots, Father, finding expression of feeling difficult in his own person, was most himself when playing a part. Now he was the exiled Jacobite gazing from the flatlands of Picardy back to Schiehallion or Bennachie, pining by Arno or Tiber for the swelling Tay or the green haughlands of the Don. Now, misfortune crowding still harder on him, he saw the tall towers of Ilium aflame. Now, stumbling into darkness, he was Job himself: 'Dost thou still retain thy integrity? Curse God and die.'

He turned away from the window, letting night have its way, and knocked his pipe out.

'I have made of here my Sabine Farm, my *arx*, a pleasant retreat, too pleasant it may be, where it seemed I could deny what I knew of the mischief and knaveries of the world. "*Naturam expelles furca, tamen usque recurret.*" I gave the boy all my love, too much, perhaps.'

Self-pity is repellent. Everyone knows that, it's axiomatic. Self-pity is sentimentality run riot; true also. Yet, faced with Father's abject self-pity, I felt pity for him myself, pity and love. In acting out his grief, he made it real to me. Yet I had no words of comfort, none that I could utter. I could not match my insincerity against his dramatic willing of himself into sincerity by means of old tags and impersonations. And I could not speak the truth: that his love for Alastair had been inadequate, being endlessly indulgent and, therefore, self-indulgent too. Nor could I say that Alastair had been reared incapable of loving, except in as much as his love was the reflection of his own rays.

So I said: 'Alastair lives too much in the intellect. He argues himself into a course of action and is indifferent to feeling.'

He offered no response. That wasn't surprising. It wasn't,

perhaps, the moment to analyse Alastair's character. Certainly it would have served no purpose but the killing of time to do so. It could hardly have eased his pain, applied a balm to his perturbed spirit. And it might be that if he had talked it out his verdict would have been quite the opposite of mine. There was a case for saying that Alastair was guided by emotion, incapable of reflection. Father had been accustomed, I recalled, to speak of the boy's 'ardent spirit'. Yet, years later, talking the sad business over, late at night and on the second half of a bottle, with Toby Macrae in Edinburgh, I found him in agreement with me.

'As it happens, I must be one of the few people who actually heard that broadcast,' Toby said. 'Not at the time, you understand, but later, when I was employed by the army's psychological branch to draw up profiles, as I don't think we called them then, of the various traitors, or possible traitors. And it was very logical. It was argued out perfectly. If you accepted the premise, which was essentially the commonplace one that the Nazis were the defenders of European civilisation against the destructive nihilistic force of Bolshevism, then it made excellent sense. The trouble was it was divorced from reality, because it was so bloody lucid. And reality's never lucid – not sane reality or not in that way. Madmen are always intellectuals, you know, in a manner of speaking; they've lost the sympathetic connection between intellect and feeling. Going on from that premise, a lot of what he said made excellent sense: the need to construct a European state that was opposed to both Bolshevism and soulless American capitalism. It's become almost a cliché, hasn't it? I mean, it's the common wisdom of the day. Alastair's political aims weren't very different from Jean Monnet's, or from Ted Heath's, come to that. They made perfect sense, if . . . But the "if" was what he couldn't see. Come up to the Royal Edinburgh and listen to some of my patients and you'll find exactly the same dissociation between feeling and intellect. It's only possible if you live in your own mind and have no sympathetic understanding of anyone else's. I daresay there are tycoons who display the same characteristics, only they don't come my way.'

'Are you saying he was mad?'

'No, I'm afraid not. He was capable of functioning in daily life.'

'It would be a comfort to be able to think he was mad.'

'Sorry, chum. He wasn't mad, he was just crazy. It's not exactly the same thing.'

XVI
England 1940–1

As autumn slid into winter and the bombs fell nightly on London, I extricated myself from the paper and was recruited by the Special Intelligence Service. The final interview was almost comical, conducted by a First World War colonel and an even more aged Oxford don.

'Isn't it,' I said, 'a bit odd that you're about to accept someone whose brother has been branded a traitor in the popular press?'

The colonel sniffed, doubtless to indicate his opinion of the popular press, and the don giggled.

I never saw either of them again, and often wondered if they had any other function in the organisation. I was sent on a training course held in Oxford. We were billeted in Oriel, but after a couple of weeks, I arranged to remove to Blankets, travelling in daily by motorbike. In December, Van wrote to say she was going to the States with Jukes; Rose would naturally go too. If I wanted to see them, I should come up to London. The tone of the letter suggested we were no more than acquaintances.

Two days later, while I was making arrangements for leave to travel up to London, a bomb fell on the house in Dorset Square where Jukes had a flat. There were no survivors.

Since Van's parents had chosen not to return from a visit to South Africa, where her father had business interests which he had ostensibly gone to attend to a few weeks before war broke out, it fell to me to arrange the funerals. It seemed proper to have Van and little Rose buried in the parish churchyard of Blankets. There was indeed nowhere else that would serve. Alfred Moss accompanied me on the train that carried the coffins from Paddington. He wept much of the journey, but I could find no tears myself. I was oppressed by my own failure, my inability to love, that had sent her to Dorset Square.

Alfred took a drink from his flask. 'War claims the wrong victims,' he said. 'It was the same last time.' Then, looking out of the window, while we halted for no obvious reason, as trains frequently did then, he said he found it impossible to paint, so couldn't earn any money, so was in ever deeper trouble with the Inland Revenue.

'It seems absurd to worry about money now,' he said, 'but I suppose the war has to be paid for. But every time I pick up a brush and approach a canvas, I feel physically sick. In the last war, when I was a war artist, I felt full of zest even in the front-line trenches. And the sights you saw there were worse than anything I've seen this time. Actually I haven't seen anything awful this war. And now this poor girl's gone.'

That evening Father held forth at the dinner table, almost in his old style. He quoted Henry Adams: 'After all, man knows mighty little, and some day may know enough of his own ignorance to fall down and pray.'

'Since the news of these poor girls was brought me, I have been reading in my old favourite, *The Pilgrim's Progress*. I have often feared, in recent years, that the whole world was being turned into Vanity Fair, for the cackle of the town seemed lighter than vanity. And vanity, I have ever held, is a mere enamelled despair. I said to you, Alec, that I have been attempting a little memoir of my grandfather. It's an attempt to catch something of the serious purpose of life. He had no time, he used to proclaim, for anything he could not apprehend by the senses, or that failed his test of common sense; and yet he drew on a rich store of confidence in the future. Recalling him has fortified me against the whips and scorns of experience.

'When Rhodes died, his last words were: "So little time, so much to do." Since I was *dégommé*, I've found so much time, so little to do. But my grandfather never felt like that. In his nineties he retained a zest for life and drew on a seemingly inexhaustible store of energy . . .

'Is Colin dead? Well, it is a good death, whatever the *New Statesman* thinks.'

Could his own death, a few days later, be called that? Has the term any longer a meaning in a world that has ceased to believe in the afterlife?

'History,' he said, 'takes centuries to determine the justice of a cause or the folly of a course. For a hundred years, men wondered at Napoleon. I did myself. Now we look on him with disgust. History has altered our perspective. And look at the vicissitudes of Cromwell's reputation. His body was exhumed and hung in chains. And now we see him as the Great Man of his century, the one strong, truly moral figure. Reputation's a whirligig, blown in the wind. The wise man is content with the judgement of his own conscience.'

Those were almost his last words. He was thinking of Alastair.

When he keeled over, the upper part of his body pressed against the solid mahogany of the dinner table, a silver locket, delicate eighteenth-century work, was forced upward and out of his waistcoat pocket. In the morning Mrs Haskins found it on the floor by his chair and gave it to me. The photograph it guarded showed Alastair as a child, laughing.

Wartime funerals couldn't be expected to be well attended. Shortage of petrol, weariness, general dislocation, all combined to keep people away. The sparse attendance was to Mother's taste. If it had required a considerable love on her part to welcome to the house all those who were professionally connected with Father, or came to pay what they might choose to call homage to him, that didn't – he being gone – oblige her to look for their presence now. On the other hand, in years to come, she would often remark on hearing some particular name: 'One of those who drank your father's claret but hadn't the courtesy to attend his funeral.' This was especially the case with young writers – such as my Trinity contemporary Andrew Somerled – whom he had encouraged and regarded as his protegés.

All the same, though she frowned when, talking to relatives at the church door (among them Lucy Pelham-Grey, a bridesmaid of Kirstie's, whom, Mother had hoped, I might marry), she saw a Rolls-Bentley draw up and disgorge Edwin Pringle, she couldn't help but be pleased, even flattered, when Pringle's chauffeur, moving round to the other side of the car, opened the door and assisted an old and broken-down-looking figure to heave himself out and totter to his feet, only then revealed as the former Prime Minister, now Lord Baldwin. Though Mother had never felt for Baldwin's policies anything more than a mild contempt – 'It's a pity that someone who is so clearly a gentleman should also be an old woman,' she would say, having assured herself that Father was out of hearing – nevertheless, in the circumstances of his ill health, unpopularity, and even fear, it was said, of being exposed to public insult, she couldn't but take his presence as an agreeable tribute to Father.

Baldwin's unpopularity was due to Britain's unreadiness for war. No doubt his responsibility was great. I had written angrily on the subject, as recently as the summer of '39, two years after he had, as I put it, 'slunk off into private life and the House of Lords' – which in fact he scarcely attended. Now, advancing with uncertain steps towards the church, and leaning on the arm of an arch appeaser in Pringle, he suggested, as in his better moments he had always done, a native decency, and also, as he had not always done, a sturdy resolution. He was here because he was the kind of man who did his duty as he saw it, and who would not be deflected from an expression of his affection and regard for an old friend, even by the knowledge that that friend's son had written brutally about him. If he represented the weakness that had brought the country and its Empire to its present desperate state, he possessed also the qualities that were giving us a chance – no more than that in January '41 – of seeing it through.

In any case he now seemed too frail and gentle, almost like Lear in the fifth Act, to bear reproach.

'My cousin Kipling always said your father had the root of the matter in him,' he murmured. 'He deserved to die happy, but, whom the Lord loveth, he chastiseth.'

I understood then that what had kept some away was the reason for his determination to be there.

It started to rain as we lowered the coffin into the grave. The old Prime Minister stood bare headed. His dark overcoat glistened with the soft raindrops, and then, unable to bend, he gestured to Pringle who put a few crumbs of earth in his outstretched hand. He opened his fingers and let them trickle down.

'Just the two of us.'

Kirstie sat before the fire, a Shetland shawl round her shoulders and a mug of Ovaltine held between her hands.

'I'm glad it's you, if there was to be only one of you, and not Hector or Alastair.'

'Or George?'

'I come close to forgetting old George.'

'Perhaps he's been the wisest of us, cutting himself off.'

'You sound bitter. Don't be bitter. You mustn't be bitter. We've no right to bitterness.'

'Despite everything?'

'Despite everything. Father's well out of it though.'

'Yes.'

Kirstie was pregnant. The child, conceived on Colin's last

248

leave – 'The last night actually, it was the only time we made love, does that shock you?' – was due in a fortnight.

'Father would have liked a grandson.'

'I hope it's a girl,' she said and sipped her Ovaltine. 'Col was oppressed, right to the end, by the burden of the dead hero father. You remember? I wouldn't wish that on the next generation.'

'You wouldn't be like Colin's mother.'

'Perhaps not. Listen, the wind's rising . . .'

That was appropriate. If Father's soul was hovering in the vicinity the sort of wind that blows through the Border ballads in which he delighted was just what he would have welcomed. However much he liked to pretend that he had put down his roots in the tranquil beauty of the South, the element that gave his Romances their peculiar quality, lifting them at their best above the common run of such things, belonged to a sterner and wilder landscape. I drew back the curtains, briefly (risking the unlikely wrath of a warden) and opened the shutters. The upper branches of the trees were caught up in a wild dance, the moon scudded behind flying clouds so that the lawn was now lit like a stage set, now thrown back into invisibility. As I closed the night out, the owl called, hunting far down the valley.

'The last time Alastair was here, we listened to the owl.'

'I can't feel as you do,' Kirstie said. 'I feel only shame and anger. How could he, I ask myself, lying in bed and not sleeping.'

'He's doing what he thinks right,' I said. 'It's just a pity he's so wrong.'

'I'm not going to argue. I don't want to quarrel. We've both lost too much to quarrel. I couldn't write to you about Vanessa. I just couldn't find words. I felt guilty because I disliked her so.'

'She rather disliked herself, poor girl. That was part of the trouble.'

Kirstie laid down her mug and lit a cigarette. 'Col was like

249

that too, you know. I never came to terms with it. Perhaps I never would have.'

'You're quite certain – forgive me – that he's gone?'

'Oh yes. I've seen his ghost, you see. He's come to me a couple of times, very gently. I shouldn't be surprised if he came and sat between us now. After all, he's always done that, in a sense, hasn't he?'

Kirstie remained at Blankets for the birth of her child. My Oxford course came to an end. I was summoned to London to work in the assessment of what was called HUMINT – intelligence garnered from agents, newspapers etc., all of which required to be collated, scrutinised, presented in accessible form to the High Command and the Cabinet offices. It was demanding work, not immediately rewarding, much of it done in an atmosphere of miasmic futility, since one so rarely saw its results. It was easy to feel one was living in the world as described by Kafka, himself enjoying among intellectuals a very understandable vogue. The hours were long, and that was welcome, private life put on hold. The spring of 1941 was the bleakest time of the war.

Hector returned from Bucharest, for six weeks, before a posting to Washington, which itself dismayed him in prospect. Habitually melancholy, he was at a lower ebb than I had ever seen him, complaining that the direction of the war was all wrong, even futile.

'We can't win the war without a social and political revolution,' he said, 'and there seems no chance of that unless we have defeated Germany.'

As to his personal life, he was saying nothing. Remembering him at that time, I think of storks I have seen huddling wretchedly in the rain, in a muddy pen at a poor quality zoo. I suggested we should have dinner one night. He said: 'I can't eat anything.' He went down to Blankets for only one night. Mother said: 'He's not fit to go to Washington, but I suppose he will. I don't understand him, of course, and he has no time for me.'

A letter came from Kirstie, some weeks after the birth of her daughter, Hattie; at least I think that must be when it was written – the first page, which may have contained only trivia, is missing. What I have now reads:

I think you were shocked when I told you that Col and I made love only once on his last leave, but that's because you had such a romanticised view of us as a couple. Like most such views – like so many of Father's, you may say – it wasn't, of course, entirely wrong. But it was askew. I adored Col, of course, and admired him, and he tried to adore me. But really he only needed me. He needed me to let him believe that he was grown up. But he wasn't. He had never escaped adolescence. Like Alastair, I suppose. Or at least that's what you say of Alastair, isn't it? Col was oppressed by a sense of futility which he couldn't admit. It felt all wrong to him and yet it was what he felt most deeply. Toby Macrae knew that, and even warned me against it. He said: 'You're very brave to take on someone who doesn't like adult life.' Col could never put feelings into words because he couldn't admit them to himself, and that may have been because they were never more than half-formed. He really adored you, right up to the end, and you moved away from him, growing up, while he remained sixteen. He was good at soldiering because there was make-believe in that, and I suspect he rather welcomed death.

That sounds horrid and bitter. I don't mean he didn't want to go on living, just that he didn't know how to do so in a grown-up world. Our marriage had got more and more silent, but it wasn't the silence of contentment.

When you were down here, you said something about being no good at loving, or inadequate at it. I can't remember exactly, but I know it was with reference to Vanessa. (I think the same was true, probably more true, of her too.) When I look around, we all seem to be stranded in an emotional desert.

Does that sound hysterical?

At least I've got the children, I keep telling myself that.

Hector, I suspect, blames Mother for his frozen condition. I wish I could think he was wrong.

You once said: 'Perhaps old George is the wisest of us.' It seemed nonsense at the time, but now it seems you may be right. I would like to know his Malay wife and I wonder if they are really happy. I think they may be.

This is a horrid wintry letter, not like me. Sorry.

The news from Greece fills me with anxiety.

Love K.

XVII
Paris 1944

Two photographs: they are captioned 'Retribution'.

The first shows a French collaborator being taken into custody in Paris. He is held by a policeman and surrounded – guarded – by four other men carrying guns. One, a very handsome boy, seen in profile, has a pistol held low at waist level. There is blood on the collaborator's face. His suit looks as if he had been rolled in the street. All he wants immediately, you think, is to be got out of sight.

The second shows two women collaborators being led barefoot through the streets. Their heads have been shaved and their brows daubed with swastikas. One, middle-aged, has had her blouse torn off. Her brassière just manages to support sagging breasts. They are followed by a crowd, and most of them, especially the women among them, are smiling broadly. A young man walking just ahead of the shaven women, is laughing.

Recently, I read a news item about a woman who had been found dead in a lonely cottage in the Auvergne. Evidently, she had been dead for some weeks. The report said that she had been found guilty of collaboration by a People's Court in 1944, and had her hair sheared. She had become a recluse, and then mad.

Memories revived: of the heady mixture of exhilaration, terror, and sadism that was France in the days of the Épuration.

In the Boulevard St Michel I saw such a miserable

example. This time the woman must have been fifty. She hadn't been thoroughly sheared, so that some grey locks hung like rats' tails down the side of her face which was swollen and bruised. She had lost her shoes and one stocking; the other hung loose about her knees and flapped. She walked slowly, limping, in the middle of a jeering crowd, and her lips were working. They seemed to frame denial: '*Non, non, non* . . .'

Barbara had climbed on to her chair outside the café to get a good look. She said: 'Trust the French to take their revenge on the women. It's medieval sadism.'

No doubt it was. But wasn't it also the case that in turning on the collaborators in the manner that they did the French were expressing their own self-hatred, which they could not admit to themselves? No doubt many who howled abuse and curses at these women had applauded Pétain a few years earlier, been guilty also of their own tacit collaboration and now despised themselves for the fears and relief that had led them to do so?

'You'd have behaved as badly in England if Hitler had come,' Barbara said. 'It's not just the French.'

'And you Americans?'

'My first editor once recounted the lynching of a negro he had witnessed in Alabama. He's never been south of the old Mason-Dixon line since.'

I had secured my release from the army a few weeks previously. The war could not now be lost. My work, little though I valued what I had achieved, seemed redundant. So I was a newspaperman again. Comfortably off since Father's death, distrusted still by Harbottle, I was happy to work for a liberal weekly. It could pay little, but supply what I required, which was accreditation.

In coming to Paris, I had an ulterior motive. I sought to pick up Alastair's trail. Watching that parade of the condemned, it seemed urgent to do what I could to rescue him from the consequences of his choice. If that was possible.

Nothing had been heard of him since 1942 when reports had come through that he was working on a film in Paris. It was impossible then to say how reliable this news was. News, as anyone who has worked in the media knows, often arrives in distorted form even in quiet times. How much more so when the Four Horsemen are galloping unrestrained across the earth. Still, it provided at least a possible starting point.

Just being back in Paris, even that Paris, was exhilarating. I felt more alive than I had done since 1939. I even began to keep a diary again – or rather, a sort of journal, for I used one of those thick grey notebooks which are supplied to the students of the *lycées*, and I didn't trouble to date the entries.

Journal: Barbara disapproves of my concern for Alastair. 'I know he's your brother, but all this Bloomsbury E. M. Forster stuff about personal relations and betraying your country not your friend makes me sick. Why can't you just lay off? If something's coming to him, it's coming and what he deserves. But no, you go all English upper class and think you can pull a few strings here and a few more and it can all be swept under the carpet.'

She went on in this vein for a long time, and in the end I made her more angry still, by asking what we had been fighting for if it wasn't for personal relations.

'A new social order,' she said, sniffily.

This morning I went to see Armand de Balafré. He's close to de Gaulle, and I used to meet him sometimes in the Café Royal. He's one of the few Frenchmen I have ever liked, and I hoped I would gather some information about de Gaulle's intentions – Barbara's Communist friends have already made their distrust of him clear. He's said to be 'authoritarian', sympathetic to Action Français. To listen to them you can't understand why he didn't join Vichy. The

255

truth is of course that they recognise that he is the principal obstacle to a Communist takeover, which, extraordinary though it may seem, some of them believe Roosevelt would favour. (I put this down, though it seems crazy to me; they wouldn't even believe Barbara when she said it was crazy.)

Eventually, after we'd covered that subject, and de Balafré had confessed that, though he is on the outer ring of the General's inner circle (that was precisely how he expressed it), he really doesn't know what his intentions are – beyond maintaining the prestige of France and re-establishing the authority of the State – I ventured on the subject of my quest.

De Balafré looked weary. And wary.

'Why do you choose me to enquire of?' he said.

I thought that was oddly put and replied that I hadn't exactly selected him. There were others of whom I'd enquired and there would be still more, I expected.

'You must realise it's a peculiarly delicate question to put to me, nevertheless.'

'I'm afraid you've lost me,' I said.

'Put it like this,' he stubbed out his Caporal and straightway lit another, 'it's a matter I'd rather not talk about here.'

'But elsewhere and some other time?'

'Yes . . .'

He paused a long time before he said that, as if he would have preferred to deny me. So we arranged that I would visit his apartment tomorrow lunch-time.

In the Ritz bar, an English officer: 'These Yanks, they come over and want to make a New World or tell us how to make it. Don't they understand that we're simply too tired to be interested?' Contrast with Sergeant Riddle in the department who had also no time for Americans, but in his case because he regarded them as the obstacle to the creation of a New

World. 'They'll just try to force their lousy rotten capitalist system on us again.'

The curious thing is they're both right. When I suggest this to Barbara, she tells me I understand nothing.

De Balafré's apartment was off the Boulevard Haussmann. It had that over-furnished look characteristic of the French bourgeoisie. A maid had admitted me. It was inconceivable that only a few months before, the master of the house, who now stood bulky before me in a (pre-war) double-breasted suit, heavy silk shirt and Charvet tie, should have been on the run, hiding in barns, moving only by night, after he had been parachuted into Occupied Normandy to liaise with the Maquis. But I knew this was the case. Now he opened a bottle of champagne with a deft twist.

'The appearance of normality is easily restored,' he said. 'There are things we have to hold on to if we aren't to be swept entirely away.'

As I looked at him I felt like apologising for my own tepid war.

He said: 'In twenty years none of this is going to mean anything to anybody.'

Then he turned away from me and stood looking out of the window. It was clear and frosty. The rooftops were sharp against a harsh sky. Still with his back to me, he said: 'We've rather a lot in common, I'm afraid. I spoke to Malraux about you, he says he knew you in Spain and you did rather well there. Why didn't you approach him?'

'It didn't occur to me he would remember me.'

'My brother Lucien was a Vichy minister. He's dead. That's why I say we have a lot in common.'

'Oh,' I said. I don't think I said anything more; bad news, the worst which is long anticipated, takes words away. I've never understood wails of lamentation. It's a facility civilisation has deprived us of.

'Lucien was an idealist who thought he was a practical man

facing reality. Does that description fit your brother too? I thought so. I've asked some questions. But I haven't had any satisfactory answers. I don't know where he is, whether he is, or whether he's gone the way of Lucien. He was certainly still in Paris a year ago. Someone said he was now in Germany. I trust not, for your sake. But I do have someone to pass you on to, as it were, a friend of my brother, a film director, Marcel Pougier. He has just contrived to save himself. That doesn't displease me. He's a pansy but he was a good friend of Lucien. It's rather an amusing story, but some other time. You don't want amusing stories, do you?'

Pougier was actually in the news. His film, *Le Jeune Davide*, was showing in at least three cinemas. I had liked his early work: delicate Romantic comedies with a touch of pansy frivolity. The new work was said to be sterner stuff. I went to it that afternoon: if I was to see Pougier it seemed good, knowing the vanity of artists, that I should be able to say something intelligent about his latest work. That wasn't, as it turned out, easy. He had abandoned the subtlety and charm of the pre-war films. *Davide* was tricksy, with much use of montage. Everything was exaggerated, even shrill. The analogies he drew between the Biblical story and contemporary France were grotesque. David was the heroic youthful Resistance. The Philistines were the Germans; Goliath, even, was got up as a parody of the Reichsmarschall Goering. Licence had been taken with King Saul; he was an octogenarian pederast, prepared to collaborate with the Philistines. That was harsh as well as absurd; whatever else he had been accused of, Pétain had never been charged with a preference for boys. He was known to be an indefatigable womaniser even in old age. But his lust for David, expressed in long brooding shots in the cunningly-lit darkness of the royal pavilion, must be taken to represent, in some oblique manner, the relations between the Marshal and France. Only Jonathan was allowed to escape crude analogical treatment.

Perhaps he represented the ideal soul of France, but the point, uniquely in this movie which to anyone who had admired Pougier's earlier work must seem a prostitution of talent, wasn't laboured.

And yet there was something endearing about it, just as there had been in Noël Coward's absurd celebration of Dickie Mountbatten, *In Which We Serve*.

Barbara said: 'Makes me sick, should have stuck to petit point.'

Pougier had certainly gone over the top. Yet the audience, predominantly French, adored it. Murmurs of appreciation were audible. It was a movie that made them feel good about themselves, sweeping away their own memories of whatever accommodation they had made – would now say, as ordinary Parisians, been forced to make – during the years of the Occupation. And perhaps it was no more absurd than so many of our own patriotic movies.

That at least is how I remember it. Curiously, my journal merely notes that I went to see it, and Barbara's disparaging comment.

Pougier had some excuse, he was scared stiff. He had remained in Paris throughout the Occupation, and continued to work. Someone said at the Flore that he had even had a lover who was in the Gestapo. That may not have been true. It's the sort of malicious story that went the rounds. However, there's no doubt that Pougier, as the Axis began to crumble, had felt the need to put himself right with Gaullists and the Resistance. He couldn't be blamed for that. And he must have been cunning, as well as enterprising, in managing to make such a film during the last months of the Occupation.

Journal: Pougier greeted me with a show of eagerness that couldn't hide a wish that I hadn't come. I suspect he would rather the last few years were blotted out. *Le Jeune*

Davide has undoubtedly saved him a deal of unpleasantness – national disgrace and so on. You've only to look at him to see that he could never be politically serious. He is an artist of some delicacy, but I doubt whether he has ever given a serious thought to anything outside his personal life and the problems of making a movie. He has the sort of innocence that enrages, because he is too intelligent to be permitted that degree of irresponsibility.

And yet, I couldn't help liking him. It was partly because he was still frightened. Ever since Spain I've found that I can't dislike anyone who is in a funk.

There were a couple of pretty boys in the apartment which was cluttered with knick-knacks and signed photographs in frames – flowers everywhere. I wonder how he came by them in this austerity of Paris. He shooed the boys away, and they went into another room with squeals and giggles.

'Armand sent you to me?' We spoke in French, his English is, he apologised, very poor. 'That's a surprise. He's never liked me.'

I could see that he was wondering whether there was something to be wary of. 'His brother, poor Lucien, was a great friend, of course.'

'But it's my brother whom I've come to ask about.'

'Yes, of course.'

He bounded, theatrically, from the sofa where he had stretched himself, and straightened a picture.

'Oh dear,' he said, 'it's so difficult.'

I assured him, as best I could, that all I was interested in was trying to find out, for his own good, where Alastair might be now. Nothing that had happened during the Occupation was any concern of mine.

'Oh, I believe you,' he said, and rubbed long fingers over his forehead. 'It seemed so certain, you know, back in 1940, that the only thing we could do was find some means of accommodating ourselves to the situation. Your brother felt like that.'

'But he didn't entirely dislike the situation?'

'I don't know.'

'You made a film together?'

'He was always full of ideas. They weren't very good ones, you know, or very practicable if they were good. Which comes to the same thing really.'

The film, it seems, was never made. (Have any of Alastair's projects come to fruition?) As Pougier described it, this didn't seem surprising. It was to have been a version of *Coriolanus*, set in an unidentified Balkan country in the decade before the war.

'There was a certain ambiguity that pleased me about the concept,' Pougier said.

Philippe Torrance was to write the script. That was apparently the beginning of the problem. First, his Coriolanus-figure was unacceptably vulgar to Pougier. Then Torrance himself got cold feet.

'He sniffed the changing wind before I did.' Pougier smiled. 'He's a sly bugger.'

And the finance was wrong – story again, I thought, of Alastair's life. 'Moreover,' Pougier said, '– and this may be of some assistance to you, even comfort – it began to seem as if your brother was no longer looked on with favour by the authorities. I don't know why. You must understand that in those years many of us preferred not to speak openly of things which it seemed might be safer to leave unspoken. All I know is that your brother fell under some sort of suspicion. But of what I am ignorant. He even spent some weeks in prison, you know. They didn't trust him, ultimately.'

'They, being?'

'Ultimately, I suppose the Germans, though it was the French police who arrested him. Beyond that I don't know. I haven't seen your brother since the spring of '43, which was a few weeks before I heard he was under arrest.'

He lit another cigarette and lay down on the couch again.

'That makes you feel better, doesn't it? You're all the same, you want people to suffer.'

I didn't know in which 'you' he included me.

'Nevertheless,' he said, 'I'm grateful to him. In an odd way, it was his *Coriolanus* which gave me the inspiration for *Le Jeune Davide*. And now I think you'd better talk to him.'

'Who?'

'My David, only his real name's Fred. I wasn't sure at first if it would be a good idea. I'll arrange it. He can tell you more than I. You see, his cousin was your brother's girl.'

Journal: Pougier, anxious to be rid of me, gave me an address where I would find Fred. 'It's no use trying to telephone,' he said. 'He lives with his mother, I've tried to persuade him to leave, but he's devoted to her. She always distrusted your brother, so the best thing will just be to go there, do you understand? Oh dear, it's all so difficult. Give the boy my love. The mother's a Breton Countess, an old cat.'

It was too late to go there after I left Pougier, and so I went round this afternoon, when I thought they would have finished their lunch. It was a studio apartment near St-Germain-des-Prés. I was admitted by a maid in mobcap, black dress and apron, as in a Feydeau farce – extraordinary, I thought. But of course there were domestics in service throughout the Occupation. You might say it was the reason for accepting German rule – to keep your domestic staff.

The maid showed me into a pale blue room, full of colonial furniture – an armchair covered in ox-hide and bronze tray-tables from Indo-China. They sat rather uncomfortably with a couple of good eighteenth-century pieces – a writing desk and a chest. A sheaf of whips and riding crops hung over the looking glass.

A thin woman dressed in a severe, well-cut, black costume entered, followed by the boy, easily recognisable as Pougier's David, even in the pre-war suit which had, perhaps, been made for his father, since it was a couple of sizes too big for him. He looked both eager and nervous.

The Comtesse gave me an appraising stare, motioned to me to sit down.

'I would have you to know,' she said, 'that I did not approve of my niece's liaison with your brother. If her uncle had been alive' – her glance flickered to a framed photograph of a naval officer on one of the bronze tables – 'he would would have put a stop to it.'

I explained, as politely as I could, that I wasn't concerned with that. I had come merely, I said, in the hope that they might be able to tell me something of where Alastair might be, or what had happened to him. I was sorry if my request revived painful feelings, but she would understand, I was sure, that family was an important matter, and that it was my duty etc., etc. I laid it on pretty heavily.

'Yvette was a well-brought-up girl,' she said. 'Naturally, she was. I should like you to understand that. I was responsible for her after my brother's death. I am widowed now. My husband, the Count, served his country. Admiral Darlan thought very highly of him.'

I didn't enquire about her husband. (I found later that he was killed at Oran when we bombarded the French fleet; no wonder she dislikes us.) It was obvious straight away that she neither knew nor cared anything of what had happened to Alastair, that she had agreed to see me principally to prevent me from seeing Fred alone. He sat very still and pale while she conducted the conversation. Occasionally he touched his lips with long fingers.

'Now the Communists will take over,' she said. 'De Gaulle is a fool and a traitor.'

'Maman.' Fred's reproof was no more than breathed.

'Understand,' she said, 'there are standards that I have always maintained. At first I did not disapprove strongly of your brother. Then I discovered he was married already.'

She launched into a tirade about the decadence and immorality of the English. As she spoke, Fred looked towards me and made a small, barely perceptible, disclaimer. He ventured on a quick smile, so brilliantly fleeting that for the first time I caught the charm which he had revealed on the screen.

The monologue continued. An atmosphere of intense misery pervaded the room. We were caught up in that most acute of horrors – a life lived entirely in the mind. That it was, within narrow limits, a powerful mind made the realisation more painful.

Her resentment exceeded even that which I have so often encountered at home among those who are intelligent enough to understand that society as they have known and relished it is crumbling, that a different order will be imposed, which, whatever else it portends, will have no place for them. Edwin Pringle, for instance, recognises this; and responds with resigned cynicism, which is perhaps the natural consequence of the English empirical tradition. So Edwin, with the odd inept joke and sour remark will, nevertheless, accommodate himself; he may even – probably will – learn the language which will permit him to continue to play the game, and do quite well personally out of a system he deplores and despises. Naturally Pétainist himself, Edwin will accept democratic socialism because, to him, nothing ultimately matters, except his own comfort. He is incapable of the flinty and rebarbative arrogance with which the Comtesse set her face to the future which, nevertheless, she refused to contemplate. I felt sympathy for the boy, Fred, caught in the net of her bitter clarity, wintry logic formed of impenetrable ice.

At last I was able to disengage myself. I apologised for occupying her time. She shook her head, very slowly, but whether to indicate, as seemed unlikely, that no apology was necessary, or that her time had not been wasted, or, as seemed most probable, that in the desert of her life, time was immaterial, I could not tell. I explained, carefully, that I had another appointment at the Dôme. I was late, I said, and my friend might have moved on, but I supposed I'd better go and wait there. He would probably return, and there were worse places to spend a couple of hours than the Dôme, weren't there?

It was only just over an hour before the boy appeared.

He had changed out of the unbecoming suit and now wore a black polo-neck and grey flannel trousers. Two or three people greeted him as he approached me, and others looked hard at him, doubtless recognising the star of Pougier's film. I found it difficult to connect the boy who had played David with the other who had sat so obediently and self-effacingly under his mother's tirade. Now he said he was sorry to have been so long; it was clever of me to find this way of letting him know where I would be, but could we go somewhere else, somewhere less fashionable – he wasn't comfortable here.

So we moved to a quiet café in a side street, and ordered coffee and two glasses of Rhum St Jacques, and he pushed away the curl of tawny hair that fell over his left eye, and began to speak.

Fred's childhood was (he told me) narrow and confined, divided between a gaunt, bleak house perched on a cliff above a Breton fishing port and the Paris flat I had visited.

His mother, never sociable, withdrew from the world early, even before her husband's death. Fred had scarcely known his father; he had been trained to worship an image of stern and heroic self-denial. Even so, he couldn't help suspecting by the time he was ten or eleven that his mother actually rather disliked her husband, that her hatred of the flesh was turned into resentment of the man who had compelled her to admit its demands. She was, perhaps, even pleased when news came of his death; it was as if she had been long preparing herself for the more congenial role of widow. It was then that they removed, finally, to Paris, which, however, she despised.

Fred's schooling was unhappy. A weedy child, till his beauty suddenly blossomed when he was sixteen, he was unable to form friendships with boys of his own age. He suffered bullying, ostensibly on account of his Breton accent, in reality because he was a sort of white blackbird in the flock. As a child he had adored his cousin Yvette, the older by some seven years. She was his only refuge, the only person in whom he could confide. And she constituted herself his moral protector.

Consequently, when she first took up with Alastair, he was miserable and jealous.

'How on earth,' I asked, 'was she able to do that? I mean, how did she escape from your mother? Forgive me for putting it so crudely.'

He turned his dazzling smile on me – the smile that already, in the few days since I saw *Le Jeune Davide*, I have observed half a dozen Parisian boys imitating.

Yvette was very determined, he explained. Her own mother had been 'not quite' he said, 'not born, you understand', and she saw his mother's life as an exercise in futility and self-punishment – 'as if the greater glory of God compelled one to be miserable'. She was quite right, though at first Fred resented her escape. He was still at an age when he was obsessed by his mother, and could

266

persuade himself that he adored her. Now, if he felt anything but irritation, it was pity. That held him in its sad chains.

It was only when, at last, he met Alastair, some two years after he and Yvette had taken up together, that his resentment melted away. Alastair was so full of vigour and enthusiasm. His arrival in Fred's life was like opening a window and finding winter had fled. Amazingly, at first, Alastair had this effect on even Fred's mother. Whatever she came to say later, she adored him too. Indeed, the way Fred spoke of the shifting relations between them, it was clear to me, if not entirely to him, that her later antipathy towards Alastair was, to some extent, at least, the consequence of a spurned love.

All this was interesting, but not greatly to the point. I knew enough, after all, of Alastair's ability to inspire others with enthusiasm, of the destructive effect of his charm. I willed Fred to get beyond an analysis of his family's emotional deficiencies and turmoil; and yet I heard them out, thinking that it was, perhaps, important to him to be given this opportunity, and that an attempt to move him on would throw him off course.

Fred hadn't heard Alastair's 1940 broadcasts. He wouldn't have been interested, and was then only thirteen or fourteen. It was, he thought, in the winter of 1941–2 that Alastair and Yvette had returned to Paris from the Haut-Savoie where they had been living – approved by the Vichy authorities – while Alastair worked on a book and a film script. By the time Fred got to know him, Alastair was disclaiming all interest in the war and its progress. He still took it for granted that Germany would win, indeed he spoke as if that was already accomplished. The important thing was to work to create the new Europe that must emerge from 'the ashes of war'. Alastair often used to say – Fred frowned in concentration as he repeated this – that the war had been worse than a crime, it had been a blunder. 'That was Napoleon, wasn't it?'

'No, Talleyrand, I think. Concerning the execution of the Duc d'Enghien.'

'Oh, my knowledge of history is lamentable.'

Alastair was frequently critical of the Nazis, Fred said. Their anti-Semitism was taken too far. They had got a lot of things out of proportion. Nevertheless he backed them because, unlike the English governing class, they were modern. They understood how industrial society had debased men, and made a new heroic ethos imperative. He used to say, Fred smiled, 'it's absurd to suppose that you cure the ills of the modern world by giving the working classes bathrooms.' The film he was planning would celebrate the 'Hero-Individual' who nevertheless recognises that his superiority imposes obligations of leadership.

The time of the Romantic hero wallowing in self-pity and Weltschmerz was over; film must celebrate the New European, and teach the masses to acknowledge him.

'It sounds silly,' Fred said, 'and empty, but it didn't, the way Alastair talked of it.'

'Was this *Coriolanus*?'

'Yes, but the "New Coriolanus", purged of . . . oh, I can't remember just what he was purged of . . .' Fred laughed – his first indication of any sort of sense of humour.

As the war turned against Germany, relations between Alastair and Yvette deteriorated. This perturbed Fred. Yvette complained that Alastair was unreasonable. He became more strident just when he should have been quiet, and getting ready to change tack. She didn't put it quite as bluntly as that, but nevertheless . . . And Fred could see that she was right. He was surprised, only because it wasn't like her to be willing to change her mind. She was a very determined person. As for Fred, he had never – he looked at me with spaniel eyes – felt as Alastair and Yvette had about Germany. The Nazis had disgusted him from the start. Maybe I wouldn't believe that – he could understand if I didn't – but it was, nevertheless, the case.

By the summer of 1943 Alastair and Yvette were scarcely on speaking terms. She hated Pougier, too, which made things worse. She had been furious when Alastair introduced Fred to Pougier. Fred had had to resort to tears to prevent her from telling his mother. Did I realise that his mother had no idea he had made *Le Jeune Davide*? 'She thought I was going to my studies. There's no danger of course that she will ever see it, and since she talks to nobody and reads no newspapers except for the Bourse prices, she's unlikely ever to learn of my part. That seems mad to you? Well, I agree.' Fred smiled, lingeringly. I looked past him, through the open door of the café to the street. It had begun to rain. Fred fingered his empty glass, not suggestively; but I ordered more rum.

'It wasn't over politics that they quarrelled though,' he said. 'It was on account of me.'

Pougier had fallen for Fred. He used to say, apparently, that he couldn't write a story or make a film unless there was one character for whom he felt physical desire. I had already guessed this. The way the camera dwelt on the young David, in that scene when he tries on the armour and then lays it aside; the way in which it seemed to inhabit the soul of Jonathan as he gazed on David returning sweat-stained and nervous even in triumph after his slaying of Goliath, had laid Pougier's erotic imagination bare. It had disturbed me at the time. Now, sitting opposite the boy, who had hesitated in his story, I experienced a sensation like that which Proust knew that afternoon when he entered the courtyard of the Guermantes' mansion and, stumbling against unevenly placed paving stones, found one of his feet stepping on a flagstone lower than the one next to it, so that, in that very instant, without any conscious exercise of memory, he found Venice restored to him, and was possessed again by the same felicity which had come upon him, uncalled for, at rare moments in his life. So now I was back in the cricket pavilion at school, sitting opposite Colin, who had just unbuckled his pads, and sat, half-shadowed and mouth open, as the field from which he had just departed in triumph was suddenly swept by a torrent of rain that would end the match which his efforts had brought to the point of victory.

Pougier's feeling was only embarrassing to the boy. The really difficult thing was that Fred fell – hopelessly, as he said – for Alastair. He had known and liked him for three years, and then, one evening, seeing him put his arm round Yvette, who pushed it aside in irritation, he felt a thrust of desire and anguish as Alastair's face lost its usual look of assurance and he stood puzzled by this rejection.

Fred told me this awkwardly. He had never spoken of it to anyone else. He had never let Alastair know how he felt, because, well, it was ridiculous, wasn't it? He was inexperienced, of course, but he knew that Alastair could never think of him as a lover. But Yvette, believing that Alastair – she made no bones about it – had delivered her little cousin to Pougier, either as the price of his involvement in the film or from sheer devilry – provoked a quarrel, which tore Alastair and her apart. So Fred knew guilt because their separation was a necessary first step to what he suddenly so demandingly wanted, even though he also knew he could never have it.

It was three weeks later that Alastair was arrested.

'Why was that?'

'Someone denounced him.'

'Was it Yvette?'

'I hope not. She was capable of it. But I've never been sure, and I daren't ask her.'

'So she's still in Paris?'

'Yes, but she doesn't speak to Maman or me. She joined the Resistance in time, and now Maman reviles her for associating with those she calls the *canaille*.'

'I don't understand,' I said.

But, though I did not understand in detail, I was not quite lost. In that frenzied Paris, every emotion was magnified, and therfore distorted. Resentment, jealousy, the sense of being betrayed, all might have worked together to convert the love she had certainly felt for Alastair into a hatred that demanded to be satisfied by an act of revenge. We can, after all, forgive anyone except those we have loved and no longer love. Moreover, it seemed that Yvette had joined not only the Resistance, but actually the Communist Party, and, Fred suggested, might in fact have done so some time before she broke with Alastair. Nothing was straight and simple in that world where all certainties had been disturbed, and in which people reached ever more desperately for whatever might promise to offer what had been lost.

'But it may not have been Yvette,' he said. 'It may have been Torrance.'

He had two reasons for supposing this. First, Alastair himself had one day remarked that, certainly, he knew Torrance was now his enemy and would be happy to destroy him. He said this, Fred recalled, with that light air of mastery, that sense of his own invulnerability, which so buoyantly revealed his charm, and which at the same time of course was precisely what might provoke someone like Torrance, whom Fred admitted he scarcely knew, but of whom he had heard nothing good, to an act by which he could expunge his own feelings of inferiority.

Second, soon after Alastair's arrest, Fred himself was summoned to the office of the Police Judiciaire for examination concerning his relations with Alastair. The course of that examination, which was conducted with perfect propriety, made it clear that whoever had denounced Alastair had also raised the possibility that he might be guilty of the offence of corruption of a minor.

'Of course,' Fred said, 'I insisted that nothing of that sort had occurred. But it was uncomfortable.'

He was told there would be a second examination. But that never took place. It seemed that Alastair had been released. Fred believed that some of his German friends had intervened. He didn't know where he had gone, or where he was now. He thought it probable he was in Germany.

'You don't think the worse of him?'

'I don't think badly of him at all.'

We left the café, and out into the smirr of rain, the soft sooty rain of cities, and walked slowly, not speaking, but as if we had exhausted words, to the river, and there leant, damp shoulders brushing, on the parapet that was wet enough for the moisture to seep through the broadcloth of my British Warm and the wool of Fred's jersey. The river flowed as for centuries it had carried the discarded debris of Paris out of the city, and I thought of the many who must, from our vantage, have watched the same but ever-different and indifferent water, and longed for it to bear their pain to oblivion. I wondered if Swann, his heart gnawed by the certainty that the woman he was bound to was 'not his type', had watched the same water pass beneath him. From a little street behind us came the moaning whine of an accordion, and it seemed as if the earth was turning with unusual slowness on its axis, as a haunting tune brought back the Paris of before the war.

Fred said: 'I don't want to go home yet.'

My journal stops there, abruptly, as if what followed blotted out the need, itself perhaps neurotic, to record and examine. For, as the leaves fell from the chestnuts and the plane trees, and the war stumbled into the north, and autumn turned to winter, made bitter cold by the shortage of fuel, I was rewarded, in that middle year of my progress through life, with what I had not looked for, in setting out on a bitter quest: an idyll, known even then to be short-lived, without a future, but an idyll, nevertheless, which eased the pain, staunched the guilt, lightened the burden of years of loneliness in which I had felt shame to shadow my every step, in which a sense of loss and an inability to grieve as I felt I should be grieving, had stripped from me any sense of virtue, and condemned me to emotional lassitude.

Of course, from the first, as I say, I knew it could not last. The tenderness I felt for the boy as I woke to find the aureole of tawny curls on the pillow and traced the line of his sleeping lips with gentle finger couldn't disguise from me that the delight of our being together depended – as had not been the case with Vanessa – on the certainty we both felt that this was an interlude. For Fred, too, I was perhaps at best a substitute for Alastair, and for me – wasn't what I felt for him, in part dependent on what I felt for my brother? It seemed, even as I leaned over and laid my lips on his, to wake him, that all I was doing was making for myself a brief refuge from reality; that Fred knew this, and that it was the same for him. But the future could not be long denied, and for neither was it a future that could include the other without the sacrifice of that sense of self, and self-worth, without which life itself so easily becomes something to be despised. There was happiness too in that thought, for I could not wish to see Fred held in the trap of homosexuality.

The sight of Pougier fretting in his queendom confirmed me in that opinion. So did memories of my last meeting with Hector just before I came to Paris. We met in the Reform. He knew I was off to try to find out what had happened to Alastair, and this made him nervous.

'I don't see how we are going to avoid a public scandal,' he said, 'unless he's dead. That would be the most satisfactory solution.'

'You can't be serious.'

'I can't be anything else. I've discussed the matter with Mother, you know. She agrees with me.'

'Father . . .' I hesitated, and he snapped.

'Don't bring Father into this. He always spoiled the boy. He encouraged a very ordinary boy to think himself remarkable. I'm not sure I don't blame Father for the whole disaster.'

'I can't agree that Alastair was "very ordinary".'

'No, then let's agree to differ. I'm in no mood for an argument. The Office is a terrible strain. The reactionaries are already positioning themselves to try to turn us against the Soviet Union. The opposition to switching our support from Mihailovitch to Tito was a straw in the wind. Winston's no help, he's locked into nineteenth-century imperialist patterns of thought.'

'How's your private life?'

'I have none, literally none.'

'I saw Max the other day. He's still in the Air Force. He sent you love.'

A plump young man, wearing a bow tie and looking as if he needed a bath, lurched towards us.

'I say, Hector, this club does depress me,' he said. 'Have you noticed there are no page boys?'

He slumped into a chair. Waves of whisky floated towards me.

'Don't be silly,' Hector said.

'Buy me a drink then. You know I like being stood drinks.'

'You know I don't like standing them. Just the one then.'

Later in the evening Hector, abstemious yet awash with self-pity throughout our (probably) inadequate meal, pushing his cup of nasty wartime coffee (made from a liquid essence) to the side, and frowning as I lit a cigarette from the stub of another, said: 'Father used to talk a lot about duty. But in a romantic haze which I find self-indulgent. I disappointed

274

him, I've known that for a long time. You mentioned Max earlier in the evening. I didn't respond because, as I told you years ago, I've put that sort of thing behind me. But I don't regret my affair with him. It taught me a lesson: that that sort of thing isn't for me. Ever since, I've devoted myself to duty. As far as I'm concerned, happiness is only to be had from deliberate achievement – clearing the jungle around one, and creating good order. I see myself as a useful man, working to build a just society. And nothing matters beyond that. Do you understand?'

'It sounds rather bleak.'

'It's the bleakness that attracts me, the chance to lose myself in a cause.'

XVIII
Blankets
Christmas 1945–New Year 1946

Almost nobody, Guy Holland once suggested to me, is content with being what he is, no matter how considerable his achievements or renown. Accordingly, there is a temptation to construct an alternative, more satisfying version, in which he presents himself to the world as either better or worse than he really is, but at any rate more interesting. Guy's view revealed itself with disquieting clarity in my own family. Thus, it was easy to construct for all of us other careers, to which we might have been better suited and in which we should have been each of us more comfortable.

That was certainly, and most obviously, the case with Alastair. Still, seven months after Germany's defeat, off the map, missing, perhaps dead, he had neglected to nourish the real if minor talents he possessed, preferring to take on himself the part of a tragic hero – a role which no one but himself could see as fitting him. Hadn't he, I thought, as I stood in the nipping air, listening to the beaters move through the wood beyond, chosen this part because he could not bring himself to admit that his character and abilities actually fitted him to a humdrum existence – even to the 8.40 to the City every morning?

The birds, naturally wild, came with a rush, high out of the trees. Shots were fired either side of me, but, though I raised my gun, I did not squeeze the trigger and allowed two cocks to pass unmolested over my head. Old Haskins would rebuke me for that. So would Mother. Disliking shooting, she had yet let it be known that, with Christmas impending, she would like to see a big bag.

So, when we broke for sandwiches (corned beef in these austerity days) and brown sherry, I apologised to Haskins, for my inattention.

'I don't rightly know, Mr Alec,' he said, 'as I can blame you. There's too much happening to take our minds from what we should be doing of.'

He sucked his pipe.

'Things haven't been what they were since your father left us,' he said. 'I don't know as they will ever be again what they should be.'

Haskins was perturbed by Frank's election to Parliament that summer. He didn't know now whether Frank should be a beater or a gun. The news that I had put Frank up for membership of one of my clubs had him shaking his head. It was no good joking with him that he was the last support of the feudal system left in England. He saw nothing funny in that. For Haskins, the war had been futile if it didn't mean a return to the England he had served and loved. He saw that Frank's friends were determined that that shouldn't happen.

Of course, Frank and his friends were right. To attempt to restore the England that old Haskins valued would be intolerable. Men hadn't fought and died for that. And in any case, I thought, as the mist closed in and the shoot was abandoned, it was that England which had led us into war by ineptitude and cowardice.

The path I was following through the woods led to an Edwardian folly: a summerhouse in a glade where as children we had been accustomed to enjoy picnics on the long afternoons of August. Its original purpose had been different: the Rand magnate, Sir Reuben Goldsmith, from whose widow Father had bought Blankets, had been wont to seduce the wives and daughters of his City friends there; Frank had once told me it was still known in the village as 'Sir Reuben's Snug'. Now the path was overgrown, half-choked by spreading brambles. The windows of the summerhouse had been broken, perhaps by some of the evacuees whose presence in the woods had so irritated old Haskins. A corner of the roof had fallen in. Putting my hand to the overhanging wood, I found a piece break off. Dusk gathered. The fringe of the trees sank into mysterious dark. Alarmed by some noise I hadn't heard, a pheasant clattered from its roosting place. It grew cold, but still I sat on the wet porch, and smoked, reluctant to retrace my steps towards the firelight, tea-tray and toast.

'You can't go back,' was the message that rang in my ears, 'but you don't want to go forward.'

I found this strange. Hadn't I, after all, always thought of myself as progressive? Hadn't I written pieces calling for the creation of a Socialist society?

'George has arrived.' Kirstie met me in the hall with this news. 'Unfortunately he's a little drunk. Mother sent him to lie down.'

'Not exactly the welcome the Prodigal Son received.'

'The Prodigal Son probably wasn't pie-eyed. Some American major gave him a quart of Bourbon.'

'Nice. Old George, eh . . .'

We hadn't seen him for almost fifteen years, and now he had been sent straight to bed by his mother. It seemed a poor reward for three and a half years in a Jap POW camp.

Dinner was strained. The thought of George slumbering overhead oppressed us. He wasn't exactly the Black Sheep, I thought. George had made good in a way. The rubber estate Father had consented that the trust should buy for him had, at least by his report, flourished; it had remained a going concern till the Jap invasion. His marriage to the Malay girl had produced two children. They might well be the only members of the next generation to bear the family name.

278

Best of all – worst of course for George himself, that had to be granted – his war, if not glorious, in fact hellish, had earned him more merit points than mine, or Hector's, or, certainly, Alastair's. He hadn't, it was true, done much fighting. That wasn't his fault. A corporal in the Johore Volunteers could scarcely be held responsible for the ignominious surrender of Singapore. But, though we didn't yet know much about the horrors experienced by POWs in Jap camps – sufferings which, in the decades to come, would, reprehensibly, never impinge on the general consciousness as the obscenities of the Nazi death camps were to do – it was already clear that to have survived that ordeal was to have proved yourself. The camps were schools of private and quiet heroism, which left me abashed. And now our own family hero, the only one of us whose sufferings had been physical as well as mental – and never underestimate the influence of physical suffering on mind and imagination – had returned drunk because he feared to confront his mother.

Later, when Mother and Kirstie had gone upstairs, Hector and I retired to the billiard room. A log fire had been lit there, for the first time in a couple of years, perhaps, and the chimney smoked. A cloth covered the green baize. I smoked cigarettes and gave myself a glass of Father's pre-war Armagnac. Hector talked of his disappointment with the Labour Government which, in his view, was ready to ally itself with reactionary forces on the Continent to curry favour with the Americans.

'There is still just time to create a European Union of Socialist States,' he said, 'but the twelfth hour is already well advanced.'

I said I thought the project chimerical. I talked of the Soviet Union's imperialism. He would have none of it.

'The choice in Eastern Europe,' he said, 'remains one between the progressive forces gathered together under the wing of the Communist parties, and reactionary neo-Fascism. There is no middle way.'

How hard, at this distance of time, not to make Hector seem a blind fool. Either that or a villain! Yet, with the benefit of hindsight, how many cannot be so charged?

Hector said: 'I loathed America, its ignorant optimism, its crass and indifferent materialism, its intense selfishness. There's nothing I won't do to prevent Britain becoming an American satellite – which is the fate our masters have in store for us, though they are too stupid to realise it.'

The door opened.

'Thought I'd find you chaps here. In the old lair, eh?'

I wouldn't have recognised George. Naturally, if I'd thought about it, I'd have expected him to be skeletal. His baldness was no surprise either. But, if met in the street, I'd certainly have passed by, unthinking. Yet, there was something of the old George there. That was soon apparent. The too-blue, slightly protuberant, eyes still sparkled with that disconcerting look of humorous lunacy, still gave off that determination that George would choose his own path, and that it would please him if others found it not to their liking. A large bottle dangled in his hand. He set it on the table; it was still a third full. He found a glass and poured a big measure for himself. Then he turned to look at us.

'And where's the apple of our late Father's eye?'

Explanation was difficult, unavoidable. I attempted it, briefly.

'What a fool, what a bloody fool!'

George stretched himself in the chair, looked over the rim of his glass.

'You know,' he said, 'it feels crazy being here, and hearing that sort of stuff.'

'You shouldn't have got up, George,' Hector said. 'You're still drunk.'

'And intend to remain so. I've a lot of drinking time to catch up on. You political buggers have taken years out of my life.'

He tilted his glass.

'And so the Old Man has been gathered to the God of his fathers. I don't mind telling you that's a relief. In one way. In another, I'm sorry. I've had harsh words from him over the years, and I'd have enjoyed the chance to tell him his Empire's bust. That mighty Empire, on which the sun never sets, now all in darkness. It's the great joke of our time. I knew that even as we laid down our arms in Singapore. There never was such a fiasco, you know. And what sort of a war did you have, brothers?'

Hector got to his feet.

'I think that's for another day,' he said.

'Always the little diplomat.'

His laugh followed Hector out of the room.

'And how much did the Old Man cut up for?'

One of Father's favourite sayings was: 'Cripples have a right to be cankered.' George's bitterness was forgivable. That didn't mean it was easy to accept. He hadn't been home more than a few days before Mother was rebuking him for self-pity. All the same she made an effort to get on some sort of terms with this son who had fled to the East to escape her. She failed. Overtures of affection, appeasement, even apology, were heavily rebuffed. George seemed to take pleasure in saying whatever he thought would hurt her. Even Kirstie couldn't get close to him. Her enquiry about his wife and children was snubbed. Hector said: 'George seems to regard the war as having been arranged specifically against him. He might realise that others have suffered too. Some of them haven't survived to soak up Bourbon.'

The only people whose company George seemed to enjoy were Kirstie's little girls, Jean and Hattie. He lay on the nursery floor while they clambered over him. He built farms with bricks for them, and read Beatrix Potter to them. When he finished *The Tale of Mr Tod*, and they cried for an encore, he obediently went back to the beginning and obliged. He took them for walks and told them stories of tigers and the jungle and an old Chinese hunter – 'the biggest Chinaman I ever saw' – who used to shoot jungle fowl for his supper. Years later Hattie recalled these days, and said to me: 'Of course I never realised then how miserable he must have been. We just thought he was wonderful. I'm sorry, Uncle Alec, but Uncle George was absolutely our favourite Uncle. I never liked Uncle Hector of course. Even then, I thought there was something creepy about him. But Uncle George used to throw me up on his shoulders and march through the woods singing.'

'What did he sing? I never heard him sing.'

'Oh, don't ask me now. It was so many yonks ago. But we adored him. So he must have been nice really. Children are never wrong in that way, don't you think?'

Hattie has, for long, been someone I don't argue with. So I didn't ask if she had always placed the same faith in the judgement of her own children.

Father had always insisted that we celebrate Hogmanay with a family dinner at which we were each expected, from the age of eleven or twelve, to make a speech and say something about the year that was ending and of our hopes for the one to come. It was not an occasion which Mother had enjoyed and the custom had lapsed since his death. So I was surprised when Kirstie told me that Mother was determined to revive it.

'Strange, isn't it?' Kirstie said.

'An act of unexpected piety.'

'And not, to me, a welcome one.'

Father, sentimental in such matters, had ever decreed that the dinner should be authentically Scots; that alone might have deterred Mother from reviving the custom. The menu always began with a sheep's head broth, made according to the classic recipe of Meg Dods of the Cleikum Club, even though it was no longer necessary, or perhaps possible, to send the head to the blacksmith to be singed. While we took our soup (with, in Alastair's case, some reluctance), Father would retail the story of the learned Scots professor, who, exiled to Cambridge, experienced 'a natural and national longing for this savoury food, which is, to a Scotsman, like his mother's milk'. So the professor procured a sheep's head, and sent it to the blacksmith to be singed. The dinner hour arrived and he waited in eager anticipation. Imagine, Father would say with relish, 'his horror and disappointment, when a fleshless skull was put before him. His dismay was only increased when he was presented with the sauce of a bill, which set forth the charge – one shilling and four pence – "to polishing a sheep's head for Professor Smith . . ." So little,' Father would say, 'is this most robust of our native delights appreciated in these barbarous regions.' Whereupon, Alastair, equally invariably, would remark that Professor Smith had been fortunate in getting the only sort of sheep's head that he himself would welcome – and, being Alastair, was forgiven for this blasphemous pleasantry.

If the sheep's head broth wasn't to everyone's taste (though Kirstie and I agreed with Father in applauding it), this wasn't the case with the oysters stewed in their own juice, or the roebuck venison collops, or the Kingdom of Fife rabbit pie, or the gigot of mutton with roasted onions, two or three of which dishes used to follow. There was general approval, too, for the cranberry tart with a quantity of double cream and the oatcakes with farmhouse cheese which used to end the meal. Claret was drunk throughout, and served in a tappit hen, which contained three quarts of the wine, and which provoked Father to give us the old rhyme:

> Blythe, blythe, and merry was she,
> Blythe was she but and ben;
> Weel she loo'ed a Hawick gill,
> And leuch tae see a tappit-hen.

'And what's a Hawick gill, lass?' he would ask Kirstie.

'Half an imperial pint, Father.'

Though the tappit hen was, as I recall, never filled to the brim, and (probably) never emptied, it will be understood that by the time we were required to make our speeches, we were all agreeably free of inhibitions, a state in which we were maintained when Father set himself to the making of what was known as a 'Glasgow punch'.

I have called the occasion an example of Father's sentimentality. So, doubtless, in one sense it was. But, looking back from this distance in time, I see it also as an expression of his dissatisfaction with the course on which his ambition had directed his life. It was as if, for one night in the year, he freed himself from everything that his success had brought him, as if he scraped the patina of Oxford and the Empire from his essential self, and became a mosstrooper or bonnet laird. Of course it was play acting; but play acting which revealed the certain idea he had of his deepest nature.

This first year of uneasy peace, the meal was on a diminished scale. Oysters were unavailable; the Kingdom of Fife pie contained more rabbit than pork; pheasant replaced the gigot of mutton; and the tappit hen was absent, a few odd bottles, remnants of Father's never considerable cellar, being provided in its stead.

Mother had, however, with ironical relish, insisted on the sheep's head broth, of which she herself took no more than a few spoonfuls. She presided over the meal in remote manner, like the priestess of a dying cult conducting a ceremony, necessary but no longer credible. In consequence, a certain chill prevailed, all the more because places had been laid for Father and Alastair and Colin.

When Mrs Haskins had placed decanters of port and brandy, and a box, perhaps the last survivor, of Father's cigars – Bolivar – on the table, and left us, Mother began to speak.

'You are all, I fancy, surprised that I should have insisted on maintaining the tradition of this meal. You need not feel any anxiety that it will be repeated. But this is the first New Year's Eve that we have all — or almost all — been together since your father died, and I suppose it will be the last. For one thing, the Government which your friends have installed, will make it unlikely that we shall be able to maintain Blankets. Your father lived up to his income, and in some years beyond it. You all know how generous he was to you children. Though some of his books still sell, and will, I trust, continue to do so, I can't afford to live here. I'm therefore proposing that the house should either be let or sold, while, for my part, I intend to go to live with your Aunt Elizabeth. She has been asking me to do so for the past two years. We are both widows, and, though we irritate each other, we have the bond of sisterhood. So now I should like to hear, formally, from all of you what your response is, and what your own plans are. Hector, as the oldest, should speak first, but your father wished the house to go to you, Alec, eventually. And you can't afford to maintain it, can you? Furthermore, like Hector, you have no family. George, you have a family, but I question whether they would wish to live here. So, Alec?'

It was masterly. We were all disconcerted. Mother lit a cigarette and watched the smoke from her first puff float between her and us.

I said: 'Father may have wanted me to have Blankets. He certainly said so. But I don't know that I took it seriously. I certainly couldn't afford to live here. My only child is dead — yes, there's no use pretending now that little Rose wasn't my daughter — and I don't think I'm likely to marry now. In any case, I'm a newspaperman, not a country gentleman. I'm going back to my old paper, as foreign editor. Now that Harbottle's dead, they want me again. Billy Hughes is going to take over as editor in the spring. So. But I think we should let Blankets, not sell. It's hardly the best time to put a property like this on the market. Or are there still death duties to be cleared?'

Mother said: 'Yes, there are. But they should be provided for. Negotiations are still going on. It would have been nice to have had help and advice on the matter. As for selling, there must be hard-faced men who have done well out of this war also.'

Hector cleared his throat. 'Of course I should feel slighted,' he said. 'No doubt the world will think me slighted. But it's a matter of indifference to me. Sell the place, and let's be rid of this, this affectation of gentility.'

'Isn't it,' Mother said, 'your own denial of gentility that is the real affectation? George?'

'It's nothing to do with me. I don't belong here. I never have.' George reached out for the brandy decanter, and poured himself a good measure. 'It's comical, you know,' he said, 'really comical, to hear this conversation in this day and age. As if nothing had happened since the Durbar. Don't you realise it's all gone up in smoke? The last gentleman died on the Somme, and everything since has been a charade. I'm going back East. I've a wife there. She's still alive, just. One of the children is dead. Cheerful, isn't it? Did Father leave me any money? Nobody's told me.'

'Don't be silly, George. You know perfectly well. You had a copy of the will. The rubber estate's yours, and £20,000.'

'Well, there it is. I'll sell the rubber estate, and buy a boat. I'm going into shipping. There's a bit to be made in the carrying trade between the islands. I'll fish in troubled waters, and there are plenty of them from Sumatra to New Guinea. I'm going to live selfishly, exclusively for myself and family.'

'When have you lived otherwise?' Hector said.

'That's as maybe. I haven't wasted the years, pretending to shape the world, that's for sure. The old thing shapes itself, and we cling to the turning wheel and try not to get ground under. It makes me laugh when I hear you chaps assuming airs of responsibility. Don't you know the world doesn't give a damn? I daresay young Alastair's learned that by now, if he's still alive to learn anything. So do what you want with this place, Ma. I never liked it. It was only a stage set. And Hector, forget the White Man's Burden, whether you preach the gospel according to St Paul or Karl Marx. The East will go its own corrupt beautiful way.'

'Kirstie?'

'I've nothing to say, for the time being. You'll all go your own ways, as you always have. Some day, you may realise what you owe to Father.'

'I don't know why Mother inflicted that on us.'

Kirstie and I were walking through frozen woods. Lucy, the spaniel, no longer, in her old age, ranging a hundred yards or more away, bounced out of the withered bracken between the ash trees.

'Don't you?' Kirstie said. 'She's very bitter.'

'That's clear. But why?'

'You don't know?'

'No. I never thought she had much ambition for any of us.'

'It's not that. It's rather that each of you, all . . . four . . . of you seem to have lived your lives as a criticism of hers and Father's and everything she holds dear. Which is the way things are, the way that she believes they very properly have always been. And she has a contempt for public life, tolerable in Father, but she feels you have all cheated her by following him in this respect.'

'It doesn't make sense. You make her sound like George.'

'Well, yes, but then he cares about money.'

'Does he? I hadn't noticed.'

'He's mad about it.'

It was very cold. The wind blew sharp from the east. There was a smell of dog fox in the clearing. Pheasant feathers on the path were evidence of his dinner. A magpie flew chattering out of the trees.

'One for sorrow.'

287

'Old Haskins is getting past it. Ten years ago there was never a magpie on the place. Will he retire if we let or sell Blankets?'

'It's not going to be let or sold,' Kirstie said.

'What do you mean?'

'I've had an offer of marriage.'

'Oh . . . who from?'

'Edwin Pringle.'

I was silenced.

'He's rich. I'll make him buy Blankets, I'll make that my price.'

'Kirstie . . .' I began, 'this is difficult but . . .'

'I know what you're trying to say. Don't think I haven't thought about that side of things.'

Who am I to talk, I thought . . . Fred stretched himself out on my bed, pretty as a postcard. I ran my hands over smooth thighs . . .

Kirstie and I climbed out of the woods to a bare grassland where I had made love to Van.

'So you'll say yes?'

'If he meets my terms. And he will. He's fond of me. He's been lonely since Linda died. He wants a wife. And besides it'll gratify him to be able to appear, in a sense, Father's heir. He really did admire him, you know.'

'You're very confident, Kirstie. I wish I was as sure of things as you are.'

'You think too speculatively.'

But, I thought, don't you want more out of life? A marriage of convenience sounds all right in nineteenth-century fiction. We expect its women, girls even, to be sensible. I don't believe, for instance, that Emma really loved Mr Knightley. But that marriage was eminently suitable. Only, we're not living that sort of life now.

Kirstie strode up the hill, with long-swinging country-woman's stride.

She said: 'If we cut round by Lazely woods we could do a full circuit and come home round the lake.'

'It'll be dark.'

'Doesn't matter. You don't think it will be too much for Lucy, do you?'

It was not a question she would have put about her daughters.

We walked half an hour, perhaps, without speaking. The silence was companionable, a brief recovery of childhood intimacy. Now I felt at the same time close to Kirstie and very distant. Both feelings were prompted by my admiration for her self-assurance, or for the appearance she gave of possessing that quality.

'What about you?' she said, as we turned back into the woods and out of the wind which, however, still rushed through the high branches. 'Isn't it time you got married?'

'You heard what I said last night.'

'Yes. You've rather made a mess of things, haven't you? Vanessa was a bitch, I suppose that was the attraction. Cousin Lucy would have had you, you know. Well, that chance has gone.'

'Sugar and cream? No thanks. She's made a more suitable choice.'

Lucy Pelham-Grey, Kirstie's bridesmaid, had married a Guards major, heir to a couple of thousand acres in Dorset.

'Dull as a stick,' Kirstie said. 'But you ought to get married all the same, before you turn eccentric.'

What would you say, sister, I thought, if I told you that at this moment I feel a longing, lust indeed, for a French boy of eighteen?

She said: 'I haven't forgotten Col, you know. I don't want the girls to think I'm disloyal to his memory.'

'Poor Col. Think how his father's death hung over him. You won't make that mistake.'

'No,' she said, 'poor Col, he had no ambition to be a hero. I often think, poor Col.'

'Yes,' I said, 'he could love people, but he didn't much like life.'

We came out of the trees. The lake lay before us, the wind rippling the water in the half-dark. Lucy bounded at a pair of mallards which took off with a whirr of wings. Chill damp penetrated my tweed coat.

'Look at these rushes. The lake needs clearing out. I'll get Edwin to see to it.'

'Do you think that's his style?'

'I mean, pay for it.'

The path leaving the lake led us by Old Haskins's gibbet. A couple of grey squirrels, a jay, and two carrion crows swung in the wind.

'Are you really going to Nuremberg for the trials?'

'Yes. That was my condition to Billy Hughes.'

'It sounds like hell.'

'I hope so.'

'I don't think the generals, Keitel and – is it Jodl – or the admirals should be on trial. What else can a soldier do but obey orders?'

'They'd agree with you.'

It was almost dark when we came within sight of the house. Kirstie took hold of my arm.

'And Alastair . . . do you think he's dead?'

'I rather hope so sometimes.'

'So does Mother.'

'Pride. But if he isn't dead, he might be a prisoner in the Soviet Union. I'd rather be dead.'

'Will you be asking questions in Germany? Silly, stupid of me, of course you will, but is that really the first reason you're so determined to go?'

'Let's just say it's a reason.'

'I used to understand you better, Alec.'

'So did I. God help me, so did I.'

XIX
Nuremberg–Berlin 1946

'*Wie es eigentlich gewesen*' – was that Ranke or Goethe? To see life, to tell it 'as it actually was'. Looking at the grey men in the dock, it was near-impossible to see them as they had actually been. But weren't they being compelled to confront the reality of their lives? Wasn't that the purpose of the trial? And isn't it, I wondered, the purpose of any trial, which brings the being in the dock up against the blunt fact of consequence?

'I guess,' an American major said to me, 'it's the categorical imperative in action.'

His sincerity didn't exclude irony. An intelligent man, in civil life, he told me, a company lawyer, who had, nevertheless, resisted attempts to draft him into the legal branch of the armed forces, he talked, over coffee from the US PX stores, chain smoking Camels, of his German grandfather who had emigrated from Nuremberg itself, by way of Hamburg or Bremen, in 1895, 'for economic reasons, he was the seventh child in the family', and who had seen the windows of his hardware store in a little town in Missouri broken by patriots in 1917.

'You'll have cousins still here in Germany?' I suggested.

'I'm not persuaded I'm eager to look them up,' he said.

He had been among those who were first into liberated Ravensbrück.

'Though we were good American citizens, my grand-parents talked German to each other and to us kids. We sang

German carols round the piano on Christmas Eve. It was all kind of *gemütlich*.'

The trial itself was profoundly depressing. Depressing? Inadequate word, but I can't think of a single alternative that expresses what I felt then, and still do, when Nuremberg returns to me in dreams. It was not merely the dreadful catalogue of infamy and horror. That was bad enough, awful in every sense of the poor word, of course. It was rather that the reduction of humanity of which, collectively at least, all the accused were guilty, was now performed on their own persons. There was justice there. No one could deny that. But it was as if we were all sucked into an evil-smelling swamp.

We were brought up on tragedy. I mean by that, that we were educated to recognise tragedy, in its Greek, Shakespearean, or French classical form, as the supreme point of art. But, though the form of tragedy might superficially seem to be observed here, though it might have been possible to construct in an essay, an argument that the conditions of tragedy were present, yet the horror was its utter absence. It was as if *Macbeth*, denied the language of poetry, was revealed as merely squalid.

It was impossible, looking at these grey insignificant men, to imagine the power they had possessed a few months before. Goering was an exception; the Allied doctors had weaned him from his drug dependency, and he had got a new vigour, as if the last years were wiped out. There were days when he seemed, even, to be enjoying himself.

Most who have written of the trial have stressed how Speer seemed 'different', how he alone had retained dignity. That wasn't how it presented itself to me: I saw shreds of dignity in the soldiers – Jodl, Keitel, even Kaltenbrunner – but Speer? He was too eager to say what he thought the right thing. No doubt this was because he had retained or reacquired enough integrity to be able to distinguish right from wrong. Yet I found distasteful, then, the manner in which this nearest thing to a friend Hitler knew, used his acknowledgement of responsibility to distance himself from the others in the dock.

We were lodged, us foreign correspondents, in a large villa, or Schloss, a couple of miles out of Nuremberg. It was in design fantastical, like a Wagnerian set, and that was suitable, for the regime had been permeated with Wagnerism. The villa was overcrowded, and, when it was built, in the 1880s, there had been less demand for bathrooms than there was now. The overcrowding should have bred a spirit of comradeship, but, though the bar, established in one of the salons, panelled with marble that made it look like a room decorated with butchers' slabs, was well-frequented in the evening, for much of the time men and women drank silently, not in the manner of journalists. We were the victors, but there was no sense of triumph.

I had been there a week when Barbara arrived. She had been covering the Civil War in Greece, and had travelled back through Yugoslavia. What she had seen had caused her, for the first time, perhaps, to question the Cause to which she had devoted her life and which not even what we had both known in Spain had led her to doubt.

Her figure had acquired a mid-American stockiness, and her voice a new harshness. She was all for meting out the severest punishment to the Nazis, scornful of the former head of the OSS General Donovan, a lawyer who had resigned from the prosecuting team when Jackson, its leader, had refused to countenance a plea-bargaining arrangement he had made with Goering, but her new suspicion of the Soviets was already leading her to anticipate the day when we would re-arm the Germans in defence of Democracy.

Our talk lacked its old intimacy. Barbara, conscious of what I saw as the real Barbara, was strangely uncomfortable with me. I had always, before, deferred to her, recognising that she possessed not only a will that was stronger than mine, but a clarity of vision that made my qualified assent to propositions appear a peculiarly English fault of character. But now, when I saw how she was shedding her old skin to suit the new fashion, I lost my sense of her superiority, even though, in opinion, I was no further from her than I had ever been; and she sensed this, disliked it, and went cold on me.

It was different with Helmut whom I encountered for the first time since the old days in Berlin. Still making use of the Norwegian nationality he had prudently acquired, he was covering the trials as the representative of an Oslo paper. On my first night he clapped my shoulder with a '*wie geht's, mein Alter*', which attracted the disapproving attention of some American correspondents whom he favoured with his Berlin street-urchin grin.

'So, Helmut,' I said, 'and are you still a Communist without hope?'

'But certainly. How can a Communist have hope when he considers the Soviet Union?'

'My brother retains it, but then he has never been a Party member.'

'No? But we have both come through, my friend. Did you have a good war?'

'No.'

'No, indeed. Europe has not had a good war. When I see what Germany has brought on itself, what the Germans have made for themselves, I come close to despair.'

'Only close?'

'No nearer.' He laughed. 'Now we must drink American whisky.'

I talked to Helmut about Alastair, something I couldn't do with Barbara now.

'Ah,' he said, 'I remember your brother, so young, so charming, so stupid. Even then, I said to myself: you should go back to your cricket field, young man. So I should have said it to him out loud? Yes?'

'Could he be in the East?'

'He could, if he had another identity. Under his own

name, impossible. They would certainly have produced him by now, to embarrass, you understand. But do you know if he was ever, indeed, in Germany?'

'No,' I said, 'I know nothing.'

'Ah,' he said, 'you, too, are among the mutilated of the war.'

We had dinner together. Reluctantly, Helmut said something of his work for the Norwegian Resistance. That was all in the past, of no importance now, he brushed it off. Would he resume German citizenship?

'It is a temptation not to. I admit that.' He stubbed a cigarette out with three sharp stabs. 'It is quite comfortable to be a Norwegian, you know. For us Norwegians, the war was an accident, so we can forget it.'

'But you had Quisling in Norway.'

'Oh, yes, it is of no significance.'

'And Nazi sympathisers? The novelist Hamsun, for instance.'

'That is true.' He waved truth away and lit another cigarette. 'It doesn't alter the fact that for us Norwegians the war was an accident. It did not grow out of our society. But for us Germans, it was quite otherwise. The last twenty years constitute the history of our character. Sad.'

'Us Norwegians? Us Germans? Which, Helmut?'

'Ultimately, my friend, I am a German, I can't get rid of that reality. So, yes, my future lies here, unless the Americans re-establish Fascism, as they will be tempted to do. And even then, who knows? Now, let us drink more of their excellent Bourbon.'

Later, much later, while in the background, from another salon, came the sound of voices raised in chorus – 'Is this the Chatanooga Choo-choo' – Helmut poured us yet another whisky and said: 'All the same, for us Germans, the war was a terrible and necessary drama, from which we may emerge purified and stronger. But was it that for you English? I think not.'

'So what was it for us?'

'A dream, I think. Perhaps the last Romance.'

I got the offer of a lift on an RAF plane to Berlin. The Tiergarten, where I had walked with Trude, was a vast potato patch, stretching out in the grey of the afternoon towards the immensity of the eastern plains. That is, it would be a potato patch – already the ground was being dug – while the Hohenzollern statues which Hitler had removed from Unter den Linden and hidden in the thickly-wooded park, now stood naked, amidst the stumps and broken shards of trees, and old men and women, heads bowed, as if in penitence, prepared the ground for the potatoes that would ward off starvation.

Berlin was a city of the walking dead. 'By Kafka out of Piranesi', one of my travelling companions, a Welsh infantry officer now attached to the Intelligence Corps, remarked.

'An odd marriage,' I said, 'and a terrible child.'

'I used to teach Classics before the war. I don't know if I can go back to that.'

'Surely the Greeks can teach the young something of value now. Hubris, Nemesis – hasn't their view of life been justified?'

'The Germans led the world in Classical scholarship. I was compelled to make a tour of Belsen,' he said.

The Berlin cold returned to me insistent as a leitmotif.

'On the other hand,' I said, 'Nietzsche declared that the city states of Ancient Greece tore each other apart so that the citizens of each might find peace from themselves. Or something like that. Perhaps that is the message you should carry to your pupils. Isn't it what we have been doing?'

'You mean,' he said, 'that we fought this war for our own sakes?'

'Something like that. Because we were ashamed?'

'I never questioned that we had to fight,' he said. 'My wife thought it wrong, her parents are Quakers. She's a very good person. I don't know that I can live with her again. That's

296

what this war's done to me. I taught in a public school, rather a minor one – the sort of place, you know, which has its Old Boys saying: "I was at a place called Grindlay Hall – you won't have heard of it." In the West Country. A very decent school, preparing boys to lead decent lives as country solicitors, farmers, doctors, businessmen. We thought it a triumph if we sent a boy to Oxford, it only happened three times in the nine years I taught there. But very decent in our best unobtrusive quiet English way. I took my Upper Class through Homer, Aeschylus, you know. It never occurred to me that life could be so savage – now – in the twentieth century. Was I naive? Was I a fool?'

An old woman crouched over a brazier in what had been the porter's lodge. The windows had been blown in, and the glass from those on the first floor of the block had also gone. But the block was one of only two or three in the long avenue that had more than a façade, and dim lights – candles, I assumed, for it seemed unlikely that the gas or electricity supply could have been restored in this wilderness – shone in the upper apartments.

The old woman viewed me with indifference, her gaze blank as the future. I explained my purpose. She made no response. All she wanted was that I should go. Whether I went back out into the gathering night or mounted the stairs behind me was no concern of hers. I wondered if she was the wife of the old porter who used, on my first visits, to view me with keen curiosity and with whom, later, I had fallen into the habit of conversation, or, rather, listening, as he told me, again and again, how he had been wounded in the neck near Messines and what good chaps the British Tommies had been: 'Fair, like us Germans,' he used to say, smacking his fist against his open palm.

The staircase was in darkness. The rail had gone from the balustrade on the well side. There was a stench of decay. I mounted, gingerly, feeling each step.

When I knocked, there was silence, then a shuffling of feet, and an old woman's voice asked who I was to be disturbing them. I gave my name, the shuffling resumed, and the feet receded. I stood listening to the creakings and little unidentifiable sounds of the dark building.

Then the door opened and a voice said: 'Is it really you, Alec?'

We embraced. She laughed, and rebuked the old woman for her fears. There was a note of hysteria in her voice, but she took me by the hand and led me through, along the winding passage, to what had been her father's study. It was lit by half a dozen candles, and I was able to measure the change in her.

Trude had always been thin, but it had been the thinness of energy. Now it was the thinness of exhaustion that I saw. Her hands were rough; she explained that 'like everyone else' she had spent the day clearing rubble, repairing the stricken city.

'It's not as bad,' she said, 'as it was nine months ago. Or I'm accustomed to it now.'

I unpacked my rucksack, produced coffee, biscuits, chocolate, tinned ham, and a bottle of Johnnie Walker. She thrust the coffee at the old woman.

'Quick, Marga, boil a kettle. Real coffee. Alec, I haven't drunk real coffee since 1942.'

She began to cry.

'It's the shock,' she said, 'and the thought of coffee . . .'

We talked, first, of our distant past, easier to live in than the present. Trude sipped the coffee: 'It is so good, so rich, I am afraid my stomach will rebel.' Then she spoke with what I had not yet heard in Germany, which was optimism.

'We have taken a purge,' she said, 'and will be stronger.' She smiled. 'I do not mean we shall be stronger in the old bad way, dear Alec. We shall be stronger for good.' I gave her a cigarette. 'Peter will be so glad you have come to see us. You do remember Peter, don't you? I am almost sure I told you I was going to marry him. We have often spoken of you, he admires you, Alec, he remembers you well.'

Peter's bank had, indeed, as Helmut – was it Helmut? – had predicted, lent money to the Nazis when they were on the verge of power. So he did well in the thirties, he was quite in favour with the regime, though behind his back, as Trude said, real Nazis laughed at him. 'Peter is very correct, you will remember, and the Nazis were not correct.' He was excused military service, on account of his value to the banking business. In 1941, while still a director of the family bank, he was given one of these six-or-seven-syllable posts, attached to the Treasury. Trude didn't like that, but Peter was blandly confident. 'Naturally I despise the Nazis,' he said. 'I belong to an old patriciate which they do not understand. I am not a Bavarian peasant, you know. My ancestors were great merchants in Lübeck. But now they are in power, they are Germany, and I am a patriotic German. So, naturally, I serve the State.'

'He talked like that a lot,' Trude said. 'It was not entirely convincing. Do people talk like that in England?'

'People like Peter don't talk much about the State. The State has never been quite respectable in England. But they might talk the same way about serving the Crown. My father used to.' Father would also have said that you needed a long spoon to sup with the devil. That was not an adage Peter heeded. He was commissioned to organise the financial side of the logistics by which labour was transported from the conquered east to staff German factories. It was not important to him that this conscript labour force was condemned, essentially, to slavery. He was not, you see, responsible for their conditions of work. All he had to do was get the finance right. He experienced some trouble in rooting out corruption, for there were numerous officials who saw, in the vast scheme, a chance of easy pickings for themselves. Such behaviour offended Peter's moral sense. Banking, he used to say, is an honourable profession, and can only be carried on if standards of absolute honesty are maintained. He prided himself on his integrity.

In August 1944 he was arrested. Though he had had, in fact, no connection with the July plot against Hitler, it so happened that one of his cousins was among the inner ring of conspirators. This cousin was executed in the first wave of victims; he was among those whose execution was filmed for Hitler's private viewing. Peter's name was found on a list of those who might be employed in positions of trust by the Government that would take over when Hitler and his gang had been eliminated.

'That was quite natural,' Trude said, 'unfortunately. Though nobody had approached Peter, everyone who was anyone knew that he had no real sympathy with the Nazis, is a very competent banker and administrator, and absolutely trustworthy. So he was arrested, and tortured. Peter is not good at withstanding torture, I can't blame him for that.' He was condemned to death; then, in the administrative confusion of the last weeks of the Reich, relevant papers went astray or were amended, Trude still wasn't sure which. In any event he was released early in March. They had remained in Berlin, in hiding, then made their way, with great difficulty and in danger, to Lübeck. Peter was arrested there by the British. He was having to undergo de-Nazification. He thought that terribly unfair. He was at liberty again now, but not permitted to resume his profession. They had returned to Berlin because, if they didn't, well, who knew what would happen to this apartment, which in any case had strong sentimental associations for Trude, and which the old woman, Marga, whom I wouldn't have recognised, but who had certainly recognised me, couldn't be expected to maintain on her own. That might not even have been permitted. As to the future . . . Trude smiled again, that old serious-ironical smile which had been one of the things I loved in her.

Trude's voice quickened, regained vitality, as she made a

story of her husband's progress. His misfortunes, even if the consequence, as she saw, of the deficiencies of his own character and judgement, had given her a new deeper affection, even if it fell short of love, for his rather absurd person. She had married him because it was expedient; she would hold to the marriage because it was right.

If I had come there, as perhaps I had, partly in hope that she might be the one who would give a new direction and meaning to my life, that we might resume and take further what we had once had, or almost had, that hope was revealed as vain. A candle extinguished itself.

I gave her an edited version of my affair with Vanessa, but did not mention our child. Self-pity is one thing; seeking the pity of another, intolerable. I did not tell her about Fred. I spoke of my time in Spain and of what I had learned, sadly, there. And then I mentioned Alastair.

A key turned in the lock. The outer door of the apartment opened and shut. Footsteps and a cough came from the lobby. Another door closed.

'That's Peter,' she said. 'He's gone into his bedroom. He will shave in cold water before he comes to see me. He is always punctilious still, you see . . . Alastair. Do you still hold that against me?'

'I never did.'

'Then?'

Then I told her something, quickly, but then it was only a little, of what I knew of Alastair's war. She was astonished. If there were British traitors, she had heard nothing of any of them.

'You do believe me?'

'You've never lied to me.'

'You hope he's dead?'

'Sometimes. I feel wicked doing so. It's because it would be easier. But yes, sometimes.'

Peter came through. I wouldn't have recognised him but for the pop eyes. It was his manner. He was so anxious to please, so apologetic. He had lost the assurance which had been the product less, perhaps, of his nature than of his certainty as to his social position, rank, standing in an important organisation. Now, experience of a sort that he could not have imagined had stripped him naked.

At first Peter talked in short sentences, the words coming out in little jerks. He had much to complain of, but every complaint was punctuated with an apology, or expression of his awareness of guilt or the necessity that he should suffer on account of his shortcomings. It was embarrassing to observe this naturally complacent and unreflective man wallow in self-abasement. Then he drank a couple of glasses of the whisky I had brought, and began to recover his self-esteem. Before long he was announcing how he would rise from the abyss, how Germany would recover – so long as the Allies were not so stupid as to allow the Communists a share of power. Then he frowned.

'But I cannot be confident of that. If you British and the Americans understood the meaning of Communism you would not have allied yourselves to the Soviet Union. You would not have insisted on the unconditional surrender of Germany, which, I must tell you, demoralised the opposition to Hitler and his gang – an opposition whose feelings and thoughts I know well, since I was so closely concerned and connected with its leaders.'

When, after two more whiskies, Trude persuaded him to retire to bed, saying that I would sleep on the couch in the sitting room – 'I am sorry, Alec, but the spare bedrooms or what were the spare bedrooms are occupied by cousins of mine who have lost their estate in East Prussia' – and that we could talk more in the morning, she said, sighing: 'Poor Peter, in a few months he will have been one of the moving spirits in the July Plot, even Stauffenberg's confidential adviser.'

'Perhaps it is better that he should think so.'

'How can you say that, Alec? Truth is always better. How

302

can we commit ourselves to the future if we cannot tell and confront the truth about our past?'

I said: 'I don't know. I've lived through six years of war and I am less certain of anything than I was when it began. I don't think I shall stay on your sofa, Trude. When I came here to see you, it was not only to reassure myself that you had survived. It was in some way because I hoped that talking with you, being with you, could set my feet again on a path I want to follow. I even hoped . . .'

'No, Alec, don't. We were young once, and if we were foolish then, we were perhaps, nevertheless, wiser than we are now. You talk of the absence of hope. For me, the only hope is that I can regain hope by doing my duty. I married Peter because I was afraid. I thought his position and, yes, let me be honest, what I knew of his character, would protect me. His character was less than I had supposed, but still I have come through. I have survived the hell we Germans made of the world; and now my duty is so to support him that he can work to repair what we broke. I have no religious faith. Yet, this is a duty to which in a manner of speaking I must consecrate my life. So, Alec, I am fond of you, and I am sorry for you in your distress of spirit; but I am not strong enough, I am not strong enough to shoulder another burden.'

So we kissed, like brother and sister, or old friends between whom a veil of mist has descended; and I threw on my British Warm, and with heavy steps departed into the black cold of the Berlin night.

Ten years later I met Peter again. It was at a conference in Milan. I had chosen to cover it because the Common Market was just being created – had just been created? – with Britain outside it. I thought it might be useful for the paper's readers to know something about the work the new organisation was intending to do, what its principles were, and so forth. It was

303

one of my moments of high-mindedness, increasingly rare, even by then.

Peter was there as an adviser of Ludwig Erhard, the Economics Minister of the Federal Republic, already celebrated as the author of the *German Economic Miracle*. Peter looked an economic miracle in his own person; he shone with well-being, he glowed with self-satisfaction. His suit was clumsily cut but the cloth was very good, and you could see that it had been expensive. He greeted me with a show of enthusiasm which did not conceal a certain condescension. He insisted on buying me dinner, and lectured me on the inadequacies of British economic management. He steered clear of personal topics. For a little, I thought there might be a residual embarrassment, because he had been so down at our last meeting. But it wasn't that at all. He simply said, wordlessly: 'I am too important and successful to have a personal life.'

When at last I asked about Trude, from whom I had not had a letter for several years, his reply was: 'We are no longer together. She developed a distaste for society. Eventually, she is no longer a serious person. She drinks too much. It is sad.'

XX
Nuremberg 1946–Yugoslavia 1944

Back in Nuremberg I was disturbed by a series of bad dreams. Some related to my months in Yugoslavia. They began pleasantly, almost every night. I was following a broad upland valley, with chestnut trees on the upper slopes, and a river gently flowing through green meadows dotted with red poppies. Before me was the dancing image of an elegant town, Muslim on account of the minarets. A bridge spanned the river, and I stood listening to the call to prayer while swallows and martins swooped through the soft evening air, and white houses with red roofs stood among glades of trees. I crossed the bridge and settled myself outside a café. I called for coffee and slivovitz and watched the young men dance together in the square, while the old men played dominoes and smoked their pipes. It was the most peaceful and delightful place you could imagine.

Then the scene darkened. It began to rain. But I still sat there. To my surprise the square, instead of emptying as people took shelter, began to fill. Men, women and children emerged from the shops and houses, and stood lifting their faces to the rain. There was a roll of drums and from three corners of the square – the fourth appeared to be blocked off – appeared a column of soldiers. But the soldiers were all children, boys and girls of ten or eleven. The leading figure in each file carried a light machine gun, probably a Sten. A trumpet sounded, and they opened fire, indiscriminately. The rain turned to blood, but the people in the square resumed the dance of the young men which, I could now see, had become a dance of death. With light steps and inexpressive faces, they danced over and around the fallen bodies of those who had been shot, and all the time violins and accordions continued to play in gypsy rhythms.

I woke shivering and sweating and afraid, and next night it was the same. The dream never advanced beyond the dance of the unconcerned living over the fallen who were beyond feeling.

My time in Yugoslavia in the summer of '44 had been brief and inglorious. I was sent there for a purpose which soon proved superfluous: to report on whether we should continue to support Mihailovich and the Chetniks or transfer such aid as we could give, which was in truth little enough, to the mysterious Tito and his Communist partisans. There were those in my department of Intelligence who believed that the information we were getting from Yugoslavia was distorted by political bias, and that, as a result, we were in danger of adopting a policy which was against our true interest. There was much that was true in this judgement, as I soon discovered. On the other hand it was impossible to come to a valid conclusion. As it happened, I was sent to the Chetniks, and consequently was unable to make any assessment of the partisans, for each group distrusted any British officer who had had dealings with the other.

So in that sense my enterprise was vain.

It was vain also because it was fraudulent. The decision to abandon Mihailovich had already been taken. It had been taken on the authority of the best evidence: the Ultra intercepts, which made it clear that the Germans regarded Tito as the more dangerous enemy. But this information was not generally available till many years later, and it was not, of course, available to those of us who were in Yugoslavia then.

So, I was playing, though I did not know it, in a bitter comedy. Betrayal is, of course, a characteristic of comedy: the wife betrays her husband and makes him a cuckold; Malvolio is betrayed into supposing that his mistress adores him. We were betrayed into playing the part of traitors to those who trusted us. The only one among the British officers who saw what was happening was Robin Maltravers. His selection for the role of liaison officer to the Chetniks might, itself, have been an act of betrayal. A Communist sympathiser might have picked Robin as the type of British officer most likely to disgust the Serbs and so make them distrustful of us as potential allies. It didn't work out like that. Robin turned the flamboyance with which he had forced his sexuality on the world to good account. Now, among virile young men who despised effeminacy, the old queen transformed himself into an extravagant hero. His fearlessness under bombardment had even these reckless warriors lost in admiration. He became their model, their mascot, their pet; it was quite the thing to sing praises of his dandyism. They competed to fetch him hot shaving water. (Most of us never shaved and grew beards like the Chetniks.) They even brought him roses to wear in his cap.

Robin was candid in conversation with me. Filing his nails, a cigarette held at a rakish angle in an amber holder, he said: 'Of course I adore them, my dear, but I soon saw it would never do to lay a lustful finger on any of them. So the only thing to do was to set out to make them adore me. Which they do. It helps, of course, that I've no great desire to come out of this war alive. Whatever we are fighting for isn't going to be the world I knew and enjoyed. These boys are all frightful Puritans, they don't even sleep with the girls. I don't say there isn't the occasional bit of rough-and-tumble between a couple of them on a dark night, but my sort of thing, certainly not. Now, get that bottle of brandy out, dear.'

Robin saw very clearly that we would abandon the Chetniks.

'This is total war, isn't it, dear, and the first rule of that is that you shit on your friends if it suits you. Besides, this is a civil war, you know. And our boys aren't always clever. Dear old Draza himself, who's a gent, but not the brightest, made a speech in February in which he said that his enemies were the Croats, Muslims and Communists. That didn't go down well in London when it was reported. The partisans think the same way, substituting royalists for Communists of course, but they are careful not to let on when we're about.'

'So what can we do?'

'Nothing, dear boy, except to try to make our boys so strong that when the war ends they can at least fight it out with the Partisans on terms of equality.'

How often have I thought of that conversation in recent years, as Yugoslavia drifts to catastrophe, encouraged by the ignorant and malicious.

Robin picked up his glass and strolled to the doorway of our hut. We looked over a wide valley, in evening shadow, to the black mountains beyond. The scent of honeysuckle and pine resin mingled with the smell of cooking – a lamb was being roasted on a spit in front of a neighbouring hut, and the aroma of its flesh was laden with thyme, oregano and rosemary. The evening was very soft, and the young men were singing of the brave deeds of their ancestors.

'I love this place and this people,' he said, 'I've never felt this sort of love before. It must be the Empire spirit, wouldn't you say, dear?'

He spoke ironically. Set aside by years and habits of self-indulgence from what others, Hector, for example, would consider the serious business of life, Robin had learned to resort to irony as the means of reconciling himself to his condition. Disappointment – the inevitable consequence of attachments to those who were incapable of giving him the response that he desired, precisely because what drew him to them also ensured that their own sexual and emotional impulses were directed towards girls – had bred in him a romantic pessimism, Housmanesque, which could not be satisfied with brief mercenary scuffles with trade. When he had said to me, lightly, in the Paris Ritz: 'I 'listed at home for a lancer / O who would not sleep with the brave?', he was not, as I thought then, being facetious. He could laugh at his predicament, for self-mockery is the surest defence of the wounded, but to hear him murmur, as he stood, glass tilted, and gazed at the young Chetniks going about the duties of the camp: 'The Spartans on the sea-wet rock sat down and combed their hair,' was to understand his longing, his sincerity, and his lack of illusion.

Moreover, in remarking that the sort of love he now felt must be 'the Empire spirit', or its manifestation, he spoke the truth, whatever his ironical awareness that he was the antithesis of the Empire-builder. Perhaps, indeed, that antithesis was more apparent than real. There was a sense in which Robin, like the spoiled hero of *The Four Feathers*, or my own favourite among Father's characters, Malcolm Deloraine, cashiered from his regiment, despised as a weakling, abased and self-hating, redeemed by thwarting a dastardly German plot to overthrow a native princeling friendly to Britain, and then suffering a noble death after hideous torture, could be said to have embarked on this Serbian adventure as an act of atonement for his years of often squalid self-indulgence and his failure, hitherto, to recognise that privilege can be justified only by a life devoted to service. To see Robin like this was, perhaps, evidence of my own innate Romanticism. If so, it was bred by my admiration for his ability to be what I couldn't become. There was nobility there, that nobility which, as Camus wrote, is 'based on scorn, courage and profound indifference.'

There was another sense, perhaps the one he himself had in mind, for he certainly didn't see himself in the Romantic role for which I fitted him out, in which his attribution of the Empire spirit rang true. For in this guttering twilight of Empire, when any thinking man could see that our dominion was melting away, not only because the war would leave us impoverished and weak, but, more importantly, because we were losing, had perhaps already lost, the will to exercise authority over other races, those of us young officers, who were scattered over Europe charged with bringing what poor help we could to Resistance movements, all came to feel for those we were with, something of the pride and responsibility that the best sort of District Commissioners experienced for the tribes entrusted to their care. And the more those tribes were proudly independent and difficult, the more intense our attachment to their fortunes. Though we had argued that this was a war of ideologies, yet such attachments extinguished ideological differences. So, for example, across a couple of mountain ridges from us, men such as Fitzroy Maclean or my old Cambridge friend, the novelist Andrew Somerled, had fallen as deeply in love with Tito and the Partisans as Robin with his Chetniks; and this was possible, even though Maclean, who had served in our Moscow Embassy, knew the brutality of Stalinism, while Andrew retained all the middle-class prejudices of Tunbridge Wells (the setting of his best novels) to which he would even more thoroughly revert after the war, when his conversation became utterly tedious as he inveighed against the Labour Government which confiscated so much of his income and made it impossible for his mother to employ a maid, or for him to travel abroad as he wished. Then he married an American, which solved that problem by making dollars available to him.

I spoke to Helmut about my dream and about Robin. I did not see how they were connected.

'But he is dead, yes?' Helmut said.

'Oh, yes.'

'And how did you feel when you heard that?'

'Confused, overwhelmed, envious. I wanted to follow him.'

'A good death?'

'As deaths go. A brave one, anyway.'

'Yes, of course,' he said, 'the temptation to extinction is strong.'

'Is that what you think my dream suggests?'

'I'm not Freud, my friend, to make a nonsense of dreams. Accept it as it is: a statement or, better, a narrative of the world we recognise. That's enough to be going on with. It's absurd, yes, and therefore real. Do you know what the problem is? It's to keep going when you have confessed the absurdity of existence and have no hope. When that thought strikes me, I remember the wild flowers.'

Nuremberg. I find I can't write more, directly, about Nuremberg.

Not even now.

From the notebooks of Camus: 'The concierge of the Gestapo, who took over two floors of a building in the rue de la Pompe. In the morning she clears up with tortured bodies all around. "I never worry about what my tenants do," she says.'

Like God?

I find I scribbled that question in the margin of my copy.

It's dated 1963. I started reading Camus again today when I recalled that conversation with Helmut.

As for that dream, it stopped when I left Nuremberg. A newsreel from Africa recently showed children with AK–70s emerging from the bush. 'I never worry about what my tenants do.'

XXI
Paris/Le Havre 1946

Paris again.

Journal: Autumn–October '46:

This is still a city where people have not yet recalled how to live. That is to their credit. Otherwise, it would be as if they were pretending what has been, never was. I lay in bed for two hours after waking, reluctant to get up. Before I went to Yugoslavia, when I was wretched and moping in London, Barbara said to me: 'You're suffering from war nerves. The answer is to get into the war.' For the time I found myself in the Balkans, her prescription worked. War was a sort of escape. Now, I'm suffering from peace nerves, but it is more difficult to get into the peace.

I had lunch with Fred. For an instant, as he approached, light-footed, and bent to brush his cheek against mine, I thought we might begin again. But when he settled in the seat opposite and we looked in each other's eyes, I knew it was impossible, as I had known it would be wrong because it would have twisted him from a natural course of development. That's what I told myself.

In any case, he said, quickly:

'I've got myself a girl.'

'Ah, and does your mother approve?'

'No, but that can't be helped.'

He told me he had broken with Pougier. It wasn't what

he wanted from life, to put himself on show. And it would be embarrassing working for Pougier now.

All this was, in its way, a relief. I would hate to think I'd harmed him.

He asked if I had heard anything about Alastair. Fred has made it up with Yvette. So he promised that this time, certainly, he would arrange for me to meet her. It seems his own girl's father is in prison, awaiting charges of collaboration. Now that the worst of the *Épuration* is over, he may well get off with a sentence of a temporary ban from pursuing his profession. He's apparently a university teacher who was rash enough to publish articles advocating, like Alastair, the acceptance of the New Order.

'What makes me love Gilberte is that she refuses to pretend to feeling shame on her father's account,' he said. 'As you know I disagree totally with his position. Nevertheless, her attitude is magnificent. Don't you think so?'

Well, yes, I suppose I do.

'I think I shall become a writer,' Fred said, with his face very set and lovely in impassivity. 'I feel I have been cheated of something by my mother's determined withdrawal from the world, and her disapproval of whatever is natural. But, that I shall know what it is, precisely, of which I have been cheated, only if I write. But I think today the novel has to be a sort of journalism. Because we must solve public problems, the problems of the collective intelligence, in order to make space for the private life. Do you agree?'

'You could be right,' I said; but in truth I am lost when this sort of French abstraction is offered me. I should have said: 'Go out into the street and imagine the life of the first person who takes your eye.' Or perhaps: 'Go back to Brittany, to that little patch of land your mother talked of, and plough the earth. You'll do less harm and find a deeper satisfaction.'

We embraced, parted. I think he was glad to turn away.

It had been raining while we were in the restaurant, and when, afterwards, I walked along the quays, the river was shot with streaks of blue under a now brilliant sun. As it declined and I turned up the collar of my coat, the trunks of the trees caught the light and glistened. I said to myself: we'll always have Paris. We lost it but we've got it back and it will always stay with us and be ours. And then I was irritated because I couldn't remember who had said that, or something like it, in which novel or, perhaps, movie. But, nevertheless, the lines ran in my head, sang there even, like a music hall tune.

I stopped in a café, and asked for a half litre of white and some writing paper. The wine was greenish with a long aftertaste, and I got some bread and Pont l'Évèque cheese to eat with it. Then I wrote a letter to Kirstie. I told her I was now likely to see Alastair's girl, and then I said I hoped she hadn't committed herself to marrying Edwin Pringle. 'You deserve more than that. Have you thought that, when you are eating together in a restaurant, his eyes will slide away from your conversation to follow the progress of a waiter who has just emerged through the swing doors from the kitchen?'

October 16: 'For they're hanging Danny Deever in the morning.'

The line came to me as I woke, and then I remembered that they were, indeed, today hanging those condemned to death at Nuremberg. I have stood, as a newspaperman, outside a prison in the demeaning cold of dawn, and seen a warder emerge from a little door cut into the double forbidding door of the prison, and take down one small white notice and replace it with two other bits of paper, one of which declares, in the name of a sheriff, that a hanging has been performed according to law, and the other of which is the doctor's declaration that he has examined the hanged man and pronounced him dead. There is always a crowd gathered there, and the faces of some reveal a grim satisfaction, while others show an awareness that something ugly but necessary has been done in our name and on our behalf. The ugliness stays with you for a long time into the morning. You remember that de Maistre said that society is built on the work of the executioner.

As I shaved, I pictured the men I had seen in the dock, being led, with their hands tied behind their backs, to the execution shed; and I thought of Ribbentrop as I had seen him capering in a London ballroom. He had once asked Van to dance, she told me. 'And what did you say?' 'Oh,' she giggled, 'I danced. What else could I do? He is the ambassador after all. But he's an awful dancer.'

Well, I thought, he will have danced, horribly, on the air this morning.

But when I went down to the bar on the corner for my coffee, the *patron* told me that Goering had escaped the noose.

'The scoundrel,' he said, 'I always knew he would get the better of us. I always knew he would have the last laugh.'

I couldn't disagree. Judicial execution is so foul that the thought of even a brute like Goering cheating the noose seems a victory for humanity. That was what I read in the café proprietor's response. In my case, of course, I'm an unsatisfactory citizen. Though, in principle, I approve of Nuremberg, accept that something of that sort had to happen, and that it was done as well as could be, nevertheless, something elemental in me rebels.

Rebels against justice?

Yes, if that's how you want to put it.

I'm like Charlus. 'The idea of the defeated pained him. He could not read the accounts of trials in the newspapers without feeling in his own flesh the anguish of the prisoner and a longing to assassinate the judge, the executioner, and the mob that howled in delight at "seeing justice done".'

Something like that. When I first read the passage, I said: 'This is me.'

Test of a good citizen?

Do you identify with the dock or the bench?

For me, the dock, every time.

These thoughts ran through my mind as I made my way to the address Fred had given me in the little rue du Tournon where Yvette was expecting me.

The concierge questioned me. I passed, it seemed, muster, and was invited to mount the stairs. As I turned away, she said: 'But you must be his brother! How charming he was! Such manners! He made me feel like a duchess when he spoke with me! She wasn't worthy of him, I'll tell you that, even though she is my tenant. And I don't mind who knows it.'

I wouldn't have recognised the stocky woman who opened the door to me. She greeted me by name.

'You'd have passed me in the street, wouldn't you?' she said, understanding my perplexity, and I responded with one of those meaningless remarks with which one tries to pass off embarrassment.

'I haven't seen him since the spring of '44,' she said at once. 'I only agreed to see you because young Fred made a point of it.'

'I understand.'

'Do you?' she said. 'I wonder. There are times when I hate to feel I am understood. You are fond of him, aren't you?'

Uncertain whether she meant Alastair or Fred, I answered: 'Yes.'

She fetched a bottle of *vin ordinaire* and two glasses.

'I left him,' she said, 'because I had found something to

believe in. But I've only been half-alive since. That's absurd, isn't it? But, though in becoming a Communist, I've committed myself to the future, I see nothing but absurdity. And you don't know whether he's alive or dead?'

'I've found no evidence that he's dead.'

She drank one glass quickly and filled it again. She looked at me over its rim.

'If he's alive,' she said, 'what was most alive in him is dead.'

'What do you mean?' I said, though I was already sure I understood what she was saying.

She paused and looked round the room. I remember nothing of its furnishing.

'Perhaps that was why I left him,' she said, 'because it was already dying.'

'Yes?'

She got up, like one rising unsteadily from an illness, and went through to another room. Two pigeons were making love on the rooftop across the street. Voices called out, incomprehensibly, below. I drank some of the harsh wine, and saw that Yvette's glass was empty again. I tilted the bottle towards it. Time held me in its stalled train. The clock was silent, its hands forever fixed. Hopelessness seized me with a grip as tight as the Ancient Mariner's. But it had no story to tell.

The door opened.

Yvette said: 'If you are blaming me you are wrong. He demanded that my love should be absolute, but his own was like the Ten Commandments, all broken. This is what I was looking for.'

She handed me a photograph, scuffed and torn at the edge.

'The last I had of him,' she said.

Alastair was sitting at a café table. His head was thrown back in that gesture which I recognised as accompanying

317

his richest laughter. But he wasn't laughing. The expression on his face was one I had never seen before: the defiance had lost its joy and turned sardonic.

'It's the face of a gambler whose last throw has cleaned him out,' I thought.

My own face must have revealed what was in my mind, for Yvette said: 'I see you have understood. He was desperate then, he knew he had got everything wrong, that the New Order of which he had spoken so long and with such ridiculous enthusiasm was nothing like what he had imagined, but something foul that had risen from the dark places and spread the plague, infecting all it touched, and was moreover doomed to defeat because it was against all reason. He saw all that, he knew it in his heart, and yet he refused to act on what he knew. Because, in order to do so, he would have had to admit his own weakness, and he lacked the moral courage to do so.'

As she spoke, her hands fluttered, like small birds against a window.

'I think it was arrogance destroyed him,' she said. 'He could never learn from anyone. I find that very English.'

No more English than French, I thought, but did not say so.

'The last time I saw him he still expected we would make love, even though he knew, because I had written it in a letter, that all was over between us. But he thought he had only to smile, and . . . when I refused him, he looked like a small boy, and I came close to relenting. The worst thing is, if he came through that door, I am not certain I would, could, refuse him again, even though I have another lover now, a comrade, whom I find very pleasing and satisfactory. But none of this is what you want from me, it is only what I feel I must say.'

'On the contrary,' I said, 'you are explaining to me why it is that, despite the pain and shame he has caused all his family, I feel tenderly towards him, even now.'

'Yes,' she said, 'it is because we recognise that he is Peter Pan in your English play. Or he is Hamlet. I don't know. He has never grown up.'

'He was never encouraged to do so,' I said. 'He was such an attractive boy, everyone was happy he should remain that.'

'Yes,' she said, 'he was one of those to whom all pleasures come easily.'

She drank some wine, and then I saw that her eyes had filled with tears. She began to sob, stumbled to her feet, and ran from the room. I could hear her continuing distress, and I thought with abrupt bitterness of Alastair, who had left such a trail of wretchedness in his casual wake.

I wondered whether I should leave, if only to avoid further embarrassment for myself and pain for Yvette. But I sat and smoked and waited till the sobbing subsided.

'I'm sorry. That was an exhibition. Ridiculous.'

Yvette had returned without my being aware of it, and now resumed her seat, perfectly composed, and picked up her little tumbler of wine as if it was the second half of a sentence which had been interrupted by some extraneous event.

'I stopped believing in his films,' she said. 'That may have been part of the trouble.'

I explained that I was puzzled by the circumstances of his arrest. Was Torrance, perhaps, responsible?

'Torrance is a cunt,' she said.

She sipped her wine, too eagerly.

'What will the English do if they find him?' she asked.

'I don't know. They might prefer not to, they might prefer now that he disappeared. A year ago it would have been different.'

Then she said: 'Fred speaks well of you. You helped him to escape Pougier. I'm grateful. There was a priest

319

Alastair formed a friendship with. I'll write down his name and an address where you may find him.'

'You think, then, Alastair is still alive? Really?'

'I tell myself I would know if he wasn't.'

I thought: that's the language of the cinema, which doesn't, however, mean it isn't sincere. After all, who doesn't have recourse to readymade, even cant, phrases when it is a matter of giving expression to feelings which, if not, perhaps, newly-admitted, nevertheless haven't been put into words before? We all trade in a small stock of phrases, and new-minted ones are rare as white blackbirds.

Yvette then proceeded to give further justification to this theorising, by saying: 'After all, when everything's said and done and taken into consideration, he has been the great love of my life. I don't suppose I shall ever love anyone again as intensely and recklessly as I loved Alastair. If I live to be ninety he will remain my one great passion. That's why I was able to endure his wife that awful evening in London. I told Alastair afterwards you were in love with her. Do you know he hadn't seen it till that moment?'

'Egoism,' I said.

'Or innocence. Do you still love her?'

'In a way,' I said, 'but it's different. You see, she's dead, a bomb.'

'Oh,' she said, 'she was very beautiful. That was what pleased me so much, that she was so very beautiful, and I was not, but he preferred me.'

October 23: If I delay in Paris, it is not only in the hope that the letter of introduction which Yvette gave me for this Father Dominic (from whom, in truth, I expect very little) will lead to a meeting, or because I have been enjoying some agreeable society of different types – that dinner at Armand de Balafré's, for example, where I certainly had useful conversation concerning the political outlook – de Gaulle's increasing frustration, A. thinks he is already planning a return – or my encounter with Barbara's niece, Jackie, and her friend Jacey, a long-legged beauty from Harlem, but also because being here is not being there, in London, resuming life, career, duty and its various impositions.

Billy Hughes is wonderfully understanding. He says he needs me because Harbottle ran the paper into a swamp of dullness and mediocrity, but he doesn't need me till I'm ready to be needed. This sort of sympathy disconcerts me. Or perhaps it is being apparently valued that does that. I have only just begun to see how the self-contempt I have indulged in since Van's death has damaged me.

October 25: And, perhaps, I am beginning to revive. At least the erotic nerve jumps several times a day. It is different from my time with Fred. It was consolation, reassurance, I sought then. Yesterday at the Select, when Jackie went to make a telephone call, Jacey gave me a full welcoming smile, and we made an assignation, for this afternoon, here, at three o'clock. It's half-past two now, and I feel eighteen.

There was a letter for me, from Kirstie, at Thomas Cook's which I have been using as my poste restante. She isn't offended. Or is she? It's hard to tell. So often when people say they are not offended it means the precise opposite. But she assures me that she 'understands' Edwin, and that they can each supply what the other lacks. 'Anyway,' she adds, 'you are mistaken in supposing that Edwin doesn't like women, just because he runs after boys. We are actually very cosy together. I think we shall be happy. You must remember, too, he is still ambitious. I like that.' She goes on to say that Edwin has a great admiration and affection for me. 'So stop being beastly about him.' Hector is being sent back to Washington, 'Kicking and screaming, I hadn't realised just how much

he loathes Americans. I can't help thinking his appointment has been inspired by someone who doesn't have our
good relationship with our closest ally to heart. George, it
seems, has bought a second boat. His business is already
flourishing. I wonder how much of his trade is legal. As
Father used to say, sadly, George isn't straight.'

When Jacey arrived she wasted no time in conversation.
She slipped out of her shoes and skirt, and lay down on the
bed.

'Take my stockings off,' she said.

As I did so, unsnapping the suspenders and easing the
silk down the long thighs, the colour of milky coffee, she
unbuttoned her blouse and drew my head down to have
me nuzzle the flat belly which smelt faintly of sandalwood.
When, a little later, naked myself, I lay down beside her,
she wrapped her legs round me, and swung over and then
astride me, and lowered her head so that her lips brushed
my leaping cock. She drew back, and smiled for the first
time, and brushed loose hair off her face and opened
herself to my thrust . . .

Even as I write this, two hours later, with her scent still
warm on the bed, excitement renews itself and I have to
stop.

Afterwards, we lay still, my fingers running over her
damp flesh, and smoked cigarettes.

She said: 'I have to go very soon. Jackie will be mad at
me.'

I took the cigarette from her mouth and kissed her.

'No,' she said, closing her lips against my tongue and
turning her head away. 'Once only, for today. You
understand about Jackie and me?'

'Oh, yes.'

'I get love from her, I need love.'

She left. We fixed that she would come back tomorrow
at the same time.

Jackie's father is a director of the Chase Manhattan Bank. Jacey is the ninth of eleven children. She is twenty-three, hasn't known her own father, but has experience – unhappy I would suppose – of several stepfathers. She sings in a *boîte* on the Left Bank, which is where Jackie found her.

October 30: I am intoxicated with Jacey. For the first time in years I am in the grip of a purely sensual passion. For four days I have existed for that half-hour in the afternoon. We talk very little, but she says enough to make it clear that I mean nothing to her beyond what we do together. Yet that itself is as important, for the moment, for her as it is for me. When she goes, I lie sniffing where her body lay till the scent fades. Existence, Sartre says, precedes essence, and this affair (which it scarcely is) represents the most intense existence.

Last night I went to hear her sing. She was uncertain when I said I wanted to. It might make Jackie suspicious. So I recruited Fred and his girl, Gilberte (who is a very nice well brought-up girl whom Mother would approve of) and we went to the *boîte*. It was dark and smoky and lit by candles stuck in bottles, so that it was difficult to see who was sitting on the other side of the little cellar. Gilberte was nervous, she had never been in such a place before. I don't think she realised that most of the girls there were lesbians, but she did remark that it was strange that there seemed to be more girls than boys. Fred cottoned on and wasn't best pleased.

Jacey sang without any affectations half a dozen songs, in both French and American. There was a guitar accompaniment played by a fat girl who might have been Scandinavian or Polish. She didn't play very well, nevertheless it was effective. Jacey's singing voice was unexpectedly deep and the absence of expression, the sense that the words and music came into being quite independently of her, her utter passivity, were striking, and to me, disconcerting. When she finished she paid no attention to the applause, ignoring it as if it, too, like the music, belonged to someone who wasn't there. She crossed over from the little stage and sat at a nearby table. The upper part of a body advanced itself towards her, and an arm crept round her neck. Then I saw Jackie's profile which had been obscured in the shadows.

Fred said: 'But yes, you were right to bring us here. She is remarkable. She expresses exactly the emptiness we all feel. Don't you think so, Gilberte?'

'Oh, I loved it,' she said, looking at him and meaning: I adore you, Fred.

Jackie and Jacey looked round, saw me, and crossed over to our table. Jacey made no response to our congratulations, but sat very still and watched Jackie, who called for more beer and then began to talk about the need for writers to accept and proclaim commitment. Fred expressed some hesitancy. She responded with the authority of one who has had a play produced off-Broadway and is now working on her first novel.

I thought: I have heard this conversation before – in Berlin, Madrid, London. Are the young doomed to repeat everything we have done and said?

Then, I thought: I am thirty-six. By this age I should know myself the way a farmer knows the fields he has cropped for so many years. I should know exactly what my defects and qualities are, how far I can go, dare risk going, should be able to predict the falls I will have. I should be capable of being myself. And that means giving things up, settling for less than the absolute. At the age of thirty-six, at this near mid-point of the twentieth century, I am at once too old and too young for religion. Or for any faith. I have experienced enough to surrender almost everything.

There was a great, a welcome, calmness in that thought, and then I saw the white flecks of beer on Jacey's lips . . .

★

November 2: Today, at last, a letter from Father Dominic. He is in Le Havre and cannot come to Paris. But he expresses a cautious readiness to see me. I arrange to take a train tomorrow morning. This evening I have an invitation to dinner from the Marquise de Vaugoubert, old snob, half-Belgian cousin of Mother's. Now I am waiting for Jacey.

When I told her this was the last time, for now at least, having waited to do so till she was dressing, all she said was: 'I guess that wraps it up then.'

November 3: The train has been standing in a brown-grey landscape for at least twenty minutes. Thin rain seeps from sullen clouds. A single figure in dark suit and slouch hat had started to cross the beet fields on a long straight path, when we came, unannounced, to rest. He is still walking. There seems no reason why the train should ever move again. He leans forward as if into a wind which is not blowing as he tramps his way to what, where? In the distance beyond the fields, a line of beech trees makes a yellow stain on the indifferent country.

Last night the Vaugouberts' salon was brilliantly lit. Furnished in the gross style of the Belle Époque, the profusion of ornament was disgusting. What, I thought, had paid for this display of affluence without taste? Were the hothouse flowers with which tables and sideboards were laden, designed to banish the acrid smell of poverty which had been the lot of those who toiled in the squalid industrial landscapes of the Nord to create the Vaugoubert fortune?

It was ten or eleven years since I had seen Marguerite, perhaps on the last occasion she came to Blankets. Mother was never pleased with her company, but they had been to finishing school together, in Dresden, and they would talk of their time there and of how its citizens despised the

Prussians, whom they regarded as crude barbarians. Now she greeted me as if I was a favourite nephew, and did not notice my recoil from her suffocating scent. She was fatter than ever after five years of Occupation and eighteen months during which the mass of the French people have endured even greater privations. Isn't there an Italian proverb – 'beware the fat Neapolitan; he has eaten his brothers'?

Now, Marguerite, having enquired about Mother, sighed, so deeply that the garnet necklace that rested on her voluminous bosom quivered, and said: 'Like me, she must weep for our beautiful Dresden. That was the real crime of the war. And now it is occupied by Russian barbarians.'

The company was unrepentantly Pétainiste, mostly elderly, embittered, pessimistic. Indeed, a portrait of the Marshal still stood in a gilt frame on a side table. Talk of the injustice and barbarities of the *Épuration* was batted to and fro. A couple of old ladies recounted the excesses of the Resistance.

'And now the traitors who corrupted the will of France before the war are back in office,' said one. 'Communists, Freemasons, schoolteachers, Jews.'

Resentment of the British defiance of Hitler (and abandonment of France in 1940) mingled with expressions of surprise or contempt that we had elected a Labour government. No doubt it was part of the Anglo-Saxon conspiracy. If it wasn't that, it was evidence of our lack of seriousness. To elect Socialists, with the Russians in occupation of half Europe, was madness, surely.

I have never doubted that if we had been compelled to accept a Peace in 1940, our own Pétain would have appeared, or that he would have commanded general support, appealing to the weariness of the time. But even so, I can't think we would have sunk to the depths of prejudiced imbecility I endured last night. Yet, underneath

326

it, like the little tune of a symphony that is never quite submerged, there recurred an awareness which I haven't yet discerned at home: that Germany won't remain as she is, but will recover and must, therefore, be accommodated in some European system.

An old professor of ethnology observed, with a throaty chuckle, spilling snuff on the lapels of his dinner jacket that had turned green with age: 'Eventually Laval was right. He was a man of no breeding or manners, but when he said: "France will always have a frontier with Germany, and there will always be more Germans than Frenchmen. So we must either fight them every generation or come to an accommodation with them," can you gainsay that? And have you English understood it? Moreover, Germany, whatever the excesses of the Nazis, who were, I grant you, terrible people, is a civilised country as Russia is not and never will be. You English,' he pronounced with ancient malice, 'with your empiricism and your incapacity for abstract thought, do you suppose your Empire will endure? In twenty years it will have been swept away, for you have lost the will to govern and will sell it for American gold. And where will you be then? Will you be ready to become Europeans, or will you withdraw into dreams and mist?'

He stretched out and seized my wrist between crooked fingers.

'Your brother, young man, used to come to talk with me, or rather to listen, for he was eager to learn. He understood that all our values – the values of Greece and Rome and two thousand years of Christendom – are now being challenged. The barbarians are at the gate, and we must present a unified front to them if we are not to go the way of Rome. But I am pessimistic. Can this so-called democracy summon up the moral resolution to face that challenge? This democracy with no sense of what pertains to enduring national interests, but only of what is most immediately convenient or comfortable. There is no aesthetic of democracy. Your brother understood that. Is he alive or dead? Free? Or imprisoned by those who do not care to hear the truth spoken . . . ?'

The train has begun to move, jerkily. The peasant still crossing his field is left behind, to trudge, in the imagination, for ever, as unchanging as the malice and grievances of that ancient professor. The France that now presents itself to my eye is indeed *la France profonde*, which has endured and outlasted every regime since the time of the Bourbons, but wasn't what I encountered at the Vaugouberts at least as characteristic of the nation for which I feel simultaneously such admiration, affection and distaste?

There was another there whom I had met in London at a party given by Vanessa's parents. A woman of great beauty, with a profile declared to be Greek, and of brilliant intelligence, if quickness of wit, the ability to catch references and to embellish stories can be said to amount to intelligence. She fascinated Vanessa then. This was partly on account of the audacity which had carried her through three marriages, the second ending in scandalous divorce – she alleged that her husband, a baron who was also a newspaper proprietor and sometime ambassador to Tsarist Russia, had compelled her to submit to the vilest sexual practices, while he, in his defence, claimed that not only had she made the running in that respect, but that she had had recourse to love potions and black magic, possibly even trying to procure his death by such means. I do not know what truth there was in these various accusations, which were doubtless exaggerated in any case. What impressed me – and amazed me – at the time, was the manner in which she had so complacently surmounted what would have destroyed other women, forcing them into some sort of exile. She had already discarded her third husband, a poet a dozen years her junior. Van, I remember, couldn't take her eyes off her. Now I wonder if she saw in her an encouraging example of shamelessness.

I did not immediately recognise her last night; the skin of her face had cracked like the shell of an egg. It was only when she moved, that the grace of her walk recalled her to me. She enquired of Marguerite who I was. At least I suppose so, for she came over to speak. She first said, rather gently, how sorry she had been to hear of Vanessa's death; she had had a letter from her old friend, Lady Stuart-Styles, and she remembered Van perfectly, as a girl of an unusual radiance. (At once I wondered if there had been something between them; if she was another with whom Van had betrayed me. I use the word though Van would have denied me the right to do so.)

Then the woman – I never learned what she is now called – spoke of Alastair. She had known him only during the war, here in Paris where almost everybody was 'contemptible'.

'Your brother was an exception. He remained radiant.'

She saw him, she said, every day, for almost a year. I at once concluded they had had an affair, that it was on account of this derelict that he had broken with Yvette. Perhaps it was. She would have flattered him, as Yvette had ceased to do.

She said: 'Of course, you reproach me, as you reproach him. Very well, I accept that. We miscalculated. But it wasn't because he was a coward that he acted as he did. On the contrary, he was one of the bravest men I have known. It was for his courage that I loved him.'

'You say "was" . . .'

'I do so because what we had is now in the past. We are now condemned to mediocrity.'

'But you believe he is dead?'

'Certainly. He had too much pride to have survived.'

She talked, at length, of Alastair, but all in generalities. She might, as she bombarded me with abstract nouns, have been speaking of a hero of Romance; the personal was absent. And isn't that what I have discovered in the memories of all those to whom I have spoken of him – Pougier, Fred, Trude, Yvette, even the concierge – the sense that he did not exist as an individual, that he was a blank sheet on to which they transferred certain desires and needs of their own? Isn't it what Van used to complain of: that he had no substantial existence, so that when he was away from you, it was impossible to retain, or rather form, an idea of what he was truly like? But then, of course, I wonder, as I do not think Van did, whether we can ever know what another person is 'like'.

Nevertheless, it is strange that Alastair, who possessed such vitality or animal magnetism that you were more aware of his presence than of anyone else in the company (unless there was one there, another, with whom you happened to be in love), should be so hard to make to live in memory, except as an image. Max, I know, felt this. Curiously immune to Alastair's charm, he once remarked: 'I'm not saying he's a vampire, and crawls back into his coffin at dawn, but I do wonder if he doesn't just evaporate when he's alone, and materialise only when there is someone there to play off.'

On the other hand, everyone who has known him wants to talk about him, and acknowledges his importance in their life. When Van took up with Jukes she was avenging herself on Alastair, not on me. We might indeed have been happy together if his shadow hadn't hovered between us and lain dark on our love. Or is that sentimental self-deception? Trude said to me: 'You hope he's dead.' I took it as a question. Now I think it was, perhaps, a statement of what she recognised, or thought to see, in me.

Later, 10.30: Here I am again in the solitude of a hotel room, and as I look out on the wet street, on the little

330

group of people under umbrellas, or with the collars of their raincoats turned up and their hats pulled over their eyes, as they stand waiting under the gaslight for the tram that will break the silence of the night, my situation appears appropriate. In the old novels, the inn was always a place of animation; it was where adventures began. Now the hotel room is where adventures end. The sociability of the tavern − Father loved to write a tavern scene − has been replaced by the vacancy of the hotel room where one feels less oneself and yet more conscious of self, and where the furniture appears to have been always there, but never chosen. From my window I see, flickering, the red and white light of a café, the Rendez-vous des Cheminots.

Tomorrow, in the afternoon, I see Father Dominic.

The rain drifted from the Atlantic up the narrow street which still showed signs of war damage. There was scaffolding round the little church and the upper windows of the parish house were boarded up. I pulled the bell handle and listened to the hollow ring, like a message from another time.

Father Dominic himself opened the door. Before he greeted me, his gaze flickered either way along the empty street. Then he drew me in and led me into a little parlour to the right of the hall. There were screens, creamy yellow with age, across the lower half of the window, and the leather of the two armchairs was scuffed. He motioned to me to sit down. A case of brightly-coloured stuffed birds stood on top of a piano.

For a moment, he stood looking at me. His tongue twitched at the left corner of his mouth. Then he said: 'Your brother told me you were a Communist but honest. It is not a combination I find easy to believe in.'

'He was given to exaggeration,' I said.

Father Dominic is very thin. He looks as if he is preparing himself for martyrdom, but though I knew from what Yvette had told me that he was an old adherent of Action Français who had not, she believed, repented of his faith, martyrdom has eluded him.

He sat himself on a straight-backed chair and began to fill a pipe, stuffing the tobacco in with fingers that trembled so that wisps fell to the floor.

Conversation was long in starting. We were nervous of each other, and there were two or three false preliminaries. At last, I explained that, whatever our political differences, Alastair and I remained affectionate brothers.

'I have been interviewed by British Intelligence,' he said. 'They got nothing from me.'

'What would there be to get?'

'The vanquished are always vulnerable. In any case, let's not pretend. In the eyes of the State your brother is a traitor.'

'I think of him as a misguided patriot.'

'I cannot agree that he was misguided.'

At the third or fourth attempt, he contrived to light his pipe.

'Don't think,' he said, 'because you see me here in the parish house that I have not suffered. There are streets in this town I cannot walk without hearing insults hurled at me. My own brother denounced me. With that experience in mind, why should I trust you, merely because you are his brother?'

'The first thing I seek to know is whether Alastair is alive or dead. That commits you to nothing.'

'He is alive.'

'You are certain?'

'Certain.'

'And is he safe?'

'Are any of us?'

'Is he as safe as could be hoped for?'

'I believe so.'

The short sentences fell like stones lobbed into a

stagnant pool, only momentarily disturbing its surface. The priest rose, and, crossing to a sideboard, took out a bottle of Calvados and two small glasses.

'It was not a matter of politics,' he said. 'I have made many political mistakes. I see that now. So did your brother.'

He handed me a glass. 'His politics were naive, I saw that from the first. Perhaps, it was his naivety I found attractive. That may be. I have been so incapable myself of acting spontaneously. Do you understand? Nor is it a matter of my faith. I am not certain where that now lies, though I continue with my offices. No. Nor was I immediately drawn to him when my brother Philippe introduced us. I thought him callow. At the same time, he diminished me. His confidence was repulsive. All my life I have felt myself to be exceptional, and even when I discovered that in one respect I was less exceptional than I had supposed, that, indeed, in this matter many others felt as I did, nevertheless I suppressed what I felt, believing it to be wrong to give expression to it . . .'

He paused, drank off his Calvados and filled our glasses again.

'I am talking about myself, which is not what you came to hear. But if I do not, then you will not understand the story. And, besides, it is a relief to unburden myself to someone whom I shall never see again, and to do it face to face in my own person, and not in the confessional box. So bear with me. I felt myself exceptional, and incapable of belonging. It was in the search of something I could belong to that I entered the Church, and then later engaged in politics. But though I did so with ardour, my loneliness was not healed. And so, when I came to know your brother, I first resented him for his light-heartedness, for the impression he gave that life, which I found so demanding, was a joyous game. But then I found in him a remarkable sympathy. He understood me, was gentle with me, and did not condemn. There was rare spiritual goodness there in him. Soon, aware of that, I was also aware of his innocence. He had ventured into a world he could not fathom, for he had no knowledge, no comprehension of its iniquity. And then it was Philippe, whom he had befriended, who betrayed him, told lies about him. As a result of which he was arrested.'

'Your brother Philippe? Philippe Torrance?'

'Yes.'

The little priest shook his head.

'I didn't wish to speak about him. I don't trust myself to do so. But he was responsible. I would carry that shame if I had not been permitted to expiate it. Nevertheless it was a crime, for it forced your brother to learn what had been hidden from him: the vile nature of man. Even those of us who feel a need to come to that knowledge would wish it hidden from the innocents. So he was then imprisoned, tortured, by those whose cause he had supported. I learned of his arrest, was fortunately in a position of sufficient influence to intervene. He was released. But the damage had been done. His faith, his child's faith, in the goodness of man was destroyed. On the surface he recovered. For a few weeks after his release he gave the same beautiful impression of buoyancy, of being that rarity in the world today: a man who rose when the dew was still dancing on the grasses and smiled upon the world. I am sorry. I grow lyrical. I become absurd – it has often been remarked – when I am lyrical. Let us have some more Calvados.'

For a little we sat in silence. From beyond came the long-drawn-out wail of foghorns.

'Let me try, then, not to be lyrical. And, indeed, the temptation has passed, for what followed was, to me, truly horrible. When it became clear that all was lost, that the cause to which he had, with such careless abandon, attached himself, was doomed, doomed to defeat and ignominy, and that a terrible revenge was being prepared,

334

he suffered a complete moral collapse. He broke down and wept like a child whose mother has abandoned him. He shook with terror.'

'Are you sure it was terror, and not guilt?'

'It was terror. Believe me, a priest learns to recognise abject fear, and the annihilation of the will which is its consequence. I had not expected it. It was horrible, and yet — now you will think badly of me — it pleased me.'

'Pleased you?'

'Yes, because now, you see, I could repay him. As his vitality had enriched my life, so now, I could save him and even, I hoped, restore him to health.'

'I see. But are you so sure he did not feel guilty?'

'He had done nothing of which he felt ashamed, but he was afraid. I suppose he had always been popular, and now to be reviled and punished . . . it didn't bear thinking of.'

He got to his feet and walked about the room. When his restless waving hand touched the crucifix which he wore on a chain, he clutched hold of it.

'It was clear,' he said, 'that he was in no fit condition to save himself. So I had to do it. Fortunately, the Church has experience in such affairs.'

What this meant, apparently, was that Alastair and Father Dominic were passed from one religious house — mostly monasteries — to another, till they reached the Spanish border.

'It was safe for me to leave him there,' Father Dominic said, 'in any case I was not empowered to cross.' Once in Spain Alastair was halfway secure — 'It was not thought that he was of a rank which would require him to be extradited — in any case, that could not be done legally, for the United Kingdom, we ascertained, has no treaty with Spain that would cover his case. Even so, it was thought better that he did not remain there. It would not do to strain General Franco's tolerance.'

'So, where is he now?'

Father Dominic looked away, declining to hold my gaze. He knocked the ash from his pipe and, again, began to stuff it with tobacco. Again, some strands escaped and fell to the floor.

I said: 'I'm grateful, more grateful than I can say, for what you have done. So' – I added with no great certainty – 'will our mother be. I can see you are reluctant to tell me more. You're wrong, but I can understand why. Will you, however, arrange that a letter should be delivered to him, wherever he is? Is that possible?'

He gestured towards the writing desk.

Then he said: 'You will not object if I read what you have written? Otherwise, I cannot undertake – yes, I read English fluently.'

XXII
Edinburgh: January 1947

'It's a matter, isn't it, of what you can live with?'

Toby Macrae stretched his long legs before the wood fire in his den, and drew on his pipe.

'Well, marriage seems to suit you,' I said.

'I've waited long enough for it. I'm a lucky man.'

But he hadn't been referring to his own circumstances.

When I came back from France, I straight away fell ill. My doctor assured me I was suffering from nervous exhaustion; it manifested itself as a plague of boils, painful and ridiculous. I couldn't concentrate on any task beyond a few minutes. My temper was short. Sometimes I broke down weeping. A fortnight at Blankets exacerbated my condition. That wasn't in itself uncommon then. The return of peace proved more than many could endure; in my case the symptoms were merely late in arriving. People had been bound to duties which, though often seemingly trivial, wearisome and nerve-racking, were justified by the assumption that they contributed, somehow, to the great enterprise. Now that was completed, they felt flat. Many broke down.

Billy Hughes was understanding, though his own nerves were none too good. 'People won't see we're just one cheque away from national bankruptcy,' he kept saying. Nevertheless, he told me to get away, get fit so that, restored to health, I might 'gird my armour on again'.

So I had come north to see Toby as my oldest and wisest friend rather than as a medical man.

Toby walked with a limp now, the consequence of a bullet in the knee during the Italian campaign. It had been serviceable, that bullet. Taken prisoner, as a result of the wound, he escaped as soon as he could hobble, and fell in with a band of Partisans, who had sheltered him and been happy to make use, themselves, of his medical skills. His wife, Maria-Serafina, was the widow of one of the Partisans.

'Awfully nice chap, a railway worker and red-hot Communist, as brave a man as I've ever met. Blown up by his own explosive as he was trying to fix it to a bridge. You can imagine that Dr Pangloss doesn't approve of Maria, and young Torquil is fair affronted: a wop, a Red, and working class, not the thing at all for my brother, who – to be fair to him – had rather a good war himself.'

'How does she find Edinburgh?'

'Ask her yourself. Difficult, I should say. But we're happy.'

'Do you remember Morag? and how you held her up as an example of the robust good sense of the working class, in comparison with the sort of girls we met at dances?'

'Oh, I often see Morag. She and her husband keep a bar in the Gorgie Road. It's very proper, very well run. She's a patient of mine now. You think Maria-Serafina's a substitute for Morag? Perhaps you're right.'

He laughed.

'That really would upset Torquil. Not that I see much of him or of Dr Pangloss. Mother died, you know.'

'I hadn't heard.'

Maria-Serafina had accepted me, with natural courtesy, as a friend of Toby's, without suggesting, as wives are apt to do in such circumstances, that our shared past represented any sort of threat to her present. After an excellent meal of macaroni with smoked haddock – these were still austerity days, but she was fertile in adaptations of what was available to her own inherited cuisine – she shooed us off to Toby's den to drink whiskies and soda.

★

'So, with one bound,' he said, 'our hero is free.'

'Hector,' I said, 'is furious. I believe he would really like to have seen Alastair arrested and put on trial. Mother refuses to allow his name to be spoken in her presence.'

'Whose? Hector's or Alastair's?'

'Oh, Alastair's. She has, when it comes down to it, the old view of patriotism. My country, right or wrong. If only it was so easy.'

'If only. But Hector can't see it like that?'

'No, of course not.'

'Maria-Serafina and Aldo – that was her first husband, a lovely man – would be on Hector's side.'

'Yes, and you?'

'Oh, for me, it's a matter of indifference. I don't mean that callously. I mean that nothing Alastair has done matters to me. It's not, after all, as if he was in any way effective. He couldn't have been less so, by your account. And what concerns me now, in the public realm, is preventing these clowns at the head of the BMA from wrecking Nye Bevan's proposals to create a real National Health Service. Beside that, what do the posturing and preening of people like Alastair – or even Hector – signify? Not a docken. But, as I said earlier, it's a matter of what you can live with.'

In the morning, a north-easterly had scaped the sky clean as a washed plate. It was very cold and there was snow on the Ochils which I could see from the bathroom window of Toby's house. The wind threw the upper branches of the poplars at the bottom of the garden into a dance of dervishes, and the sky was as blue as the dart of a kingfisher. When we stepped out into the street, the schoolchildren breasted the wind like swimmers launching themselves on the waves, and their satchels flew behind them.

All morning the wind blew as I accompanied Toby on his rounds, and it made mischief with whatever was ordered and settled. Turning a corner into its exuberance, Toby caught an old lady flying through the air, and when he set her on her feet, in the shelter of the wall, she laughed at the predicament from which he had saved her.

'It just picked me up like a stray branch,' she said. 'I thought I micht be off to heaven like Elijah.'

We mounted tenement stairs and climbed the worn stone steps to single-ends where old men and women lay in beds from which they had not stirred in a long time, or where bairns grizzled at their confinement on a day when the glimpse of the world flying past the window called them out to play. Everywhere, Toby was greeted with respect and affection. For everyone, he seemed to have the right word, if rarely a medicine. More than once, as we left some mean but spotless apartment, he sighed and shook his head.

'How's your mother, how's your father, how're the bairns?' Or: 'I brought you into this world, you scamp. What do you mean by falling ill? We'll have you up and out in no time.'

To the old men he was as likely to talk football as medicine, and assure them they'd soon be on their feet to see the Hearts play at Tynecastle.

But that didn't stop him from cursing as he left.

'Conjunctivitis should be cleared up in five days. That woman's had it for a month now. It's the diet, you see. She gives her share of the ration to the bairns, and lives on bread and margarine herself. No wonder she's no resistance to infection or the resources to respond to treatment. But try telling her to behave differently! You haven't a hope!'

Yet hope was precisely what he seemed to bring. In his presence, the will to a better future was made manifest.

'One more call before lunch. You are not unconnected with this patient, I should warn you. So up to you . . . it's Mrs Milligan . . .'

'Mrs Milligan?'

'You knew her husband. In Spain. He died. Remember?'

'Yes. I do. What's wrong with her?'

'What's wrong with every working-class woman of her age in Scotland. Too much work and worry; too little food and selfishness, too much living for others – in this case, her children.'

The flat was clean as a Presbyterian conscience, not a spot of dust on the carved wood back of the dresser that dominated the living room. Mrs Milligan wiped bony hands on her apron, and told the Doctor he shouldn't have wasted his time. Hadn't he any sick people to attend to? They chaffed each other, all the while Mrs Milligan darting little suspicious looks at me.

'Is this some sort of inspector you've brought with you, Doctor?'

'Aye,' said Toby, 'he's got the power to put you in hospital on my say-so.'

'Never,' she said, 'be off with you. You ken fine what I think of hospitals.'

Then he told her I had known Jim in Spain, and added my name.

'Aye,' she said, 'I mind. You wrote me he was dead. And I've aye thought it was you sent me some money by way of the Doctor here. I was grateful. I'll no insult you by saying I'd like to be able to pay you back, though I would . . .'

She sat down at the table, and lit a Woodbine. Catching Toby's eye, she said: 'Och Doctor, it's no more than ten a day. See here, it's a ten packet.'

'With your lung, Dolly, it's ten too many.'

'Aye,' she said.

She held the cigarette between thumb and her first two fingers, and blew smoke at me.

'I was that angry,' she said, 'when he went to Spain. He'd a good job in the brewery, and a bairn, wee Jessie. He used to take her in his arms and croon that she was his lily o' the valley, and then he was off to fecht for a set of furriners. It's for democracy, he says. I tellt him where he could put his democracy. And then he said it was for Jessie. I couldna see

341

it. I was that wild I threw the flat-iron at his heid, and he lauched and said he micht be safer in Spain at the Front. Poor laddie. And now I think that if he hadna gone there, then mebbe Jerry would hae had him, and it's a' the same. But I couldna speak the day he went awa and I've aye been sorry for that.'

'I think he understood,' I said, 'the way he talked of you.'

'Aye, he had a gift that way, he talked me into marrying him after a'. Weel, Doctor, that's my tatties biling. Gin you see the bairns in the close, gie them a skelp and say their denner's ready. I'm glad to have seen you, Mr Allan, just to say thank you. Poor Jim, the brewery would have had him back. He was a good worker, see. And that's no sae common.'

At the bottom of the stair Toby turned aside and into the close where a group of children were playing marbles.

'Jessie,' he called, and a thin girl with brown hair in pigtails and a serious face turned round. 'Your mum says the dinner's ready.'

The girl left her game at once, and taking two other children, a small boy and even smaller girl, by the hand, came towards us. 'How is she, Doctor?'

'She needs to rest more. See if you can get her to.'

The girl shook her head. 'She'll no dae whit she disna want tae,' she said.

'I'll not argue with you on that point,' Toby said, and patted the wee boy on his tow-coloured head.

'That's a good girl,' he said.

We turned into the wind.

I spent a week with Toby, drinking, even in icy northern winter, from the well of his new happiness. Though he was weary with overwork, and would shake his head and say; 'The whole country's exhausted, and we're trying to make a social revolution without bloodshed – it's magnificent, *c'est magnifique, mais ce n'est pas la paix*,' yet he retained a vitality

342

that communicated itself to me, while the strength he drew from his unexpected marriage suggested that here, at least, was a point of stability to which I would be able to refer for reassurance. It was true that a casual observer might have thought the marriage ill-balanced, might even have seen Maria-Serafina as an exploited victim. Toby harried her with questions and demands, expecting her, for instance, to produce tea and scones for a needy patient, or even to take soup – in these days before the Social Services provided the Meals on Wheels which I sometimes think I shall myself soon look forward to – to some old man or woman incapable of managing on their own. He had the unthinking wilfulness, amounting, indeed, to selfishness, of the bachelor who has always had someone to wait on him. It might even have seemed that he regarded Maria-Serafina as a domestic servant herself, and one whom he didn't have to humour since she wasn't in a position to give him notice.

But all this would have been wide of the mark. Though every marriage contains in it something mysterious to the outsider, something which cannot be grasped, because we can never have any certain idea of how different the picture which a couple present to the world is from the way they behave when alone together, and also because the way their marriage appears to the outer world is never, and can never be, the way they see it themselves, which, moreover, doesn't exclude the possibility that each sees it and understands it quite differently from the other, yet it seemed to me then that Toby knew that in everything except economic circumstances, he was ultimately the dependent partner. I don't mean by that that he couldn't without marriage have continued to function as a doctor, popular with his patients, many of whom, I had realised, would swear blind by him, but rather that he who had, all his life, shunned intimacy, so that even though we saw each other so seldom and had had no regular intercourse for so many years, he was sincere when he once let out that I was the only one among his friends – most of whom he said, were, in reality, no more than acquaintances, suitable to partner him on the golf course or at the bridge table – to whom he could ever disclose his real sentiments, had found in Maria-Serafina what he had never hoped to find and knew he could never replace. But she, on the other hand, precisely because she had already loved – and still mourned – Aldo, knew in her heart, despite her reticence, that she lived most naturally in companionship and communion. I doubt if any of his Edinburgh acquaintance – most of whom, as he confessed, thought his marriage a bit rum, and didn't really know quite how to accommodate Maria-Serafina – guessed how the balance of the marriage hung.

'Of course,' he said to me, over our evening whisky and soda, 'there's a part of me resents the conjugal state, a part of me feels it as an unnatural and artificial condition. But Maria-Serafina recognises this herself, and makes allowances for it. She knows that, for a man, home is something he likes to know is there, but doesn't want to be tied to, whereas for a woman it's a nest, a lair. That's an antique inherited knowledge which women of our class in this country have lost. They don't see that a woman is most independent when she is most completely at, and of, her home. The poor painted things believe they are free when they encroach on male territory.'

It amused Toby that the wives of his acquaintance – 'Oh, good women, you know, good,' he would sigh – made so little of Maria-Serafina, and that she regarded the well-bred Edinburgh condescension with which they treated her – condescension that was as inherently stupid as it was well bred – with utter indifference. She, in turn, couldn't understand their concerns, and it pleased him to observe that the closest friend she had made in Edinburgh was Dolly Milligan.

'I often wonder if they speak of Aldo and Jim,' he said, 'but I'm inclined to think, you know, that they probably don't. Of course Maria-Serafina understands why Jim Milligan went to Spain, which Dolly never will, but I fancy she doesn't try to explain it. She wouldn't see the need. What they do talk about is an utter mystery. How wise Jane Austen was never to offer us a conversation between two of her male characters.'

'I've been meaning to ask,' I said. 'She's still Milligan, I notice. Who is the father of the two little ones?'

'Oh, a Pole. Naturally a Pole. It means Dolly suffers a bit of disapproval, which is another reason why I'm delighted that she and Maria-Serafina have taken to each other.'

'I take it the Pole is no longer on the scene.'

'He was a good Pole as Poles go, and, as Poles go, he went,' said Toby, chuckling, and reaching for the decanter.

A scab began to form over my wounds. Toby and I had fallen so immediately into the old ease of communication. It was like those nights of youth, in the study bedroom we had shared in the Lower Sixth, when, over cocoa, we talked the night away, setting the world to rights and elaborating each other's future, nights when we spoke more frankly than I – and I suspect this goes for Toby also – have ever spoken to anyone else. Much that we had promised each other had never come about, and much that we had said then was no doubt absurd, for middle age finds the hopes and fears of youth as absurd as youth, with perhaps greater reason, finds those of middle age. But we still marched sufficiently in step for neither to be embarrassed by these memories.

And so it was to Toby that I was able to speak as to no one else, not even Kirstie, for with her, too, I felt the obscure need to protect Alastair, if only by defending his memory. Moreover, I couldn't to Kirstie – though she subscribed no more than I did to what I thought of as Father's cult of Alastair – lay bare the complicated web in which my feelings for our brilliant younger brother – that Joseph for whom Father's imagination had woven a coat of many colours –

were enmeshed. I could not confess to her that my love for Alastair was corroded by resentment, that even the delight I so often took in his company was soured by my jealous awareness that his charm was effortless and indifferent. Nor could I tell her of the shame I now experienced at the thought that the most triumphant moment of my life was when I took possession of my younger brother's wife, and that even that triumph was sullied by the knowledge that he had already thrown her aside in careless abandon. I could no more speak of these things to Kirstie than I could have spoken to her of Fred.

But none of this required to be concealed from Toby. So also, only to him, could I fully express the shame that I felt on account of Alastair's treachery – or, more correctly, treason. His conduct had given aid and comfort to the King's enemies. That neither aid nor comfort had been of the slightest use, didn't alter the case. Indeed, by adding something contemptibly inept to his offence, it sharpened my sense of shame. We had been brought up, I said to Toby, in a simple faith, which insisted that conduct must be guided by a sense of honour, and rejecting that, Alastair, lightly, frivolously, seemed to mock and hold worthless everything on which successive generations had built the house we lived in.

I spewed out all my bitterness to Toby, putting into cruel and vile words what I had, even to myself, denied as thoughts. It was as if the barriers I had laboriously constructed to defend Alastair against the judgement of the world, were now swept away in a flood, and I with them. No doubt there was much madness in what I said, for I included myself in the reproaches I directed at Alastair, but Toby listened, and took me seriously.

'I've always distrusted the word "honour",' he said, at last. 'It's a self-serving housemaster's word, often, as you may remember, on Dr Pangloss's lips. Of course we should try to live decently, but people have such different conceptions of what decency is. And I recall you arguing years ago, over the dinner table at Blankets, that we were living in an age like your father's favourite seventeenth century when ideology set up its own loyalties that cut across other inherited ones. I've always thought there was much that was true in your argument, though I've come to detest ideology myself. Even Maria-Serafina's Aldo, who was, as I've told you, a good and brave man . . . well, let me tell you a story.'

He paused, lit his pipe and re-filled our glasses. The siphon gave an expiring hiss, and Toby rose to fetch another from the glass-fronted cupboard. Then he opened a drawer in his desk, and took out a photograph. He handed it to me. A high wall ran across the lower half, and above it were cypress trees and a Baroque bell tower. In the foreground lay several bodies.

'It was a little village called San Demetrio in the Apennines. As it happens it was Maria-Serafina's home village. You will know that everywhere the retreating Germans followed a policy of reprisals. For each German soldier killed by the Partisans, they took appropriate revenge. Everyone knew that. So there was argument among the Partisans as to the right course they should pursue.'

'Yes,' I said. 'I saw some of that in Yugoslavia.'

'Well, the group I was with ambushed a German staff car. We took a colonel prisoner. He was in the SS. He was put up against that wall and shot. Oh, he died bravely, but that's no matter. The trouble was we were unable to hold the village. So, when we withdrew and the Germans moved in, they shot ten villagers. One of them was Maria-Serafina's father, a peasant who asked nothing more than to be allowed to cultivate his little patch of land, and who had no time for Mussolini or the Pope or Stalin. Aldo was one of those who had insisted that the SS colonel must be shot. I have never known what Maria-Serafina's opinion was, how she feels about it; she certainly didn't reject Aldo as a result, though I believe she mourned, still mourns, her father. I don't know what the story proves. It's arguable that both shootings were

347

necessary. But it confirmed my rejection of ideology. You see, afterwards, one of our band argued that it was not a bad thing that rich peasants – kulaks – should have been got out of the way. He was a law student, a boy of nineteen, and as brave as a Highlander.'

He paused, his long, sad Jacobite face in shadow. Beyond the house was silence. The orange cat leapt onto Toby's knee, and dug its claws in, till calmed by his stroking hand. I drew on my cigar, waited.

Toby said: 'You must remember, we, unlike the English, have an innate tendency to take things to extremes for the sake of an idea. Revert to the seventeenth century. Have you ever thought how it was that in England, Puritanism, after the Restoration, so quickly transformed itself into a decent civic dissent and nonconformity, while here we had the Covenanters obstinately, blindly, fanatically still setting themselves to establish God's kingdom on earth, and absolutely indifferent to suffering caused and endured?'

'You're not suggesting that Alastair's conduct is explained by ancestral Covenanting zeal. That's too ridiculous. He scarcely thinks of himself as a Scot.'

'No, I grant you that would be naive, but I do suggest that he is, in spite of Eton, Oxford and an upbringing in salad country, enough of a Scot to feel the magnetic attraction of an Idea – whatever its relation to reality. As a race we're an odd mixture, Alec. We like to think of ourselves as hard-headed practical men, building the railways and bridges of Africa, and Asia and America, traders, manufacturers, and engineers, servants of Empire and the rest – though that last one is a giveaway, for the Empire has been important as an Idea as much as a Thing. But there's the other side of it – the madness for theology and disputation concerning matters that no Englishman would give the time of day to considering. And I think he had at least a touch of that.'

'Well,' I said, 'I don't know. Give me some more whisky,

348

please, and let us drink damnation to all those bloody egotists who take up causes.'

'Yes,' he said, 'I feel like that too, often.'

'Only I can't, still, drink damnation to my brother.'

'No,' he said, 'I understand that. Affections last. Despite everything, they endure. And you're a faithful old body, Alec, it's one of the things I've always liked about you. That, and your ability to find something remarkable in those for whom you feel love. Your geese have always been swans. Colin's pretty face and, of course, the beauty of his cover drive blinded you to his dislike of a fast ball on the leg stump and to the fact that he always lost his nerve when things got tough. It used to make me laugh. Now I see you behaving in the same way still. But you're not doomed to repeat your mistakes. It's time you began to live without that sort of reference to others.'

'Oh, I'm selfish enough,' I said. 'I'm more selfish than the next man. I couldn't, for instance, live, working for others like you, Toby.'

'I work first for myself,' Toby said. 'You need to be more robust in your selfishness. As for me, yes, I despise – or rather, distrust and fear – ideology. I'm Scottish enough to know I'm capable of going mad for ideas – or for whisky. I suppose you could say that the democratic socialism I now desire and work for is a sort of ideology, but I don't think of it like that. Ethics, not ideology – that's my watchword. And ethics requires you to ask of a suggested course of action, not whether it accords to theory, but whether it will do some practical good.'

XXIII

The wheels of the night sleeper south hammered out Toby's message, though the words slipped out of rhythm, as ethics had, I thought, out of fashion. Keep it simple, Toby had said. For him, that seemed to serve. Yet was it as easy as that? After all, hadn't Hitler kept things simple? 'The objects of society are of the greatest possible complexity,' wrote Burke. Quite so. In any case, was Toby's ethical simplicity so very different from the public school creed, from 'the bumping pitch and the blinding light . . . the colonel's dead and the Gatling's jammed . . .' How did it go?

The train slowed and then came to a halt. Silence enveloped us. Shivering, I swung out of the bunk, and released the blind. The compartment was lit only by a pilot light, and outside the world was white. Snowflakes danced past the window, blowing in when I pulled it more widely open. In a little, the attendant knocked on the door, and explained that we had run into a drift. He was sorry he couldn't make tea. The device that heated the water had failed. We had hit the beginning of the great snow of the worst winter of the century. It was late in the afternoon before we limped, tired, cold – for the heating had failed likewise – and hungry, into King's Cross.

XXIV

London: January 1947

Arriving back at the rooms I then occupied in Half Moon Street, rooms advertised as 'Chambers for Gentlemen', a sign that would soon vanish from London, I found an anxious and perturbed landlady. I had had a caller: 'Very respectable, but not what I would call a gentleman,' said Mrs Hayward. He had left his card. He was from Special Branch. It was not what Mrs Hayward was accustomed to. I had often, in old novels, come upon the expression 'to look askance'; now I encountered the thing itself.

The post waiting for me included a letter with a French stamp. I put a match to the fire, and, still in my overcoat, sat in the armchair beside the fireplace, and read its contents.

Father Dominic explained that his correspondent was pleased to have heard from me. He could not say at present just where he was, but it was unnecessary for me to feel any further or immediate anxiety. Nevertheless, his correspondent was not free of worries on his own account. Though safe, he found himself in straitened circumstances. He believed that there was family money due to him. Would I communicate with Father Dominic please?

The following morning I telephoned Billy Hughes and told him I would be back in the office on Monday.

'Boils gone?'

'Job also ran.'

'Good.'

Then I called the number left for me by the man from Special Branch.

Hastings was tall, lean, and wore a drooping moustache and thick spectacles with tortoiseshell frames. He laid his hat on the table, but did not remove his mackintosh. He settled himself, choosing a hard-backed chair.

'I suffer from lumbago,' he said, 'it catches me nastily if I settle myself in the sort of chair I used to like.'

He accepted my offer of a drink.

'Does this mean you're not on duty?'

'You know better than that, sir, being a newspaperman. That's the sort of idea that's put about by the people who write 'tec novels. I daresay most of them have never encountered a policeman. Steady with the soda, if you don't mind.'

He sipped his whisky, and let his gaze wander round the room. It settled, or seemed to settle, on a print of Winterhalter's portrait of the Empress Eugénie, a lady for whom my landlady, who had started in service in her household in Sussex, professed a devotion, which was indeed the only warm feeling I had discovered in her.

'You're not much of a homebird, are you, sir?'

'I've been up in Scotland.'

'It wasn't that I was referring to. You give the impression that you are camping here.'

'Inspector,' I said, 'as you've remarked, I'm a newspaperman.'

'I always like to see a man in his own home, tells you a lot about him, that does. This is a very agreeable whisky, sir.'

'Have another?'

'I don't mind if I do. Awful, isn't it, the way we pick up these catchphrases from the wireless. You won't believe, sir, perhaps, having been abroad so much lately, just how great a part of people's conversation now is made up of ready-made expressions they've heard on the wireless.'

'I daresay I wouldn't.'

He lapsed again into silence. Through the window, behind him, fog gathered smoky-yellow in the narrow street. Major Berkeley, who occupied the rooms above mine, began to play Chopin on his piano. Halfway through the opening bars of a waltz, he stopped, then repeated what he had already played, before continuing, hesitantly, too slowly for dance time.

'I'm a great admirer of your late father's books,' Hastings said. 'Matter of fact I have one with me now.' He patted the bulky pocket of his mackintosh. '*The Towers of Illusion* – what a story that is. I often say to Mrs Hastings, there's no one today can tell a story like he could. But, of course, my favourite is *Corners of Foreign Fields*, now that is a book. I was in the trenches myself, and it rings true, every word. And yet I understand he never saw action. Remarkable.'

He lifted his glass and gave me a half-unexpectedly charming smile.

'The title comes from a poem by Rupert Brooke, doesn't it? "If I should die . . ." that's how it goes, isn't it, sir, ". . . think only this of me, that there's some corner of a foreign field, that is forever England!" "Forever England", it still moves me. But things are more complicated now, aren't they, sir? And it's the same with his adventure novels. Amazing how they leap to the right conclusion! I expect you've found that yourself. And then the coincidences. We accept them in a book, but in real life. Does this mean anything to you, sir . . .'

He took an envelope from his inside pocket, withdrew a photograph, and passed it over.

'Look closely, will you, and think before you reply.'

But I didn't need to think. A hat concealed his baldness, and he wore dark glasses, but the turned-down corners of his rather prim mouth and the way, even in the photograph, he was caught picking at the cuticle of the little finger of his left hand, were unmistakable.

'Ah,' Hastings said, 'so you do know him?'

'Know is a strong word. I've met him. Or I think I have . . .'

'Boris Popov, he was called, when I think you knew him, sir. In Spain wasn't it? Of course he's gone by other names, before and since. Long-serving Comintern agent. Must be clever to have survived. Clever and adaptable. Not a nice man, I'd say.'

'That was my impression.'

'So, what do you make of this?'

He passed me another photograph from the envelope. It was grainy, taken outdoors, in poor weather conditions, probably with a telephoto lens. It showed two men sitting on a park bench. The one nearer the camera was identifiable, if only because I had just seen the previous print, as Boris. The other was Hector.

'That's Central Park,' Hastings said. 'New York,' he added, helpfully. 'An American friend passed it to me. Interesting, wouldn't you say? Of course there may be nothing in it. Mr Popov – or whatever he calls himself now – is, I understand, a well-authenticated diplomat. A Trade Mission, is it? Something of that sort. But my American friend, an old colleague, thought I might be interested. And I am.'

'Mr Hastings,' I said; then, playing for time, offered him a cigar, which he declined, and occupied myself in removing the band from one, snipping the end, and lighting it. Through blue-grey smoke, I said: 'Special Branch, aren't you? Is this quite your line? I mean shouldn't the photograph have gone to MI6?'

'Of course it should, sir, you're quite right. And that's another point of interest. My American friend may have sent a copy there, but again he may not. It appears that he is not altogether confident about these boys, not completely happy with them. So he passed it on to me, as a matter of security, you might say . . .'

'Might I?'

'Well, you might, sir. Or again you may tell me there's nothing in it. And I might believe you. Only it's difficult to know what to believe these days, where you can put your trust. "For now we see through a glass darkly." Mrs Hastings is fond of quoting St Paul, with reference to my job, it's a family joke, you might say, but that text always makes me wonder if St Paul wasn't something in the security line himself. As he may have been. Isn't there a theory that he played some part in the arrest and stoning of St Stephen? I like to think there's something in that. It's a comfort when you find yourself engaged in what can be a dirty business, to think that the Apostle may have walked the same mean streets before you, in a manner of speaking.'

'It must be. I hadn't thought of that.'

'Ah, now you're being ironical, sir. Central Park, it's very innocent. But it looks a nasty day to be holding a conversation in the open air. Could be raining, couldn't it? But you think there's nothing to trouble myself about, then, do you?'

'I expect there's a simple explanation.'

'Do you now? That would be a nice thing to come upon in my line, a simple explanation that happened to be both innocent and true. It does occur, occasionally. So, shall I tell my American friend he's barking up the wrong tree?'

'My dear man, tell him what you like.'

He took the photographs back and replaced them, neatly and almost tenderly, in the envelope.

'Caesar's wife,' he said, 'that's a diplomat's duty, wouldn't you say, to be like that lady. But of course she wasn't, was she?'

'Wasn't what?'

'Above suspicion. Caesar divorced her, didn't he, as I recall, because she didn't measure up to the standards he demanded. I daresay there was a degree of hypocrisy there.'

He stood up, and smoothed the front of his mackintosh.

'Mrs Hastings will be interested to hear I've met you. She's a great admirer of your father too, though she prefers the biographies. Strange that, isn't it, or maybe you don't think so. She leads a very retired life, so she likes reading about men who have done great things, but I run up against nasty reality every day, so I turn to fiction.'

He took the book from his pocket, and tapped it, perhaps to prove that it really was one of Father's.

'A grand story,' he said, 'I've read it four times at least, but you know I can never believe till it happens, that they are going to escape from the fix they're in east of the Bosphorus. A very nasty prison that is, too.'

He pushed the book back, out of sight, and picked up his hat.

'Do you know, Mr Hastings,' I said, 'I thought you had come upon quite different business, another brother indeed . . .'

'Another brother?' Again he released that charming half-smile. 'Last year I might have. I won't insult you by pretending not to understand your meaning. But, though we are naturally concerned with the past if it forces itself on our attention, it's today's and tomorrow's dangers that occupy us now. And that's as it should be. Fascists – why, they have as much life as cold mutton, it seems to us now.'

XXV
Blankets: January 1947

'But it's obvious,' Kirstie said, 'you must arrange that he has the money that is his due.'

'Steady, old girl,' Edwin Pringle said. 'Granting that I'm new to the family and strictly speaking this is no concern of mine, all the same, hold your horses, I say. There are all sorts of considerations.'

Marriage to Kirstie seemed to suit him. He had put on weight, settled himself in Blankets snugly. The shooting had been more successful than old Haskins had predicted. The large Labour majority made unnecessary regular attendance at the House, where Edwin had never in any case made much contribution to debates, and which he regarded principally as a club, agreeing with his friend Chips in thinking it 'a tawny male paradise'. Now he was settling contentedly into the life of a squire, who spent Tuesday, Wednesday, Thursday, up in Town. His first wife had had a title — she was an Earl's daughter, but had brought him no land. It was clear that he felt he had found his niche.

Kirstie smiled at his intervention, not entirely pleasantly. If he hadn't yet discovered, he would soon find, she had a powerful will. But probably he knew that. They were rubbing along happily. Though I didn't care to admit it, she found in him qualities desirable in a husband, qualities that poor Colin had lacked. A power of decision was one.

'What sort of considerations were you considering?' I asked.

357

Edwin clipped the end off a cigar, and pushed the box towards me.

'Four, at least.' He stuck the cigar in the corner of his mouth, rolled it round his lips, and held up four pudgy fingers. 'One, this French priest. We've only his word for it, don't we, that he is in touch with Alastair. Two, even if he is, can he be trusted? Three, there are strict exchange controls. Transferring money isn't easy. You need Treasury approval. Four, apply for that, and even if it's granted, some nasty cats are let out of the bag to go yowling through the streets. There are questions of sensitivity, you know. Some of your friends, Alec, in the press, could raise rather a stink. Oh, and five, I forgot: we have only this officer's word – what's his name, Hastings? – for it, that they've lost interest in the boy, that he's in the clear.'

'Well,' I said. 'Father Dominic's trustworthy. That disposes of your first two objections. As for Hastings, he may have been up to something, but what he said makes sense. Fascism's dead meat. Tom Mosley's farming somewhere in England, isn't he, and either publishing or about to publish a newsletter?'

'Oh, yes,' Edwin said, 'Tom's farming at Crowood, having a great time. We went to lunch with him and Diana actually – just don't tell the Chief Whip. He was in tip-top form, all cracks and then long philosophical disquisitions, just like the old days. But Tom didn't live in Vichy France and broadcast on Vichy radio. There's a difference, Alec.'

'Certainly,' I said. 'Tom was locked up in Brixton and Holloway, that's the difference.'

'You know it's more than that.'

'Stop it, boys,' Kristie said. 'The money is Alastair's. He needs it. To keep going and, I hope, branch out in a different direction. So he must have it. That's simple. The question is, how. There may be some royalties in New York that could be diverted. That might be the easiest way to handle it. I'll speak to the trustees. Alec, you'd better let me have the address of your Frog priest. And now let's play canasta. It's our new passion, Alec, ever so much more fun than bridge.'

After church, Kirstie stayed behind to discuss parish matters with the vicar over a glass of sherry, leaving Edwin and me to walk home together. The sky was leaden. There would be more snow before night, and the wind blew sharp from the east.

'Kirstie enjoys being the squire,' Edwin said.

There was affection in his voice. Pehaps it was my surge of warm feeling that prompted me to tell him the other part of my conversation with Hastings, of which I had intended to say nothing. Edwin had a reputation as a gossip. Nevertheless, his own way of life had schooled him in the practice of necessary reticence.

'I've never found Hector easy,' he said. 'I knew him when he was at school, not very well, and then a little better at Oxford. And we had close friends in common, poor Robin Maltravers for instance. But Hector has always had that air of disdain, nose in the air as if he had just sniffed a bad smell. There's something buttoned-up in him, and a certain vanity. Of course he's a clever chap and I'm not, but he's never been clever enough, or cared enough, you might say, to disguise his knowledge that I'm not in his league. And intellectuals have a hard time in England, we're apt to let them see we think their brains have gone to their heads. Do you see what I'm getting at?'

'Yes,' I said, 'and I don't like it. Because I've come to the same conclusion myself.'

'Hector feels unappreciated, you know,' Edwin said. 'The first thing is to get him away from Washington. I'm glad you told me. I still have some friends in the FO, you know. I'll have a word in the right quarter. Sooner the better.'

We turned into the woods. Edwin began to speak of the Labour Government. They were doing better than he had expected, less harm anyway. Of course the level of taxation was intolerable. It couldn't last. But, when you came to think of it, in the present state of the world, Winston might have done much worse.

'You were always a Chamberlain man, weren't you?'

'Poor little Neville! But could Winston have brought himself to let India go? That's what I ask myself. And it has to go, I realised that ten years ago. The days of Empire are past, far-flung, our navies fade away, you know . . .'

Edwin was a realist. Perhaps he was wise. Endlessly adaptable, pliable, he would never be found in the last ditch. He would probably make Kirstie a satisfactory enough husband. Perhaps I was wrong to advise her against the match. If so, it was one mistake in a long line. All the same, looking at the soft complacency of his jowls, as he strutted beside me, I couldn't resist asking: 'What do you do about boys nowadays, Edwin?'

'I don't let myself fall in love, that's what.'

That wasn't, I thought, Hector's way; better, perhaps, for him if it had been.

Edwin said: 'Don't get me wrong. I'm not going to do anything that will disturb Kirstie or make her unhappy. I'm too fond of her for that. Owe her too much, too. By the way, talking of such matters, do you ever hear anything of young Max now?'

'No,' I said, 'he's dropped quite out of my life.'

'Mine too. Pity.'

Snow began to fall, thickly, in big fleecy flakes. A heron rose from the rushes by the edge of the pond, circled twice above us with heavy-beating wings, and, legs out-thrust, came to rest in the upper branches of a big Douglas fir.

'I think I'd better try to get back to London tonight,' I said.

Envoi
Glasgow 1984

When the ceremony and the offical lunch were over, and I had divested myself of my academic robes, it had started to rain, a smirr coming in from the west. Craig Cabell, the Professor of Journalism, to whom I owed my honorary degree, guided me through the corridors of the 1960s functional building to his office, remarking that we would neither of us have supposed, when he came under my wing, as he put it, near forty years previously, that we would find ourselves taking part in that morning's archaic theatre.

'But,' he said, 'sometimes I think that's all that's left to us – theatre.'

Craig's office was the dog kennel which universities now apparently think appropriate for professors. A desk, with computer, telephone and fax; two bookshelves able to hold, at most, five dozen volumes; a cord coir carpet of indeterminate colour; a stack of steel-rimmed chairs. It gave on to a blank wall across a lane.

'Yes,' he said, 'it depresses me, too. I often think about that Irish boy in an Angus Wilson novel who let loose a stream of blarney about what a great thing it was for him to meet a professor. He was lying of course, but he couldn't even venture on such a lie today. Still, I mustn't complain, it will provide me with a pension.'

'Real life begins at retirement? Wish I could think so.'

'Still, there are rewards, even now. This girl who wants to interview you, she's really bright.'

'I can't think I have anything to say that would interest her. I must seem Neanderthal.'

The taxi carried us, through streets in which what were either new developments or expensive refurbishments, alternated with continuing evidence, as it seemed, of a city that had emerged, battered but still breathing, from a long siege, this last an impression which the number of shuffling derelicts seemed to substantiate. There were frequent stops at intersections, during which the driver turned to favour us with his views on the city council, the rise of feminism, and the disgraceful showing of Glasgow Rangers in Europe. Craig parried his arguments to which I lent only half an ear.

The girl was waiting for us in the pub which had the air of one that would not till very recently have admitted a female on the drinking side of the counter. Pub wasn't, of course, the right word; this was a bar, nothing more. A jar of greenish pickled eggs offered the only concession to the possibility that any of the customers might wish food.

Craig fetched us whiskies while the girl, who had been one of his students, exchanged introductory remarks. Those who have since seen Kate Byrne interrogate politicians on *Newsnight* may suppose that even then I felt a tremor of anxiety. But in reality, my first thought was that she was beautiful, and my second that I was old.

She was a big girl, with a lot of blonde hair worn loose, and a mouth that would have invited kisses if you hadn't heard the sharpness with which she uttered. Sharpness perhaps isn't right, but her way of speaking was decisive. She wore jeans, frayed at the knee, and a blue donkey jacket, and she had been sitting, waiting half an hour she told us, in that bar which had at least hired out to be tough, and she had frozen off approaches and hostile innuendo. I was impressed, first by her beauty and then by her air of certainty. I found myself remembering Barbara as she had been in Berlin.

The meeting had been arranged by Craig. A feature piece in the recently launched Sunday paper for which the girl

362

worked would do him no harm at the university. Academics, long shy of newspaper publicity, were already growing greedy for it; it served as a visible support in the new climate wherein they were required constantly to justify themselves and their departments. Not, of course, that Craig Cabell experienced too great difficulty in that respect; journalism was, after all, an eminently serviceable discipline.

He nodded but said little as the girl led me on a routine canter through my career. It was all stuff that she could have got from my entry in *Who's Who*. I was tired after the ceremony, and wary of the effect that the whisky might have on me. The questions, delivered with admirable brevity and coming at me through the cigarette smoke, were brisk and intelligent. All the time, however, I was more aware of her body than of her words, and ached with the sad, shaming, never-to-be-gratified lust of old age.

Then she shut her notebook, lit another cigarette (soft-pack Marlboro), and gave a look at our empty glasses which sent Craig scurrying back to the bar.

'Thanks,' she said, 'that's what my features editor wanted, picture of old Fleet Street, schmaltz. I can do it nicely with what you've given me.'

'I'm sure you will.'

'Yeah.'

Craig returned with only two glasses, said he hadn't realised how late it was, must get back to his office to finish some tasks, didn't want to be late home, thanked me for coming, hoped to see me again before long; and left, awkwardly.

'His wife gives him hell,' Kate said.

For a little we sat in the trance-like state that drinking in the afternoon can induce. Men entered the bar, shaking the rain from their shoulders. Laughter came from a group, mostly in overalls, at the far end of the room.

Kate said: 'Was your brother the Fifth Man?'

The question was not surprising. Four or five years earlier, soon after the exposure of Anthony Blunt, there had been renewed newspaper speculation concerning the identity of the so-called Fifth Man who had tipped off Blunt who had tipped off Philby – I forget the details. Hector's name had been among those mentioned. A couple of reporters from the *Sunday Times* had gone to interview him in Provence, where he had then been living for more than twenty years. They had got nothing from him.

'He is perfectly well, physically, you understand,' Giulio, his companion since he settled there, explained to me. 'He reads a lot, watches television, goes to the cinema, takes long walks. He just refuses to speak.'

It was four or five years since Hector lapsed into silence. Giulio, who had grown very fat, continued – continues – to look after him with what it is convenient to call devotion. That, anyway, is how I prefer to interpret it.

'Is this on or off the record?' I said.

'Could be either. Up to you.'

'Well,' I said, 'I don't suppose it matters, now. There is no one to whom it could matter.'

'So?' she said.

'So, I don't know, but I think it probable. Hector resigned from the Foreign Office in 1955, or thereabouts. I'm no longer much good on dates. It was, anyway, a bit after Burgess and Maclean decamped.'

'Did you know them?'

'Maclean quite well, and never liked him. Burgess, I think, I met only a couple of times. Once, in Hector's club. He complained about the absence of page boys. Philby not at all. Maclean had principles. He wasn't, in some ways, unlike Hector. Though Hector was never a drunk.'

'So why did Hector resign? He wasn't suspected then, was he?'

'Almost certainly. Very few who had ever been on the Left escaped suspicion. The Cold War probably seems silly to you. Your generation doesn't believe in it, does it? Or in the Evil Empire? But in the 1950s, things were different. In any case, waging the Cold War was a substitute for the loss of our own Empire. But Hector needn't have resigned. He chose to. He loathed the Americans, you see, and he regarded our subservience, as he saw it, to American policy and interests as shameful and wrong.'

'Was he a Communist?'

'In principle, yes. Communism was on the side of history. It represented the progressive forces. It all seems awfully remote now.'

'And he was gay, like Burgess and Blunt?'

'Ah, the old Homintern.'

I got stiffly to my feet, and took our glasses over to the bar. How to explain that she had got it the wrong way round? That version was too easy. It might hold – I didn't know – in the case of Burgess and Blunt. Certainly the equation was simple. Homosexuality made you an outsider; therefore provoked an inclination to betrayal. Q.E.D. I settled myself at the table.

'It wasn't like that at all,' I said. 'Anyway, Hector thought of himself as "queer". The word "gay" hadn't yet been appropriated. And his queerness was something he disapproved of. Or was something which, intellectually, and with considerable willpower, he turned away from. It got in the way of whatever commitment to Communism he had.'

She was a bright girl, but I could see she didn't follow, or more probably, couldn't accept, my argument. So I didn't go on to talk to her about Max, who had offered Hector the prospect of happiness which he had rejected as incompatible with his austere commitment, Max who had continued to talk affectionately of Hector as 'the old dear', in the antique and curio shop which he had opened in Notting Hill sometime in the 1950s.

Instead I said, merely, deprecatingly: 'It doesn't matter. He became a journalist, you know, he thought he could serve the Cause more effectively in that role, but he wasn't much good at it, a very dull writer, and in the end he didn't so much leave the Party as was left behind by it. He became irrelevant.'

When, eventually, he settled with Giulio, I didn't add, it was an admission of failure. No wonder he retreated into silence.

Instead, I said: 'Hector really was an authentic example of what no longer exists: the ruling class.'

'But a Communist?'

'Oh, yes, he believed in the Marxist dogma. Absolutely. But Communism was also, for him, the means by which Britian could continue to be great, escape American domination. It was a tenable argument, at the level of argument.'

'My grandfather was a Communist,' she said, 'still is, really. He used to work in the shipyards. He thinks my dad sold out.'

'And did he?'

'Probably. He's the manager of a travel agency.'

'Sending the toiling masses to Benidorm?'

'Aye, that sort of thing.'

Her smile was affectionate as well as mocking.

'But you're fond of him?'

'Couldn't not be. Anyway, he's a good Labour man, solid Labour.'

'Your grandad might say that's the worst sort of sell-out. Better the class enemy than the false friend.'

'Aye, he might.'

I asked her if she had a couple of hours to spare. There were one or two places I'd like to visit, I said, and I'd be glad of her company.

The rain was heavier now, set in for the night. The taxi stopped before locked and rusty gates. Beyond them could be seen a waste land of derelict buildings, willow herb, and scrub that tangled its way to the long-abandoned wharf. Two small boys, kicking a ball, looked round at us, and, indifferently, resumed their game.

'They haven't built a ship here in my lifetime,' Kate said. 'The council took over the land years ago. For development. There have been several different plans. But nothing bloody happens.'

'It's where it began for us,' I said. 'The *Christina Johnstone* was built here, launched from that dock. My great-grand-father's first ship, the first of the Allan Line. You wouldn't think so.'

'No,' she said, 'it's like trying to imagine life at Skara Brae.'

If the shipyard's dereliction exceeded what I had imagined, Ardlochish House was a different matter. I had last seen it during the war, when it had already been, for five or six years, an asylum, and had taken on the forbidding aspect of such institutions. Now its Scottish baronial fantasy blossomed again, transformed into a luxury country club hotel, with a golf course laid out in the park, running down to the lochside, and Jaguars, Mercedes, BMWs and a couple of Bentleys parked on the great sweep of gravel. It had been a sentimental whim, of the kind that grow common in old age, which had prompted me to ask Craig Cabell to book me a room there, and now I found myself regretting it. But we paid off the taxi, and entered the lofty hall which had been decorated with stags' heads, absent in old Sir William's day. The prevalence of tartan was as depressing as the confident babble from the cocktail bar. Kate's frayed jeans and donkey jacket attracted disapproving looks.

'Doesn't worry me,' she said.

The paintings hung in the hall, drawing room, and bar were all Highland kitsch, landscapes some way after Land-seer, featuring stags and tweeded sportsmen, ghillies and garrons.

'I expect the Americans like it.'

'Oh, aye, Scotland as Maggie Thatcher's theme park.'

'Old Sir Willie collected Post-Impressionists. Sorry, am I boasting, or just being pathetic?'

'I don't doubt,' she said, 'that you are looking to me for a word of condemnation. That's why you've brought me, isn't it? To indulge your guilt?'

'Oh, I don't think so.'

But I couldn't say I had asked her to come with me because she was beautiful, or, more flippantly, because it would cheer the ghost of Sir Willie to feel her presence there, or even, simply because I didn't want to be alone. All truthful responses were ruled out by the gap between us. So, instead, I didn't answer her directly, but, when we had settled ourselves with drinks, told her about Sir Willie and my memories of visiting him there, trying to conjure up for her the impression of dynamism which, even in his old age, he had so vividly conveyed to me.

'He told me to make things,' I said. 'It seems now as if he saw the way we were going and still hoped that by warning me, it could be averted. Fanciful, that is, sorry.'

'You don't need to apologise,' she said.

'You see,' I said, 'though he was what you might disapprovingly call a robber baron – and I daresay if your grandfather ever mentioned his name, it would be with reprobation – it seems to me now that he was still in what I can only call the tradition which is the central core of western thought. By that I mean that his habit of mind depended on three unquestioned dogmas – even though he called himself a free thinker and a pagan who had rejected the idea of a personal God. But he still believed that all genuine questions had one answer, one true answer; that the true answer to any such question was, in principle, knowable, and that since true answers can't clash with each other, for one true proposition can't, by definition, be incompatible with another, then together these answers formed a harmonious whole. The world made sense to him.'

368

'It did to my grandad too,' Kate said.

'I'm not trying to claim superiority to your grandad, if I say that this makes no sense to me, that I think we've outgrown it, and say so even if I am, I suppose, the same age, at least the same generation, as your grandad. But that's how it is, for me. Hector, on the other hand, committed to Marxism, still held the old Classical European view, as if Tieck and the other romantic irrationalists who in fact came before Marx had never written. And, though I hadn't meant to mention it, I had another brother who thought the same way in this respect, though different in others, the same as Hector, I mean.'

'What happened to him?'

'He went to Argentina, and died there. Squalidly.'

Then we went through to eat. The head waiter objected to Kate's jeans.

'Press,' she said.

We ordered lobster and a bottle of Hock.

'They tell me German wine's unfashionable. The Victorians always drank it. Make things, he said. Well, all we made was mistakes.'

'You've used that line before.'

'Too often.'

'How did your other brother die?'

'Oh,' I said, 'he had too much charm. It killed him. A jealous husband. Argentinian husbands are given to jealousy, I suppose.'

'You make it sound as if you were all failures.'

'Well, yes. George made money, a very successful businessman, based in Hong Kong. Died of drink.'

The lobster was delicious.

'You'd have liked my sister,' I said. 'Perhaps, anyway. You wouldn't have agreed about anything, except what's important.'

'How do you know what I'd agree on?'

369

'I don't, do I?'

'Who was Tick anyway? I've never eaten lobster before.'

'Tieck, not Tick. German writer. In one of his plays the Prince despairs of reaching the end of his journey and orders the play to be put into reverse.'

'I see,' she said. 'Is that how you see your life?'

Even that evening was some years ago. Now I try not to miss Kate on television, but we've not met again. She comes to me sometimes in dreams. They say lobster is an aphrodisiac, don't they? Such a lot of nonsense. In any case, if that was indeed her first lobster – odd that she should have admitted it – it was my last.

Every day I try to walk three miles. Takes me an hour and a half.

Kirstie died last year. I didn't go to the funeral. Couldn't. Couldn't face Edwin blubbering. In his way he loved her, was (she said) faithful, but his tears would have been tears of self-pity.

Now this young man, friend of her grandson, can't remember his name, wants to write a play about Alastair. Coming to see me this afternoon. It's absurd. Set the dogs on him? One terrier losing her teeth.

Absurd, but who cares? Now. Who's left to care?

'The great object of life,' Byron thought/wrote, 'is sensation, to feel we exist – even in pain.'

But he died at thirty-six, before the years of frost.

Hector still lingers silent. George, shoved out of his company by his younger son, sat for years drinking whisky and gazing on the cold sea. Alastair used to write me from the Argentine, letters on thin grey paper, full of typos, promising still great things to come. They stopped years before the news of his death.

They say Father worshipped success. They say the gods are just.

I suppose I can give this manuscript to the boy and send him away. Tell him to make what things he will of it. Or shall I take him up the valley to the ruined keep and show him desolation?